A Novel with Musical Accompaniment

❖ The Dancing Master ❖

MURDER
&
MISS AUSTEN'S BALL

Books by This Author

The Richest Man in New Babylon

The Incompleat Sound Operator

A Novel with Musical Accompaniment

◈ The Dancing Master ◈

MURDER
&
MISS AUSTEN'S BALL

BY A GENTLEMAN
as it was recalled and recounted to
RIDGWAY KENNEDY

Copyright and Credits

Hedgehog House Books
28 Yale Terrace
West Orange, New Jersey 07052
973-400-9738
www.hedgehoghousebooks.com

ISBN: Print Edition: 978-1-951989-08-8
ISBN: KDP Print Edition: 979-8780265-34-4
ISBN: E-Book Edition: 978-1-951989-09-5
Publisher's Cataloging-in-Publication Data:
LCCN 2021924156
Names: Kennedy, Ridgway, author.
Title: Murder & Miss Austen's Ball / Ridgway Kennedy
Description: First Edition.
Hedgehog House Books
West Orange, New Jersey

Identifiers: LCCN: 2021924156.

Cover Design by Damonza
      www.damonza.com
Christina Boyd, Editor, The Quill, LLC
      www.thequillink.com
Typesetting by Affinity Publisher

10 9 8 7 6 5 4 3 2 1

Dedication

For My Miss Jane

Of Histories, Mysteries, and Twice-Told Tales

C aution, dear Reader,

In the preparation of this manuscript, experts in literature, most especially those with detailed knowledge of the life of Miss Jane Austen and her works, have examined it and found it wanting.

They have informed me of verifiable errors and report that several events have been exaggerated beyond their true import. Indeed, a few have gone so far as to say that some incidents might never have actually occurred.

Regency era historians, familiar with the customary behaviour of ladies and gentlemen of the time, have discerned displays of impropriety that would never be countenanced. Authorities in Regency era music and dance have questioned several of the musical references and dance customs contained in the tale.

Yet, the elderly Gentleman who related the story to me swore, based upon his firsthand knowledge of the events, that all is true.

My responsibility in the creation of this narrative has been that of a scribe, the penman who has written the tale as it lives in this Gentleman's memory.

How then can we account for faults contained herein? Has it, like many a time-worn tale, been embellished in his recollection? Did he dissimulate in his desire to provide amusement? Might his faculties have been failing?

For my own part, I can only offer this as a faithful narrative of the Gentleman's experience as it was given to me.

Your faithful servant,

R. Kennedy

An Editor's Note Concerning Music

Several extraordinary musicians have worked to create recordings of music to accompany this volume. The tracks include samples of many of the tunes mentioned in the story in addition to longer recordings, including a dance-length recording of *Miss Jane* or *The Dancing Master's New Tune* by Sarah Gowan.

Please visit www.hedgehoghousebooks.com for up-to-date information about how to access and enjoy this book's "audio illustrations."

Dance leaders will also find dance instructions for *Miss Jane*, an English Country Dance created to go with the music, written by Tom and Susan Amesse.

Dramatis Personae

The Principals
Freddy Worth, dancing master
Jane Austen, lady and Author

The Austens of Chawton
Cassandra Austen, sister of the Author
Mrs Cassandra Austen, mother of the Author
Henry Austen, banker and brother of the Author
Edward Austen, master of Chawton House and brother of the Author
Francis "Frank" Austen, naval officer and brother of the Author
Flora, maid at Chawton Cottage
Hotchkiss, stable master at Chawton House

The Ellicotts of Kellingsford Manor
The Right Honorable Horatio, The Viscount Kellingsford
The Honorable Percival Ellicott, eldest and heir to Kellingsford
The Honorable Letitia Ellicott, daughter of The Viscount Kellingsford
The Honorable Aloysius Ellicott, younger son of The Viscount Kellingsford
Simon Sloat, Mr Percival Ellicott's man of business
Mr Jerome, butler at Kellingsford
Marryat, in service at Kellingsford
Hinch, gamekeeper at Kellingsford

Kellingsford Estate Tenants
Admiral William Harwell, gentleman farmer
Robert Morgan, tenant farmer
Jimmy Morgan, son of Robert Morgan

Of a Regiment of Dragoons
Captain Reginald Wembley, newly made captain of the dragoons
Corporal Doggett, of the dragoons
Several more officers and gentlemen; a number of additional privates.

Townspeople of Alton
Bolabus Claypoole, greengrocer, dry goods merchant, inn owner, and parish constable
Eli Turkle, driver and assistant to the constable

In addition...
In London
Richard Crosby, principal of Crosby & Company, Publishers and son of Benjamin Crosby
Kendrick, Lefty, and Walker, seamen who served on the *HMS Victory*

In Bristol
Sophie Croft, sister of Freddy Worth
Isaac Croft, husband of Sophie Croft
Nate Woodman, carpenter's mate

In Bath
Mrs Dorothea Jones, widow of Llewelyn Jones

A Consort of Musicians
William Quinn, violin
Sarah Quinn, pianoforte
Thomas Thomas, wind instruments of various sorts including unfortunate noisemakers such as the krummhorn

Joining our cast in supporting roles...
Surprise guests, kind innkeepers, hostlers, a baker, several musicians, bartenders, patrons, drunks, ruffians, clerks, bystanders, a few farmers, numerous sailors and other good and honest men and women; along with several horses, including **Caesar, Daisy,** and **Dalrymple**.

Chawton Cottage

Residence of the author
of *Sense and Sensibility*
located on the grounds
of Chawton House
close by the Town of Alton
in Hampshire, England

RIDGWAY KENNEDY

❦1❦

"N o! No! No!"

A boy…a lad, not a man—but doing a man's work—ran toward a tall figure wearing a grime-streaked, oilcloth greatcoat.

The pistol in the man's hand went off.

"No!" wailed the lad.

The man returned the bulky flintlock to his coat pocket.

A red stain spread on a white patch of fur on the animal's hindquarters. The man's greasy black hair spread out from under an oilcloth cap and dangled around his face as he leaned over the creature, taking the two forepaws in his left hand and the hind paws in his right. The dog growled, then cried with pain but did not try to fight. In three strides, the man reached the fence and heaved the animal over. The dog landed hard with a short, agonized yelp.

"Your damned cur will live," the man said, turning toward the lad. "Nothing but a nick on his arse."

The man approached the boy, close enough to strike him if he so chose. Close enough to poison the child with his rank breath and spatter him with spittle.

"Now, are you going to believe me? Ha? Now do you understand?" The man snarled. "This ain't the commons! 'Tis His Lordship's land and you're trespassin'!" The boy wept but did not cower. "It's always been—"

"Not anymore."

"Mr Hinch, it's always been—"

"Not anymore!" the man roared back. "The old commons was enclosed. We told you that again and again. Act of Parlymint. Your pasture's across there."

"But we were only crossing—"

"You're trespassing on His Lordship's land!"

"But—"

"They's no buts! Now gather up your woolies," Hinch said, gesturing toward seven sheep grazing nearby. "Gather your woolies and get 'em out."

But the boy, still crying, walked to the fence. He slipped between the rails and knelt beside the dog.

Hinch cursed. Then, working slowly with the patience and craft of an experienced gamekeeper, he moved around the sheep guiding them toward an open gate a few yards away down the fence.

"Damn sheep," he muttered, as he chivvied the animals. His gaze darted to the boy and his dog. "Damn sheep."

❧ 2 ❧

"Turning off here," the driver said. The brawny young man with a cap of shocking red hair slowed the wagon and halted at a crossroad in the tiny village of Bentley.

"I'll be off then," the man seated beside him said. "And many thanks, lad."

"Let me give you a hand."

"That would be a feat." Both men chuckled as they heaved a large wooden box—a sea chest it was—from the back of the wagon.

"Such a day," the driver said. "And it being November."

"Fair weather and a following wind," the passenger said. "You canna want for more."

The men set the trunk down in a sunlit clearing just beyond the crossroad and returned to the wagon. While the driver regained his perch, the passenger removed a small, oblong leather case from below the seat. He slipped his left arm through a strap and slung the case over his shoulder.

"Will you be visitin' us later? Coming back this way?" the driver said. "Now we've traveled together, I'd like to hear you play that thing. See if you're any good."

"Well, will you give your beast a rest?" the passenger said, nodding at the bony gray horse in the wagon traces. "I'll be playin' for my supper now."

On this unusually warm day in late November, there were no fields to plow or reap. The young man would be home in good time for his chores. "Aye, it's a good time to rest the nag," he said.

Heavy traffic plied the Winchester Road that day. The usual wagons and coaches traveled their routes. Additionally, the warm weather encouraged pleasure outings in a variety of open carriages.

While the driver attended to his horse and wagon, his passenger opened the sea chest, took out a plain wooden plank, and set it on the ground. He placed his instrument carefully on top of the chest and was tightening the band of well-rosined horsehair on a violin bow when the driver rejoined him.

"Looks mighty old," the driver said, admiring the violin. "Nice looking wood."

"She's a fine, old fiddle," the passenger said as he picked it up and seated himself on the sea chest, his feet on the board. "Got her in Italy. Man who sold her to me said she was from Cremona. That's a town famous for makin' fiddles. 'Course, that might'a just been talk. Still, she's a good old girl. Now put the fiddle case right in front there. Leave it open. If I can inspire 'em, it might pick up a copper or two."

With his instrument tucked firmly under his chin, the fiddler placed the bow on the chest next to him. With his left hand, he released the strap on the tan leather glove he was wearing on his other hand. He gave his right hand a shake and the glove fell off. It hit the top of the chest with a noticeable thud.

The better parts of three fingers on his right hand were missing.

Grasping the bow in an odd way with just his thumb, the bit of one finger, and his little finger, he began tuning his instrument.

The driver had recognized the glove and knew what it meant when he picked up his passenger. Farm life is full of accidents that can cut off a finger or two or three. He showed no surprise.

"All right," the fiddler said, plucking the strings of his instrument with the fingers of his left hand and raising his bow. "That'll do. Are ya' ready, lad?"

The driver nodded.

The fiddler tapped his feet on the board, setting up a rhythm that sounded like an ironshod horse trotting on cobbles. "Here you go—a tune just for you. It's called the *Red-Haired Boy*."

And he was off.

It was only one instrument, out of doors—no walls or ceiling to contain the sound and resonate—but it was glorious. As the tune tripped along brightly, the red-haired lad's face split with his broadest grin, and he shuffled his feet to the music.

Soon, he was not the only one.

A passing chaise stopped. Two ladies stepped out to join the young man while their driver stood nearby holding the horses. A minute later, four passengers from a double phaeton joined the listeners. Two elderly men with pints in hand emerged from the Red Lion House across the road and wandered over to listen. A crofter and his boy halted their wagon and joined the group.

The London-bound mail coach from Winchester stopped at the Red Lion to drop off two more ladies. Passengers within and atop listened and begged the coachman to stay a while.

"Nay, nay. I have a schedule to keep," he said. "You can get off and listen, and have yourselves a good, long walk." The coach moved on.

A beautifully appointed curricle arrived; a two-seater drawn by two horses. The driver, a fashionably dressed young man with flowing blond hair, edged his conveyance onto the verge. He descended to hold his horses and listened intently, a little bit apart.

Several more coaches and wagons stopped, leaving just enough room for others to pass through. Many of the onlookers just listened, but there were dancers, too.

Six of the gentlefolk in the crowd organized themselves into a country dance set. The fiddler recognized the pattern they had chosen and called on them to return to their places. Then the music flowed into the proper tune for the dance. The couples squealed with delight and resumed their caper.

Copper and even a few silver coins began to populate the fiddle case. The red-haired boy noticed and grinned. The fiddler knew what he was about. He ended the dance tune, then stood to begin a different piece.

"Here's a sailor man's dance." He began a quick-stepping, heel-clicking dance while playing a sprightly tune. "'Tis a hornpipe," he said, turning about on his tiny stage. When he ended the dance, more copper and silver appeared in the fiddle case.

"Have we any Scots about?" he asked.

A young gentleman gave a hesitant wave. "I am attending the University in Edinburgh. Will that do?"

"Fair enough," the fiddler said. "Here's a tune from Robbie Burns."

He played a new melody, with the fiddle crooked in his arm, bracing it on his shoulder rather than tucking it under his chin.

> *"There's not the care on every hand,*
> *in every hour passes-oh"*

The listeners quieted. Couples joined hands and gentlemen passed their arms behind the backs of their ladies. Some recognized the song and joined in when the chorus came around.

> *"Green grow the rushes oh*
> *Green grow the rushes oh*
> *The sweetest hours ere I spent*
> *Were spent among the lassies oh"*

By the end of the second refrain, all the bystanders were singing in a grand chorus. The song ended to great applause.

Now, grasping his fiddle and bow in his left hand, he raised his right hand and addressed the gathering.

"As you can see, a poor mathematician such as m'self will have difficulty counting to ten. One, two, and a half, maybe? And where do you go from there?" he said, waving his maimed right hand. "Me mathematical skills got addled on Monsieur Bonaparte's account, but I got back payment enough. We settled our business at Trafalgar!"

Applause and grunts of appreciation. The red-haired boy put two fingers in his mouth and let out an piercing whistle.

"On board the *Victory*, I was, with Nelson himself."

The noise from the crowd doubled.

"So, I'll ask you to sing with me to celebrate the men, the ships, and the immortal memory."

Then, with a triumphant scrape on his fiddle, he set out.

> *"Cheer up me lads*
> *it's to glory we steer"*

The start of *Heart of Oak*, the well-worn naval anthem. The onlookers knew it well when the chorus came around.

> *"Heart of oak,*
> *are our ships"*

…they sang with feeling.

> *"Heart of oak*
> *are our men"*

…they sang, even louder.

By the end of the second chorus, everyone in the crowd had joined in. As they reached the final strain, folk as far away as London might have been able to hear them.

After decades of war, protected by the wooden walls of the Royal Navy, all Britons were prepared to celebrate their fighting sailors.

Twice through the chorus, and then, to great applause, the concert ended. Satiated, the departing audience took time to double the layer of copper and silver in the fiddle case. The fiddler took the stage once more.

"Is there anyone takin' the road west with room for an old sailor and his chest?" the fiddler cried out.

No offers were forthcoming.

"Anyone travelin' toward Winchester? Give us a ride?"

More quiet. Then the young dandy who had arrived in the two-seater waved a hand.

"We must show respect for our fighting navy men, must we not?" the young man said when the fiddler approached him. "I can offer a ride, most certainly, but not all the way to Winchester."

"That's just the direction," the fiddler said. "I'm for Alton. I'm told it's the nearest town to the village of Chawton with an inn."

"Then indeed, I am your man," the curricle driver said. "Aloysius Ellicott. My home—Kellingsford— Perhaps you've heard of it? A league beyond Alton."

"Worth," the fiddler said with a polite nod. "Freddy Worth."

The musician collected his earnings and placed his tools in their softly padded home. He repacked his chest and swung the instrument case over his shoulder. Poking his right hand through a spliced loop on one end of the sea chest and grasping the handle on the other end with his left, he hoisted the trunk, then frowned as he approached the elegant curricle. His face brightened when the young gentleman unfastened a tailgate to accommodate the chest.

"You can put your instrument here," Aloysius said. "Plenty of room."

The fiddler laughed. "Nay, she stays close with me."

As the evening chill settled in, the young Mr Ellicott and Mr Worth buttoned their coats. After taking a quick turn around his conveyance, inspecting the harnesses and patting his horses, he climbed aboard the springy carriage. Worth followed, sitting to his right.

"Two hours, I'll say," Aloysius said. "Possibly less. You'll have your pick of the inns this time of year. The Rose and Crown is nice. I would avoid the Kings Arms as a landlord is a bit of a prick. Oh, shame on me. I shouldn't speak ill. Still if it were my choice…"

Aloysius continued a spirited monologue in this fashion, praising the area's delights, alternating between sincerity and sarcasm. Occasional humorous comparisons to Piccadilly and the Pall Mall made it clear the young man viewed Alton as a rustic village. *A country gentleman with a yearning for city life,* Worth thought.

"So, what *actually* caused your injury?" the young gentleman asked, taking a sudden, sharp turn in his discourse. "That story was marvelous. Trafalgar. Nelson. You had them enraptured. Enthralled. What a windup." He looked directly at Worth. "So," he continued, in a sly tone, "What really happened? Your hand?"

"Like I said, I was serving on the *Victory*—"

"Oh, come now," Aloysius said. "Just between us. I won't spoil your performance."

Worth looked at the young man, his immaculate attire, his flowing blond hair. The older man's features clouded briefly, then eased.

"Just an accident. On board ship. Got me hand caught."

"I knew it." Aloysius said. Then he quickly added: "Bloody bad luck. Has it been difficult? With playing the violin?"

"It's not easy," Worth said. "Most folk look at a fiddler and think it's the left hand dancing on the strings, what's doing all the hard work. They don't know that the bow is an instrument all by itself. A fine bow has just as much music in it as a fine fiddle. And playing the bow takes a touch, and skill, and a lifetime o' practice. So, no, Mr Ellicott. It's not easy."

❧3❧

"Intolerable, I say. That's what it is. Intolerable."

Admiral William Harwell, a bluff man, wide and fit, wearing a navy dress uniform, placed two fists on the desk and leaned in. Again, he smashed his fist down on the table.

"Do you hear me?"

The confrontation in the middle of the library echoed out into the marble and stone hall. The reading table generally found in such a room had been replaced by a much smaller, flat-topped writing desk. The Honorable Percival Ellicott sat at the desk with his back to the fireplace, centered between two large windows. He continued to peruse his papers and make notes.

The navy man fronted a delegation. Three men, wearing coarse wool garments in shades of gray and brown, waited close behind as the admiral continued his effort to drive home his point.

In the farthest corner of the room, his brother, Aloysius Ellicott, fastidiously dressed, slouched in a large armchair, holding a book, suggesting that he might be reading. The gamekeeper, Hinch, lurked in the darkest corner of the room.

"Do you hear me?" the admiral bellowed again.

The man seated at the desk gave no indication he did. He continued with his papers, made a note with his pen, blotted it, and shifted the foolscap across the desk. Then he broke the seal on another letter, without acknowledging the officer's tirade.

The admiral addressed the men who accompanied him. "This is what you have been given from Mr Ellicott? This silence? This…nothing?"

Admiral Harwell turned away, looked up toward the ceiling, and paced in a small circle. His companions backed away to give him room. The angry officer took a deep breath and returned to face the seated man.

"Listen to me now, sir."

No response.

"Percival." He spoke the seated man's Christian name with a snarl. "These men have reason for concern. I have reason for concern. You have divided their crofts, taken possession of fertile soil and good pasture, and left them with steep, rock-strewn, fallow ground. They are my tenants. My income rests on the success of their harvest. Can you not see? Your action has injured them and injured me!"

Silence.

"It's not just the income for my estate that's damaged. There's your portion as well."

Still no answer.

"And then, your damned gamekeeper shot Mr Morgan's dog. A herder. A damned fine sheep dog!"

All the visitors eyed the unkempt man in the stained oilcloth great-coat, standing in shadow, shifting from one foot to the other.

"Ah, that," Percival said, turning toward the estate's gamekeeper. "Hinch, did you kill it?"

The gamekeeper looked at each of the visitors before answering.

"Nay, sir."

"Might have, just as well, sir," Mr Morgan shouted. "The dog can't run. He's ruint."

"Hinch, go fetch Mr Sloat for me," Percival said.

"There is no good end to it, sir," the admiral said. "This 'enclosing' makes no sense. The income from my estate will be halved, as will your own. You must—"

"Must?" Percival asked. "You must not tell me what I must do. The land must be put to the most productive use. We must be efficient, you see. We must make improvements. The Enclosure Act reflects Parliament's wisdom on the matter."

"Wisdom? Wisdom, you call it?" the admiral said, coloring. "Parliament's wisdom will ruin me. While I have been at sea, my debt has doubled. Your man Adderly—you were the one who recommended him—has managed to turn my property's small income into a heavy loss. I should've left my steward, Radford, in charge. He's no good with numbers, but it couldn't have been this bad. Your Enclosure does nothing but cause losses, sir. And my tenants' losses are my losses! Is this how you reward a man who defended you from the Bonaparte? Is this my reward?"

The admiral took a breath.

"We thank you for your service," Percival said, glancing up at the admiral. "Perhaps your prize money will see you through this difficult time?" He addressed a small man with a trim, black moustache entering the room. "Ah, Sloat."

"Yes, sir," the small man said, approaching the desk. He donned a pair of spectacles from his breast pocket, opened a notebook, and peered at Percival, head cocked to one side and a pencil poised.

"Mr Morgan here," Percival said, "his dog was injured on our property. Trespassing to be sure, but I am confident it was only a misunderstanding. Give him five shillings to...to compensate him for his trouble. You may withdraw the funds from the gamekeeper's account."

Hinch's lip curled with only the slightest quiver.

"How stand our accounts with the good admiral here?" Percival continued.

"We've extended credit several times now at Mr Adderly's request," Sloat said.

"There!" the admiral exclaimed. "Mr Adderly, not me. Not by my request."

"Quite true," Percival said. "But he was properly designated. All perfectly legal. Now, let us find our way through this, shall we? Sloat, what is our current return on capital?"

"Right round five percent," Sloat said.

"And the sum?"

"A little more than five hundred pounds, sir."

"Five hundred!" the admiral shouted. "No. I saw the figures—"

"Calm yourself, Admiral," Percival said. "Sloat, you're sure?"

The little man turned several pages, squinted at his notebook, and read a list of transactions, fees, and interest charges. He concluded his recitation with the description of a promissory note, signed by Mr Adderley, in lieu of rents, for the five preceding years.

The admiral stood speechless.

"So that's five hundred twelve and six," Sloat concluded. "I can, of course, supply all the letters of agreement."

"Sloat, you know the admiral has been of great service to the nation," Percival said. "This seems rather a rude homecoming for our fighting navy. Can you suggest any remedy?"

"Well, sir," Sloat said, "we can certainly give consideration to the terms."

"Yes, that might signify. Place the debt in abeyance. Temporarily. There, Admiral. We have a solution. You can have additional time—let us say six months—to settle your debt. See to it, Sloat. Oh, and go fetch my sister," Percival said, turning away from the admiral. "I have some papers for her to give to our father."

Sloat stepped to the side to pass the admiral.

Harwell again placed both fists on the desk and leaned toward Percival.

"You…miserable! Why, I…! This shall not…! You...!" the admiral choked, seething.

Percival returned his eyes to the papers.

"This shall not stand!" Harwell said, drawing a white glove from his uniform pocket. Holding the fingers of the glove, he stepped close to the desk and lashed the left side of Percival's face with the glove's gauntlet. The kid leather burned a pink rash on Percival's cheek and jaw. The admiral threw the glove down on Percival's papers as the stunned gentleman looked up to meet his eyes.

Then, Percival smiled.

"What is this?" he said, still smiling, *smirking*. "A challenge? An affair of honor? Oh, my dear admiral. How quaint." Percival laughed. "You demand satisfaction?"

"This has become a matter of honor," the admiral said.

The laughter continued. "Honor? What is honor? A word, is it not? Oh, my poor admiral, I must inform you that dueling is decidedly out of fashion. But you were away, so it is likely you did not hear. We settle these matters in courts today. Far more civilized."

Movement in the vestibule caught his eye.

"Ah, Father!" Percival said.

All eyes turned to the doorway where a stout but still handsome older gentleman strode into the room, wearing a bright burgundy coat trimmed with cut silk velvet. Ruffles peeked from the coat cuffs, and the white satin, flowered-brocade waistcoat, trimmed with gold braid, set off the embroidered collar. Stripes on the pantaloons, gold and red, carried the eye to glistening buckles and gleaming leather of his dress shoes with tall, beautifully curved heels.

The Right Honorable Horatio, The Viscount Kellingsford, presented himself in the fashion ideal from the middle of the previous century. Miss Letitia Ellicott, his daughter, a plump lady in an equally outdated gown, followed him.

"Percival, my good boy, have a look at this," Lord Kellingsford said, pausing in front of the writing desk and turning once around. "Perfect fit. Perfect. No need to touch a seam. Where is the glass? There was a looking glass—a tall, standing glass right here."

"Lord Kellingsford," Admiral Harwell said, striding toward the lord of manor. "Lord Kellingsford, I must have a word."

"Ha," Lord Kellingsford said, turning to face the admiral. "Navy man, I see. Decent uniform, but rather plain, do you not think? Have you no more ribbons? Or some medals? And your sword? You need a sword, sir. That would dress you up proper. Nothing better than a fine uniform," Lord Kellingsford continued. "Have you considered a dragoon? Or possibly a hussar? Something with a bit more color? I'm very partial to the dragoons, myself. Most striking."

He stopped speaking abruptly, looked at Admiral Harwell, and walked up to him.

"I know you."

"Yes, my lord," the admiral said.

"Navy man."

"Yes, my lord."

"Nelson! Lord Nelson! How good of you to come," Lord Kellingsford said, beaming at the admiral and executing a deep bow. "Your Lordship."

"Ah, not Lord Nelson, sir. Not the viscount," the admiral said. "Harwell, Your Lordship. Admiral William Harwell. Your tenant, sir. I have urgent business to discuss with you."

"Not Lord Nelson?"

"No, my lord."

"Are you sure?"

"Quite sure." A pause. "Lord Nelson is dead, my lord," Harwell said. "He died at Trafalgar."

"Nelson is dead?" Lord Kellingsford said. "No. No, it can't be! Nelson is dead?"

The admiral opened his mouth, but, before words could arrive, His Lordship addressed his daughter.

"Letitia, my dear. I bear sad tidings. Nelson is dead. Dead," he concluded with a great sigh, bowing his head. "Dead." Then, as if awaking from a brief slumber, Lord Kellingsford brightened and faced Letitia again. "Mourning. We must be in mourning dress. I have just the thing. The black velvet. And the breeches—sateen, I recall. And there's the crepe neckcloth. We shall have mourning…" And he left the room.

"Sloat. Hinch," Percival said, rising from his desk. "With me, if you please."

As he stepped around the desk, he picked up the white leather glove. He approached the admiral and held it out.

Harwell glared at him. Percival dropped the glove.

"Oh, how clumsy of me," Percival said. He turned his back on the admiral and walked out of the room.

The room fell quiet.

"A very pretty sight, the old man, eh?"

Lord Kellingsford's younger son rose from the corner armchair to approach the admiral and his tenants.

"My father may have lost his wits but never his love of fashion."

"Aloysius," the admiral said, "your tongue."

"'Tis naught but the truth. We are such a beautiful family," the young gentleman said. He spread his arms and offered a deep bow to the naval officer.

"We need your father to step in—to be reasonable," Harwell said. "Percival will ruin us all."

"Then, we shall all be ruined," Aloysius said. "Whilst father looks the part of lord of the manor, he is insensible to his duties. Percival rules in all but title."

"Damn, damn, damn," the admiral muttered. "Enclosure. How long has that been about?"

"Percy has been pursuing it for at least three years now. He finally slipped his Act through in the last session of Parliament."

"What's the purpose? Enclosure is ruining his tenants which, in time, will ruin him."

"He thinks otherwise," Aloysius said. "He plans to enclose all the land after the tenants fail. The larger fields and pasturage will be very profitable, Percy says. It all seems like far too much work to me."

"This must not...will not...stand," the admiral said, his color rising again.

"That seems...improbable," Aloysius said. "Percival has my father's voice. But then, something might change."

As the admiral conferred with the tenants, a strong, deep voice echoed in the front hall.

"I know the way. No need for an escort."

An army officer appeared in the doorway, resplendent in his regimentals, and entered the room.

"Reginald," Aloysius said, greeting the new arrival with a warm handshake.

"Lieutenant Wembley," the admiral said. "You look well."

"Admiral Harwell," Wembley said, with the click of his heels and offering an easy salute.

"I am mistaken," the admiral said. "An additional bar and pip, I see. It is Captain Wembley now."

"A recent addition," Wembley said, touching the board on his shoulder. "I came into some money and invested in the commission."

"Money well spent," the admiral said. "Trying business, you landsmen have. Purchasing commissions. I like the navy way—fight for 'em or die for 'em. Good living though, with peace coming now. Our lot, we navy men, will be put ashore on half pay in double quick time. You army chaps will have a billet and full pay, even if they muster out all the troops."

"One can hope," Wembley said. "Your ship?"

"*Audacious*," the admiral said. "An old three-decker. She's been sent up the river to the breakers yard."

"Well, that's a sorry business."

"Not so. She was slow and frequently missed her stays. Unfit for pursuit or attack. And with the sad state of her lower futtocks—it was her time. A sorry old lady, I'll warrant, but I will miss her.

"Now men"—turning to Mr Morgan and the other tenants— "it's time to retire, clear the decks, and plan our next action against this enclosure business." Nodding to Wembley and Aloysius, he said, "Good day," and gathered his delegation and exited the room.

Alone, Aloysius approached Wembley, reached up, and touched the badge on the officer's uniform.

"Captain."

❧ 4 ❧

Standing under a small portico that protected the front door, Worth found a porcelain knob fastened to a fine chain and pulled it gently. A small, mellow bell sounded on the other side of the door. *A perfect D*, he thought. *Neither sharp nor flat. Pleasant.*

The substantial brick house stood on the north side of the Winchester Road, about one and a half miles from his lodgings in Alton. With his instrument slung over his shoulder, he traveled lightly. Sunshine, mild weather; it had been a pleasant walk, but he remained uncertain about the reception he would receive.

A maid came to the door and greeted him skeptically.

"I'm answering a summons from Miss Austen," he said. "She sent an inquiry to Mr Wilson." He withdrew a letter from his coat pocket.

The maid still looked suspicious, but recognizing the familiar hand, she allowed the visitor to enter and took the stairs up.

Worth surveyed the tidy parlor. *It looks, in some ways, like a library,* he thought.

Several books rested on tables, one upon a chair, and another upon on the settee. He saw place markers in a few of them. On the interior wall that formed a right angle with the front of the house, there stood a large bookcase—nearly full.

He noted the duplicates of some editions. Two sets of the three-volume novel *Sense and Sensibility* sat next to two more three-deckers of *Pride and Prejudice*. On the bottom shelf—he counted them off with surprise— no fewer than five sets of the volumes for *Mansfield Park*.

Worth knew the books well. Musicians frequently had long, quiet times between engagements; time for reading. As a musician who must engage with his patrons, for the most part ladies, he had no end of reading recommendations and offerings of book loans. He had even subscribed to a circulating library for a time. He knew the works of Mrs Radcliffe, Charlotte Lennox and, of course, the poetry of Lord Byron and Mr Scott.

A square pianoforte against the wall opposite the door spoke of music in the house. A classical score, a challenging piece and not some mere étude, occupied the music stand. The musician or musicians in the house possessed most respectable skills.

The maid descended the stairs and exited through a rear door of the house. Then, the lady herself appeared.

"Miss Austen," Worth said with an appropriate bow.

She was of medium height, wearing a lace trimmed morning gown, and approached him with a puzzled expression.

"You are…?"

"Worth, ma'am. Freddy Worth. But," he added quickly, "I am here at the urging of Mr Wilson. You see—"

"Mr Wilson?"

"Aye, Miss Austen. Now, of course, in your letter you asked for him, but as it approaches the holidays, he's extremely busy. So, he asked me to come in his stead."

"My letter?"

"Aye, requesting his—or rather our—assistance. You see—"

Worth's speech was cut off as another person entered through the back door of the house, closing the door with a brisk kick from a large boot. Looking more closely, Worth thought she was a woman.

"Mr Wilson!" the newcomer said.

Decidedly a woman.

"Flora told me you had arrived."

The removal of an oversized hat and man's greatcoat revealed a shorter and slighter lady, dressed in a well-worn frock and a mud-spattered apron. As she kicked off the oversized boots and discarded her apron, hair tumbled around her face.

"I see it now," said the lady who had come down the stairs. "You are expected by my sister, Miss Jane Austen."

"Good day," the new arrival said as she stepped into slippers. "So nice to meet you. I have heard such wonderful reports about your assemblies in Town. It is so very kind of you to travel all this way."

She spoke quickly, in a cheerful soprano. She tucked her hair under a white, lace-trimmed cap.

"You have met my sister, Miss Cassandra Austen," she said. "I am Miss *Jane* Austen." She approached Worth and dropped a polite curtsy. He bowed. "Now, shall we have some tea and discuss our business?"

"Your business?" Cassandra asked.

"Yes," Jane replied. "Very important business, and no, I have not discussed it with you."

She spoke to her sister with a mixture defiance and humor.

"Mr Wilson," she said with an air of confidentiality, "being the little sister can be such a trial."

"Then, little sister," Cassandra said, "you will surely want to know that this is not Mr Wilson."

"Oh," Jane said, turning toward the man. "Not? But, the letter…?"

"Worth, ma'am. I am called Freddy Worth. And I am…ah…well…Mr Wilson, y'see…like I said, he's a wee bit busy and he asked me t' take his place."

"Well now," Jane said. "I am not at all certain this will do. And now the truth is revealed, I am also quite sure that you do not sound very much like a proper dancing master."

"A dancing master?" Cassandra asked. "And what is your business with a dancing master?"

"I am planning a ball, Cass. For my birthday. I shall be forty years upon the earth and descend permanently into spinsterhood. I am decided that before I am so resigned, I shall have a ball. But," she continued, turning to face Worth, "to have my ball, I must have a proper dancing master. None but the best will do."

"Now, Miss Jane, I'm sure—"

"Mr Wilson is the top of Town. He is much in demand. He has volumes and volumes of dances published and he even puts his advertisements in rhyme," Jane said. "They are terribly clever, Cass."

"This is not Mr Wilson, Jane," Cassandra said. "He may not even be a fair facsimile."

"A poor reproduction?" Jane asked, circling to Worth's side, observing his shabby travel cloak.

"He most certainly does not sound like a proper dancing master," Cassandra said. "More likely"—she fixed Worth with a glare— "Mr Worth, are you a Scot?"

Worth took a half step backward.

"English, ma'am," Worth said. "But from hard by the Borders, so there's a wee bit of a lilt. Now if I was to say 'Noo, thaur is a braw sassenach chiel, weel dressed in a frock jeekit and breeches.'"

"What was that?" Jane said.

"Sounded like the grumbling of a distressed highland *coo*," Cassandra said, pronouncing the word "cow" in a proper Scottish burr.

"A close approximate," Worth said. "'Tis how a *mon* from up north o' the Clyde might describe a gentleman from London or thereabouts."

The ladies offered slight smiles, but Jane remained concerned. "What is wanted is a proper English ball," she said.

"And you're thinkin' that some dour old Yorkshireman canna manage such a feat?" Worth asked, with a hint of anger. He caught himself, took a deep breath and continued. "Miss Austen"—nodding to Cassandra—"Miss Jane"—nodding to Jane— "I'm most hopeful that I can set your minds at ease."

He unslung his fiddle case, opened it, and prepared to play. He removed his prosthetic hand.

To the Austen sisters, as country dwellers, the sight of such injuries was not uncommon: disfigurement since birth, work injuries, and, in the recent years of war, far too many battle scars. Still, in genteel houses, ladies' eyes were shielded.

Worth stood, tucked his instrument under his chin, and touched the strings with his bow until the pitch was satisfactory. He addressed the sisters:

"Ladies and gentlemen," he said in an accent that would suit a lord, or at least the most proper butler. "Our first dance is about to begin. Gentlemen, please choose your partners. It shall be longways, for as many as will."

The ladies stared at him. First Cassandra, then Jane, took places on the settee, facing the bookshelves. Cassandra folded her arms in front of her.

"Now, Miss Austen, Miss Jane, what sort of dance shall we have?"

"A country dance," Jane suggested, "familiar to us all."

"Something from Mr Wilson or Mr Budd, perhaps," Cassandra said.

In an aside in his natural voice, Worth said, "At a proper ball, we'll play one time through the tune to announce the dance to the hall while sets are assembling. Being as our set is already waiting, we'll begin."

Then, the dancing master transformed into the fiddler. After two quick notes, he launched into a lively melody. The ladies seemed to recognize it immediately: *My Love She's but a Lassie Yet*.

A bright tune for a quick step. In Town, many a lady asked for it and selected lively steps to go with it.

Cassandra remained unmoved, Worth saw. Her younger sister, he could see, struggled to contain a smile. One foot was keeping time with him.

After three times through the tune, displaying improvisations and double stops, he brought it to a smooth, graceful conclusion.

Jane gave a small smile, patted her hands together, and nodded. Cassandra offered only a curt nod.

Worth thought humor might soften her mien and ventured *abroad*.

"Perhaps ze ladies would prefer something from ze continent," he said in an exaggerated French accent. "Shall we dance ze quadrille...or a new dance created to fit ze melody from ze Scottish bagpipers—Monsieur *Bonaparte's Retreat*."

At this, both Miss Austens replied with small smiles.

"*Ach du lieber*," Worth said, speaking with a Germanic inflection. "You vants de German danze. For da danzin der Deutschland, you vill haff to settle for *ein Valtzer*."

He raised his bow and, with jerky motions suggesting a clockwork musician, a comically precise waltz flowed from his instrument.

When Worth ended the piece, he detected a thawing in the ladies' demeanors, in Jane somewhat more than her sister. But an air of disappointment hung in the air.

"Mr Worth, you are a most surprising dancing master," Jane said.

"An unwelcome surprise, I fear," he said, as he put away his instrument, "and a poor substitute for Mr Wilson. I'll refrain from troubling you any longer. I'll return to Town as quickly as possible and speak with him. Possibly he'll have another person to recommend."

"No, no, good sir. You mistake me," Jane said. "Your demonstration was excellent."

"Parlor tricks, ma'am. A busker's antics. As your sister kens, I'm not a proper dancing master."

He did *not* confess he was an apprentice of a sort who was learning while working with his fiddle and bow. He did *not* admit he was equally as worried as they might have been about his ability to create a program and provide prompting if it was necessary. He did *not* divulge his lack of experience dealing with the disasters that occurred when unskilled or inebriated dancers—always men—took places in a set and caused chaos. He was *not* going to disclose he had never been responsible for organizing a ball before.

"Hold, Mr Worth," Cassandra said. "You must not be routed on my account. My sister has sent for a dancing master. You must hear her out."

Worth finished putting his instrument away and replaced his prosthetic. He said nothing.

"I meant no offense when I teased you regarding your brogue," Cassandra continued. "It is ...mellow. Pleasing to the ear. And your dancing master's voice is very fine."

Worth glanced briefly at Cassandra, shrugged his shoulders, and finished securing his instrument case.

"I thank you for your courtesies," he said, slipping into his coat. "I ken that time is fleeting. I'll get back to Mr Wilson on the morrow."

"You had better not do that, sir." Jane spoke up. "That would not be at all wise."

The dancing master looked at her, a question on his face.

"Mr Wilson sent you here in the belief that you were a capable dancing master. He received my letter. He sent you to assist me. Am I not correct?"

Worth narrowed his eyes as he looked at her. She took two paces toward him, stopped, and placed her hands on her hips.

"And now," Jane continued, "you plan to scurry back to London and ask him to send someone else? He will most certainly not be pleased with that result."

No, Worth knew, *he would not.*

"You are a competent musician. You have the voice of a gentleman when you have a care to use it, and you seem to have some understanding of my wants. Would it not be better for you to allow me to decide whether you are 'a proper dancing master' or not?"

Her arms folded, she looked sure of herself, he thought. And she was smiling. And she was right.

"Cass, will you see what Flora has done with our tea? We must have tea, Mr Worth, I am sure you agree?"

He much preferred coffee but nodded and removed his coat.

"Now, we must discuss the details. Please sit here," Jane said, indicating a chair by a small table. She drew an additional chair and sat opposite him. "The date is 16 December. All else we shall determine."

Cassandra returned shortly with Flora and a tea service.

For the next half an hour, Jane described her feelings about dancing and balls, proper music, the scourge of war and dearth of gentlemen, and the perils of old age that sent ladies to the sides and gentlemen to the card room. Or, with the gentlemen, was that simply a lack of civility?

"How is it, that once a man is married, he loses interest in dancing and turns into one's father?" she wondered aloud, among many similar observations.

Worth listened attentively and penciled notes in the small book he carried. He took in the furnishings and the room. He wondered at this lady and the shelves full of books.

By the time the teacups were emptied, Jane and the dancing master agreed to inspect the assembly rooms. They would meet at ten o'clock the following day in front of the Bank of Alton, her brother Henry's bank.

"It is directly across from the assembly rooms. I will send word for the landlord to meet us," she announced decisively.

Worth prepared to depart, but the bookshelves again caught his notice.

"Miss Jane," he said, "upon my arrival, I could'na help but notice your library. It's a very large collection."

"Yes." Jane nodded.

"And there seems to be one author with precedence over all others. *Sense and Sensibility*. Lovely story about two quite interesting sisters." He glanced at Jane and Cassandra. His lips curled. He removed the first volume of one copy and gently opened it. "Written by 'A Lady.' Two full copies of the novel," he said, replacing the volume. "And here's *Pride and Prejudice*. Two more copies; all three volumes. And I confess it's a favorite of mine." He had taken another volume out and gently opened it. "By the author of *Sense and Sensibility*. Down here," he continued, as he put the volume back and bent slightly, eyeing the lower tier, "is an entire shelf filled with *Mansfield Park*. Which, I noted when I read it, is also by the author of *Sense and Sensibility*."

The sisters looked at Worth with surprise, Jane with the odd expression of someone straining to hide her delight.

"It would seem to be a most curious collection, unless——? Miss Jane, I'd like know, if it's not too bold, would you be that lady?"

❧ 5 ❧

"A very…interesting…person," Cassandra said, watching Worth turn on to the Winchester Road. "You might have mentioned your plans."

"He is talented," Jane said. "Thomas Wilson is, by far, the most popular dancing master in London today."

Cassandra remained silent.

"While Wilson is most excellent, I'm sure, his proxy…this Mr Worth…I am not displeased."

Cassandra crossed her arms, maintaining her silence.

"I did not want to dispute the matter with you, my dear sister," Jane said after a pause. "As well you know, I attend your gifts of prophecy. I have heeded you well. Likely too well. I have given this plan great consideration, and I did not want to risk a dire prediction from my closest, dearest advisor."

"Inviting a meeting with a complete stranger," Cassandra said. "A man, and a ball…this plan…what is this all about? This ball?"

"We love to dance," Jane said. "It is for my birthday. Is that not sufficient?"

"Is this to be a public event? Will it have subscribers?"

"No, no, good sister. It will be private, and by our invitation."

"Then, consider the price," Cassandra said. "The cost of a proper ball is no small undertaking, no mean expense."

"True, true, but I am now not without means," Jane said.

"The tide flows against us. Peace brings joy, but hardship as well. Henry's bank—"

"His concern is with the Alton establishment. His London bank remains steady, he says, and, Cassandra, I have nearly three hundred from *Mansfield Park*. I possess capital. I have the means."

"Your success has been remarkable, Jane, and we love you all the more for it. But, is it wise at such a time to diminish your reserve…for a party?"

"Now here is my dear sister, weighted with worry and concern," Jane said, approaching her sister and gently embracing her. She continued, her face close to her sister's, speaking with the greatest sincerity. "Did you hear me? I have a plan."

"Then, will it please you to share your plan with me?"

"Today, my dear sister, I shall not," Jane said. "No previews. No early pages. No drafts, revisions, or printers' proofs. You will have to wait to discover the faults of this little scheme of mine in their full flower."

"But…but, Jane. This is not…and the expenses…" Cassandra struggled to find an argument to move her younger sister. "This dancing master—this Mr Worth. He may very well not be what he seems."

"Mr Worth!" Jane exclaimed, and then laughed. "I am quite certain that he is not what he seems."

"Jane!"

"Cassandra!"

Jane pressed on. "My course has been laid and the wind is fair. You must prepare yourself for society. What gown will you wear? New dancing slippers? We are going to host the most wonderful ball."

❧ 6 ❧

The Ship, a tidy little inn, occupied a corner on the Alton market square next to a bakery. Ever a loyal navy man, Worth chose it for his anchorage over the much grander Rose and Crown across the way. Upon his return from his first meeting with the Miss Austens, he found an unoccupied corner in the public room to take his supper.

"Mutton stew. Four pence. Includes a nice bit o' brown bread. Or," the man behind the bar said, looking at Worth carefully, "if you've got a taste for finer food, we've got a fine ragout du Mouton. Very tasty. Includes the bread and only another tuppence."

Worth raised an eyebrow. The barkeeper shrugged. Worth was soon back in his corner table with a brimming bowl, bread, and a pint of bitter.

He was not the only navy man to be drawn to The Ship. Three sailors, just paid off in Portsmouth, were sharing a parting glass before going their separate ways. *Graftons,* they were. The *HMS Grafton,* Worth knew, was a 74-gun, third-rater, decommissioned, and sent to be broken up. Listening to the shipmates' loud conversation, Worth gathered she was a creaky old lady but a happy ship to the end.

Worth stood and offered the lads and their former ship a toast.

"The *Grafton,*" they replied. And then they returned a volley.

"Wives and sweethearts," they called back.

"May they never meet," Worth joined the chorus.

The public room at The Ship felt like a safe harbor that night. Worth was carrying a second pint to his corner when three men came in. Two boisterous, big men ordered pints and exchanged greetings with the landlord. The third man, thin, wearing a long, greenish oilcloth greatcoat, stood in the center of the public room and stared at the fireplace. Then he looked around at the other customers, then back to the fireplace.

When the big men slid into a settle and bade their companion to join them, he continued to stand, studying the fireplace.

"Hinch," one of the newcomers said. The man in the green coat disregarded him and turned toward the barkeeper.

"Me usual," he said. "Me usual place by the fire there seems to be occupied."

"True, Mr Hinch," the host said. "Them lads is staying over. Just the night."

The public room grew quieter then.

"Mebbe you can explain it to 'em?" Hinch said, staring at the sailors. "Ask 'em to move it around just a bit?"

"Ah, it's always first come, first served, Mr Hinch," the barkeeper said. "Now, can I draw you a pint? With our compliments?"

"Certainly. And I'm thinking I'll enjoy it even more seated right here by the fire."

Hinch went over to the seated sailors and tipped one's pint, splashing the other two men.

"Clumsy me," Hinch said. "Maybe you boys can shove off? Make us a little room here?"

The seamen were already on their feet, preparing for battle. Hinch's companions, *reluctantly,* Worth thought, came to his side.

The barkeeper, clearly wanting no part in a brawl, stayed safely behind his taps. *Not the owner of the inn,* Worth observed as he stood.

"Avast!" Worth roared out the naval command to halt all activity. He was on his feet. "Stand down!"

The dancing master, promoting himself to bosun, stepped between the warring parties. Hinch alone remained ready for battle.

"Another jolly tar, eh," he said. As he took a pace toward Worth, Hinch reached inside his greatcoat, pulled out a long black pistol and gripped it by the barrel, preparing to use it as a club. Worth waited—no retreat—as Hinch moved closer.

"Stand down, y' damned fool," Worth said.

Hinch took another pace. He never saw the blow coming. Worth raised his left hand, as though preparing to ward off a blow, and stepped a little to the left and forward. While Hinch watched the dancing master's face and hands, Worth raised his right foot and stamped the thick, hard leather heel of his shoe down on the middle of Hinch's foot. The greasy man dropped his pistol and collapsed to the floor in pain.

Worth picked up the weapon. Blackened steel with black wooden handle. *An unusual weapon,* he thought. Deadly looking but still a flintlock. Slow to load and like to misfire in a pinch. Worth opened the frizzen and shook the priming powder out on the floor.

He looked over at the barkeeper.

"These men need new pints," Worth said, gesturing to the *Grafton* shipmates.

Then he handed the pistol to one of Hinch's companions.

"And your man here needs fresh air," he said to the two big men. "Help him along now, lads. Tell him to soak it in cold water—cold as he can find. He'll be dancing a jig in a day or two. Or three."

One of the big men supported Hinch and helped him hobble out the door. The other, still holding Hinch's weapon, moved close to Worth.

"Never—don't never, ever, turn your back on that man," he said before following the other men out the door.

᭞7᭞

"**G**ood morning, Miss Austen," Worth said. She nodded politely.

"'Tis a good day for the banking business," he said. "But then, a bank canna be doin' a great deal of business when the front door is locked."

Jane's face reflected the shock she felt.

"There are people within," Worth said. "You can sometimes see two or three of 'em working on papers and moving things about, but…"

He tried the door briefly, looked at Jane, and shook his head.

"Henry will be seeing to it," Jane said. "I heard something about Mr Gray, one of the partners, and a shortage. I'm sure Henry will set everything right."

"Aye."

"It will be settled."

Worth nodded.

"The money for my ball is secure in Henry's London bank. And as we are on the topic, let us talk about the expenses. I am prepared to pay as much as fifteen pounds for the ball," Jane said. "Will that be sufficient?"

"Possibly," Worth shrugged. "A great deal depends on the cost of the rooms. Will you want a full suite? Ballroom, tearoom, and card room?"

"We must have a suite."

"And the date is a Saturday, the most expensive night. Are you fixed on it?"

"It is my birthday," Jane said. "That cannot be changed."

"There will be costs for service, tea, cakes, and so forth. There will be an expense for musicians."

"Of course."

"I will have to write it up, but it seems possible. The cost of the rooms still bein' a question—but fifteen pounds will likely be sufficient."

"You are omitting one additional charge, Mr Worth. What will you be paid?"

Worth paused before replying. "Silver and tin. The usual. Coin of the realm." He looked away from her.

"That is the most difficult part, is it not?" Jane asked. "It is for me. 'Here is my book. Now, how much will you pay me for it?' The publisher must answer. It is impossible for me to ask."

"It surprises me to hear you say that, the way the characters in your books go on about incomes and interests. For me, I have no trouble negotiating the fees to pay musicians," Worth said. "I know them, and I value their work, and I have high expectations for their pay. But when it comes to negotiating for m'self, I am terrible."

"It is the bane of artists, this issue of money. Yet, it is essential."

"Essential? To you? A fine lady?"

"Yes. For me. In these times? Essential." She took the slightest involuntary glance at the closed bank office. "With all of the uncertainty surrounding us, the opportunity for a lady to convert her mere scribblings into an income is a great temptation."

"Why then...? A ball...?"

"You take your cues from my sister," Jane said, smiling. "Cassandra worries profusely, and unlike her mythic namesake, she has the ear of all around her. I appreciate her concern. I have given this matter great consideration. As you are to be the master of these revels, I shall share the whole of my purpose with you. I am gaining some experience in this writing business now—" Then she caught sight of someone across the street and changed course. "Aha! Now, a personage of interest arrives."

Across High Street, a man, very close to spherical in shape, came out of the grocer's store at one end of the building. He accosted a delivery boy entering the neighboring dry goods shop and gave him some direction. There was a brief pause while the large man peered in the window of the bakery, his head moving from side to side to observe the activity within. Bolabus Claypoole, the lord and master of this High Street fiefdom, approached the entrance to the assembly rooms that occupied the level above his ground floor establishments. Jane and the dancing master crossed the street to meet him.

After the briefest pleasantries, Mr Claypoole unlocked the doors and, breathing heavily, ponderously led his guests up the stairs to the assembly rooms.

Upon achieving the summit, he grasped the handles of the double doors and held on, panting. Then he straightened himself. Taking a stained kerchief from his coat sleeve, he dabbed his temples lightly and threw open the doors.

"Here you shall see the finest assembly rooms in all of Hampshire. Winchester included."

Light from a wall of windows flooded the room. The width of the hall from the doors to the windows would accommodate three sets easily, four without distress, and five in a pinch.

The ceiling arched twenty feet or more above the floor. Large chandeliers would provide good illumination. To the left, a small stage offered accommodation for musicians. A pianoforte stood ready.

It is, Worth thought, as he entered the room, *an agreeable space indeed, especially for a small country town.*

Mr Claypoole and Jane stood in the center of the room while Worth walked the perimeter and then passed through the archway at the end of the hall to visit the tearoom and card room. The dancing master reappeared and took another turn around the ballroom. At length, he paused at the stage, unslung his instrument case, and prepared to play.

Mr Claypoole withdrew a snuff box from his coat pocket and inhaled two pinches. The landlord grunted and darted a quick glance at Jane when Worth removed his prosthetic. She smiled, placidly. She was growing accustomed to the sight of his disfigured right hand.

With his fiddle in tune, Worth launched into a country dance melody.

"Oh, *The Persian Ricardo*," Jane said, clapping her hands.

She faced Mr Claypoole and tried to engage him in the steps. He stared at her, mouth slightly agape, and shook his head. Jane nodded politely, moved up toward the stage, and continued the dance with imaginary companions.

Worth, observing her capers, played the tune a second time through. Jane applauded.

"Miss Austen," Worth said. "I should like to sound the hall with more than one instrument. I noted the pianoforte in your home. Do you play?"

Jane hesitated before responding. "A little. Just a little and very poorly."

"Will you give me a chance to hear how the instrument sounds? 'Tis not a recital. Just a wee melody to sound out the room."

"I have no music," she said. "I cannot play without music."

"Just a few chords," Worth said. "You can manage without the dots, I'm sure. Come now. We need to hear the instrument."

Reluctantly, she sat at the pianoforte.

"What shall I play?"

"Any old tune," he said. "A *gavotte*, a prelude, a country dance. Something you have to heart."

Jane paused for a moment, ran her hands up the keys with a scale, struck two notes, and began playing, emphasizing chords, and adding a simple melody line.

"Ah! *Knole Park*," he said. "Excellent choice."

Worth took another turn around the floor and when he returned to the stage, bade her to continue.

Then he moved to stand beside Jane and joined in the tune. He pressed the tempo forward, slightly, and she moved the tune at a livelier pace. Toward the end of the third time through, they exchanged glances, Worth nodded to her, urging her to continue another time through the tune.

While she navigated the chords with her left hand, he assumed command of the melody. He quoted from the proper tune, then improvised new lines around it. She caught his new lines and underscored them with right hand chords. The tune took on a new complexion, soaring and swooping with energy.

Somehow, magically, she found herself taking the lead. Worth doubled her, playing a harmonic parallel with a joyful touch, musical capering that forced a broad smile to her lips. As they reached the last two bars, he looked at her with widened eyes and a quick nod. She understood. *Rinforzando,* an abrupt crescendo, on the final note.

They reached a happy conclusion and listened to the reverberations in the hall.

Worth smiled and said quietly, "Very fine, indeed." Then his face became grim as he walked up to Claypoole.

"D'ye have no draperies for the windows? And something for the wall behind the musicians? Oh, and the stage needs a carpet—somethin' to soften the sound."

Claypoole drew himself up to say something, but Worth continued.

"All the hard surfaces," Worth said, shaking his head. "It's like playing in a pump room. All the echoes. Floor looks nice enough but look here"—moving toward the windows— "this is like a rocky beach at low tide, all uneven. Dancers may even trip and fall. And the card room. Cramped. And only four tables."

"We can add tables," Claypoole said. "We have had as many as eight."

"What? Have 'em sitting in each other's laps? And there's no windows for the card players," Worth continued, turning to Jane. "You know the gentlemen will be smoking. And no windows? Ah, I suppose the gentlemen can suffer, but the ladies…"

He turned back to Claypoole. "Steps. Two steps going from the tearoom to the ballroom. For ladies, you want them to be clambering up and down stairs? I know it's assembly rooms in the country—not Bath or in Town—but…" Worth's shoulders sagged, he shook his head and sighed. "How much are you charging?"

"Well," Claypoole said, rubbing his chin with his hand. "The rental for a Saturday night is two pounds—"

"Two pounds!" Worth said. "In the dead of winter?"

"That's the usual. But as this is a special occasion…"

The two men went back and forth, discussing the costs: fees for coal and candles, linen, tea service, servants, assistance with horses and carriages, and hours—when will rooms open and when must they be vacated. The price of one pound, twelve shillings was on the table when Worth ended the negotiation.

"We'll have to think on it," he said. "Miss Austen and I will discuss it and be back to you presently."

They descended the stairs to ground level, leaving Claypoole to lock up.

"Is it really so bad?" Jane said, on their walk back to Chawton along the Winchester Road.

"Oh, no, not at all," Worth said. "Quite nice, in truth. Much nicer than many of the assembly rooms in Town. And a very fair price."

"So, all your complaints…?"

"All part of the dance around the dance," Worth said. "A fine gentleman inquires, it's one price, and he pays it. Then there's the extras. The gentleman is already committed so he pays up for them, too. A poor, hard-working musician comes to hire the hall, now that's a different story. Just part of the dance."

Jane smiled. "So shall we take the rooms?"

"I can confirm the booking when I come back to the inn," Worth said. "But, are you sure? You have no other halls hereabouts?"

"My brother—"

"Aye."

"He has a great house with a ballroom."

Jane stopped on the bridge across the River Wey. She continued, speaking not so much to Worth as to the water rushing away toward the sea. "No," she said. "Independence. That is what is wanted. That is my purpose."

She stared down the river.

"Aye," Worth said, prompting her. "You spoke of this before. Your purpose."

"To understand, you first must have some knowledge of the book writing business," Jane said, turning to face him. "A book can be written and sold on commission. This is not unlike a wager. I, the author, bear the cost of the preparation and printing. The publisher maintains the supply of books and earns a commission on each book that is sold. If the books are not sold, the author, or authoress, bears the loss. Do you see the sticking point?"

"Risk of loss. A requirement for capital even to proceed. As you said, a wager."

"Well done," Jane said. "You have it."

"A risky business then."

"That would depend on how confident you are in your work. If you lack confidence, or capital, a publisher may offer another scheme."

"Indeed," Worth said. "And that would be?"

"The purchase of the copyright," Jane said. "The publisher offers a price, owns the work, bears the cost of printing, and keeps all profits from the publication."

"And the author? If the book is successful? Popular? If they print more copies?"

"The author has already been paid in full. No additional income. Ever."

"But surely—"

"The end," Jane said. "*Finis.* Selling one's copyright is like the selling of a horse, a bolt of cloth, or a bag of corn. A simple exchange of goods for money."

"I see." Worth observed a peculiar look on her face.

"It is very like selling your own child," she said, looking down the river again. She sighed. Then she addressed Worth with some energy. "I have achieved some success with my novels. And I rather enjoy it. I have gained a little experience in this book publishing trade. I have a much better understanding of how it works. I can imagine a pathway that will allow a modestly successful authoress to achieve some independence. My ball—our ball, perhaps I should say—will take me a step or two in that direction."

They stood without speaking for a while, listening to the river.

"I must return to Chawton," Jane said at length.

"May I walk with you?"

She nodded her assent and they set off.

"Tell me now, Mr Worth, how does a musician and dancing master maintain a living?"

"For the musician, it's a simple trade. We're hirelings. It's a job of work. Do your job and you gets paid. Don't work, no pay. You gets to know people, ones you can count on. When something comes along, maybe they put in a good word. Maybe you gets hired."

"And is it…rewarding?"

He laughed. "Just enough to keep body and soul together. Oh, there's a few lucky ones—gets employment with a great house or the Palace or a church. Mostly though, you finish the job and hope somethin' will turn up. Maybe there's not much for a while, and then you starts wondering if you'll ever work again."

"But surely…you play so beautifully."

"Music makin' were never a plan o' mine," Worth said. "Just sorta happened. I learned to play a flageolet—a wee whistle. It seemed like I had a knack. And a while later, an old shipmate who'd lost most of his hearing, he gives me his fiddle."

"Was he your teacher?"

"Teacher?" Worth laughed again. "No teachers when you're at sea. You just learn by the doin' of it. If it sounds good, you must be doin' it right."

"Very much like writing, now that you say it."

"Sometimes you meets other fiddlers on a ship or while you're ashore, and you learns bits and pieces and tricks. And then you just keeps on playin'."

"Yes. Yes. Just keep on…playing…writing. And you joined the navy?"

"You either join up or get pressed. Getting pressed, that's where they knocks you out and drags you on board."

By the time they neared the Selborne Road, Jane had most of Mr Worth's history. Going to sea at thirteen, a ship's boy on a packet. Growing up to be an able seaman and then going into the navy. Music kept his spirits up, even in the darkest days of the war. His music gained the attention of Captain Thomas Hardy. That good officer took him on as a follower; made him a steward. Worth maintained the captain's larder, poured his wine, cooked for the captain's table. Much of his time was spent in the company of officers—nearly all gentlemen. He saw their manners, learned their ways, and in private—with his shipmates—mocked them endlessly.

He was with Captain Hardy at Copenhagen where Nelson famously raised his telescope to his blind eye and said that he saw no signal to retire from the battle. When Hardy shifted to *HMS Victory* as the viscount's flag captain in the days before Trafalgar, he brought Worth with him.

"It were a good life," Worth concluded. "You could'na ask for more."

"But your hand?"

"Small price, that," Worth said. "The ship's surgeon worked it round so's I can still make music. And there was a pension. Not much but it helped."

"What was it about Nelson? How? Why did men follow him so loyally?"

"He kept it all so simple. When you spied your enemy, you went after 'em. You engaged. 'Never mind the maneuvers,' that's what Nelson said. 'Just go straight at 'em.'"

"Hmm." Jane nodded her head. Her mind turned to books and her feelings about the publishing trade. She repeated, mostly to herself: "Never mind the maneuvers. Just go straight at them."

≈ 8 ≈

At the widening where Jane and the dancing master passed the turning to Selborne, a pair of horses, moving at a quick trot, came up from behind. The walkers stood aside, but the vehicle halted as the driver drew next to them.

"Ahoy there," the driver said. "Mr Fiddler, you old sea dog."

Aloysius Ellicott stood in his place, bobbing up and down gently with the carriage, and doffed his fashionable hat.

"You know him?" Jane said softly.

"We are acquainted," Worth replied.

"And Miss Austen," Aloysius said, offering a sweeping bow that left his dangling blond locks askew. He brushed his hair back, resettled his hat. "Now this is portentous. The writer. The fiddler. The author and the musician. In concert. A chance meeting? I think not. Pray, tell us what does this tête-à-tête foretell?"

Worth, astonished by the man's impudence, gave Aloysius a hard stare and looked at Jane. She laughed.

"Oh, Mr Ellicott, if you must know, I am planning a ball." She turned to Worth: "It can hardly be a secret now that we have surveyed the rooms."

"A ball, you say!" the young man exclaimed. "How delicious. And when will this grand fête occur?"

"Upon 16 December," Jane said. "My birthday. And you need not exert your charm so extravagantly as you shall most certainly be invited."

"In Alton?" Aloysius said. "The assembly rooms?"

"Yes. We have just come from there."

Aloysius drew in his cheeks and squinted as though deep in contemplation. Then he said, "Tell me, Mr Worth…ah, do I recall your name correctly, Mr Worth?"

"Aye."

"Then tell me, sir, a man of the cultured world such as yourself, what you think of the assembly rooms in Alton?"

Worth paused, unsure where this was leading. He looked at Jane. She shrugged.

"Entirely adequate," he finally said. "They will suit the purpose nicely."

"Adequate?" Aloysius said. "Adequate! And this is how we shall celebrate the joyous anniversary of our most celebrated lady of literature? With a ball dressed in the dull habiliment of the Alton assembly rooms? It cannot be! Come. Up with you both. Ride with me!"

"There is not enough room," Jane said.

"Silly goose. Of course, there is room."

He slid to the far end of the bench and, indeed, for the slight Miss Jane Austen and the trim Mr Worth, there was room.

"Now," Aloysius said more quietly with Jane seated next to him. "You know Kellingsford: the gardens, the drive, the stables, the portico, the great hall… And the ballroom! You must, you must, you must host your ball at Kellingsford."

Jane opened her mouth to reply.

"I insist," Aloysius continued. "The library for cards. The second salon for tea. We have not hosted a grand event in ever so long."

For the remaining short drive to Chawton, Aloysius encouraged his idea. He cited all the advantages, proposing it as a gift to the community and the literary world, promising the assistance of his servants, access to the stables, and, of course, the use of the first plate and silver.

By the time they reached the Chawton Cottage, Aloysius had obtained a promise to consider his proposal. He would send a coach in the morning. The author and the dancing master would visit Kellingsford the next day.

"Quite an…energetic young man," Worth said as they watched Aloysius continue down the Winchester Road. "Is he always so…enthusiastic?"

"Aloysius Ellicott is…unusual."

Worth nodded. "Aye. Unusual."

"Tomorrow?"

"Tomorrow."

❧9❧

"I played a duet with him," Jane said, sitting next to her sister. "*Knole Park*. It went beautifully. He played it as I knew it to be written; then played variations, lovely inventions that fit perfectly within the chords. He communicated with the slightest gestures, a glance or a nod, yet I realized exactly what he was saying. He is remarkable—that is—he is a remarkable musician."

"And still, he claims that he was a seaman," Cassandra said.

"He was. He rose from ship's boy to able seaman living between the decks. Only later, he was plucked from the ranks to be a captain's steward," Jane said. "He is truly modest about it. A steward is neither fish nor fowl, he says. Certainly not an officer but, I think, truly something more than a common sailor."

"That may well be, but take care, Jane. You know nothing about this man."

"I know he is a musician. About that, there can be no doubt."

"Yes, but the rest? He has demonstrated his skill at impersonation. He is a very fine actor. His tales of life at sea and the source of his injury may prove to be a grand illusion."

"If so, it is uncommonly well done."

"That does not make him honorable."

"But it does make him interesting," Jane said. She rose and began pacing, thinking.

Cassandra opened her mouth, closed it, and looked to the ceiling.

"He might make a very fine character for a novel. Not the hero, of course, for that must be a gentleman. But, let us say, the hero's close associate. A batman or a trusted lieutenant. I believe the world should enjoy a story about a man of modest birth who works his way up in the world through hard work and talent."

"Such as the opportunity the navy provides?" Cassandra said.

"Promotion and prize money, yes. But one must be an officer of some rank. A commander or lieutenant would barely do. An ensign, never. No, he must be like Frank or Charles, a captain, I believe."

"Then your fearless Mr Worth shall not become your hero."

"He is not fearless," Jane said after a moment. "Not at all. He spoke to me of ordinary, mortal fear in the face of the enemy. More resonant to me, he spoke of the worries that now accompany his musical life. Will one fine performance lead to the next opportunity? Or will he be supplanted by someone new and more fashionable? It is the same fear I face. I remember, after the public celebrated *S&S*, I worried so much. Would they care for *P&P*? I was the more confident then." She looked at her sister. "You feared it would fail. Heroes face innumerable fears. To some, the fear of being spurned may outweigh one thousand times the power of an enemy broadside."

"You need not search so far," Cassandra said. "You have models for your characters—true heroes—within the bosom of your own family. They have faced our nation's foes, engaged with valor, and carried the day. You need look no further."

"Frank and Charles are, indeed, very fine naval officers. 'Tis a provable fact. They have prize money." Looking out the window, she said almost to herself, "That is an odd thing, is it not?"

"What is an odd thing?"

"Oh, the manner in which we measure one's worth by measuring one's worth. But," Jane continued, "to your point, Frank and Charles are officers with all the distinction of character and spirit that distinguish gentlemen. Mr Worth was a sailor—a common sailor. But one with extraordinary musical gifts. And he can act the part of a gentleman, and possibly many other roles, I daresay. Will you not agree with me, Cass? Would he not make a most interesting literary character?"

❧10❧

Aloysius slid into a settle next to Captain Wembley, the latter dressed in subdued browns and grays rather than his splendid uniform.

"I am undone," Aloysius said. "I must have a claret. Or better, a brandy."

"Cheer up, Ally. You have no cause for complaint."

"Oh? You think it a proper life dwelling under the martinet gaze of my sanctimonious elder brother?"

"Bide your time."

"Percival is a prig," Aloysius said. "He is a pompous, preening, parsimonious prig. He deserves—"

"Bide your time."

"My life in Kellingsford is hell. My days have degenerated into dreary humdrum. There is no gaiety. No society. No romance."

"Stop whining," Wembley said. "Truly, Ally, how do you think barracks life would suit you? A lean table, stinking quarters, and decommissioning in the air? I tell you, my life was a damn sight better in the middle of the war. We commanded fine lodgings. The best in every town. The food was excellent, especially when we were in France. And the wine! Ah! Good that, a soldier's life. Eat well. Drink well. Sleep well. Then kill or be killed."

"Your memory betrays you," Aloysius said. "Recall the blood, gore, and losses you have also endured. Good sir, would you rather be tramping through mud and blood in France, or enjoying the pleasures of the country life hereabouts?"

"Country life hereabouts is a business of living among snakes, your brother chief among them. Ever so polite they are, and ever so appreciative that we saved them from the frogs. And ever so ready to stab you in the back. They have earned some discomfiture."

"It is a matter of time, is it not? That is what you said?" Aloysius looked at Wembley closely. "Bide my time?"

"Yes. That is what I said."

"So, there's an end to it. All's well that ends well, saith the bard." Aloysius put his right hand to his chin and smiled. "And I sayeth, methinks the time is at hand. I am delighted to inform you, dear captain, that we are to have a ball at Kellingsford."

"A ball?"

"One of the spinster sisters of the Chawton House heir. She proposes to celebrate her birthday with a ball, and I am determined to host it at Kellingsford. It will be a great commotion. A large gathering, upwards of one hundred, I should say. Guests from all corners of the county and beyond."

"Interesting," Wembley said.

"Percival will object, of course. Letitia and I will persuade him. We shall enlist dear Papa. I expect he will bend to our entreaties. And Percival, as heir, will preside over the fête, if only to keep watch over the silver."

"An interesting development. Possibly…"

"*Fortuna audaces iuvat*," Aloysius said, calling on his schoolboy Latin.

"Virgil?" Wembley said. "Fortune favors the bold."

❧11❧

Percival glared out the window of his upstairs sitting room, shook his head, and resumed pacing. On every third or fourth turn, he again returned to the window, searching.

Jerome appeared at the open door.

"The gamekeeper, sir," the butler said and stepped aside. The man in the oilcloth greatcoat entered the room, limping slightly, favoring his right foot.

"Hinch," Percival started. "Mr Hinch. You have served this house for some time now, have you not?"

The gamekeeper, holding his oilcloth cap in a tight roll in front of him, nodded.

"It is good service, you will agree?" Percival continued. "You have accommodation: a comfortable cottage. There is a fine table. You are compensated handsomely."

Percival resumed his pacing.

"You oversee our grounds. You know the woods, the fields. You alone have the greatest knowledge of the comings and goings— Aha, there!" Percival exclaimed, rushing to the window. "There, Hinch. Do you see?"

Hinch joined his employer at the window. Of course, he could see. One of the tenants—a man, but he could not say which one from this distance—leading three cows across the field that was once the commons.

"You see, Hinch. Back and forth they go. All day long."

"They's not grazing, sir," Hinch said. "I have spoken with 'em—"

"They are trespassing, Hinch. They are ignoring the law. They are flouting an Act of Parliament."

"I've spoken to the constable, sir."

"And yet, there they are," Percival said. "I see them, again and again."

"The admiral, sir. You know he's encouraging 'em. Sayin' that enclosing ain't right. If you've a mind to convince him…"

"This is not my problem, Mr Hinch," Percival said, turning on the gamekeeper. "I don't spend my days in the fields. I don't track the comings and goings of my tenants."

"Sir…"

"What is it that a proper gamekeeper must do?" Percival continued. "Is it just to watch? To see what happens? Keep count of the animals and fowl taken from His Lordship's lands?"

Hinch made no response. Percival ended his pacing and came close to the gamekeeper.

"You have shown yourself to be a man capable of taking action— when confronting a twelve-year-old boy. Perhaps I should find someone more...?" He left the words in the air and resumed his pacing. After three turns, he returned to address the gamekeeper. "Hinch, they are no more than poachers," he said, spitting the words in the gamekeeper's face.

"Deal with them," he said as he left the room.

❧12❦

K ellingsford Manor stood tall above a vast lawn dressed in winter hues of ochres and browns. The great house served as a golden crown of fine English stone. The drive, leading to the front portico, wound ingeniously up the hillside, across the lawn, through gardens and evergreen hedgerows of yew and holly, and back across the lawn to display the house to its best effect.

The butler and two footmen met Jane and Worth at the coach. Aloysius greeted them under the portico as they ascended the steps and ushered them into the vestibule. They glimpsed the grand staircase to the private rooms and passed under the gaze of the portraits of several generations. The guests entered the first salon and encountered Percival Ellicott.

"What is this? Oh, Miss Austen," he said, tugging at his red cravat. "To what do we owe the honor?"

"Tea, dear brother," Aloysius said.

"Tea? Ah, well, go on then."

He turned his attention to the little man with the small black mustache who accompanied him.

"Sloat and I have more correspondence on this wretched matter with that tenant Morgan. We must put an end to it," Percival said as he took Mr Sloat by the elbow and stepped toward the hall, then halted as two new figures swept into view.

"The Viscount Kellingsford and his daughter," Jane said in an aside to Worth as His Lordship and Letitia entered the room.

"Percival, my lad, what think you?" Attired in knee breeches, doublet, and a cloak of colorful silks and satins, Lord Kellingsford stood in front of his eldest son and made a leg. "Is this not the finest?" he asked, then twirled in place, admiring the folds of his cloak as it swirled around him.

"A pretty little ballet," Worth said gently to Jane.

"Why must you always be so dull?" Lord Kellingsford asked, looking at Percival. "Now look at this one bit of color, your red cravat. See how it brings the roses to your cheeks. Eh, Letitia?"

His daughter, similarly attired, nodded. Her tight blonde curls bobbed.

"More color, Son, more color. Brighten our spirits. And you, Aloysius? What? All in black? Are we a house in mourning?"

Percival and Sloat continued out of the room as His Lordship approached his younger son.

"You cut such a fine figure," he said, walking around Aloysius, conducting a survey. "Waist, neat. Handsome brow. And hair? A glorious crown. I should trade with you in an instant, 't'were possible," he said as his hands made a slight adjustment to his own wig. "But look here, not a hint of calf. I'll warrant you have just as fine a leg as I," Lord Kellingsford said as he went to a tall glass near the hearth and made an extravagant ceremonial bow, extending his left leg.

"Ah, just so," His Lordship said, admiring his image in the glass. "Now, look at yourself, cloaked in black and hidden away."

"'Tis the fashion, Father," Aloysius said. "In the manner of Beau Brummel."

Lord Kellingsford disregarded his son's reply, his attention caught by the image in the glass again.

"Letitia," he said, snapping his fingers twice. "Letitia, bring me my stick."

The lady darted into the vestibule and returned with an ornate, gold-capped walking stick.

"There," His Lordship said, taking the stick and resting both hands on it, frowning into the glass. "Oh, but of course." Tucking the stick under his left arm, he withdrew a pair of white gloves from his doublet. "There, there, there! What think you now?" he said, twirling and striking the same attitude for the others in the room. Focusing his gaze on Jane and Worth, his eyes brightened. "Letitia, we have guests!"

Moving toward Jane, he made a leg and took her hand.

"How do you do, my lady..." Then he puzzled. "Yes...my lady..." Then he looked to Miss Ellicott.

"Miss Austen," she said.

"Yes, yes, yes, Miss Austen," he said, and bowed over her hand. "And Lord Austen," he said, honoring Worth.

"Worth, my lord," Worth said.

"Worth what?"

"My name, my lord," Worth said.

"Indeed," His Lordship said. "A man's good name is truly his worth."

Miss Ellicott giggled. Aloysius looked skyward. Worth opened his mouth but was interrupted.

"Come to see the new portrait, eh?" Lord Kellingsford said as he went to the far end of the room where an object the size of a door, propped on a stand, stood draped in purple velvet.

Lord Kellingsford stood next to the object.

"Aloysius," he said. "The drape."

Aloysius went to the other side of the object and untied a cord. The velvet drapery fell away to reveal a life-sized portrait of Lord Kellingsford in the same attitude the gentleman had assumed.

"A wonder, is it not?" he said, after allowing a pause for admiring gasps.

It is a wonder, of a sort, Worth thought. A very flat representation by a second or third tier artist—likely an apprentice. The face was well done, however, possibly by the master. The remainder seemed to be from a different hand. But he had to allow, it was colorful. The gaudy clothing in the portrait was from the same era as the garments His Lordship wore. Altogether, it seemed like a very apt portrait.

Aloysius stepped forward, applauded, then stopped as though suddenly struck with a new idea.

"We must have an unveiling!" he said. "Yes, Letitia"—turning to his sister— "an unveiling. I say, we shall have a ball!"

"A ball!" His Lordship exclaimed, clearly delighted. "A ball! Yes, that's just the thing. A ball."

Lord Kellingsford handed his stick to Aloysius. He then approached Jane, bowed, and extended his hand.

"Miss...?"

"Austen, my lord," Jane said again.

"Yes, Miss Austen, shall I have the pleasure of your company at our ball?"

"Our ball?" Percival said as he entered the drawing room followed by Sloat. "Our ball? What's this?"

"It is such a wonderful idea," Aloysius said. "A grand ball a fortnight hence for the public display of Papa's new portrait."

"Just the thing," Lord Kellingsford said. "We are having a ball."

"And we shall redouble the joy for the occasion," Aloysius continued, "for we shall also celebrate the birthday of the renowned author, Miss Jane Austen. It will be ever so delightful. Letitia, we must have a ball!"

Miss Ellicott giggled, her curls quivering.

"You did not consult—" Percival started.

"Father said we must," Aloysius said.

"There will be no—"

"Oh, please. Papa, speak with Percy."

"Yes, of course. Percival," His Lordship said, clearing his throat, "yes, indeed now, but what were we speaking of?"

"Your portrait," Aloysius prompted.

"Oh, yes, and…it was…? Oh, I know! A ball, Letitia. We must choose our habiliments," His Lordship said, taking his daughter's arm. "Mayhap, I should wear the very accoutrements shown in the portrait itself," he said as they swept out of the room.

"What do you think you're playing at, Aloysius," Percival said, turning his brother. "A ball? Without consulting me? What is this scheme?" Percival hushed, aware of the others in room. "Ah, yes. Miss Austen and…"

"Mr Worth," Jane said. "A dancing master."

"A dancing master! A scheme indeed!

"Miss Austen, you must forgive us. I require a few moments with my dear brother." Percival rounded on Aloysius. "Since it seems my father may have become enamored with the idea, we must give it deep consideration."

"Hospitality, dear brother," Aloysius said.

Percival caught himself. "Yes, of course. What shall…ah…would you like to see the ballroom, Mister… Mr Worth?"

"Ah, yes," Worth said.

Percival had already tugged on the bell pull to summon the butler.

"Jerome," he said when the butler promptly appeared, "we need someone to show…Miss Austen and her dancing man…the ballroom. Get Father's man, old Marryat. He can manage it."

"Just so, sir," the butler said, smiling at Jane and Worth. "If you will follow me."

❧13❧

"Marryat, show the lady and the...ah...gentleman to the ball-room," the butler said.

"Aye, sir," the man called Marryat replied in a deep, rasping voice, touching his forehead with his right fist.

Jerome retreated, leaving Jane and Worth in the company of a short, gnarled tree stump of a man wearing shabby, well-worn house livery. He looked cautiously at the guests through his good left eye. The right side of his face, sightless, was a mass of old scars.

"Navy, then," Worth said, addressing the servant.

Marryat smiled. "Aye. On the *Temeraire*, sir."

"I know her well. She was in the thick of it at Trafalgar."

"That were the new *Temeraire*, sir. My time, long ago, a third-rater she was then. We was putting down the Spaniards. Never did get a chance t' go hunting frogs."

"Well, shipmate, no time for tales now. Let's not keep the lady waiting."

"Aye, aye, sir. Follow me." The old man led the way down the hall.

"How did you know?" Jane said quietly to Worth. "That he was a navy man?"

"His salute to the butler," Worth said with a laugh.

"Navy men don't salute, eh, Marryat?" he asked, loud enough for the old sailor to hear. "We just show 'em a knuckle."

"Aye."

"A proper sailor has too many other things to learn," Worth continued. "No time for practice like parade ground fancies."

Worth was rewarded for his remark with a raspy chuckle.

At first sight, the ballroom may well have been Kellingsford's finest feature. The view from the grand staircase: a ceiling sparkling with chandeliers, glittering with gilded moldings; the dance floor, an expanse of warm, glistening oak bordered with intricate parquet, spread out below. As they descended the staircase, celestial images depicted in frescoes within the arching ceiling panels came into view.

The stage was set in a massive frame of ornate, gilded woodwork. Gold-trimmed, maroon velvet stage curtains dressed its edges creating a platform worthy of works by Shakespeare or Sheridan. A pianoforte and a harpsichord held pride of place center stage between the parted curtains. Steps on either side of the stage led from the dance floor to stage level. Black drapes masked the wings on either side of the stage. Peering offstage, Worth saw doors that provided access from the garden, hidden entrances to the stage. *A little gem of a theatre,* Worth thought.

Looking out onto the dance floor, Worth imagined it filled with elegant ladies, fine gentlemen, and soaring music.

"It's a beauty," Worth said as he returned to the center of the ballroom. "A rare beauty."

Jane had attended balls at Kellingsford in the past; she smiled and nodded.

"Shall we sound her out?" Worth said to Jane, nodding toward the pianoforte. He was slipping his instrument case off his shoulder. "Will you try out their instrument?"

"I have no music—" Then, seeing the impatient look in his eyes, she continued. "But if you insist."

They mounted the stage and Jane proceeded to the pianoforte. She warmed her fingers with scales while Worth tuned his fiddle.

Jane smiled. In the past, she had called his instrument by its proper name: a violin. But, in his hands, she seemed to regard it as a fiddle.

"*The Persian Dance?*" he suggested.

"Something different. But spirited," she said.

"*Down the Brae?*"

She made a face. "I have not played it so often. Ah, I have it. *The Fandango!*"

He nodded. After she struck two bold chords, they launched the melody.

On the second change, Worth began dropping out during certain measures of the first strains of the tune. Jane responded by emphasizing the melody, resulting in a delightful conversation between the instruments. Worth tempered his playing, encouraging Jane with his eyes to lead. And so, she did.

They played a third change. Of course, they must, to give the third couples in each set an opportunity to lead. As they rounded into the final eight bars, Worth added a soaring harmony that led into a resonant, satisfying ending. As the sound faded, Jane found herself slightly breathless.

A noise from the hall; the old servant, Marryat, had given one tentative clap. Worth smiled at the old man. Another tentative clap. Then

Worth gestured to Jane and bowed to her. The old man then applauded with great enthusiasm, adding a hearty "huzzah" to his approbation.

"Do you have *Roast Beef of Old England?*" Worth asked her softly.

"With two brothers in the navy?" she said with a laugh. "*G* major?"

"Perfect."

They played the melody of the patriotic song widely thought of as a sailor's anthem and frequently played as a call to navy mess dinners.

Their audience of one moved closer to the stage, clearly delighted by hearing the old song again. Then Worth lowered his fiddle to his shoulder, played a spare accompaniment and began to sing.

> *"But since we have learned from all vaporing France*
> *To eat their ragouts, as well as to dance*
> *We are fed up with nothing*
> *But vague complaisance!"*

Now all three voices in the room joined in the chorus.

> *"Oh, the roast beef of old England*
> *And Old English roast beef"*

Worth signaled Jane to repeat the chorus which they did with gusto. Laughter filled the hall, along with more applause from Marryat.

After putting away his fiddle and adjusting his right hand, Worth and Jane joined Marryat.

"How d'ye come by your souvenir?" Marryat said, eyeing Worth's hand.

"A little action off Gibraltar," Worth said. "And you?"

"Accident on shore, wouldn't you know. No glory in it. But it did set me on a course."

"How so?"

"There were a fire. A public house. In Portsmouth," Marryat said. "I got clear straight away, but we seen that some o' the lads was still inside. Well, this damn fool midshipman gets thinkin' that he ought to rescue 'em."

"There's your problem, right off," Worth said. "A midshipman and he goes and starts thinkin'."

"The other lads come out fine, but the young gentleman's still inside. So, I had to go back in and find 'im."

"You had to?" Jane said.

"Aye, o' course I had to," Marryat said. "He weren't nothin' but a damn fool middy, but he were a shipmate. The lad weren't cut out to be an officer, but he were a good man."

"This midshipman?" Jane said.

"Aye," Marryat said. "Good lad. He growed up to be the lord here. Lord Kellingsford. He quit the navy after that fire. Took me on. And he's always done right by me. You should'a knowed him afore…well…you know. He were a grand man."

They arrived at the hall and were greeted by Aloysius and Percival.

"All is as it should be," Aloysius said, greeting them. "Kellingsford shall host your fête, Miss Austen. It will be magnificent."

"That is a generous offer, and it is a most satisfactory hall," Worth said, looking at Jane. "We may need to take some time for consideration."

"My dear sirs, are you certain?" she said.

"I am certain my younger brother is a dandy and a fool," Percival said. "As well, I am certain this proposed revelry will not stand against the house accounts. My brother's allowance will provide security against any costs for breakage or theft."

Jane looked at Aloysius. He grimaced, smiled, and shrugged.

"Ordinary house service will be on hand. Any additional needs must be met from your purse. Yours, Miss Austen, or my brother's. And, you will arrange for the most striking unveiling of my father's portrait," Percival added. "At the height of the festivities when it will gain the most notice."

"What do you think, Mr Worth?" Jane said. "I have placed the event in your hands."

"Ah…but…" He saw a gleam in her eye. He nodded.

"Your terms are most generous, sir," she said to Percival, and then to Aloysius, "Thank you for your inspiration, Mr Ellicott, and your security. Advise your house servants, if you please: on 16 December, we shall have a ball at Kellingsford."

Percival frowned, glared at his brother while shaking his head, stalked back into his library, and closed the door behind him.

"Thank you again, Mr Ellicott," Jane said gently to Aloysius. "The ballroom is quite the loveliest in all of Hampshire. I am thrilled to have it. And we will have your father in fits of delight. Mr Worth has a gift for arranging memorable moments."

"Yes, yes, yes," Aloysius said. "Spectacular. Memorable. I can see it all now."

"It was so kind of you to send your carriage," Jane said. "Might we have use of it to return me to Chawton and Mr Worth to his lodgings in Alton?"

"Oh, of course, but...lodgings in Alton? At one of those shabby inns? For our dancing master? No," he said decisively. "That simply will not answer. You must stay here at Kellingsford, Mr Worth. We shall provide you with the perfect accommodation."

"That is a most considerate offer," Worth said.

"It is not an offer, good sir," Aloysius said. "It is a command. As your benefactor, I insist. We have a suite that will suit you perfectly, and this will allow you to bask in the atmosphere of the great hall, all the better to inspire your program."

Aloysius rang for the butler.

"'Tis most generous of you," Worth said.

The butler appeared.

"Ah, Jerome," Aloysius said. "We must arrange for the coach. Miss Austen returns to Chawton, and then Mr Worth hies himself to Alton where he'll retrieve his belongings. You'll have a maid make up the tutor's rooms. And the ball. Did Percival inform you? On 16 December, we shall have a ball. Oh, Miss Austen. This shall be so much fun."

❧14❧

"Sling my hammock in a great manor? Like some visiting nabob? I could never…" Worth said, shaking his head in the carriage on the way back to Chawton.

"It is an offer of free accommodation," Jane said. "Consider it? Take it under advisement? It is a great saving."

"Once again, our theme returns to money, Miss Austen. As in your novels, it seems a matter that canna be escaped."

"Not easily, that is true. Unless one has the means to escape."

"Around and around, it goes," Worth said.

"What is wanted is not great wealth," Jane said. "What is wanted is independence. But…"

"But…?"

"But… Mr Worth, can you apprehend the difficulty a lady faces in the world today? How difficult it can be to have everything placed just out of one's reach? To be required then to ask some…some man—even when he is as kind and caring as my brother Henry—to ask him to take all of one's matters in hand? To beg favor any time you want to do something? My trials bear no comparison to your own. Your service. Your sacrifice. And yet, in some small way, I have faced adversity and encountered setbacks—in some instances not of my own making."

"Aye," Worth said. "These times can be difficult."

"These times, yes. And these people as well."

She faced Worth. "I told you about the publishing business. My first novel, *Sense and Sensibility*—we call it *S&S* amongst ourselves, Cass and I. *S&S* was published on commission. As a woman, of course, I had no control over the business arrangement. Such activities are unbecoming of a lady. So, it was Henry who selected the publisher, the Military Library, a house operated by Thomas Egerton."

"The Military Library?"

"Indeed. Verifiable accounts of battles and wars. Tactics, strategies, battleground maps, and indexes. And among their books, not a single novel. But of course, it is the Military Library. Egerton agreed to publish *Sense and Sensibility* on commission. Henry—his banking business profiting nicely through his navy, army, and government connections—arranged financing. Our capital expense was one hundred and fifty pounds. Nearly one year's household expenditures in Chawton. Risky business, eh, Mr Worth?"

"Aye. I have a sense of the apprehension you must'a felt."

"*S&S* proved to be a success," Jane said. "After printing costs and commissions, I earned more than one hundred and forty pounds."

"One hundred and forty! That's a fair prize. Huzzah!"

"Yes, it was, and with no great assistance from Egerton. He arranged no reviews. There was no advertising. Yet it was a great success. By this time, *Pride and Prejudice*—*P&P*—was already well in hand. Now, with the success of *S&S* already known, we should have had confidence that, with *P&P*, my success would be repeated. Yes?"

"Certainly."

"Egerton agreed with you," Jane said. "He informed Henry that he was willing to purchase the copyright..." She stopped and looked out the coach window. "And Henry agreed."

"But that would mean—"

"One payment. No subsequent income. The loss of my child," she said, turning her gaze away. "I insisted on a price of one hundred and fifty pounds, the amount we profited from *S&S*. Henry settled for one hundred and ten."

"And you agreed?"

Jane remained silent, composing herself, then turned to Worth.

"Henry said it was the practical business choice. A bird in the hand and such. And Cassandra, being a Cassandra and always fearing the worst, supported him. The success of *S&S*—perhaps it was mere chance? Perhaps *P&P* will be noticed, reviewed, and reviled. Perhaps the sky will fall, and England will sink beneath the waves. Perhaps, perhaps, perhaps. I had to agree."

Nothing but the sound of the horses' hooves and the harnesses filled the vehicle.

"*P&P*, I confess, is my favorite of your works," Worth said.

"A parent must not have favorites among her children. But many of my readers agree. Mr Egerton certainly agrees. He has now gained, by my estimation, more than four hundred pounds in profits and he is printing a new edition."

"Four hundred?" Worth murmured.

"Nearer to four hundred and fifty. It has been an extraordinary success…for a 'minor, female author' such as myself."

"What have you said…to Mr Austen? Did he…?"

"I said I was perfectly delighted with the payment of one hundred and ten pounds. I said everything was quite satisfactory. I said certainly Mr Egerton can publish *Mansfield Park*, as it had already been set in type." Facing Worth again, she continued. "And, I told Henry that I would never, ever, under any circumstance, sell a copyright again. And I bade him retrieve the copyright for *Susan* that he sold to Crosby for ten pounds."

"What's this? Another novel? Ten quid?"

"An exuberant, somewhat immature work—and yet, a complete manuscript," Jane said. "I was much younger—it happened twelve or thirteen years ago. It was a whimsy. My father took it on first. 'Would it not be amusing to see your words in print?' Papa said. 'Of course.' I replied. 'Well, here is Mr Benjamin Crosby, publisher, of London. He will take it on. And you shall receive ten pounds!'"

"*Susan?*" Worth said. "That was the title? But I saw no copies on your bookshelves. How did it fare?"

"Aye, there's the rub," Jane declaimed and then continued quietly. "Crosby never published it."

"That makes no sense."

"Henry has corresponded with him. Henry has spoken with him. Crosby told him that his firm purchased the copyright but has no obligation to publish. At one time, they offered to sell it back to us for the original price, but Henry did not pursue the matter. With my current work occupying so much of my time, *Susan* was left to the side. Now, with the success of my other novels, I fear that Crosby will decide to publish it, an inferior work that will tarnish my reputation. So, Henry must retrieve the manuscript and my copyright. He must." Jane looked at Worth, a determined gleam in her eyes. "He must!"

The coach neared Chawton. Worth saw the bell tower of Saint Nicholas gleaming in the late afternoon sun.

"Will you remain in Alton or take Mr Ellicott up on his offer?" Jane said. "It is most generous."

"Generous. Yes, generous," Worth said more to himself than Jane. "A saving. And it's not a hard journey from here to Kellingsford. We'll see," he said, louder. "We'll see."

When the coach stopped, Worth exited quickly to hand her down.

"Shall we meet on the morrow?"

"That'd be best," Worth said. "I'll have arrangements to make that'll take time."

"Here at the cottage? At two?"

"Certainly," he said. "Four bells of the afternoon watch."

"Navy time." She laughed. "I must master it. Frank and Charles would be most impressed." She glanced at her right hand still in his.

"Ah." Worth released the hand and he bowed to her. "Yes, tomorrow."

"*Au revoir*, Mr Worth," she said, curtsied, and turned to her cottage.

❧15❦

Two footmen in Kellingsford livery swung Worth's chest down from the back of the coach and placed it at the bottom of the broad steps under the portico.

"Worth, is it?" Jerome said. "Our worthy guest," he continued with a chuckle, amused at his own wit. "Mr Aloysius Ellicott said you might be returning. Marryat will be along for you shortly." The coach continued around the front of the great house, then in the direction of the stables.

Left to himself, Worth looked around the place, noting the fine white marble steps, worn in the center by two centuries of lords', ladies', and servants' tread. He sat on the third step, placing his fiddle case next to him, and considered the drive, lawn, and gardens spread out before him. Even in early winter, they were clipped and well-tended, wearing coats of gold, russet, and brown. Two holly trees on either side of the steps made a bold showing. Decked with red berries, they foretold the gaiety of the coming holiday season.

After several minutes, Worth resumed pacing. The drive was eight paces wide under the portico, then another eight steps in the open on the other side. The portico spread twenty paces wide and at least thirty deep, Worth estimated. And the house—well, it was just bloody, damned immense.

At last, the old servant Marryat rounded the northerly corner of the house.

"Ahoy," the old man rasped as he approached and greeted Worth warmly. "I'm sent to fetch you. Got a fine berth for you. The old tutor's quarters."

The old man made to manhandle the sea chest.

"Let's have a hand," Worth said, taking one end of the chest with his left hand. "Makes it a damn sight easier to navigate."

With the chest between them, they circled the house.

Away from the primary aspect, Kellingsford took on a humble air. Over the years, ivy-covered red brick additions extended the great house. The place was still enormous, but this side was somewhat less imposing, Worth thought.

A plain oak door in the back opened to the hidden web of servants' passages and stairs. Three flights up, just below the garrets, the old footman opened the door to a warm, cozy room furnished as a study.

"Bedchamber's there," Marryat said, nodding to an inner door that stood half open.

Fine lodgings, indeed, Worth decided.

"They's a washup room in the stable," Marryat said. "When you're on the stable path, look to the right and there's a path to th' privy."

"Comforts of home."

"Better than hangin' yer arse over roarin' great waves."

"Aye. Yes, indeed." Both men laughed as they recalled the common sailor's shipboard facilities.

"Ye can take your meals with the servants," Marryat said. "Six bells on the morning watch, and eight bells on the afternoon. Make a friend of Mrs Crumb, the cook, and she'll find you a crust of bread an' a cuppa."

"The keys to her heart?"

"A friendly word in passing," Marryat said, "and bold praise for her scones, if you have the good fortune to taste one. She's right proud o' her scones."

"Thank you."

"Now, I've got fires to tend," the old man said. "Twenty-eight fireplaces in this house. Not all of them in use, but they's got to be looked after."

"Avast." Marryat stopped. "For your trouble," Worth said, offering the man a shilling.

Marryat's smile dropped. The brow above his good eye furrowed.

"Nay, sir," he said. "You're bunking with the crew here. No call for vails among shipmates." And he was gone.

Worth surveyed the lodgings—the suite—recognizing it as far superior to his room at The Ship. The glowing fireplace warmed the study. The chambers were bright, each having a window. As Worth shifted his chest into the sleeping chamber, he was struck. His fiddle!

Moving quickly, he navigated the steps and path around the house and found his instrument exactly where he had left it. The panic he had not fully realized subsided as he slung it comfortably over his shoulder and retraced his steps.

As he rounded the second corner, he saw a redcoat leaving the house from a door further along the back of the house. As they approached each other on the path, Worth saw the boards on his shoulders—a captain—and campaign ribbons that marked service on the Peninsula and the continent. And Waterloo. Worth also noted the man's thin smile and cold eyes as he approached.

"The fiddler," the officer said when they were six paces apart. "Mr Worth, is it not?" He offered the slightest bow.

Worth returned the greeting with an equally meager acknowledgment.

"You have me at a disadvantage," Worth said.

"Wembley," the officer replied.

"Captain Wembley, you've done hot work in your time."

"Took the grand tour of the continent with Wellington."

"Cavalry?" Worth said, noticing the man's boots and spurs.

"Dragoons. Sabers and muskets. More ways to kill frogs."

The officer spoke the words without heat, without bluster. *This is a man who found joy in battle,* Worth thought as he looked into his eyes.

"Aloysius says you told him you served in the navy. With Nelson. At Trafalgar."

"That's the story I tell," Worth said. "It dinna fool him."

Wembley's face twitched and hardened. "You do not fool me, Mr Worth."

Then the officer's demeanor changed entirely. He smiled, or at least his mouth smiled.

"So, we are to have a ball, is it?" he said. "That could prove to be a welcome diversion. Shall I muster the troops so you will have enough gentlemen to make up a proper formation? We have a number of young officers who you can employ as cannon fodder to help fill out your sets."

"Miss Austen will be the author of the evening."

"The author," Wembley said. This time, his eyes echoed a trace of his smile. "Well, Mr Dancing Master, the house demands confidence in your orchestration of the program. A proper ball demands the same attention as a military campaign. Troops. Logistics. The program itself. The timing, of course. The timing is everything. Good day." Wembley nodded and resumed his march in the center of the path, forcing Worth to step aside.

When the captain rounded the corner, Worth shook his head and returned to his lodgings.

❧16❦

"A ball? What is this about a ball?"

Mrs Cassandra Austen commenced her inquisition as she entered Jane's writing room with this new information. Jane turned from her desk, and her sister looked up from her needlework.

"Indeed, there is to be a ball," Jane said. "At Kellingsford. On my birthday. Aloysius learned about my plan and proposed—truly insisted—that it be at Kellingsford."

"This is what that odd tradesman was about?" Mrs Austen said. "Mind you, Flora has told me all about his comings and goings. Have you any idea…?"

"Mama!" Jane spoke sharply. "This is my business."

"Your business?" Mrs Austen said.

"Your daughter is an authoress," Cassandra said, coming to the aid of her sister. "An authoress who has achieved success and who has a growing reputation."

"Jane," Mrs Austen said, "your volumes are lovely. Most entertaining, I will say. But you must be careful. Propriety demands—"

"Propriety?" Jane stood. "Oh, Mama. I am a spinster, soon to be forty years old. I am long past the age of innocence."

"Your reputation still matters," Cassandra said to Jane. "And reflects on your family."

"Of course, dear sister. Of course, Mama," Jane said. "We shall observe all propriety. This will be a ball, not a bacchanalia. But it will serve a purpose. As a young lady is presented to society that she may find suitors, so shall an authoress be presented to society that she may find readers and, possibly, a new publisher."

"Jane!" Mrs Austen said. "What will people think if they find out that you are the 'lady' who authored those novels?"

"Mama, everyone in our society already knows Jane is the 'lady'," Cassandra said.

"Yes. Well, possibly," Mrs Austen said. "But now, you propose to flaunt it? To shout it to the world? Next you will be placing advertisements in the newspapers."

"An interesting suggestion," Jane said. "I shall make a note of it."

"No Mama," Cassandra said. "What Jane proposes is a proper, dignified celebration."

"A birthday party, Mama. For our family and friends and a few special guests."

"Society, Jane?" Mrs Austen said. "What will society think?"

"Society will think kindly on it, Mama," Jane said. "If the Prince Regent approves, what objection could society possibly hold?"

"The Prince Regent?" Mrs Austen said. "What is this?"

"I had not wanted to tell you," Jane said. "I am still of two minds."

"Two minds?" Mrs Austen said. "About what?"

"I have been asked to dedicate my next novel, *Emma*, to the Prince Regent."

"Oh, Jane. Oh, my…why, that is…" Mrs Austen said. "What is this being of 'two minds'?"

"The Prince Regent is a terrible person, Mama," Jane said. "I do not want to dedicate my novel to him."

"You cannot possibly refuse such an honor!"

"The man is a contemptible spendthrift and philanderer," Jane said. "How my novels even came to his attention remains a mystery. But, Mama, you are correct. Much as I should prefer to do otherwise, I cannot refuse. As an authoress, it seems there are too often these things that one must do, and one must say. I cannot refuse."

"The blessings of the Crown," Mrs Austen said.

Jane sighed deeply.

"This is portentous news indeed," Mrs Austen said. "Royal favor. And now, a ball at Kellingsford. Aloysius insisted. This is truly portentous." She took a seat next to Cassandra. "Now who will be attending our ball?"

Following nearly an hour in discussion, Mrs Austen left the sisters to complete the invitation list. The Austen brothers, of course, would all be invited. Jane would prefer not to see dour James, but he must be included. Edward, residing at Godmersham, seemed unlikely to attend but must be asked. Frank, temporarily residing at Chawton House, would have to stand in for Charles who was presently at sea commanding the *Phoenix*, snapping up pirates in the Mediterranean. Henry, of course, if his health permitted. He was still weak from the fever that had recently struck him down.

Friends and neighbors from all around Chawton joined the list. More from Steventon, Bath, and Winchester were added, though again, the travel made their attendance less likely.

All the residents of Kellingsford must be included as well as the officers of the dragoons billeted in Medstead. "Just to decorate the dance floor," Cassandra said.

"Indeed, there is nothing so weary as seeing ladies sitting when dancing is at hand."

As she identified a few additional invitations, Cassandra began to fully appreciate Jane's scheme for the ball.

"We must, of course, ask Mr Egerton," Jane said, naming the publisher of her first three novels.

She gave her sister the names of principals at three other London publishing houses to include.

"And I shall invite Mr Murray," Jane said, naming the publisher of a wildly popular cookery book and, more recently, of successful volumes from Lord Byron and Mr Scott.

"So many?" Cassandra said.

"Printers and booksellers inhabit a tight society in Town. They goad one another," Jane said. "In my dealings with Egerton, I have learned something of their workings, ways, and reputations. I believe my novels need a new home."

"Jane, Mr Egerton has been so kind."

"Kind?" Jane said. "Kind? He and his brothers in trade do not traffic in kindness, Cass. He seeks profit."

"Of course, as all men of business must," Cassandra said. "As an author, your needs must rise above such petty matters."

"Oh Cass." Jane sighed and shook her head. "Oh Cass."

"Is this not Henry's domain?"

"Henry is my dearest brother, you know that."

"Yes, and he is your man of business."

Jane paused, considering her next words. "Perchance, dear sister, I am in need of a woman of business."

❧17❧

Worth entered the washroom in the stable block.

Marryat, the old seaman, knew the ropes, of course. Mrs Crumb was fully justified in taking great pride in her scones. Worth had captured two of the delicious pastries as the platter circled the servants' breakfast table. As the table was cleared, he seized the initiative with a foray into the kitchen armed with words of high praise for the cook and took a third scone as a prize in a frayed napkin. He patted his jacket pocket. It would go well with a cup of coffee. Or failing a proper beverage, a cup of tea.

He stepped out of the washroom and found himself face to face with the tall, thin, greasy-haired man he had encountered at the inn.

The name came to him: "Hinch." The face. The glare. It was not easy to forget.

"The sailor man," Hinch said. His eyes filled instantly with the same malevolence Worth had seen in their first confrontation. No, that wasn't true. His belligerence was inflamed by personal malice.

Then, in an instant, the fire in Hinch's eyes burned out. He turned, found the horse he wanted and saddled it.

Worth watched him. The gamekeeper was in a hurry.

The dancing master started out of the stable, back toward the great house. Warning words came back to him. *"Never, don't ever turn your back…"*

Worth whirled around.

Hinch was already mounted. Worth watched him guide the horse out of the stable onto a track that led to nearby crofts and urge his mount to a gallop.

❧18❧

Reginald Wembley dismounted under the great portico of Kellings-ford. He handed the reins of his black gelding, a four-year-old, quivering with energy, to a groom. "Water and a handful of grain," the captain said. "But keep him at the ready. I shan't be long."

Aloysius had been anticipating the captain's arrival and emerged from the house. "Wembley."

They shook hands.

"Aloysius." The captain returned the young man's greeting with warmth. "Shall we take a turn in the garden? It is such a fine day. You may find it bracing."

Aloysius grimaced slightly then tendered a bright smile as he followed the officer into the hedgerows. Drawing aside his friend, in privacy, he spoke. "A turn in the garden? You find this preferable to hot tea in the drawing room by the fire?"

Wembley laughed.

"Really, Reggie, are you conducting some military exercise? Training up the troops?"

Aloysius had already wrapped his arms around himself against the cold.

"I cannot be long, Ally. I must be in Bath by this evening."

"Bath? On what mission?" Aloysius said.

"Details, Ally, details. We have a party to arrange. Now, are all the preparations in place?"

"Yes, yes. The day and the time are settled. It will be 16 December. We must expect early arrivals at sunset—about four. Supper can be had at—"

"The presentation of the painting?" Wembley said. "What time?"

"Nine o'clock," Aloysius said. "It has been set for nine o'clock, as you suggested."

"Precisely?"

"As you suggested."

"No, I mean to say, exactly at the hour?"

"It is a ball, Reggie, a dance. These things have a way of wandering about the clock. Certainly, I can pursue the dancing master to be precise about it but..." Aloysius shrugged.

"Fireworks," Wembley said. "Tell him there are plans for fireworks to celebrate the unveiling."

"Fireworks? Oh? And what will they think if there are no fireworks? Truly, Reggie, your penchant for military precision must take some leave."

"As close as can be then," Wembley said. "You must keep watch and chivvy things along if need be."

"You are confident in this action, Reggie? Of its effect?"

"You can never be certain how men under fire will respond, Ally. Still, the threat of danger does concentrate the mind."

"But...change a mind?"

"Stay the course, Ally. Be a good soldier and follow my commands."

"Yes, Reggie. Yes, sir." Aloysius saluted and Wembley laughed.

"Oh, my Ally. Dress you up in a red rag and you would prove to be a bad bargain indeed."

"Captain Wembley, you have dashed my fondest dream—marching about in the mud and bedding down with fleas. I am inconsolable. Now, good sir, this turn in the garden is turning me blue with cold. Come in that we may warm ourselves."

"No, I must be going."

"Tea, surely there is time..."

"Ally." Wembley faced the younger man and braced him with hands on both shoulders. "The threat is real. We cannot hide. We must embrace the trial and take action, whatever the cost."

Aloysius looked back at Wembley and managed a wan smile. "Yes, my captain."

"Go now. Plan your party."

❧19❦

"C'mon now, lads, I needs you," Hinch called out. "There's a bit o' work we got to do."

The gamekeeper stood in the doorway of the barn on a sizable croft near Kellingsford.

"Apologies, Mr Hinch. We can't now," a burly lad answered Hinch from behind a massive armload of straw. "Me and Sully got to sort this place out today or old man Keith says they'll be the devil to pay."

"He's right, Mr Hinch," came a voice from the loft. "The old man told Joe he'd dock our wages for the whole month if we let him down."

"This won't take long," Hinch said, calmly striding into the barn. "You come down here for a minute, Sullivan. Lemme give you the way of things."

Hinch was not a man to get crossways with. It would be a good thing—the careful thing—to remain friendly with the gamekeeper. Sullivan came down from the loft to hear Hinch out.

"Now, like I said, there's this little bit o' work what needs to be done and it's gonna take a couple of extra hands," Hinch said when he had their attention.

"We can't," Joe said. "Mr Keith—"

"Old codger Keith ain't gonna trouble you," Hinch said. "This won't take no time at all."

"But," Sullivan started.

The gamekeeper's face hardened. His voice quietened, filling with venom.

"Now listen to me, lads, 'cause here's how this is gonna go. You're gonna help me, right now, or you're gonna find the constable at your door and the constable's gonna find hides and meat and bones that proves you've been poaching game off His Lordship's lands. And you can believe me on this, too. I know the folks that you passed some o' that game on to—to your sister, Joe, and you, Sully, you give it to your mam and da and your brother. And you know that takin' poached game— that'll get you thrown off the land faster than not payin' your rent. Now, I'm thinkin' that you boys understand things just a little bit better, eh?"

The men looked at each other.

"You'll be helpin' me out, now, will ya?"

They nodded.

"Now, Mr Sullivan, you see to my horse. A stall and water, if you please. Joe, that small cart," Hinch said, pointing across the yard. "It'll prove useful. Bring it round. Let's be at it then. We've got us a little tangle to sort."

❧ 20 ❧

"Ve are in complete agreement then?" Percival glared at his
brother.

"Certainly," Aloysius replied. "Any decoration—greens or flowers—
must be supplied by Miss Austen at no expense to the household accounts."

The men stood at the center of the floor surveying the Kellingsford
ballroom. Jerome stood close by, making note of the preparations while
Miss Ellicott wandered aimlessly around the perimeter of the ballroom,
occasionally curtsying to invisible guests.

"No holly. No ivy. Not a sprig of mistletoe from the gardens or
woods," Percival continued. "Do I make myself clear?"

Aloysius nodded.

"The silver and plate," Percival said.

"We have discussed this."

"To be certain. Jerome is to take inventory before and after the pro-
ceedings. Any losses shall come from your allowance. Are we clear?"

"Yes, Percy."

Percival addressed Worth, standing close by with Marryat. "What of
your preparations, Mr Dancing Master?"

"Preparations?" Worth asked, taken by surprise.

"Yes, man. Preparations. What do you want? What little additions will
you ask for?"

Worth collected his thoughts.

"Entry to the room. We shall have musicians arriving and need to be
able to come in and arrange things, sir," Worth said.

"Any time after noon. Jerome, see to it."

The butler nodded to Percival and made a note.

"The pianoforte," Worth continued. "It would be expected to have
your man stop by to tune and temper the instrument."

"We don't do that in the winter," Percival said. "If you want it tuned
and tempered, Jerome can give you the man's name and you can arrange
for it."

"I understand," Worth said.

"And pay for it," Percival added.

"Ah yes, sir." With a slight smile, the dancing master continued. "Some of our players will be coming from a distance. Might there be some room to put them up for the night?"

"What? Do you think we are operating a hotel? This time of year, there are plenty enough rooms in Alton. Your musicians must shift for themselves."

Worth grinned, unsurprised by the response.

"The portrait," Miss Ellicott said, entering the conversation. "We need to make arrangements for the presentation of the portrait. It will be the crowning moment of the evening."

"What is there to be done?" Percival said. "You have the portrait. The frame. The stand. The cloth. What more is needed?"

"I thought we might add some trim for the drapery," Miss Ellicott said. "Perhaps some gold braid and cord?"

"Nonsense. It is satisfactory just as it is," Percival said. Then seeing his sister's expression, he continued. "Adding too much color to the wrapping, Sister? Will it not detract from the art itself?"

Worth glanced at the ceiling. Miss Ellicott seemed satisfied.

"It is the timing that is most important," Aloysius said, directing himself to the dancing master. "Nine o'clock—the height of the evening when we have the most people present. Mr Worth, you have made special note of that?"

Worth nodded.

"We shall assemble a presentation party in advance. Ten minutes before the hour, Letitia and I will confer," Aloysius said.

"This will be so thrilling. We will place the portrait just here," she said, moving to the bottom of the grand staircase. "Papa will descend. Ah! Mr Worth—shall we have music? A noble march?"

"Why, of course, ma'am."

"Oh, Percy, it will be so lovely," she said, coming back to her elder brother and making a tentative move toward embracing him.

"Such nonsense," he said, turning away.

"Percy, you are such an old grumbler," Aloysius said. "This will be lovely. We should be hosting a ball every season."

"Wasting money every season," Percy replied.

"You think that by being a miser you increase your lot," Aloysius said.

"Adding to capital and preserving capital. That is paramount."

"And yet you throw money away," Aloysius said. "You save pennies and squander pounds."

"How so?" Percy said, his voice rising. "What the blazes do you know of capital?"

"I know Enclosure is costing you far more than it earns," Aloysius said. "Our tenants are failing. You are foregoing rents, and your shares, and all you have to your credit is title to now-fallow land. What a bargain."

"We have increased our capital."

"Only if you sell it," Aloysius said. "And who is there to buy it? Your tenants are now penniless."

"We shall run sheep in it."

"Buy sheep? Employ shepherds? Erect facilities?" Aloysius said. "When you might have left the commons to the tenants and enjoyed the same income? And rents in addition?"

"You understand nothing."

"I understand that you, dear brother, have been bamboozled."

Percival rounded on Aloysius; his fists balled. Jerome set himself between them.

"Gentlemen," the butler said.

A footman approached, breathing hard.

"A lad at the door…horse in a lather…Mr Morgan—"

"Whatever is it, man?" Percival said.

Another footman appeared in the company of a boy, weeping.

"I wants to talk to His Lordship, sir. It's my pa. He's dead. It's my pa. He's been murdered."

❧21❧

The vehicle defied description. At one time, it had been a common farm wagon. But in place of the box where grain and goods might be loaded, sat a house, giving the thing the look of a sort of carriage. The house, however, built of plain boards and painted black, showed no trace of fine workmanship. The strange vehicle had only one door, a rectangle on the left side that showed some signs of recent modification. In place of glass or shutters, the window openings were covered by metal bars.

A pair of ancient, spavined horses labored to a halt in front of the barn.

A rail-thin man with not a hair on his head set the brake, dropped down from the box, and went round to the back of the vehicle. While he loosened the ropes binding some sort of wooden construct tied to the back of the conveyance, the wagon commenced to shake, groan, and sway. The driver placed the wooden assembly, a short set of steps, in front of the carriage door.

The driver unlatched the door and, when it swung open, Bolabus Claypoole, the parish constable, appeared.

Clinging to any available handhold, the great man cautiously began his perilous descent down the steps. The treads bent and moaned. When he, at last, stood safely on the ground, he took a moment to recover his breath, removed his snuff box, took two large pinches, dabbed his nose with his kerchief, and looked around.

"Very well," he said, then delivered an enormous sneeze. After pressing it to his upper lip, he pushed the damp handkerchief up his sleeve. The constable then spied Admiral Harwell and addressed him. "What is this business that demands my attention?"

A moment later, Constable Claypoole stared down at the body and shook his head. His jowls wabbled, and the plume in his fashionable black beaver hat waved about with unsuitable gaiety. Claypoole stepped with care around the pool of blood from the man's mangled leg.

"Terrible. Terrible."

The body lay near the foot of a ladder that leaned against a sheep barn. As the constable conducted his examination, he was attended by his driver—the walking skeleton of a man called Turkle. The two men circled the corpse. Admiral Harwell, summoned from his nearby residence, followed closely.

The several farm workers, some of the estate's other tenants, their wives, and children, completed the tableau. The ladies gathered to comfort the suddenly widowed Mrs Morgan and her boy, Jimmy.

"Terrible," the constable repeated, looking closely at the body, seeing the cuts and blood on the man's hands, then gulping, and turning away.

"Tell us, now," Claypoole said, when he recovered himself, "Who discovered this tragedy?"

At first, there was no response. Then, as though prodded from behind, a brawny laborer stepped forward.

"Aye, sir. It was me."

"And you are?"

"Sullivan. Seen him. I just seen him, was all. We heard the dogs barking."

"'We' you say? You and...?" Claypoole asked.

"Me and Joe here," Sullivan said, pulling another laborer forward.

"You heard dogs?"

"Right enough," Joe said. "I went round in front. And Mr Hinch and Sullivan, they looked back here."

"Mr Hinch?" Claypoole said. "Mr Hinch?"

"Here, sir."

Now the Kellingsford gamekeeper stepped out from between the two farm workers who eyed Hinch more carefully than they did the constable.

"Yes, sir," Hinch continued. "Terrible accident here. We was over on His Lordship's land and heard the dogs, you see. So, we come over, see what was amiss. Sullivan here"—taking the first laborer by the arm and pulled him forward— "he's one what found the body. Eh, Sullivan?"

"Aye sir," the young man said. "Aye."

"And what did you see?" Hinch said.

"I seen the body, lying right there," Sullivan said. "I just seen him lying there."

"And did you see anything else?" Hinch said, his eyes darting to the right, the direction of the barn. And upward.

"The ladder," Sullivan said. "I seen the ladder right there and I knowed it must have been a terrible accident and the poor man must have fell down from it and that's how he got killed."

"You were sure he was dead?" Claypoole said.

"Oh, aye, sir. You just look at him, and I was sure, sir. He was dead."

"Fell from a ladder, eh? Make a note of that, Turkle. And get his complete name, birth date, and occupation. We will use that to complete the entry in the parish registry upon burial. Inform the rector. Alms for the family. Terrible, terrible, terrible," Claypoole mumbled, turning away, and withdrawing his snuff box. He took two good pinches and made his way through the circle of neighbors and family toward his carriage.

"Sir. Sir! Mr Claypoole. Constable Claypoole," the admiral said, following the constable. "Will you be collecting evidence? Inspecting the scene closely? Will there not be an inquest?"

"An inquest?" Claypoole said. "Why should we want an inquest? The death was an accident. Fell from the ladder," he said, looking back toward the barn. "Or possibly from the roof. Clearly, a terrible accident."

"The leg injury, sir," the admiral said. "Surely not the result of the fall?"

"From such a height," the constable said, gesturing at the roof.

"The blood—"

"Blood, oh"—turning his head— "do not speak to me of blood." After a large gasp of air, Claypoole continued. "No Admiral, the thing is plain enough. An accident."

"Claypoole," the admiral said, following the constable towards his conveyance. "Oughtn't you take this to the magistrate?"

"The magistrate?" Claypoole said turning on Admiral Harwell. "The magistrate? All the way to Winchester? To deal with a barnyard accident?"

"You are the constable, sir," the admiral said. "It is your duty."

"Duty? Oh, my good admiral, sir. Might you consider the honor of becoming the parish constable? My term, blissfully, will be ending shortly. I shall speak to the rector on your behalf."

Claypoole warmed to the subject.

"'Tis a great honor, to be sure, to be named parish constable," he said. "'Tis such a great honor that there is no need for a stipend or any other recompense. No, no, no. You are covered with honor. You delight in your privilege; your obligation to pursue petty criminals, house the indigent, chivvy vagabonds, punish drunks, transport soldiers, and, the most enjoyable task of all, collect taxes. Oh, how the townsfolk love you for that. While you bask in the glory of your position, you are entitled to the services of the deputy constable, the estimable Mr Turkle here, and the use of this magnificent carriage."

The constable swept a bow toward his odd conveyance.

"Oh yes," Claypoole said, turning back to face the admiral and striking a declamatory attitude. "And you will be entitled to visit the scene of every barnyard accident and report the death for the parish register. The position will become vacant on the first day of January."

The constable withdrew his handkerchief, searched for a dry corner, and dabbed at his brow.

"All of you," he said, gesturing to the crowd gathered around the body, "assist this poor widow! Help…help her prepare for the funeral and burial. All the rest, disperse. Disperse, I say, or I shall read the Riot Act. Turkle, come now."

The constable turned his back on the admiral.

"Good day, sir," he called over his shoulder with a casual wave.

The large man carefully ascended the portable steps. When he stepped into the wagon, it groaned and listed precipitously, but Claypoole managed to board the craft without capsizing it. Turkle closed the door, stowed the steps, and took the reins. The wagon jerked forward, and Constable Claypoole concluded his investigation into Robert Morgan's death.

❧ 22 ❧

"Worth! Wait," Aloysius called out from the top step of the portico and hurried down the stairs. "Just the man I wanted to see. We have need of your services."

"I'm on my way—"

"It is for the good of the ball," Aloysius said. "This is such a splendid plan. Miss Austen will be delighted. You shall see."

Worth waited for Aloysius to recover his breath and make his request.

"We have a squadron of new dancers to add to the guest list."

Worth frowned.

"A dozen of the dragoons," Aloysius continued. "Young lieutenants and cornets. They have such beautiful uniforms. They will add ornamentation to the festivities. And being under the orders of Captain Wembley, they will be commanded to dance every dance. No sitting about idly or running off to play whist for these chaps. There are never enough men wanting to dance, is that not true?"

Worth nodded slowly. Young ladies were frequently left seated on the sides when they wished to dance. The practice of ladies dancing in the drawing room with other ladies could not be countenanced at a ball.

"'Tis a fair point," Worth said cautiously. "I'll discuss it with Miss Austen."

"Oh, that will not be necessary. The young men, all single, I might add, have already been invited. They will form an honor guard for Papa's portrait, you see. All single," he said again, brightly, "and from noble families...or at least gentry...minor nobility, perhaps, and a few...wealthy merchants..."

"I see," Worth said. "Then it is decided. We shall have additional men. Good fortune to the ladies."

"Yes..." Aloysius said. "Yes..."

"There's more," Worth said. "What else?"

"They...well...you see..." Aloysius started and stopped several times. Finally, it came out in a burst.

"They do not know how to dance."

Worth looked at the young gentleman and then closed his eyes, hoping he would go away. When he opened his eyes, Aloysius was still there, rejuvenated by his confession.

"With the war and all, you see, some have not had a proper gentleman's education," he continued when he saw he had Worth's attention. "They have not had dance instruction."

Aloysius continued in a rush, "I am of the mind that we ought to host a small dance in the assembly rooms where you can teach them how to dance. I shall arrange the hall. Wembley will form them up and march them over. Is it not a splendid idea? I'll make the arrangements and send a letter to Miss Austen with the details. We shall invite ladies from hereabouts to join us in the instruction. It will be great fun."

Aloysius had more to say about his brilliant idea but was interrupted by the arrival of Admiral Harwell on horseback. A groom came running from the stable to take the reins. The admiral, clearly in a fury, rounded on Aloysius.

"Where's your brother?"

"What is wrong, Admiral?" Aloysius said.

"Wrong? Wrong? Damn man, what is there that's right? A man is dead. Dead. In an accident, or so your constable claims."

"What?" Aloysius said.

"Morgan. My tenant. Good man."

"Oh, yes, Mr Morgan. Yes, Percival is quite aware. Yes, we all heard. Tragic. And the constable has completed his investigation?"

"Your Constable Claypoole is an idiot," the admiral said. "Took him half the day to get there. He arrived, looked about for a minute, saw a ladder, and declared it an accident."

"Oh, my," Aloysius said. "A fall?"

"You think it was not?" Worth said. "Not an accident?"

The admiral looked at Worth, at Aloysius, and back to Worth.

"I don't know. I can't be sure."

"But," Worth prompted him.

"I've seen men who have taken falls, bad falls from the topmast of a three-decker and worse, and I have never seen an injury like this. I've seen bones snap and splinter and limbs curved and bent all crooked. But Mr Morgan's leg was mangled," the admiral continued. "It looked like a leg run over or pinned by a loose cannon."

"Smashed, was it?" Worth said. "Like a limb caught on a gunwale rubbing up against another ship?"

"Aye," the admiral said. "You've been to sea, have you?"

Worth nodded.

"His hands were cut and bloody, too—raw flesh," the admiral continued. "Some fingernails torn off. Now how did that come about in a fall? Come, Aloysius, where's your brother? We need to demand an inquest."

Admiral Harwell was halfway up the steps with Aloysius following in his wake.

Worth was left standing in the drive wondering what to tell Jane.

There's been a death at Kellingsford. An accident perhaps. Or perhaps not?

A squadron of dragoons are coming to your ball, but first we must teach them to dance.

He was not sure which news would be more unpleasant.

❧ 23 ❧

"Mr Worth, you have my full attention now."

Worth gave the slightest start. He had been so deeply engrossed in thought, he had not noticed Jane's return to the parlor.

Cassandra disregarded her sister's arrival entirely. She continued her needlework and did her duty, respecting her mother's insistence, lending Jane's meeting respectability.

"Ah, yes. Just so," the dancing master said, recovering. "I am just from Kellingsford where Mr Aloysius Ellicott has devised a plan to increase the number of men who will be attending your ball." Worth proceeded to describe the gentleman's scheme.

"This may not prove to be an ill thing," Jane decided. "But as it is proposed by Aloysius, not the most dependable of the Ellicotts, we will meet again on the morrow and see if this seed of an idea grows and bears fruit."

"Let us attend to our main purpose," she continued. "Your list?"

Worth opened his book, reviewed his notes, and commenced.

"Now, on the question of music, you've said you have no musicians hereabouts you favor. Are you sure? Possibly in Winchester? It's not so far."

"The cupboard is bare, Mr Worth," Jane said. "Certainly, we have those who can strike all the correct notes but…"

Worth waited.

"Their music is not uplifting," she said. "They plod along gamely, as you have heard me do. We shall want much better."

"You undervalue your powers, Miss Jane. But I take your point. How many musicians shall we have?"

"What do you recommend? Many of our dances around here include only the pianoforte. I think we will surely want more."

"Two or three, I would think," Worth said. "At times, I will be able to join in so you could have four."

"A proper orchestra."

"It's a lively hall," Worth said. "A quartet will fill it nicely, even with a crowded dance floor. So, two? Or three?"

"You suggested three. Why consider only two?"

"The cost," he said. "More players, more money."

"We shall not scrimp, Mr Worth. Three musicians, in addition to yourself. Please do your utmost. We want wonderful music."

"As to the dance program, what sorts of dances will you want?" Worth said. "Minuets seem to be the rage in Town. And with the war ended, quadrilles from France are coming into fashion."

"Country dances, Mr Worth," she said. "We shall have country dances that are known and well loved by all. Oh, and we must have a waltz. Or two. I have become rather fond of the waltz."

"Now, there's a nod to fashion," Worth said. "Waltzing has become very popular in some quarters. It's the rage at Almack's."

"How is it that our strait-laced Saxon cousins in Germany should have brought us such a delight?" Jane said.

"Have you read Byron's satire: *The Waltz*?" Worth asked.

"His *Apostrophic Hymn*? Of course. The most amusing thing he has ever written, I think."

"It's amusing, but there's truth in it. There's many, even in Town, that think the waltz ain't a proper dance."

"Oh, the scandal!" Jane said, laughing. "Mrs Radcliffe may construct an entire novel around the shame of an innocent girl, tempted, seduced, and ruined by a waltz."

"You jest, but there's disagreement still."

"We have danced in triple time forever in longways dances. Waltz music abounds. Yet we had not the courage to embrace the full pleasure of the meter. Our German cousins have shown us the light," Jane said.

"Your English cousins may show you contempt. We're not in London."

"Times are changing, Mr Worth. And I, doubly shamed as a spinster and an authoress, have naught to fear. It is my ball, and we must, and we shall waltz."

"So, we shall," Worth said, writing in his book, then to himself he said, "Oh that..."

"Oh, what?" Jane said.

"The presentation, ma'am. The portrait. The Ellicotts are keen on it and particular about the time as well."

"Go on."

"They want it in the ballroom."

"Yes."

"And to have His Lordship come down the grand staircase."

"Yes."

"And they wants music for that—a march or something else that sounds grand."

"Of course. What is a *grand* entrance without music?"

"And it's to be at nine o'clock, prompt."

"Is that all?"

"Well, when His Lordship is down by the painting, they'll drop the cloth."

"No military salute? No firing of cannon? No oration? An ode from Lord Byron, perhaps?"

"They dinna go that far," Worth said, "least ways not yet, though Mr Ellicott, the younger, did make some mention of fireworks."

"How much did we save by staging the ball at Kellingsford, Mr Worth?"

"Well, the assembly room cost. Some of my expenses. I reckon four or five pounds."

"There you have it," Jane said. "Cost of doing business. We have a splendid ballroom, saved money, and all for the price of this little ceremony."

"As long as you're willing."

"Lord Kellingsford deserves some kindness," Jane said. "We knew him when we first moved to Chawton, before he—"

"Lost his wits?"

"Yes, that," Jane said. "He was slightly eccentric then and obsessed with fashion. But he was also a capable landlord. He was very well liked and considered just by his tenants. A good man."

"Those times have gone by," Worth said. "This latest…oh."

"Latest? What, Mr Worth?"

"Nothing," Worth said. "It'll have no effect at all on your ball."

"What will have no effect?"

"It's not for polite—"

"Mr Worth, you must know by now, there are no secrets in this village. What?"

Worth shook his head and finally replied.

"There has been a death on the estate. Sudden and unexpected. One of His Lordship's tenants."

"What were the circumstances?"

"That's not clear. I've heard the man's son, come to fetch His Lordship, still weeping for his pa, and then the mutterings from the servants. The body was found in the farmyard. No one saw what happened."

"Tragic for the family—he has family?"

"Aye, wife and the lad."

"These things happen," Jane said.

"He seemed a very hale man when I met him," Worth said. "Of a sudden, he's dead."

"There's something more to this, Mr Worth? What else?"

"Mr Morgan was in a dispute with his landlord, with Percival. His old grazing was enclosed. His plots were cut off and relocated. And his boy, Jimmy, had a runin with the gamekeeper."

"I see," Jane said. "So, the incident will not have any effect on our plans, but—"

"You know sailors, ma'am. We're a superstitious lot."

"An omen."

Worth shrugged. "An ill wind."

❧24❧

"N o, Hinch. I can't be taking them things."

"It's just for a while," the gamekeeper said. "Just take 'em and stick 'em in some dark corner o' your master's barn."

"They's dangerous," Sullivan said. "What if someone was to—"

"Not a bit, boy," Hinch said. "They's no more dangerous than an old iron gate."

"Come on, Hinch. I seen what one of 'em can do…"

"They's completely safe," Hinch said. "You can't open 'em. Go ahead. Give it a try."

The men stood next to a shed connected to the gamekeeper's cottage. A cloud passed in front of the moon making the night even darker.

The lad took one of the devices, seized the handles on the jaws, and pulled. He was strong, but he could not move the jaws, not even an inch.

"They's locked, you see. When one closes, you can't open it at all, lessen you gots the key." He withdrew a small ring of keys from his pocket. "So they's no danger at all on account of I got the keys."

"But, Hinch—"

"Listen to me, laddie!" Hinch put a hand on the young man's arm and pulled him close. Foul words were accompanied by foul breath.

"Ya don't want to be spending your time talkin' with the constable or the magistrate, do you? If that's what you wants, I can… But that's not what you wants, is it? Nah, you'd rather be spending time with me and your mates. Enjoying a pint or two?"

Now Hinch moved even closer to Sullivan's face.

"And the last thing you'd ever be wanting to do is to make me angry? Ain't that right? You seen what can happen when I gets angry? Or Mr Ellicott gets angry? And you knows that I'm the arm of Mr Ellicott? You knows that?"

Hinch backed away, bent down, and picked up the second device. He handed it to the young man.

"Like I said, just take these here little snappers and put 'em away someplace safe. I'll let you know the next time I needs 'em."

❧ 25 ❧

"There is an end to it," Jane said. "I've received a letter from Mr Aloysius Ellicott. The rooms are let. We dance two days hence."

Cassandra had served the tea in the parlor and withdrawn to her needlework. Jane sipped; Worth allowed his cup to grow cold.

"And dancers?" Worth said. "I know he can marshal the troops, but-...ladies?"

"He has raised the hue and cry," Jane said. "The war effect will likely fill the room."

"The war effect?"

"With so many men at war," Jane said, "the news of a parcel of young, eligible men at a dance will have mothers across half the county hastening their single daughters to attend. There will be ladies enough, I warrant."

"Music?" Worth said. "With young Mr Ellicott's dragoons to instruct, I'll have m' hands full. We will need you to play."

"Should we not find a more accomplished player?"

"Someone we would have to pay?" Worth said. "And for that matter, you're a fine player. Superior to many in Town, I'd say."

"You are flattering me, sir."

"I'm no flatterer, Miss Jane, especially when it comes to music. It's the plain truth," Worth said.

"Well, if you think—"

"Done," Worth said.

"You are very persuasive, sir. I shall have a letter carried to Mr Ellicott completing the details of our plan."

"I'll carry it for you, if you like."

"Good, very good. But before I take up my pen, tell me of your other news. Poor Mr Morgan."

"Like I said, he was found dead. No witnesses."

"And the constable?"

"He saw the body. Saw a ladder. Said it must've been an accident."

"But you don't think so."

"I canna say," Worth said. "I wasn't there. But Harwell, the admiral, he was mighty upset. First, with a man being dead, o' course. And then the constable saying it were a fall. He dinna think that was right. He wanted an inquest."

"But the constable—"

"Wouldna' hear of it. He seen the ladder and that was that."

"And if he had seen a horse grazing nearby instead of a ladder?" Jane asked. "The constable would have said that poor Mr Morgan died when he tumbled off the horse. That is how it is with stories. We see what we want to see. In a novel, there are times when an author uses that to her advantage, to create illusions, suspense, or surprise. The constable knew what he wanted to see. The admiral did not think it matched the circumstances. What were his concerns?"

"Part of it was the man's hands. Cuts. Blood. Nails pulled off. Looked like he had been in a terrible fight, the admiral said. But he allowed that somehow, it could've happened in a fall. But the man's leg," Worth continued. "The admiral said it looked like it'd been crushed. Not just broke; even badly broke in a terrible fall. Said it didn't look right."

"How did he describe the injury?"

"Terrible crushing of the leg just below the knee. Trousers ripped. Lots of blood on the wound and his clothing but not much on the ground. He said it looked like it was smashed."

"You and Admiral Harwell—sailors," Jane said. "You would not—"

"What?"

"Even military men," Jane said, talking almost to herself. "Honorable military men."

"What are you thinkin'?"

Jane looked at him quite seriously.

"The constable ought to have spoken to the other onlookers—the tenants and their families. They might have knowledge of such things. But with the enclosing. The dispute. Perhaps they were afraid to speak out on their own accord."

"You sound like you have an idea about this story, Miss Jane. Can you skip to the end?"

"A mantrap," she said. "I have seen one in a museum, but I've never known one actually to be used."

"A mantrap?"

"Metal, very heavy. Jaws with teeth." She held her hands out, her wrists together, palms open. "Placed in a path hidden with gorse and leaves. And if a man steps on it"—clapping her palms together, her fingers interlaced— "a very powerful spring snaps the trap closed. Some of them even have locks such that only a person with the key can release the device."

Worth stared at her for a long moment. Finally, he spoke. "Who…? What bas— What kind of terrible person would use such a thing?"

"Gamekeepers," Jane said. "Gamekeepers have used them for centuries. To deter poachers."

❧ 26 ❧

Seated at the pianoforte, Jane shuddered at the sound of swords clash-ing. The ballroom looked more like a site for military exercises than dance instruction. The dancing master, surrounded by a circle of red-coated dragoons, demonstrated a basic movement of a country dance.

"It's a step-change-step, starting on the right," Worth said. "And then the same to the left. Step-change-step."

The soldiers, amid the clatter of sword scabbards, imitated his move-ments.

"Now, walk around your partner, a quick march. Eight steps, like this. It's called a 'back-to-back.'"

He demonstrated the steps. The soldiers followed suit, initiating an-other clash of swords. *At least they are all safely sheathed,* Jane thought with a small smile.

"Now, I told you lads," Worth said, "I know it's your proper uniform, but you're going to have a hell of a time trying to dance while wearing a sword."

The warriors nodded.

"So, can we disarm? Then come back and we'll join forces with the ladies and have a dance. And your bleeders, too," Worth said, calling after the men. The troops removed their spurs as well as various straps, swords, and scabbards.

Worth heaved a great sigh as he stepped back up on the small stage and joined Jane. She smiled and laughed.

"You're amused?" he said.

"Well, it is rather amusing. Seeing all these fit young lads, venturing into unknown enemy territory."

"I'm going at it all wrong," Worth said. "We need music. We need to just get 'em moving."

"*The Spaniard?*" Jane suggested.

"That's a good one," Worth said. "Has all the important bits. But let's save it for later. How are you with *The Hop Ground?*"

Jane smiled, played two chords in the key of *D* and then launched into the proper tune.

"Aye, that'll do it," Worth said when she stopped after the first few measures. "A bit slower if you please. Give 'em time to catch up when they fall behind."

He turned back to the assembly room.

"Gentlemen, find partners, please, for *The Hop Ground*." He nodded to Jane, and she played one time through the melody while the men approached the seated ladies and begged leave to dance. When the music stopped, Worth organized the couples for the dance.

"Longways, for as many as will," he said. "Form the set, please."

The couples continued to move about aimlessly.

"Ladies," Worth said. Jane heard a change of the tone in his voice. Somewhat more forceful. "Ladies, please guide your partners into a longways set."

The dance began to take shape; dancers faced their partners, gentlemen in one line and ladies facing the men in another.

"Attention!" Worth barked.

A voice for the parade grounds, Jane thought.

"Gentlemen, form a rank. Straight now. Standard spacing."

The dragoons stood straight, each holding out his right arm and moved this way and that to form a proper military line. The ladies adjusted to their partners' movements, then encouraged them until a perfect set was formed.

"From the top," Worth ordered. "Count off by twos."

"One," the soldier closest to Worth barked.

"Two," said the next.

"One."

"Two."

"One."

"Two…" and down the rank it went.

"Gentlemen, if you're a number one, you are the lieutenant. Number twos, you are mere cornets. In the order of battle, by virtue of rank, lieutenants precede the cornets in all maneuvers. We are about to go on a scouting mission. You're in pursuit of the finest ingredients for beer, so you must capture *The Hop Ground*. Are you ready?"

Then with something like military precision, Worth drilled his dance recruits.

They assaulted and retreated—in good order, of course—a maneuver called advance and retire. The men surveilled the field of battle by joining hands with partners in two-hand turns. They learned to march in small circles, avoiding collisions, and admiring their partners, ending their travels well-positioned to repeat their maneuvers.

The ladies all knew the dance well and reinforced the instruction. Worth added a few extra details while ordering the men through the dance a second time: reading the dance compass; turning up or down to find the next couple; resting and reloading at the top or bottom of the set before resuming battle.

Then he propped his fiddle against his shoulder, nodded to Jane, and the dance commenced.

The troops made a ragged start of it. Worth prompted the men for the first five or six changes. But then, with the ladies' experience and the soldier's pluck and parade ground skills, the dance took shape and went on nicely. On the tenth change, Worth caught Jane's eye and tilted his head to the right slightly. *A little quieter,* she thought. She eased her touch on the keys. He smiled and nodded. Toward the end of the change, she dropped the melody entirely, providing only a spare bed of chords. Then she read his lips as the change was ending. *One more time.*

Glorious. They began to play full strength; Jane still emphasizing the chords. Then they traded roles, with Jane seizing the melody and Worth underlining it. As they approached the end of the dance, they restored musical equality and began a slow descent from the heights. In perfect accord, they slackened the tempo and reduced the musical intensity. They watched each other, blending the instrument voices, slowing the dancers through the last four measures.

The final notes, a chord, resonated in the room. The musicians smiled broadly at each other then turned, distracted by the boisterous applause of the dancers. A few of the soldiers stamped their feet. One of them gave a piercing whistle.

How rude, Jane thought, observing the indecorous behavior. *How delightfully rude.*

"Now, form up ranks. Another longways set," Worth announced as the applause abated. He said to Jane, "Let's see about *The Spaniard.*"

⇗ 27 ⇖

"Bank business," the well-dressed man said as he embraced Jane. After five dances, Worth had called for a brief intermission.

"Mr Worth," Jane said, calling him over. "My dear brother, Henry. I'm pleased to introduce you to our wonderful dancing master, Frederick Worth."

Henry Austen, Jane's brother, had been standing on the side for the last half an hour.

"Freddy," Worth said to Jane. "It's Freddy," he repeated to Henry as the men acknowledged each other with nods and polite bows.

"Now, Henry," Jane said. "Whatever can be so important? With your illness. So soon? You ought not be traveling."

"It was necessary, dear sister," he said. "There have been some problems. Matters that demanded my personal attention."

"Yes, the bank. We noticed."

"Your deposits are protected," Henry said. "You are banked in London."

"That is good to hear," Jane said. "Still, have you consulted your physician?"

"Yes, yes," Henry said. "He did not forbid it as the business demands immediate attention. I shall be returning to Town tomorrow. I am feeling better now. A little tired, but that's nothing."

"We have just a few minutes before we recommence our instruction. Come, Henry. You must have some tea." Jane led her brother to a sideboard where two or three pots of tea remained.

Henry Austen bears something of a family resemblance to the Austen ladies, Worth thought. Tall, nearly six feet. A shock of straight sandy-brown hair. He had the look of a proper gentleman, a jolly good fellow, fit for a club or a hunt or a trip to the Downs.

The gentleman had been ill though, Worth could see. He still had a pallor, the look of a landsman getting his first taste of a proper gale. But whatever was ailing Henry Austen, it did not appear to be fatal.

The dancing master looked about the room. Most of the teacups had been set aside and the dancers were chatting amiably.

"Gentlemen, will you please find a partner," he said. "Dancing school will continue."

Henry stayed for the remainder of the instruction. He even joined in for two slower dances where he proved himself to be positively terrible. He clearly enjoyed the music and the company of the dancers. He looked about, smiling, and nodded as his partners tried to prompt him into action. He went right instead of left, then left instead of right. When confronted with a circular hey, he wandered away from the set, paused, turned about, and searched for his partner. While the Austen ladies might demonstrate great acumen on the dance floor, Henry proved it was not a shared family gift.

Aloysius arrived as the dragoons and ladies dispersed. Henry and Aloysius were soon engaged in conversation. As Worth restored his hand and put away his instrument, Jane joined him.

"A successful exercise, General Worth?" she said. "Are the troops ready for battle?"

"They'll do, as long as there is a mix of lively folks around 'em."

"Playing the music with you," Jane said, "it was—"

"You're a fine player, Miss Austen. Your technical skills are excellent. I'll warrant you can play anything that's put before you."

"But this felt different somehow."

"Aye," he said. "Playing from paper, that's playing from inside your head. If today felt a little different, perhaps it's because you're playing a wee bit from your heart."

Jane's brow furrowed. "Yes." She looked up at Worth with a small smile. "Aye. Mr Worth, I have a favor to ask of you."

"A favor? What sort?"

"Henry will return to London tomorrow," Jane said. "I should like you to accompany him."

"And why would that be?"

"He has been ill. Terribly ill. Having a man with him—I think that would be a good thing."

"I see," Worth said, nodding.

"I will pay for your passage."

"Well, it might serve for me as well. Talk to the musicians. Confirm our arrangements."

"And, on the return," Jane said.

"Yes, on return?"

"Henry will be providing you with a sum from his London bank. It seems there is a shortage of funds here in Alton. Only temporary, he believes. But he will arrange to provide the funds from his London bank. And we shall have our ball."

❧ 28 ❧

Upon his arrival at La Belle Sauvage, the coaching inn on Ludgate Hill, Worth clapped the driver on the back, gave the old man sixpence, and clambered down from the box.

Travel atop a coach was a perilous affair. As for a sailor up in the rigging, every lurch and sway of the carriage is magnified by the distance above the ground. Riding on the box, next to the driver, gave a man a firm seat. This coach even had rails to grasp, and the old coachman had rigged a sort of well-sprung bolster to cushion the worst jolts.

A comfortable passage and the saving of a shilling that he could pocket—all the while avoiding uncomfortable conversation. Worth contemplated his good fortune in getting a place with the driver while waiting for other passengers to disembark. Henry, among the first to board, was last to exit.

"Here you are," Henry said as he located Worth. "Good passage? Not too rough?"

"Easy enough," Worth said as the banker adjusted his hat and smoothed his cravat.

Henry stood about two inches taller than the dancing master. While he still looked pale—Jane's brother had been at death's door only four weeks before—he cut a most gentlemanly figure. His coat, made of fine black wool, reflected the conservative, staid values of the established gentry. Worth envied the man his coat; the best quality wool in a tight weave that would repel rain and block the wind, likely lined with silk.

Henry exchanged cards with a gentleman and tipped his hat to the two ladies with whom he had completed the journey. It was easy to see why Jane or anyone else would have affection for the man; he was amiable and genuine, even with a common sort of cove like Worth.

"I have promised my sister that I would call on Mr Crosby on a literary matter," Henry said. "Will you accompany me? When the business is complete, we can stop by the bank and then you can be on your way."

"Aye, aye, sir."

Crosby & Company, located on Stationers Row off the Ludgate Road, surprised Worth. One window had been replaced with a weatherproof case, displaying a dozen or more books with *good*, *better*, and the very *finest* bindings. Within the office, the smell of books and paper. A small sales counter stood on the left and new volumes packed bookcases near the doorway.

Henry stepped to the railing that divided the room from side to side, and tapped on it with his gloved hand, gaining the attention of a man at one of the busy desks.

"I need to speak with Mr Crosby, please. My card," he said, offering it.

The man looked toward the back of the office. "Mr Crosby," he called out. "Gentlemen."

A man with sharp eyes and black, bushy eyebrows, wearing but a waistcoat and linen shirt sans cravat, rose from a desk in the back and approached Henry. He looked over spectacles, perched on his nose, and took Henry's card.

"Austen. Austen?"

He stared at the card in his right hand and rubbed the top of his completely bald head with his left. "Austen, eh? Well, what's your business?"

Henry looked at the man, puzzled.

"I am here to speak with Mr Crosby. We have done business together and I have been in further correspondence. There is a matter that must be settled."

"And what's that?"

"What?"

"The matter what needs settling."

"I need to speak with Mr Crosby," Henry said.

"You're speaking to Mr Crosby."

"Pardon, sir. I have met Mr Crosby," Henry said. "We have done business."

"We've done business?" the man said, then stopped. "Oh, I see it now. You done business with Mr Benjamin Crosby—old Ben—me father. I'm afraid you're outta luck, sir. He's died five years ago. I run the place now. Richard. Richard Crosby. I goes by Dick. All right, now we got that sorted, come back here and let's see what this business of yours is about," as he opened the gate in the railing and led Henry back to the publisher's desk.

Receiving no instruction to the contrary, Worth followed Crosby and Henry back into the office and stood close by as Henry seated himself.

A little behind Henry's chair and a little to the side; near the wall, a familiar position. Through his service as a steward, he had learned how to take on a particular demeanor. Eyes cast down, and not a hint of interest in the conversation, a man becomes invisible.

"It's a matter of a copyright," Henry said. "And the manuscript, of course. For a novel. *Susan*."

"I've no recollection of that title," Crosby said. "You're sure it was our house?"

"Quite. My father made the initial arrangements," Henry said. "A present for his youngest daughter. Unfortunately, your father failed to publish the work as agreed. I took up the matter. I spoke with your father on one occasion and corresponded with him further. He agreed to return the manuscript and copyright upon payment of the original price."

"Original price?"

"Yes. Ten pounds."

"Ten pounds?" Crosby appeared amused by the sum.

"I will provide you with a draft on my bank," Henry said. "I have come today to collect the manuscript and copyright."

"That's all very well, Mister...?" he asked, glancing at Henry's card. "Ah, Mr Austen. But there's a problem, you see. While you have the look of a fine gentleman, I cannot collect who you are and what it is you are going on about."

"A manuscript, Mr Crosby. The manuscript and copyright your firm purchased from my sister."

"Your sister sold us the book?" Crosby said.

"My father. He made the original arrangements, selling it to Crosby & Company on behalf of my sister."

"Your father, is it now? And who is your father?"

"Reverend George Austen. He is now deceased, but he first put the manuscript in your hands with the agreement that it would be published immediately. When the publication was delayed, I took up the matter and your father agreed to return the property for the original sale price of ten pounds."

Crosby leaned back in his chair, brought his hands together touching the tips of his fingers. He looked up toward the ceiling and closed his eyes as though in deep contemplation. Then he leaned forward, eyes locked on Henry.

"What rubbish," Crosby said. "Complete nonsense. I never heard of any such business. Me old dad's been gone these five years since. When do you say this business took place?"

"In the early months of 1803."

"In aught three! My god, man, what is that—twelve or so years ago! And you ask me to remember this—some scribblings that come in here more than ten years ago?"

"I believe that when one reads a novel of such merit, one most certainly remembers it," Henry said.

"Read it? Oh Mr Austen, I'm in the business of printing and selling books—not reading the damn things. Gordon," Crosby said, getting the attention of a man working at a desk behind Henry.

"What's the name on the sale?" Crosby said to Henry. "The seller of the book?"

"Austen. George Austen. And my name may be included as well. Henry Austen."

"And the title? I think you said it was called *Susan*?"

Henry nodded.

"Look for the sales record in the office books for 1803," he said, shaking his head and handing a note to the clerk. "It'll be under my father's commissions."

"There will be correspondence," Henry said.

"Ha! Do you think we have an open file on every damn thing we ever handled? We're lucky to have a copy of the damn books themselves. We can't be about saving every scrap of paper. What's your interest in this, anyways?" Crosby said, turning his focus on Henry. "It's twelve years now, and you've got to have this book back? What're you about?"

"It was written by my sister," Henry said. "Your company was supposed to publish the work and did not satisfy its obligation. Now, she wants it back."

"For what?" Crosby said. "This sister of yours pens some silly tale and sells it for ten quid. And then, twelve years later, she wants it back?"

"It requires some revisions," Henry said. "Because of the delays in publishing, caused by your company, some of the allusions and satire in the novel have become dated and she wishes to remedy the text. As taste and fashion have changed, it must be revised."

Gordon, the clerk, came back down the narrow flight of stairs with a volume comprised of business papers. He set the book open on Crosby's desk and pointed.

"Here we are," Crosby said. "George Austen. Manuscript and copyright. Novel, *Susan*. By a lady. What is it about these novel writers,"

Crosby said, looking up at Henry. "If you goes to the trouble to come up with all them bloody words and get 'em set in type, put your name on it! That's what I say. Gordon. Look at this reference here. See if we still have the manuscript."

The publisher turned back to Henry.

"So, your sister wants to play around at authoring again?" Crosby smiled and leaned forward toward Henry. "Here's the real story. It's no good. My father must'a read the blasted thing, realized he'd wasted ten quid, come to his senses, and scrapped it."

Henry sat straighter, raising his chin. Worth noticed that he had balled his fists.

"Nothin' in the bill of sale says we promised to print it," Crosby continued, glancing up at Henry. "Yeah, me old da probably read it—he did read 'em sometimes—and saw it was childish, romantic babble."

"Sir!" Henry said.

Worth sensed what was coming next.

"…can't believe…waste of good money…" Crosby was going on.

"Sir!" Henry said again.

Crosby ended his unsolicited opinion with the words "…load of—"

"Damn you, sir!" Henry said, standing up. "My sister is the author of *Sense and Sensibility* and *Pride and Prejudice*! Even if you are illiterate, you know the titles."

Worth cringed and closed his eyes. *Oh Henry,* he thought. *Oh Henry.*

"She is the author of *Mansfield Park*, a great success in recent days. Her publisher, Mr Egerton, is readying a second printing."

Now Henry had Crosby's full attention.

"*Sense and Sensibility?*" he said. "*Pride and Prejudice?* Egerton. Yes, now I do recall some noise. I did hear something."

The clerk came back down the stairs again, this time carrying a wrapped bundle. "Found it, sir," he said, placing the bundle on Crosby's desk.

"Very good," Henry said, still standing in front of Crosby's desk. "Now I will take the manuscript and provide you with my bank draft."

Crosby drew the manuscript toward himself.

"You agreed, sir," Henry continued. "Your firm agreed."

"Will you show me the agreement?"

Henry said nothing.

"Here's a thing," Crosby said, folding his hands together on top of the manuscript. "Here I sit with an early work by the esteemed author of *Sense and Sensibility, Pride and Prejudice,* and *Mansfield Park.* A somewhat minor author to be sure—not the likes of Byron or Scott—but popular in some circles. Here I sit with a bill of sale that says Crosby & Company owns the copyright to this early work by this modestly popular author." He patted the office volume with his left hand.

"And you, Mr Austen, tell me, without offering any papers to support your claim, that I should return this manuscript and copyright to you for the sum of...ten pounds? D'ye take me for a fool?"

Henry glanced at Worth. Stunned, he turned to Crosby and cleared his throat.

"What do you propose, sir?"

Crosby stared at Henry, then sat back in his chair. There was a long silence while Crosby nodded his head, closed his eyes, and contemplated his reply.

"Egerton is reprinting *Mansfield Park,*" he said aloud to himself. "He's already done a second printing of *Pride and Prejudice.* I actually did read that one, by the way. Good book. But," Crosby said, tapping the manuscript, "this is an early work."

Crosby paused again, then came to his conclusion. He looked up at Henry.

"Two hundred and twenty-five pounds."

๛29๛

Worth left Henry seated in a small coffeehouse on Ludgate Hill across from Stationer's Row.

"I'll be returning shortly," Worth said. Henry did not speak. The outcome of his meeting with Crosby and the effects of his illness had left him drained, pale, and speechless.

"Mr Austen," Worth said, "you'll wait for me here?"

Henry gave the slightest nod.

The Thames-side taverns frequented by sailors stood only a few hundred paces from Ludgate. Worth seldom haunted them, but he knew The Mermaid to be a popular spot.

So, it proved to be. Though it was still the forenoon watch, the place was nearly full. Musicians occupied one corner. More than half the tables were filled; a lively scene.

Worth stood in the doorway briefly. A fiddle, a whistle, a guitar, and a mandolin played *Fisher's Hornpipe*, a sprightly tune. It put him in mind of lazy days on the fo'c'sle, making merry music with a mate or two. Truth be told, even in the navy, sailors had lazy days. Life on a man o' war comprised vast stretches of tedium punctuated with hours of grueling work and moments of bloody terror.

Worth sighed deeply and took three strides into the middle of the public room. Then he called out.

"*Victorys!*"

The room quieted. The music stopped.

"*Victorys!* To me!"

A small, wiry old man with the look of a gunner—blue-tinged scars on his face and arms—rose from a settle and started toward Worth. Another, even older man, missing an arm, half an ear, and most of his teeth steered to Worth, carrying his pint.

A strapping young lad, the musician with the whistle, left the circle of players and joined Worth and his growing crew.

"Kendrick," the first old sailor said. "Cruised on 'er under Jervais. Made it to the Battle o' the Cape."

"Saint Vincent," Worth said.

"Aye," the Kendrick said.

"Hot work, that."

"We done our duty."

"Young pup," the toothless man said, grinning. "I were aboard her in the Ushant, first and second."

"Left me wing tip there on 'er deck in the second go-round. So that's why they calls me Lefty!" He accompanied his self-reference with a hoarse laugh that sounded like he was choking and a wave of the stub of his portside flipper.

"Lad?" Worth said to the musician.

"Walker, sir," he replied. "Not a patch on them. The Old Lady had got the hell beat out of her by my time. I sailed her on troop ship duty. A ferry boat we was, back and forth across the channel. Got paid off after Boney took his first scamper—afore they turned her into a prison hulk."

"So, what's your story?" Kendrick asked, addressing Worth.

"Follower with Captain Hardy."

"Ah! So was you…?"

"Trafalgar? Aye," Worth said.

The men were quiet for a moment, looking at each other, savoring the kinship that sailors felt when they all had trod the same decks and slung hammocks below.

"To the *Victory*," Lefty said, hoisting his pint.

"*Victory*," the shipmates chorused.

"And wives and sweethearts," Lefty continued.

"May they never meet," came the reply, with laughter all round.

"I'm in need of crew for a sort of cutting out party," Worth said after regaining their full attention. "A nest of pirates, armed with pen and ink and paper, what needs cleaning out. Won't take but an hour—be back here by eight bells."

The seamen were all grinning.

"I need a full crew for a captain's gig—say eight oars. You know the lads here. Can you find me some trustworthy men to fill out the boat? It's two shillings a man."

Ten minutes later, Worth had his crew assembled on Ludgate Hill hard by Stationer's Row. The mission, he explained, was to do nothing. Stand around, pace the decks, and keep an eye on things. If anyone tried to hoist anchor, gently, very gently, discourage them.

"Stand by and follow my commands."

Worth found Henry in the coffeehouse. He had not moved even so much as to take a sip from the now-cold cup.

"Let's be about it, man," Worth said.

Henry did not move.

"Now!" Worth said. Then after a little pause, "Sir."

Henry stirred. "What's this about?" he said. He seemed foggy. A relapse of his illness?

"You're going to speak with Mr Crosby again," Worth said. "See if he can be a wee bit more reasonable."

Henry shook his head, but he stood and started moving in the right direction. With Worth and Henry in the lead, the cutting out party arrived at the door of Crosby & Company.

"Lefty, you and the lad here. Mind the door. Nobody comes in or goes out," Worth said. "Anyone comes, just tell 'em the shop's closed. Doing the inventory."

Worth led Henry and the rest of the men through the front door. He banged open the gate and led Henry up to Crosby's desk. The navy men took up stations all around the office. The clerks, struck mute, remained frozen at their desks under the sailors' watch.

"Mr Crosby," Worth said, as Crosby stood and backed away from his desk. "Mr Austen would have a word with you, sir." He addressed the room. "All the rest of you, rest easy. Don't get up. Don't try to leave."

Henry stared at him, and Worth nodded encouragement. "Give him one last chance to behave like a respectable, honest man. To honor his word."

"Yes. Well, yes," Henry said, turning toward Crosby. "As I explained earlier, you...or your father...your firm agreed to return the manuscript and copyright for the novel *Susan*. For the price of ten pounds."

"No," Crosby said. "I have a legal contract. You have nothing. No papers spelling out this agreement you say exists. So, my answer to you, Mr Austen, is no. But... Maybe I can lower the price. I'm a most reasonable man. Let's say, two hundred? But ten pounds?" He laughed. "No."

Henry looked at Worth, who nodded to him. "There now, that's an end to it. You gave him a fair chance."

Worth moved behind Henry, around the desk, and stood two paces from Crosby. The man clenched the back of his chair with two hands and dragged it between himself and Worth.

"Now, Mr Crosby, sir. Dick. D'ya have a place here that we can go to have a wee chat? Just the two of us."

Crosby shook his head.

"You've got a room up above," Worth said, motioning toward the stairs.

Crosby clutched the back of his chair and drew it toward himself, gripping it as if to defend himself. He was still shaking his head.

Worth reached out with his left hand, took one arm of the chair, and tore it from Crosby's grip. He raised the chair to shoulder height and threw it down. Worth advanced to within a pace of Crosby.

"D'ye want me to ask a couple of the lads here to carry you up yon steps? We're just goin' to have a talk," Worth continued. "Words only. Man to man."

Worth stepped back. Crosby remained frozen, staring at Worth. Then, with the slightest nod, he edged around Worth and led him up the stairs.

The greater part of the upper floor was filled with shelves stacked with ledgers, bound books of documents, and boxes of letters. Crosby opened the door to a small private office illuminated by a window and furnished with a desk and two chairs.

Crosby sat down behind the desk, regaining his composure.

"You don't frighten me," he said. "I won't be bullied."

"You're a very brave man, Dick. Or more to the point, you're a very greedy man, and it's that greed that stiffens your spine. Yes, I think it's the greed that makes you such a very brave man."

"I can lower the price more," Crosby said, settling back in his chair.

"Nay. That's all Mr Austen's business. I want to speak to you on another matter."

Crosby was tapping the desk with his right hand and rubbing his bald head again with the left. "What is it?"

"It's a book I been thinkin' about writin'," Worth said. "A work of nautical fiction, celebrating the adventures of our brave navy lads. Jolly tars and such. Patriotic. With the end of the war, it'll sell very well, I think."

Crosby watched Worth warily but leaned forward.

"D'ye know much of naval tactics, Dick?"

The publisher shook his head. "Navy, army, belong in the Military Library. That's Egerton's line."

"I'm thinkin' this is more of a novel. It's a story with villains—some rubbish—pirates, maybe, or frogs. Oh, it's patriotism we want, so then it must be frogs. It's a fleet action, y' see, and the French are holed up in a safe harbor. There's forts with guns to protect 'em. These *crapaud* is sittin' in the harbor, smug and happy, going ashore and drinkin' wine. They's making fools of our brave British tars who wants to drag 'em out of hiding. Make 'em fight like men."

Crosby nodded. "There's a nice bit of plot there. A premise. Go on."

"You're interested, I see," Worth said. "So how will our brave sailors bring this enemy into action? Tell me, Mr Crosby, have you ever heard of a fire ship?"

Crosby shook his head.

"You have to wait, be very patient. The wind and the tide must be just right. Then you puts a small crew on your oldest, least useful ship. Maybe it's a hull what's been damaged badly, or an old merchantman. Or better yet, we'll make it a frog prize. You tie a longboat astern, and in the dead o' night, when the watch is light and the French crews are asleep and maybe the officers are all ashore and getting drunk and whoring, you douse all your lights and sail that old barkey right into the enemy harbor. Am I keepin' your interest?"

Crosby nodded and leaned forward, his elbows on the desk.

"So, you gets some way on that old barkey—get her going at a good clip, sailing with the wind, steering straight at your enemy. They're just sittin' there at anchor. Can't move about. And then you know what happens?"

Crosby, listening intently, shook his head.

"The crew ties down the wheel. And then they sets that old barkey afire. Wood, canvas, pitch, and tar. Oh, Mr Crosby, a fire on a ship is a fearful thing. Ah, but you've got an understanding of that, you do. Look at you here, with all this paper and these books."

Crosby's expression changed, his jaw slowly dropping.

"Our brave tars scramble down into their long boat and rows back to the fleet. Imagine it, Mr Crosby. You're resting comfortable in your hammock and then a fire ship, a blazing torch, a hundred foot tall, comes bearing down on you in the night. You can't maneuver to avoid the thing. The great guns are loaded. Your powder stores are full. The crews gets into a panic. They cut their anchor cables and try to make sail, but the ships tangle. The fire ship sails in and sets 'em all ablaze. What d'ye think of my story? D'ye have a burning interest in that sort of tale?"

Crosby sat back, staring at Worth. He nodded. He understood the proposal.

"You have naught to fear—not a bit of worry—as far as Mr Austen is concerned," Worth said. "He is a gentleman. Me. My shipmates. We are not gentlemen. A greedy man such as yourself knows the benefit of property assurance. I saw the mark on your building here—the Sun Fire Office—best fire brigade in London, so I've heard. For a little extra assurance, the return of a certain manuscript and a proper bill of sale...no money exchanging hands. That might be a wise...ah...but no, you've made your position perfectly clear on that matter. As for me and my book, *The Fire Ship*, I'm thinkin' it's a capital idea. I know you'll say it's more in Egerton's line, but you think on it. Give it your full consideration."

Worth stood. "I'm takin' my leave now, Dick. But you can be assured, I'll be back from time to time—me or some of my shipmates. We'll keep an eye on your wee, snug harbor here."

After telling Henry to meet him at eight bells—four o'clock—at La Belle Sauvage, Worth and his crew departed. Crosby, showing signs of some sort of agitation, stopped Henry before he got out the door. Somehow, his recollection about the Austen manuscript was clearer. Crosby wanted to settle the matter quickly.

Worth distributed prize money to his crew, and they toasted his good health. Then he found his musician friends, the Quinns, at home where they were both giving lessons. They confirmed plans for the Austen ball. The Quinns would be seeing Mr Thomas, a talented wind player, that evening and would remind him.

"And please," Worth said to Mr Quinn, "ask him to bring only the recorders, flutes, and flageolets. Tell him not to bring any of his damn noisemakers—the krummhorns and rackets and that nonsense." Mr Quinn smiled knowingly and said he would pass the message along.

Henry left Crosby & Company with a manuscript under one arm and a bill of sale in his coat pocket. His bank draft was not needed. In light of the various misunderstandings, Richard Crosby said he felt that his firm ought to compensate Henry for his inconvenience.

Henry called on his bank, tended to matters there, withdrew Jane's draft, and found Worth waiting for him at the coaching inn.

"I am not at all sure what you could have said that would be so per-suasive," Henry said, after describing the end of his meeting with Crosby and giving Worth the manuscript to convey to its author. "But I cannot quarrel with the ending. You did threaten him?"

"Mr Crosby has a good head for business," Worth said. "It came clear to him that the profits from *Susan* might not warrant the possible risks."

"And you suggested that some harm—"

"The man was fortunate. He was bein' a pirate. In the navy, we hang pirates. He's a brave man, I'll warrant him that," Worth continued. "A brave, greedy man. But he's not a fool."

"My sister will be grateful—"

"Nay, Mr Austen. She must know nothin' o' this," Worth said. "Upon your honor, sir. It would be a great betrayal if you were to tell her about…any of this."

"You have saved her a substantial sum."

"Nothing," Worth said. "Not a word."

"If you insist, I shall have to take the credit, but you must take some share. A guinea," he said, offering a gold coin.

Worth refused the offer, but not so resolutely that Henry was discour-aged from persisting and carrying the day.

❧ 30 ❧

"Oh, no. This is terrible…surely not…oh no…ah, and there it is, repeated—Udolpho, Udolpho, Udolpho!"

Seated at the writing desk in the parlor, Jane muttered the comments to herself as she made notes in pencil. Cassandra and her mother easily overheard them. Mrs Austen and Cassandra exchanged glances and small smiles.

"Not again," Jane said, with greater annoyance. She made another note on the manuscript page in front of her and shifted it to the pile on the left.

"Agh! Again. The blasted Udolpho. I had better to purchase advertisements in all the papers…print hand bills…notice to all readers—please go away and read Mrs Radcliffe's ponderous *Mysteries of Udolpho* prior to undertaking this."

Jane pushed her chair away from the writing desk and addressed the ladies who were politely engrossed in their needlework.

"We, the Austen family and the world at large, I warrant, shall forever be grateful to Henry for rescuing *Susan* from Crosby & Company," Jane declared. "Think of the tragedy. They might have published this dreadful thing!"

The ladies looked up at her, smiled, and returned to their stitches.

"The manuscript is terrible," Jane said, rising to warm herself near the hearth. "Wretchedly plotted with clumsy conversation, what there is of it. Far too much declaration. How could you, Cass?"

Cassandra looked up, this time without amusement.

"I trusted you," Jane went on. "I believed in your good taste and judgment. How could you have allowed me to come so close to publishing this…nonsense?"

"Jane!" Mrs Austen exclaimed, and then quietly, "Civility. We all heard the story as you read out the pages, and we all found it wonderfully entertaining. It is well-developed, the characters are engaging, and it is quite amusing."

Cassandra took up the defense of the manuscript. "Time may have dulled some of the wit—"

"Dulled it? The humor is worn to a nub. The moment has passed. The satire is lost. And the conversation? 'Tis stilted, awkward, and clumsy. Nouns tripping over verbs before plunging into an ocean of adjectives. Such utter nonsense—nothing like the way real people speak."

"Jane, it was your first true novel," Cassandra said. "Your epistolary manuscripts fit comfortably to your pen. You had only to write letters— imagined letters to be sure—but letters, as you have done a thousand times. Drawing characters and giving them speech, that was a new trial, and you succeeded admirably, I thought."

"Admirably! Ha!" Jane went back to her chair. "The evidence is here on the page. It is dreadful."

"You are being much too critical, dear," Mrs Austen said. "Go and look at your needlework from your childhood and compare it to your work today. The old work is very nice—I would not trade it for anything. The work you do today is much finer, more perfect in every way as you have gained skill with practice. It is the nature of things."

"The nature of this manuscript is ill."

"Stop pouting," Cassandra said. "It is unbecoming. *Susan* is an early work by a woman now recognized as an accomplished author. You went about it in fits and starts, you recall? Yes?"

Jane nodded.

"Now you have it back in hand, you can remedy its imperfections as you wish."

"Or let it lie or consign it to the hearth."

"Jane, do not say such a thing," Mrs Austen said, provoked. "All of your letters and writing are precious to me. They must be preserved."

"I understand, Mama. Yet there must be exceptions. If something is too personal, too private, too revealing of intimate family matters. Cassandra and I have spoken about such things. Or if it is horribly dreadful," she said quietly. She started bundling the manuscript again. "Enough of *Susan* for now. If I am to be remembered, let it be for the Dashwoods and Darcy, and not this insipid *Susan*. I have much more important matters at hand. We have a ball on the morrow, and we have not selected the music for the grand march."

"A grand march?" Cassandra said

"'Tis a country dance tradition north of the Borders," Jane said. "Mr Worth described it, and it sounds like the most splendid way to begin the evening."

"A Scottish dance?" Mrs Austen asked. "Some sort of fling?"

"A dance for men in skirts?" Cassandra said.

"That hardly seems appropriate for a ball," Mrs Austen said with real concern.

"No Mama. No flings or reels, or *chassées* or rants. Just a pleasant stroll about the ballroom. It will be wonderful. You shall see. Now, what music shall we have for it?" she said, taking a music book and sitting down at her pianoforte.

"Something from Mr Haydn or the great Mozart? It must be lively and uplifting." She shared her thinking aloud. "Or simply a medley of country dance tunes. Let me see... *The York Fusiliers*, that will do nicely. Ah, *The Campbells are Coming*, now there is a lively tune. *Brighton Camp*, possibly. With a nod to the dreadful Mr Wickham. Would anyone with a musical bent twig to that?"

Jane pursed her lips and turned another page.

❧ 31 ❧

Magnificent, Jane thought. *Truly magnificent.*

She had seen the coach and four when it was nearly a quarter mile off as it entered the Kellingsford grounds. The carriage, black-lacquered with glistening silver fittings and the team, a spectacular double pair of black Hackneys, was upon her as it emerged from a colonnade of laurels. Lordly prerogative had spared the brilliant horses from military service.

"Magnificent" was the only word for it, Jane concluded. She must give her thanks to Edward for the loan of the carriage and team for her use during the ball. *Edward would certainly be surprised by his own generosity,* she thought, as he was in Kent, nearly one hundred miles away.

Her brother Frank had placed the coach at her disposal. With Mary expecting her fifth child at any instant, Frank had excused himself from the guest list to attend to his wife. But he showed his—and his brother's—generosity with the loan of the Chawton House equipage.

Hotchkiss, the stable master at Chawton House, was on the box when the carriage stopped under the portico. The old man, his skin as brown and leathery as the tack for his fine saddle horses, had taken the early turn on the coach, shuttling provisions and people between Kellingsford, Chawton, and Alton. The uniformed coachmen would take the reins when the guests were at hand.

Jane waved to Hotchkiss. He put two fingers to the brim of his flat cap in salute, smiled, and winked at her. She had a confidential relationship with the old man and had grown to have great affection for him.

The dancing master, two men, and a woman emerged, along with numerous small cases, bags, and satchels. Musicians would never trust their instruments to the coach's boot.

After the briefest introductions, the travelers hurried within to escape the cold. Within the warmer vestibule, they exchanged pleasantries while removing their coats.

Mrs Quinn, a tall woman, slender, with a guileless and cheerful, round face, smiled broadly. Her chestnut hair was tucked under a bandeau and twisted in a neat chignon.

"When Freddy told us of your event and asked us, we were delighted," Mrs Quinn said with an Irish lilt. "We have a patroness who I knew to be a great reader, and I asked if she had any o' your books."

"Mr Worth has been…injudicious," Jane said.

"You mustn't blame Freddy," Mrs Quinn said. "We pried it out of him. He's quite giddy about it all. Did you know this is his first turn at being the dancing master for a ball?"

"His first?" Jane asked. "Why, he never—"

"So, now you have him in your power. Please do feel free to tease him without mercy after it all comes off wonderfully."

"I certainly shall."

"To my point," Mrs Quinn said, "my patroness did have a copy of your *Pride and Prejudice*, and she loves it."

"I am flattered, of course."

"She was kind enough to lend me the volumes. I have read it and I esteem it, too. Her loan came with a condition, though, I must warn ya."

"A condition?"

"She said I must bring the first volume with me and ask you to inscribe it for her. Will you do that? Please say you will. She is an excellent woman and promises she will acquire all of your titles."

Jane was momentarily speechless.

"Of course, I will," she said, smiling. "After the ball."

"Wonderful," Mrs Quinn said.

"Ah, now we must see to our preparations."

Marryat led and Jane followed the musicians to the ballroom. Mrs Quinn settled at the pianoforte and tested its tuning and temper. Mr William Quinn uncased his fiddle—never a violin, always a fiddle—and hung it on a small floor stand he had placed by his chair. Mr Quinn cut a manly figure, tall and broad with a handsomely trimmed beard and moustache, light brown but with hints of gray.

Mr Thomas, whose Christian name was also Thomas, was the tallest and thinnest of the trio. He looked dapper, with closely cropped black hair and a neatly trimmed moustache. *He has the most extraordinary hands,* Jane thought. His long, slender fingers seemed to dance as be busied himself with a variety of stands and boxes which he decorated with a colorful array of recorders, flutes, whistles, flageolets, and some other instruments Jane could not identify.

Worth neared Mr Thomas and said, "No krummhorns? No rackets? No bombard?"

Mr Thomas looked up at him with a terribly hurt expression. He placed his hand on his heart and shook his head.

"Good," Worth said and walked back across the stage to join Mrs Quinn at the pianoforte.

"How is it?"

"Not bad," she replied. "Mr Broadwood makes a fine instrument."

Worth drew a tuning fork from a pocket, struck it lightly, and pressed the base of it against his head, close to his ear.

"An *A*." She struck the proper key. "Perfect," he said, and tucked the tuning fork away.

"Now, where are the clinkers? We'll take 'em low to high."

"B-flat," she said, striking a black key at the far end of the keys. Worth listened, damped some strings with his fingers, and then fitted a T-shaped tool over the metal peg that anchored the end of one of the strings.

"Again," he said. She struck the key. "Again." The note sounded. "Ah, there 'tis."

Mr Quinn settled himself into his chair between the pianoforte and Mr Thomas. Worth finished tuning his fiddle, then launched a tune. Jane recognized it. *The Rights of Man* it was called. An Irish tune with slightly revolutionary title, Jane was thinking, but a lively, enjoyable hornpipe, even to the ear of a monarchist.

As Mr Quinn began a second change, another full repetition of the tune, Mr Thomas joined with a soprano recorder. Mr Quinn held the melody. Mr Thomas danced around it, above and below. *Such a joy,* Jane thought, as she listened. *Such joy.*

Jane found herself in the middle of the ballroom, dancing in a wide circle with a skip-change step, enjoying the caress of her gown—her lilac sarsenet—the one she had trimmed with black ribbon. It floated around and behind her like a summer mist.

The music ended. She raised her arms and pirouetted. Her gown wrapped close around her. She felt very much alive.

The sounds from the stage told her that the pianoforte was in tune. Worth and Mrs Quinn had turned their attention to the harpsichord.

Worth had suggested to Jane that she might join the musicians for a dance toward the end of the evening. She would play the pianoforte; Mrs Quinn, the harpsichord. The name of the Irish tune they suggested was unfamiliar, yet, on first hearing, she thought it perfect. "*Si Bheag, Si Mhor* by Mr Carolan. We call it the *Fairie Waltz* in English*,*" Mrs Quinn said. *A waltz. Another scandalous waltz.*

Pleasant anticipation carried Jane up the grand staircase and through the corridor. She found her cloak in the vestibule, wrapped herself up, and stepped toward the portico.

A footman swung the great doors open. She surveyed the scene, imagining the coaches arriving—Cassandra, Mama, and Henry—coming up the marble steps.

The famous authoress…no, not famous. But successful. Yes, the successful authoress greeting her guests arriving for her ball. *It is the stuff of novels*, she thought. Yet it was undeniable; this was her true life.

A movement on a garden path caught her eye. She would never have noticed had the leaves not stirred. The mottled green coat and slouch hat blended into the laurel and holly of the hedge.

The gamekeeper. She knew him.

What was Hinch doing there?

❧32❧

"Best wishes, dear."

"Happy birthday."

"Good health to you, my lady."

"Splendid evening."

"Our best to you!"

Waves of compliments and kind greetings washed over Jane as guests surrounded her.

Henry made a splendid entrance with Mama on one arm and Cassandra on the other. She looked around to see fine ladies and gentlemen from as far away as Steventon.

All the Ellicotts were present, of course, even Percival. *Watching after the silver*, Jane mused. Captain Wembley led his company of young dragoons, and they were joined by several senior officers from the brigade. Admiral Harwell conversed with them.

The ballroom was alive everywhere without feeling crowded. The servants had been instructed not to serve tea or open the card room, so everyone was coming to the ballroom for the start of the evening.

"Are you ready, Miss Austen?" Worth stood at her elbow, wearing a black coat, looking as one with the musicians.

"It is such a fine gathering. From Winchester. From Town. I never…"

She took Worth's arm as they made their way through the crowd to the stage.

"Thank you, Mr Worth," she said. "It is everything that I had hoped."

"Then you must elevate your expectations, milady," he said, smiling at her, "for we've not yet begun."

Worth nodded to the three musicians on stage.

"Ladies and gentlemen!" he said, using his best gentleman's voice. The room quieted. Worth glanced at the musicians. As one, they stood, and then, like magicians, each of them produced a stylish black hat festooned with jaunty yellow and red ribbons. Their tops in place, they took to their instruments and struck several chords in a rat-a-tat fashion, a sort of fanfare.

"Miss Austen invites you to join her, accompanied by her brother, Mr Henry Austen, in the Grand March. 'Tis not a dance," Worth continued.

"No footwork or figures. 'Tis a promenade, a grand opportunity to take several turns about the ballroom, acknowledging Miss Austen, admiring all the ladies, and greeting all your friends."

He looked back at Mr Quinn and nodded. With four brisk chords from the pianoforte, the music commenced.

"Follow Miss Austen," he commanded.

Worth had prepared Jane and Henry for their roles as leaders of the festive promenade about the ballroom. The dancing master was everywhere, prompting, encouraging, guiding, and chivvying people here and there, and drawing reluctant guests in from the sides.

"It is for Miss Austen," he would say. "You must, you really must." And very nearly everyone did.

The soldiers—his young dragoons especially—proved to be excellent guides for the others with their smart stepping and sharp turns. Within moments, the ballroom resembled a beautiful quilt: lines of gaily dressed guests moving *en ensemble*; turning left, then right, forming and dissolving ranks, parading in single files, the living warp and weft of the dancing master's loom.

For Jane, the effect was magical. She and Henry paraded up and down the hall between lines of friends and relatives and guests. Every lady could smile on every other lady and admire her habiliments; every gentleman could admire every other lady, as well.

Familiar, dearly loved faces appeared suddenly, flush with smiles and joy. *What a wonderful way to begin a ball,* she thought. *This ought to become a custom.*

After numerous turns up, down, and across the hall, after seeing all the guests once or twice or more, the music swelled and, in another instant, stopped.

Of a sudden, due to some clever maneuvering by the dancing master, the grand march ended with Jane, standing alone, in the center of the ballroom, surrounded by her guests and warm applause.

She smiled, curtsied all around, and blushed. She raised her hand to quiet her guests and, as Worth had prompted her to do, made an announcement.

"Welcome. The card room is now open. Tea is served. Gentlemen, please choose partners. It is time for the dancing to begin."

The first dance passed in an instant. Henry played his part in taking possession of *The Hop Ground*. Jane saw that the young dragoons, making their second foray into the dance, were acquitting themselves with honor.

They reached the bottom of the set a few changes before the music ended, and Jane drew Henry aside. "Have you seen Mr Egerton? I've searched in vain."

"He has sent one of his men—a Mr Tolliver. I have his card."

"And Mr Crosby? He was invited."

"Jane, I have given you a fair report of my dealings with Mr Crosby. You cannot possibly expect—"

"Yes, I understand. Well, I don't understand, but I take your point. What of Mr Murray? Has he come? Has he sent someone?"

"Not the man himself, but he has sent a man, Mr Sanders, a knowledgeable young fellow who has read all your novels. I have promised him an introduction to you after the unveiling of His Lordship's portrait."

"This is most encouraging."

"Yes, very promising, I think. But listen, the music for the next dance. You must enjoy your ball, dear sister. I have done my duty. Now I must recover."

After Henry retreated to the side, Jane did not want for partners. An older lieutenant in the dragoons, a skilled dancer, took her hand for *The Spaniard*. She promised the next dance to the gentleman Egerton had sent. Though he had not made the trip himself, her publisher had shown a modicum of respect to his most prominent author of fiction, Jane thought. *His only author of fiction.*

As the dances proceeded, she wondered at the sight of every unknown young gentleman. *Was this Mr Murray's emissary?*

The cataclysm arrived during the second to last dance before the unveiling. The presentation of Lord Kellingsford's portrait was to be at nine o'clock, as Aloysius requested. Mr Worth announced that there would be a country dance followed by something new, different, and quite the sensation in Town—a waltz!

Jane heard excited whispers among the younger dancers and a few murmurs of disapproval from older ladies.

The country dance was *The Morpeth Rant*—a lively North Country caper that encouraged foot stamping and great amusement. The thing went well enough, almost until the end, when, with a terrible effect, the musical catastrophe struck.

On the next to last time through the dance, Mr Thomas rose and put a wooden instrument to his lips that made such a noise as it overwhelmed the pianoforte and fiddle. With a voice that bore echoes of the great highland pipes, it sent the tune reverberating through the ballroom, up the hall, and out the front door. It stunned ladies in the tearoom. Gentlemen at whist looked up in alarm. The dancers gasped, then whooped, and redoubled their efforts. Ladies on the sides pursed their lips and tried in vain to continue their conversations over the terrible noise.

Jane smiled, giggled, and then laughed as she danced. To her partner's puzzled look, she exclaimed: "'Tis the sweet song of the bombard, I'll wager!"

Jane caught glimpses of Worth on stage. His expression grim, yet he played in stride with Mr and Mrs Quinn as they attempted to compete with the notorious instrument.

For the last change, Mr Thomas continued with the bombard, but with somewhat less energy, ceding center stage.

When the dance ended, Worth took several deep breaths before turning to Mr Thomas. He did not have a chance to speak before Jane appeared.

"That was magnificent, Mr Thomas!" she said, clapping her hands. "I have never heard an instrument speak with such profound effect. Mr Haydn ought to compose a symphony for the bombard!"

Mr Thomas basked in Jane's appreciation and glanced innocently at Worth. The dancing master shook his head, looked around to Mr Quinn, and said, "*Northland Waltz.*"

Aloysius Ellicott appeared and asked, "Will you do me the honor, Miss Austen?" She returned a curtsy, and they proceeded to scandalize several matrons seated on the sides, arms crossed, and wearing their most disapproving expressions.

The waltz ended just before nine. Tea service was stopped. The card room was temporarily cleared as it would only be proper for everyone to acknowledge His Lordship in his moment of glory.

The musicians played a tune fit for a royal procession, *La Belle Assemblée March.* Mr Worth had it from Mr Wilson. It was a yet unpublished piece, noble and uplifting.

A moment later, Lord Kellingsford, accompanied by Miss Ellicott, appeared at the top of the staircase. He was indeed wearing the colorful garb that he had worn for the portrait.

Footmen brought out the painting draped in velvet and placed it in its stand at the foot of the staircase while His Lordship and his daughter descended ever so unhurriedly.

Lord Kellingsford walked around the portrait and stood off to the right, facing out, chin up, in the exact attitude that would soon be revealed. Percival, with Aloysius close by, stood on the opposite side of the portrait.

The music stopped; polite applause filled the ballroom. Then the appreciation grew stronger, encouraged by the dancing master, Jane noted with approval. She remembered Lord Kellingsford fondly from their first meetings—a lively man with all his wits and a fine dancer—and added her own applause with enthusiasm.

The roar from a pistol cut the applause short.

❧33❧

"*Mesdames! Messieurs!*"

Every eye in the hall fixed on the masked gentleman standing on the front edge of the stage, holding a smoking pistol in his left hand. Behind him, rough masked men armed with pistols and short curved swords poured in from behind the stage curtains. They leapt down from the stage and into the hall, scattering the guests.

The dancers gaped at the sight of the ruffians as they moved aside. Ladies tittered. A gentleman laughed and pointed at one of the masked men. *A theatrical of some sort. Surely that's what this was.*

"*Taisez vous,*" the man on stage shouted. He punctuated his command with a blast from the gun in his other hand. He dropped both pistols and took a third, even deadlier looking two-barreled weapon from his belt.

"*Restez calme! Ne bougez pas!*" he commanded. "Silence! *Personne ne sera blessé.* None among you will be injured!"

Ruffians blocked the stairs. A big man armed with a blunderbuss remained onstage. He aimed the archaic weapon at the musicians. Worth's mind focused on the bell-shaped barrel. *Useless at any distance but a murderer's tool at this range.* Worth raised his hands, still holding his fiddle and bow. He looked at his friends and they followed his lead.

"Turn round," the man growled. *English,* Worth thought as he obeyed.

The Frenchman, the leader of the gang, stepped down from the stage, holding his pistol level and aiming it carelessly around the room. An elegant mask fit for a fancy-dress ball covered his eyes and the upper part of his face. It did not hide his flowing blond hair. He wore a white uniform shorn of any braid or insignia. *A naval officer's uniform,* Worth thought. *A French naval officer's dress uniform.*

Blunderbuss Man motioned Worth and the musicians off the stage. Like the rest of the raiders, he wore rough clothes, a cloak, and a kerchief around his face. As Worth assisted Mrs Quinn to the dance floor, he briefly faced the man holding the short, ugly weapon again, getting a closer look at the tattoos circling the man's wrists and covering the backs of his hands. *A sailor.* Blunderbuss Man stayed on the stage and made it clear that no one was to look back at him.

"Pardonnez moi, mesdames et messieurs." The Frenchman strode onto the dance floor with three of his men.

Jane's guests shrank back; this was no frolic. They comprehended the threat and left a wide berth for the invaders in the center of the ballroom.

"We shall disturb you only a moment," the man in white said, still brandishing his weapon coolly around the room.

The guests and musicians all had armed ruffians standing behind them. The dragoons were unarmed and dispersed throughout the crowd. Ladies were present. Any resistance might prove fatal.

"Ladies, your jewels, if you please," the leader said. "Give to zese good men."

The men looked back at their leader. *Surprised by the command,* Worth thought. The Frenchman nodded sharply at them. They started within the circle, taking some jewelry—necklaces, earrings, some bracelets. They stuffed the loot in their pockets.

"Aha, we still have ze wonderful painting to observe," he said as he approached His Lordship's portrait, warning people away with his pistol. He grabbed the drapery with his free hand and the fabric fell to the floor in a heap.

He stepped back, as if to admire the art.

"Ah, *très bien. C'est beau. Très beau,* milord."

He moved a pace closer to the canvas and spat on it.

"How dare you!" Aloysius strode forward. The Frenchman brought his pistol around to bear and fired.

Aloysius froze, head cocked to the side, hands over his face. While the sound of the pistol echoed, Percival Ellicott tumbled backward to the floor. The blood seeping from the bullet hole in his forehead matched the bright red of his cravat.

❧34❧

The Frenchman had barely lowered his weapon when Captain Wembley was upon him. Worth could see the surprise on the Frenchman's face as Wembley reached up with with his left hand and seized the invader by his lapels.

On account of the audacity of his assault, the invader had not expected resistance, Worth thought. The Frenchman looked astonished. His eyes widened still more when Wembley raised the gleaming blade in his right hand and brought it level with his shoulder.

"*Mon—*"

Any further words were cut as cleanly as the man's throat.

Wembley released the man's lapels. The Frenchman collapsed at the officer's feet.

"Damn you," the captain said. "Damn. Damn you."

Wembley stood over the invader's body. His right hand was covered with blood. Dark stains spattered his red uniform jacket. Blood pooled around his glistening black boots.

❧35❧

Silence—a remarkably long silence—was shattered by the shrieks and sobs of women as the invaders pushed them aside and fled toward the stage. Then the low rumble of growling men swelled into bellows of rage as the ruffians disappeared. Chairs tipped and clattered to the floor as men pushed through the gathering seeking their wives.

"Ladies! Gentlemen! The danger is past!" Captain Wembley took command. Gathering his junior officers, he issued orders. "Dragoons! To me!"

Worth did not like the captain, but he had to admire Wembley's leadership; decisive with never a doubt that he would be obeyed.

"No one is to leave or enter. You two," Wembley said, selecting a pair of cornets. "Guard the stage. There's a door to the garden back there. Bar it. We won't be taken off guard again."

"Jerome!" he called, commandeering the butler. "You are to go to the front of the house. Question the servants. How did this come about? Dawkins," he called out to a junior lieutenant of the dragoons, "you're as good a horseman as we've got. Go with Jerome here. See him safe to the portico. Then take a horse and get yourself to Alton. Bring us the constable. On you go. Be quick about it."

Miss Ellicott removed her father to the chairs along the wall. His Lordship spoke sharply in confused bursts, first expressing outrage at the invasion by uninvited guests, then lamenting his son, and finally, decrying the desecration of his portrait.

"Is there no end to these horrors," he exclaimed. Miss Ellicott sat by him and held his hand which seemed to calm him.

"There's no horses!" a footman called out from the top of the stairs. "Them wretches has run off all the horses."

A wave of agitation spread through the crowd.

A colonel of the dragoons took Wembley's arm. "You seem to have the situation in hand, Captain. We shall look into this new business," he said, nodding to a small group of senior redcoats. He started away, then came back to Wembley.

"Do you think it might be helpful to put your youngsters to work searching the area where the robbers entered?" he asked. "With a bit of energy, they might capture a few of the intruders."

"They are without weapons—" Wembley started, but his superior was already leading his cadre up the stairs.

"Dragoons!" Wembley rallied the young officers and sent them across the stage, through the wings, and into the gloom behind the great house with orders to search the grounds for invaders and gather evidence.

The march of the senior dragoons up the staircase proved to be the trickle that precedes a flood; the staircase was immediately engulfed with ladies and gentlemen fleeing the gruesome scene and wondering at the fate of their carriages. When they reached the front of the house, they were greeted by a scene of utter confusion.

The attackers had first laid siege to the stable, capturing and herding all the carriage drivers, grooms, and stable boys into a tack room and locking it. The ruffians then untethered horses, unbuckled harnesses, opened stalls, unbridled, and scattered all the horses. The cattle did not go far, but recovering the animals in the dark and reassembling the carriage teams was a slow, chaotic business.

Wembley took Aloysius by the arm and walked him into the center of the ballroom, away from the guests. He spoke to the young Ellicott energetically, but in a barely audible whisper.

"Accident." Worth heard the only clear word. "Accident."

Aloysius moved away from Wembley, pacing around the rapidly emptying ballroom, not speaking with anyone.

"Captain Wembley, sir," a junior lieutenant, standing at attention, snapped off a salute and demanded an audience. "The raiders have gone, sir, escaped in a wagon."

"A wagon? You're sure?" Wembley said.

"There's wheel tracks," the lieutenant said. "And Mr Carpenter stepped in a fresh pile of...evidence...that there were horses waiting, sir. The trail crossed the lawn, but it leads onto hard-worn farm roads. They didn't leave any tracks there. Carpenter's gone to help gather our mounts, but they've stolen the march on us, sir. They're well away by now."

"Damn," Wembley said.

"Piss-poor robbers, they were, sir," the officer continued. "Left behind the best part of the jewels they seized. The men are searching and collecting them now, sir."

"A little good news," Wembley said. "Thank you, Lieutenant. Resume your search. We'll need daylight to do the job properly, but we must do what we can now."

Wembley surveyed the ballroom and saw Aloysius standing above his brother's lifeless visage and staring at the blood-drenched Frenchman. He went to the young lord and took his arm. "We're awaiting the arrival of the constable now. There's nothing to be done until he arrives."

Wembley tried to lead Aloysius away. The young man would not be moved.

Aloysius stared at the corpses with a singularly blank expression.

"Nothing," he said. "Nothing."

❧ 36 ❧

"Oh dear. Oh, oh, oh my dear. Oh, oh, oh…"

Constable Claypoole looked, then averted his eyes as he approached the bodies. "Ooh!" An anguished sound from the constable, then "oh, oh, eeew," and the sound of him scraping the sole of his shoe on the floor, attempting to wipe off some drops of blood.

Claypoole moved away from the bodies, looked heavenward and withdrew his snuff box. Taking a pinch, he inhaled delicately. The constable circled the bodies again, taking caution where he stepped.

Jane found Henry and together they accompanied Mrs Austen and Cassandra to the vestibule to find their cloaks. In a glimmer of good fortune, Edward's coach arrived. The coachmen had driven it back to Chawton House to take supper and returned to the scene of great confusion.

Descending the steps under the portico, the Austens encountered a dozen ladies waiting for their carriages. Hostlers, grooms, coachmen, and several of the male guests hurried about the drive and gardens, locating, sorting, bridling, and harnessing the horses.

With her mother and sister safely under Henry's protection, Jane refused to board the carriage.

"No, no, I must stay," she insisted. "The Ellicotts—I must comfort them. And…see to the…oh, all of the arrangements…the musicians…"

Jane disregarded whatever Henry was saying and closed the carriage door. "Come back," she called to the coachmen. "Your assistance will be wanted for other guests."

Jane returned to the ballroom to find the constable huddled with his deputy, Turkle.

"Take notes," Claypoole said. "We shall need details for the death notices."

A brief conversation with Miss Ellicott answered the constable's queries for Percival. Claypoole assured her that it would all be communicated directly to the sexton for the burial register.

As the constable turned his attention to the other dead body, Lord Kellingsford intercepted him.

"Is it not the terriblest thing?" His Lordship asked. "I am shocked. Heartbroken."

"My lord," the constable said, "you have my greatest sympathies."

"Look here," Lord Kellingsford said. "Here is a stain we tried to wipe away, but the paint was not fully dried, you see. Ghastly!"

Lord Kellingsford pointed to the lower part of his portrait, where his cuff of the breeches covered his knee, smeared with dark brown blood stains.

"Mr Richard West, the son of the great artist Benjamin West himself, shall have to return with his brushes and paints and set the matter aright. Oh, and now, look here…"

Lord Kellingsford continued to mourn his painting, spying drops of blood, and attempted to dab them off with his handkerchief, inevitably leaving the canvas worse for his ministrations.

The constable saw that there were several larger blood spatters at the bottom of the portrait.

"It will take some effort, my lord," he said. "You have my sincerest condolences."

Claypoole called his deputy. "Turkle! Turkle, come here. What do we know of the other man? The brigand?"

"Seems he were French. Sounded French, the people says. But we don' know his name or nothin' else."

"No name?" the constable said. "No name! Therefore, no family!"

The deputy shrugged.

"This is bad. Very bad. You know what this means?"

Turkle shrugged his shoulders.

"A pauper's grave, damn, a pauper's grave. That will put all the expense on our account. Blast it all. Oh. Ah…ah…" The snuff caught hold of the constable. He stepped back a pace, drew out his handkerchief, shuddered, and then discharged an enormous sneeze. "Ah." Claypoole made a satisfied noise as he returned his kerchief to his sleeve. "Well, nothing to be done now, but we shall have to make every effort to identify him and find his family. Let them pay for his burial. All right, Turkle, let's get on with our investigation. The heroic officer? Who was it?"

"Wembley, sir. Captain Wembley."

"Yes, yes. Now where is he?"

"This way, sir," Turkle said.

The constable found Wembley standing in an awkward triangle with Aloysius and Miss Ellicott. The captain's hands and face were clean, but bloodstains still darkened his uniform.

"Claypoole," the captain said.

"It is a very great debt we owe you, Captain Wembley," the constable said. "Very great indeed. Terrible business, but you ended it quickly."

"Duty, sir," the captain said. "Duty."

"There was a mob of them, I'm told. How many did you see?"

"How many robbers, sir? I can't say. I only had eyes on the leader, obviously the most dangerous man of the lot."

"Quite so, yes, quite so," the constable said. "You saw the shooting?"

"The third shot. The fatal shot, yes. The bandit also discharged two warning shots when he entered the room. I did not witness the first."

"But the fatal shot? You saw that?"

"Yes. Dreadful. The coward never dared to think that an unarmed man would confront him," Wembley said. "He was shocked and fired his pistol wildly. Simply damned bad luck he hit Percival."

"An unarmed man, you say?"

"His younger brother," the captain said. "Aloysius stepped out to confront the wretch. Charged right at the Frenchman."

"Then he was not aiming at Mr Ellicott—Mr Percival Ellicott?"

"Never," Wembley said confidently. "It was a wild shot intended for Aloysius. Percival's terrible misfortune. Aloysius is the real savior of the day. It was a courageous act that distracted the villain and allowed me to press home my attack. Truly, the glory belongs to Aloysius."

Wembley had moved over to where his friend stood and placed a hand on his shoulder. Aloysius, his face slack, did not acknowledge the gesture.

"Will we be calling for an inquest, sir?" Turkle said.

"No, no, no, no, no. No need for that," the constable said. "It's all as clear as day. Captain Wembley, Mr Ellicott, we are in your debt."

"Duty, sir. Only doing my duty," Wembley said. "Yet, Constable, you must not forget the Assizes. With the death of His Lordships' heir, must there not be an inquest?"

"Oh." The constable sighed deeply. "Oh my, oh no, yes, the Assizes. And that will mean…that will mean…"

Claypoole rubbed his chin, deep in thought, and then brightened.

"Turkle, you must prepare the documents for the Assizes—the Lent Assizes—next year. Oh, Captain Wembley, I am confident the next constable will greatly appreciate your attention to this matter. We are all truly indebted to you. Your quick action brought a swift and judicious end to this lawlessness. Do you have any idea who the man is?" the constable asked. "You say he was French?"

"I have never seen the man before in my life," Wembley said.

"Mr Ellicott—*sir*—do you know him?"

Aloysius stood, trembling; his arms wrapped tightly around himself. He shook his head.

"Miss Ellicott," the constable. "Pardon me, but I must ask if you have anything to add to this sad account?"

Miss Ellicott fanned herself. "It was terrible, so terrible, just as Captain Wembley said. And Aloysius," she went on. "Brave Ally rose to protect us. And poor, poor Percival." She lowered her head, sniffed, withdrew a handkerchief from her reticule, and dabbed at her eyes. "Those horrible robbers wanted our jewels, you know. But Captain...oh, Captain Wembley." She looked up at the officer and then gave a great sigh.

"Being of service, that's all. And doing a gentleman's duty to protect the ladies. Your brother's death—I am disconsolate, madam. You have my most sincere condolences."

The captain bowed deeply and turned back to the constable.

"What do you know of the rest of the robbers?" Wembley asked. "Have you raised the hue and cry?"

"Ah, oh, oh yes, sir. Of course, we did. Immediately." Claypoole bent to Turkle with several words. The deputy immediately found Marryat, spoke to the old servant, and sent him off.

"Constable," Wembley said, "I have a thought that may help you capture the scoundrels."

"Oh, yes then. By all means," the constable said, returning to Wembley. "Turkle, come over here now. Listen to Captain Wembley."

"Just an observation," Wembley said when he had their full attention. "The villains were armed with what appeared to me to be naval weapons. I cannot be positive about the pistols, but the swords they carried were those short, curved, navy-fashioned cutlasses."

"You're right about the barkers, too," Worth said. He picked up the weapon the Frenchman had first fired, examining it. "'Tis Royal Navy supply, this," he said, handing it to the constable. The constable took it delicately and passed it to his assistant.

Wembley eyed Worth and nodded.

"Now if that is so," the captain said, turning back to the constable, "you may want to send alerts down the roads to Portsmouth and Southampton. Where better to hunt for a pack of nasty sea dogs?"

"Very keen observation, Captain," the constable said. "Quite astute." He issued more instructions to Turkle.

As the constable went on with his investigation, Worth bent down and collected the Frenchman's other weapon. This pistol, a double barreled, side-by-side, was a good deal more interesting. It was a very fine weapon. Ah yes, engraved on the lock plate, just below the frizzen: "Joseph Manton Warranted." A pistol of the highest quality. *This was the weapon that fired the fatal shot.*

Turkle stood nearby. Worth started to hand him the pistol, then thought better of it.

"You must take care with this one," he said. He pulled one of the triggers on the weapon while holding the still cocked hammer with the thumb on his right hand, and gently let the hammer down into its "half-cocked" position. Then he opened the frizzen and turned the weapon over, allowing the priming powder to spill out of the flash pan.

"Won't go off now," Worth said, as he handed it to Turkle. "Still, you want to be careful. The portside barrel is still loaded. You'll want to draw the charge."

❧37❧

Jane, Worth, and the musicians sat on the edge of the stage, surrounded by the musicians' cases and bags. They were waiting for Edward's coach. It was one of a few pressed into service, conveying guests away to the inns of Alton while their horses had yet to be corralled.

Servants had removed the bodies and washed away the blood. Lord Kellingsford's portrait leaned awkwardly against one wall, staring out as if observing the grim aftermath.

Mr Thomas paced. Mrs and Mr Quinn continued to offer words of consolation to Jane, who remained speechless.

A clock somewhere in the house chimed twelve times, the bells loud enough to be heard in the ballroom.

"Eight bells," Worth said, translating the hour to nautical time.

"Eight?" Mr Thomas said. "Not at all. Twelve."

"Aye," said Worth, wearily. "Eight bells of the first watch. Midnight, whether on land or at sea."

Jane sat on the front edge of the stage, hands folded, head bowed. Mrs Quinn, seated closest to her, began to reach out—then stopped. She glanced to her husband and shared an unspoken message. Abruptly, Mrs Quinn was on her feet and removing something from one of the musicians' boxes.

"Miss Austen," she said, catching Jane's attention. "We can't make up for all you have lost tonight, but we can try for a better ending. Mr Quinn?"

He smiled and turned toward the cases.

Mrs Quinn circled toward the stairs to the stage. "Come now, Miss Austen. *The Faerie Waltz?* Was that not the piece we selected? Here are the chords," she said, handing Jane a small piece of paper.

Jane had no clear recollection of the next few moments. She remembered sitting down at the pianoforte. Mrs Quinn sat on the bench next to her holding a small musical instrument Jane did not recognize.

"What is it?" she asked.

"An invention," Mrs Quinn replied. "A kind of an experiment. Little Charlie Wheatstone came up with it. His da has a music shop on the Pall Mall. 'Tis a wee portable organ of a sort with buttons instead of keys.

He's thinkin' of calling it an 'organette.' I told him it's like puttin' an entire concert orchestra in the palms of your hands. So, call it a *concertina*, that's what I said."

Mr Quinn stood by the side of the pianoforte. He had mined his cases and located a small stringed instrument. Jane recognized it as a mandolin. Mr Thomas stood next to him. No bombard—only a soprano recorder.

Mr Quinn asked Jane for an *A*. She struck the proper key, and, in a moment, his instrument was in tune. Mrs Quinn looked at her, nodded and smiled. Jane realized that she was to lead off the melody and set the tempo. And so, she did.

Jane found herself playing easily, gently. There were no dancers; they need not fill the room with sound. They wove a blanket of music just large enough to enfold them where they sat or stood.

At the end of the second time through the first strain of the melody, Jane caught Mr Quinn's eyes and nodded to him: *Take the lead.* He responded, blending the mandolin's voice with Mrs Quinn's new instrument beautifully.

As they approached the second change, it was time for Mr Thomas to lead. He rose to the task, enriching the melody with trills and grace notes. Halfway through the change, he sent the lead back to Mrs Quinn, while he took off in flights of harmonic fancy. It was extraordinary how such a tiny piece of wood could produce such a joyful sound.

As the third change approached, Jane became aware of another voice. Mr Worth, standing directly behind her, had uncased his violin and became part of the ensemble. He had started playing so softly that, when the instrument appeared, it felt magical.

Jane saw Mr Quinn and Mr Thomas calling on the dancing master to present the tune while they held back. The melody took shape in the rich tones of Worth's fiddle. As it danced through the tune, Jane felt its warm embrace. She felt surrounded by these marvelous voices, each unique, distinct, and yet blended in a kind of spontaneous harmony that the finest formal composer could not match.

The third change was concluded. *Time to end? No*, Jane decided. *No, this must not be the end.*

She glanced around, catching the eyes of Mr Thomas and Mr and Mrs Quinn. *Once more*, she demanded. *Once more.*

Again, the melody soared. *En ensemble*; five equals, subtly stepping out, and then returning to support their partners. They approached the ending of the change with love and grace; building, building, building, and fading to quiet, one by one, until Jane closed the strain with one last chord.

The musicians remained absolutely silent, letting the reverberations fade. Nor did they speak as they put their instruments away.

At length, Mrs Quinn touched Jane's shoulder.

"I so regret we didn't get to play that for your guests. It would have been magnificent."

Jane, her senses awakened by the music, acknowledged Mrs Quinn but paced in front of the stage. While the musicians continued their removal and went to await their carriage, Jane recollected the evening's events. With the memory of each detail, she found her temper rising. The invasion was an affront. Percival's death, a catastrophe. And impossibly, the incompetence of the constable made it all feel much worse.

She found herself standing on the spot where the Frenchman had stood and fired the fatal shot. As she contemplated that instant, a wave of cool reason swept over her. *This is a story, a plot, an intrigue, peopled by characters and motivated by…?*

Jane Austen, the author, reassembled the details of the evening.

Worth and Jane were alone in the ballroom; the light fading as unattended candles and lamps flickered and dimmed.

"Seamen? Navy men? That is what Wembley said. Do you believe he was correct?" asked Jane.

Worth looked at her carefully, then nodded slightly. "Aye, I do."

"Do you think any of them will be caught? They must be caught. We must know who killed the heir to Kellingsford and who the dead Frenchman was and what this was all about."

"Nay, I don't think they'll be finding 'em. They'll be looking the wrong way."

"The wrong way?"

"Wembley was right. They had the look of navy men. And here in Hampshire, when you thinks of the navy, it's Portsmouth and Southampton. But sailors come from all over. Look at me, drifted all the way down from the Yorkshire Dales.

"A ship—it anchors somewhere and it puts the crew ashore in a sailortown. Spend your pay and mind the crimps. That's the way of life at sea. But a sailor's also got a berth in his heart and his dreams; a snug harbor. Might be in a port; might be a hundred miles from the water, but that's the place he calls home. No matter how long he's away or where his ship drops anchor, that's where he wants to go. Chasing them men to Portsmouth? Southampton? I'm thinking that's a bootless errand."

"My good Mr Worth, why should you think that?"

"They shipped outta Bristol."

Jane looked carefully at him, nodded, and crooked her index finger—the gesture that says, "Out with it. Tell me more."

"The man with the blunderbuss—he's a Bristol man. I know him."

❧38❧

"We need a name," Mr Thomas said, looking up from his cup. The musicians were gathered around a teapot, breakfast in their wake and the London coach ahead. Worth, having left Kellingsford before sunrise to see his friends off, was included in their company.

"I am certain of the wisdom of it," Mr Thomas continued. "We need a name."

"A name?" said Mrs Quinn.

"A name?" Mr Quinn repeated.

"For our ensemble. Our consort," Mr Thomas said. "We are a broken consort to be sure, not all strings or winds, but we are a fine ensemble and worthy of a name."

"A broken consort with a female musician," Mr Quinn said.

"Oh yes," Thomas said, "then we must be a shattered consort, broken into tiny bits and pieces. Still, I believe we ought to have a name."

"Why?" Mr Quinn asked.

"To gain recognition. Increase our earnings," Mr Thomas said. "You have seen the notices without the concert halls. Here is Mr Hayden conducting the Covent Garden Orchestra. Now, there's a notice for Daniel Auber leading the Orchestre de l'Opéra National de Paris! A century ago, persons of good taste would flock to hear The King's Consort, knowing it to be a fine ensemble. Must musicians play these authors' games and be *anonymous*? No. We ought to have a name."

Mr and Mrs Quinn nodded thoughtfully. The idea had merit.

"A musical company," Mr Quinn said, "like an acting company of a sort. Like The King's Men or The Duke's Men."

"Yes, in a way," Mr Thomas said. "But they are all named for their patrons."

"Do we need a patron?" Mr Quinn asked.

"A royal recommendation won't serve well now," Mrs Quinn said. "Mention of 'The Prince Regent's Consort' would bring his latest strumpet to mind."

"No patron is required," Thomas said. "Simply a few words that will draw one's attention. Stand out. Be memorable."

"The Hampshire Homicidicals," Worth said, reflecting his black mood. "Just the folk to help you set your murder and mayhem to music."

Worth had come to thank the musicians again and wish them God-speed. Additionally, at Miss Austen's insistence, he topped off their payment for the evening with an additional guinea. Twenty-one shillings—seven shillings apiece—unless the price of gold had made it even more valuable.

"The evening was…" Mrs Quinn started, then stopped at a loss for words.

"Memorable," Mr Quinn said.

"Aye," they all agreed.

"Astonishing."

"Unforgettable."

"Good morning!"

The bright greeting startled them. They had not seen Jane enter the inn.

There followed pleasantries which assiduously avoided any mention of the disastrous ending of the ball. With the cordialities completed, Jane addressed Mrs Quinn.

"Now, for your patroness," she said.

Mrs Quinn looked momentarily puzzled, then remembered. "The book. Yes. Of course."

Their bundles and cases were on the floor next to the table. Mrs Quinn extracted the volume while Jane, taking a place on the bench next to Worth, opened her satchel and took out pen and ink.

"And it is to Lady…?"

"Lady Gowan," Mrs Quinn said.

Jane bent over her task and provided a lovely inscription in a flowing hand, blotted it carefully and returned the volume to Mrs Quinn.

"You've gone to far too much trouble," Mrs Quinn said. "You didn't need to—"

"Mrs Quinn, my dear," Jane stopped her. "Sarah, this is just the sort of thing I want to do, that I must do." She smiled and leaned in to speak, as though sharing a confidence. "It helps sell books."

"Isn't that your publisher's task?" Mr Quinn said. "With Mr Button and Company—I see their notices frequently—they place copies of their books in any shops that carry music or instruments. Same with books by Hopkins and Wilson and the like. Doesn't your publisher do that for you?"

"It depends," Jane said. "It is a complicated business. At the moment, I think of myself very much as a peddler who must construct her wares before selling them. I write the books. I proofread and correct the text. I pay to get the books printed. The publisher may provide some assistance in advertising and distributing them—he does earn a commission on sales. But he is under no obligation to the author. If a book is to be truly successful, I must work to get it sold. It is a part of my daily labor."

"Like a hireling, of a sort," Mrs Quinn said.

"Yes, very like that," Jane said. "We are all of us hirelings of a sort."

"Well, there you have it! It is decided!" Mr Thomas said with cryptic enthusiasm.

Quizzical sounds were heard around the table as the others wondered what, exactly, may have been decided.

"The name for our ensemble. For our completely shattered consort."

"Ensemble? Consort?" Jane said.

"Thomas is of the opinion that our ensemble from last night has considerable merit," Mrs Quinn said.

"Of that, I am certain," Jane said. "You possess great talent."

"And Thomas believes we ought to perform more frequently together and become better known," Mr Quinn said. "To assist in this, he believes we ought to baptize ourselves as a consort of some sort, become better known as a group."

"A splendid idea," Jane said.

"And," Mr Thomas said with an expansive gesture, but Jane spoke ahead of him.

"It is a truth universally acknowledged, that a new consort, in possession of great talent, must be in want of a name."

Mrs Quinn and Worth, having read *Pride &Prejudice*, caught her joke immediately and laughed. Mr Quinn looked confused. Thomas, refusing to be thrown off track, opened his arms and declaimed: "The Hirelings!"

"Hmm."

"It could serve."

"Not bad, actually."

"And you, Miss Austen, shall be a greatly honored member of our ensemble," Mrs Quinn said. "Any time you're free to perform with us." This suggestion was met with even greater approval.

"But of course, with you being a famous authoress and all, when you perform, we'd have to give you greater distinction," Mr Quinn said.

"Make it Miss Austen and the Hirelings," Mr Thomas suggested.

"A Lady and the Hirelings," Worth said. "Miss Austen publishes incognito."

"The Author of *Sense and Sensibility* and the Hirelings," Mrs Quinn offered.

"No. No. Never," Jane said, speaking over their banter. "You have taught me—shown me—there is no room for rank or privilege in a true ensemble. I cannot imagine a greater musical honor than to be one of The Hirelings."

The last few minutes before the coach arrived were filled with talk about dances, music, old and new repertoire, and of playing *en ensemble*. Mrs Quinn told a humorous story about an ensemble run amok. Jane enjoyed the repartee and smiled warmly. But she thought, with some pride, that the story of "Thomas Thomas and The Bombard" was an even better, more amusing tale.

❧ 39 ❧

"Now, Mr Worth, I must discuss some business with you."
Jane sat across from Worth at the same table in the inn. She had his full attention after they had seen the other musicians off.

With a fresh pot of tea set between them, Jane said, "From the beginning. Go over it for me again. Your explanation last evening was insufficient. You say you recognized the man who threatened us with the short, ugly scattergun weapon?"

"Aye." Worth saw a new aspect to the authoress. Anger and iron. "As I said, the man had a tattoo."

"He had a number of tattoos."

"One very particular tattoo on the back of his right hand," Worth said. "The man's name is Woodman. Nate Woodman. He was a carpenter's mate. He goes by Chips. I sailed with him on *Minerve*—she were a frigate."

"The *Minerve*!" Jane said. "I've heard of her. My brother Frank was captain of the *Peterel*. They were in action together. Captured two prizes near Genoa in '99."

"My time was a few years earlier, about '96. I was an able seaman then. We was on blockade duty then. We put in for stores on the Rock—Gibraltar. Got a bit o' shore leave. I seen him in a tavern right after he got that ink. He talked about it with his mates. Couldn't see the actual tattoo then on account of it was wrapped up. Still tender, the back o' the hand. But I seen it plenty later on. Axe and a chisel, crossed. His initials, an *N* and a *W*. The tat man used colors, red and blue. That's very uncommon. I'd recognize the man by that ink scratch easier than seein' his face."

"You said you believed he was in Bristol. How do you know that?"

"His whereabouts right now, I can't say. But Bristol's his home port. That's where m' sister lives and I've seen him there enough. Maybe he even talked about it when we was shipmates. I'm sure he's a Bristol man."

"Why did you fail to report this information to the constable?"

Worth barked a laugh. "You have met your fine constable, have you not? Here's how it is," he continued, "he dinna ask me. He dinna ask and Captain Wembley was taking command, officer that he is. When you're jack tar living between the decks, you learns to stop your gob, keep your head down, and speak only when spoken to."

"Captain Wembley does seem rather sure of himself," she agreed.

Jane picked up her teacup, sipped, and then held it cupped in two hands in a moment of almost prayerful contemplation. "All right then," she said, as if to herself, and put the cup down. She looked up at Worth.

"What are your plans at present? Will you be returning to Town soon?"

"I'll be at Kellingsford another day or two," Worth said. "Mr Ellicott begged me a favor that'll keep me here until after the funeral. He said I could stay as long as I like. They sets a good table." He shrugged.

"No balls to plan? Musical engagements?"

"That's all Mr Wilson's business. I'm best suited to just bein' a fiddler—"

"Not true—"

"When I get back, I'll pick up some copper playing with other folk." He laughed, another short bark. "Reminds me, I was going to ask you to pen him a note, tell him how wonderful it all went."

"I'll think of something," she said. "Do you have a place you stay in Town?"

"Nay, I'm an old sea dog in that. I've got my sea chest right here with me. When I'm in Town, I drags it around to look for someone who'll share a berth. I can sling a hammock anywhere. After the new year, I'm heading up north. Mr Wilson recommended me to a great house, to be in service and teach 'em some music and dance. I figured I'd give it a try and see what I think."

"Nothing pressing then?"

"Nay."

He looked at her suspiciously.

"Very well, Mr Worth, I have a job for you."

"Eh?"

"Yes," she said decisively. "You are to accompany me to Bristol. You will serve as my footman or driver or some such role. You'll do as a chaperone, if necessary, to satisfy family concerns. 'Oh, what will people say?'" Jane went on with pinched lips and a falsetto. She shook her head, then muttered, "Not that anyone should care about the virtue of a spinster who has long been off the market. Your principal responsibility will be to help me locate this Nate Woodman, the tattooed man, so that I may speak with him."

"No," Worth said. "No. No. No. No. No. Tracking robbers. Finding suspicious men. Identifying criminals. That's business for constables or magistrates or maybe the army. It's not for the likes of me, and most certainly not the business of a lady!"

"You misunderstand me," Jane said, her voice calm and steady. "I will not attempt to detain the man. I only want information. Just to talk with him. A chat."

"No. There's no way that's possible. And like I said, he may not even be there."

"That is why I need you to accompany me. We need to see if he is there. I need you to be able to find him."

"Nay. I'll not be putting you in danger," he said. "'Tis a matter for the constable."

"Mr Worth," Jane said, still completely calm, smiling. "You have met our fine constable, have you not?"

He had to laugh.

"All I want to do is ask him one question," she said. "Who is—who was—the Frenchman?"

Worth sat back, crossed his arms, and shook his head.

"A man leads a band of robbers, possibly navy sailors, it seems…"

"Probably," Worth said.

"Probably navy sailors," she continued. "They break into a great house during a ball. My ball. The heir of the house is murdered. This mysterious gang leader dies for his audacity. The robbers vanish. The jewelry they took is found later, left on the ground. Do you not think all of this…curious?"

She left the question to hang in the air for a moment.

"Do you think Constable Claypoole will discover the man's identity?"

She had planted the seed. Then, like a skilled helmsman, she changed tack.

"You will be paid, of course. Let us say five shillings each day. And I will pay for all expenses—food and lodging and necessaries."

Worth opened his mouth as if to say something, then closed it and pursed his lips.

Jane took another tack.

"Shall I ask the constable to speak with you?" she said with a little shrug. "I could suggest that he ask if you have any helpful information?"

Worth's jaw dropped, and his eyes widened. "You would do that," he said. It was a statement, not a question.

"Perhaps he will refer you to the magistrate. Then you might be wanted in Winchester."

Worth stared at the ceiling.

"Mr Worth," she said, reaching out to him with her words.

"You, sir, arranged a most wonderful ball at my request. My dearest wish was fulfilled. And then it was spoiled. Spoiled by a man who is now to be restrained in the custody of a grave, but whose identity is unknown. Do you not think I deserve at least to know this mysterious man's name?"

Worth looked at her, still shaking his head.

"Please," she said. And again, "Please."

"I am going to regret this," he said, shaking his head. "My sister can put me up, but you, being a lady, you'll need accommodations. And there's the travel, changing coaches. We'll have to go through Winchester. It's a right long ways—"

"Mr Worth. I was awake more than half the night thinking of this. There is a story to be discovered, the threads of a plot to unwind. Trust me, sir. I have a plan."

❧40❧

"I forbid it, Jane. The very idea. Traveling unaccompanied. Engaging in discourse with strangers, low life ruffians. I forbid it."

Mrs Austen had abandoned the settee in the upstairs sitting room. She had seated herself in the lightly upholstered straight back armchair that her husband had so frequently occupied in Steventon and Bath when he was alive. Cassandra occupied the settee, silent and jabbing furiously at her embroidery frame.

"I shall not be unaccompanied," Jane said as she added and removed items from her satchel. "Mr Worth will serve as my driver, manservant, and defender of my virtue."

"All the worse," Mrs Austen said. "Insupportable. It is…it is—"

"Flora, here you are," Jane said as their maid came up the stairs. "I must plead for your assistance."

Jane led the young woman to the furthest corner of the room, away from her glowering family members. They would not have privacy but would, at least, escape some of the heat.

"It is too much to ask," Jane said quietly, "but I will be forever indebted to you. I should like to borrow a day dress from you."

Flora's face expressed astonishment at the request. "But Miss Jane, you're a lady?"

"Yes, a lady who is soon to be traveling incognito and without my dear maidservant. I must have a day dress I can manage with buttons in front, you see. We are of like size. Your usual Sunday—"

Jane observed the stunned look on the young woman's face.

"No," Jane said. "It is too much to ask."

"Oh Miss Jane, never—I mean, of course, I mean, I'd be honored. It'd be no trouble at all."

"You are certain?"

"O' course, ma'am."

"Only for two or three or possibly four days. And when I return, we will visit the drapers. You shall have sprigged poplin, enough to make up a day dress with more to spare, fabric and trim."

"Jane!" Mrs Austen said "You have not heard me? You have become deaf? I forbid it. I shall not alter my decision. Your scheme is completely unreasonable."

Flora glanced at Jane who smiled, giving the girl permission to flee.

"Cass," Jane said. "If you continue to stab at your whitework like that, you will tear right through it."

Cassandra looked up and scowled at her sister.

"Or is that your intent? To make it *holy* without the benefit of a clerical blessing?"

Cassandra looked up again, sighed, shook her head, and went back to her needlework with slightly less ferocity.

"Mama," Jane said, "this is something I must do. A terrible injustice has occurred. Percival Ellicott is dead. The peace of your countryside has been disturbed and, as the assault occurred at the ball I arranged, it reflects on our family honor. I must—"

"You must! Why you? Must indeed."

"There is no one else," Jane said. "The constable is a fool. He can see no further than the depth of his purse. He has neither the imagination nor ambition to discover the truth. There are threads to be followed, a plot to unravel. Someone—"

"Someone such as you?" Mrs Austen asked. "Why you? If the constable won't undertake the inquiry, what about the younger son?"

"Aloysius Ellicott is paralyzed, by shock or grief, I cannot tell. I tried to engage with him yesterday. He would not speak. He could not even look at me."

"Henry, then. Surely Henry—"

"Oh Mama, Henry is much too busy attempting to avert a financial catastrophe. The Alton bank has failed—"

"Yes, yes, I know. But there must be others. Frank, what about—"

"Frank is only at Chawton to look after Mary in her pregnancy, otherwise he would be at sea. He can hardly be expected—"

"Yes, yes, yes. But why now? Does it matter?"

"The matter must be brought up at the Assizes, Mama. If we can discover the identity of the man—the Frenchman—just his name, that will provide the judges with at least the bare bones upon which to base their inquest."

"If we? 'We' you say? You and this Mr Worth?"

"Yes, Mama."

"And who is this man? Not a gentleman. A commoner. And you—a young lady—"

"No, Mama, not a young lady. A forty-year-old spinster, unmarried, and out of circulation. With him as my serving man and driver, all perfectly proper—"

"Not perfectly proper," Cassandra said.

"Reasonably proper then," Jane said.

"How do you know you can trust the man?" Mrs Austen asked.

"He is honorable. Honorable, decisive, and he has already been of great service to us."

"Great service?" Mrs Austen huffed. "Oh, his command of the music and dancing was well enough, but that hardly merits. 'Great service' indeed."

"There is more, Mama. I have it from Henry. Much more."

"What more?" Mrs Austen asked.

"Indeed, what?" Cassandra added to the inquiry.

Jane stood still, conducting a silent debate with herself, then proceeded.

"This was all to be confidential," Jane said. "I prised it out of Henry with great difficulty. You will recall the effort that Henry made to recover the manuscript and copyright for *Susan*?"

The ladies nodded.

"Henry was unsuccessful."

"That is not so," Mrs Austen said.

"You have it all in hand," Cassandra added.

"The recovery was Mr Worth's doing. Mr Crosby was most truculent. First, he claimed to know nothing of the manuscript. Then, after locating it, he somehow associated it with *S&S* and *P&P*. With the knowledge that he was in possession of a manuscript by the author of two profitable novels, he demanded more than two hundred pounds for its return."

This news elicited gasps from the ladies.

"I am uncertain as to how the events unfolded. Henry was not forthcoming. But when I tried to praise him for his recovery of the manuscript, he demurred. Henry insisted it was Mr Worth's doing. He said Mr Worth arranged a private conference with the publisher and afterward, Mr Crosby seemed to recall the original agreement and he chose to honor it.

"Yet, he refused to take credit for assisting in the negotiations. Mr Worth insisted that Henry should hold his involvement in the matter in confidence. It was only Henry's sense of honor—his unwillingness to accept recognition that he had not earned—that gave Mr Worth away. Henry respects and trusts Mr Worth."

Her story concluded, Jane drew the chair away from her writing desk, turned it, sat down, and regarded her mother and sister.

Cassandra caught her sister's gaze, gave just the slightest nod, and returned to her needlework.

Jane looked at her mother and waited.

"I do not approve," Mrs Austen said finally. "But I can see your mind is set. I shall not forbid it."

❧41❦

Saint Nicholas Church in Chawton provided a perfect setting for blessed events: weddings, christenings, and holy days. Worth felt moved by the warm glow within. *Quite beautiful,* he thought.

Standing at the head of Percival Ellicott's coffin, Worth put bow to fiddle and filled the chamber with O'Carolan's *Farewell to Music*. He had considered the blind Irish harper's *Lament* but thought the *Farewell* had a more melancholy air.

Lord Kellingsford had removed his cape and greatcoat, despite the cold, allowing mourners to better see his doublet, pantaloons, stockings, and cravat, all in a perfect combination of textures and somber tones of gray and black.

Aloysius Ellicott, by right of primogeniture, heir apparent to the great Kellingsford estate, led the family of mourners. The funeral rite had already been conducted in the family chapel. The gathering in the church today was a memorial; a time for all who knew him to celebrate Percival's life and share memories before the removal of the body to the church graveyard.

The elegy was…concise, Worth thought. Percival's frequent contributions to the parish were noted with the emphasis on the regularity and no mention of their generosity. The rector abridged his remarks by saying that "everyone knew" about this fine man, cut down in his prime, so what more was there to say. Thus, he said no more.

The officiant asked for those who would care to say a word.

Aloysius rose and stepped out to stand beside the coffin. His Beau Brummel fashion suited the occasion perfectly. He had only to substitute a black silk cravat for white to dress for mourning.

He spoke about his elder brother and what a *fine* gentleman he had been. And what a *fine* head for business he had. And what *fine* plans he had made for the future. Aloysius also noted his brother's *fine* sense of style, so personal and unique. And the poor, deceased man had a *fine* appetite, Aloysius said, relating an anecdote about some boyhood prank when his older brother had taken all the children's Christmas treats for himself.

Aloysius continued a little longer, repeating some items but making few additions to his brother's finer points. The younger son made a brave attempt to add additional plaudits but, as he rounded into the third time through the theme, he came to a faltering stop.

Aloysius glanced at the officiant, then covered his face with his hands while issuing a great heaving sigh that might have been taken as a prelude to a sob and returned to his pew.

The grieving father seemed to realize something was required of him. Lord Kellingsford rose from the pew and stepped out into the centre aisle of the church. He lifted his chin and assumed a noble visage, a look appropriate for a portrait or even a bust. He turned around slowly, nodding to a few people here and there. Then, he returned to his pew and sat down.

With his instrument already in tune, Worth waited on the Gospel side near the front of the church, noting others among the mourners. They included a military presence: a navy man, Captain Frank Austen, Worth assumed, as well as Captain Reginald Wembley and Admiral Harwell. Constable Claypoole occupied a pew by himself in the middle of the church. Jerome, Mr Sloat, and several of the Kellingsford footmen stood in the back.

Aloysius had asked Worth to play something suitable for the service. The service nearly complete, the rector beckoned and Worth had taken up his position in the apse.

As Worth dug into the haunting melody, he thought he saw signs of genuine emotion in some faces. Sitting in a church, acknowledging the passing of a mortal being, brings thoughts of one's own mortality to the fore. Combined with fitting music, it will stir the human heart.

Worth played the *Farewell,* a fine tune, a soaring melody filled with double stops. *Aye, now that's right,* Worth thought, *give us a few tears.* When the piece ended, the rector signaled to Aloysius and the pallbearers. Worth did not recognize any of the five other men who joined the young lord.

In the graveyard, the burial proceeded quickly. Aloysius hid his face. Lord Kellingsford looked grave and lordly. Jerome and the others from Kellingsford who had been within the church joined them. An even larger group of men from the estate—coachmen, grooms, gardeners, and others—stood at the back.

The most notable visage in the crowd, Worth thought, was the craggy face of the gravedigger. Of everyone Worth had seen, this old man seemed to have the most sincere aspect of mourning. It was his job, Worth supposed, and he did it well.

As the mourners left the graveside and the first clods fell, Worth was caught by the gaze of the one man who did not turn away. Hinch.

❧42❧

"Now, you understand, she has to be kept warm," Worth said. "And she's got to have a sip of water. Wintertime is the hardest." Worth picked a small wooden box with holes in it out of the corner of his violin case and showed it to Miss Cassandra Austen. "There is this scrap of wool inside," he said, opening the box. "You keep it wet—not too wet mind you—not so it's dripping—and that keeps her happy. Keeps the air inside the case humid. If her wood gets too dry, she might crack or split."

As much as she had objected to her sister's trip to Bristol, the idea of looking after the dancing master's instrument seemed inconsequential. She discovered it was not.

"A warm place. Not too hot," he emphasized. "Nowhere near a fire."

"You have made your instructions perfectly clear," Cassandra said. "As long as she has proper indoor manners, we will not have any problems. Does she have a name?"

Worth looked at her a little surprised. And a little uncomfortable.

"Sometimes I…"

Her eyes laughing, Cassandra asked, "Yes, she does. What have you named her?"

Worth pursed his lips. He was being teased, he knew. And perhaps he didn't mind.

"Mirabella. She were a shop girl, the daughter of the master of the atelier where I bought the instrument. I was a much younger man, and she were a very pretty girl. I'm told the name means 'wonderful' in the Italian. It suited the girl. It suits the fiddle, too," he said, handing the instrument to Cassandra.

"I shall take very good care of her, Mr Worth."

Jane slung her satchel around her shoulder. Worth had a duffel on his back where his fiddle usually hung and carried Jane's carpet bag. After walking the short distance to the Chawton House stable, they were met by Hotchkiss. The stable master had the gig ready.

The bags fit easily into a small compartment behind the seat of the light, two-wheeled vehicle. It was well sprung and sturdy but provided no protection from the weather. Hotchkiss had put two blankets on the seat to supplement the travelers' coats and cloaks.

"This here's Dalrymple," the stable master said, introducing Worth to the stocky white horse standing in the traces. "She's sweet-natured, willing and able. Just give her the lightest touch."

He spoke to Worth with instructions on handling hills, giving the horse rest, feeding, and stabling her, and preparing for encounters with dogs, ill-tempered horses, and mail coaches. Worth listened carefully, nodding, and hoping he could convince the old fellow that he knew what he was about.

Seated next to Jane, both wrapped in the extra blankets, Worth took the reins and cautiously gave them a shake. The horse took off at a brisk trot, throwing him backward.

"Slow her down, Mr Worth. We need to get to the proper highway before you can give Dalrymple her head."

Worth slowed the gig to a walk, biting his lower lip, glancing right and left as he approached the Winchester Road.

"Cheer up my lads, it's to glory we steer," Jane sang out.

Worth frowned with disapproval and quickly returned his eyes to the road.

He navigated onto the Winchester Road successfully. The tension on his face began to ease, knowing it would be several miles before another change of direction was required.

"You might want to get up a bit of speed now," Jane said. "Unless you want our little jaunt to last a fortnight."

Worth gave the reins a shake and Dalrymple began to trot.

"A mail coach," he said. He had heard it before he saw it.

He slowed the horse to a walk and, seeing a widening of the road on the right, pulled over to stop, allowing the mail coach to pass. Worth observed the creaking of the carriage, the sound of the wheels, and a furious look from the coachman.

Worth let out a breath he had not realized he had been holding when the coach and four had passed. Then he noticed Jane laughing.

"The Winchester Road is a very fine, wide highway, Mr Worth. There is more than sufficient room for two coaches to pass. But if you would pull aside to give room, it would rather be on the left side. That is what is expected. What is the equivalent of 'getting your sea legs' for a sailor cast ashore?" She did not wait for an answer. "You'll get the knack of it soon enough, but as this is a rather busy highway, will you pass me the ribbons."

He handed her the reins.

"Off we go, Dalrymple," she said, and they were off at a trot.

"How is it the author of *Sense and Sensibility* could write a book on driving as well?" Worth said. "Where'd you come by this skill?"

They had turned off the Winchester Road and were headed toward Bath. Their course would take them through Bath to Bristol.

"Since we moved to Chawton," Jane said, "the stable at the Great House lured me in. I fancied the animals, the dogs, cats, and the nice horses like Dalrymple here. Mr Hotchkiss enjoyed the company, and he enjoyed explaining things to me. Men like to do that, you know, explain things to poor, ignorant women like me."

"Just an excuse. Men likes being around the ladies any time. The explaining just gives them a reason."

Jane shrugged. "Perhaps. He taught me how to handle the gig and drive it around the country hereabouts."

"You, a lady? And your family approved?"

"Mama and Cassandra disapproved most heartily. But I have the most wonderful excuse, you see."

"Aye?"

"I am conducting research! I am completing studies for my novels," she said with a note of triumph.

"If my character is to pilot a gig or drive a coach, how can I write about it if I have not experienced it? Done it myself? Do you not recall in *P&P*—Anne de Bourgh driving in her little phaeton?"

"Ha," Worth said. "Well done."

"They grumble and complain, but they have not issued an injunction."

"What do your brothers in the navy think? I'll guess they'd admire you for it. Say you're taking initiative."

"We have not discussed it. I think you might be correct, but even they might pale at the more dreadful aspect of this tale."

"There's more?"

"Much more. And it is quite appalling."

"Will you tell me?" Worth said.

"First, I must swear you to secrecy."

"Secrecy?"

"We are speaking of the most improper, unseemly, disreputable behavior. Its discovery could engulf our family in scandal and humiliation. I know you to be an honorable man, so you must promise, on your honor, never to reveal this secret."

"Milady," he said, in solemn tones. "'Pon my honor."

"You mock me, sir," she said, showing a smile when she glanced at him. Then she continued on a new tack. "I think that if I had been born a boy, I would've gone into the navy."

"What about being a writer?"

"Win the war first," she said, "then return to a village in Hampshire and write novels about it."

Jane glanced at him again.

"Truly, Mr Worth. I need your promise."

"Truly, Miss Austen," he said, resuming his ordinary tone. "I'll not say a word."

"Can I trust you?"

"Yes, yes. If you've a Bible at hand, I'll swear an oath."

"Very well," she said, glancing over at him before continuing. "With the aid of that good man Hotchkiss I have taken up riding."

"Riding?" Worth laughed. "Well, I'll not say a word about it, but that's hardly as dreadful as you suggest."

"There is more."

"In your book, *Mansfield Park*, the ladies go out riding all the time."

"They go riding in proper, ladylike fashion. They ride aside," she said. "Their author, in deep seclusion, has taken to riding astride. I have gone galloping and jumping and following forest tracks and—and I find it exhilarating."

"What's the difference?" Worth asked.

"Oh, it's the saddle, you see. A lady's saddle has a tall, wide flat pommel and only one stirrup—a slipper as it is called. The proper lady sits with both legs on one side of her horse and walks the beast about or, in a fit of wild abandon, breaks into a trot. Riding astride, like a man, you are well-balanced. It is safer and much more satisfying—even if it is not ladylike. My cousin Eliza was a great horse woman. Not caring a fig for what society thought, she rode astride."

"In your books then, why not have your ladies be daring? Wouldn't your lady readers like that?"

"You misjudge the power of propriety. No. Such a scene would cause a scandal. In secret, some readers might enjoy such freedom, but they could not acknowledge it in public. Do you know my greatest concern as an author?"

"To tell interesting stories about people. Make 'em seem real so's the readers care about them?" Worth suggested.

"*And*, Mr Worth, to sell books. To sell a great many books."

❧ 43 ❧

Dawn's glow provided the scarce light necessary for the travelers to resume their journey. Well-fed and well-watered, the little white mare was now to be known as Lady Dalrymple, the dancing master said. They set off at a brisk pace with Worth handling the reins. Jane had enjoyed the inn's finest room; Worth had insisted on a more seaman-like berth. He and the little horse had bedded down together in the stable, and he had found her to be a noble beastie and gentle lady.

"She was most generous with her hay," Worth said as they took the road out of Amesbury toward Shrewton. "She made a good meal of it but left plenty for me to sleep on. And in the middle of the night, when I was feeling quite a chill, she took a lie-down right next to me. Warmed up my bedding like a fine coal fire, and you dinna need to poke or stoke it. Lady Dalrymple. A fine lady indeed. How did she come by her name?"

Jane smiled. "Hotchkiss has a very direct way about things," she said. "After the army recruited Chawton House's draft horses, he looked far and wide for replacements. He found her in Dalrymple, a ways up north—"

"In Ayrshire," Worth said. "Near the town of Ayr and close by the Firth of Clyde."

"You've been there?"

"Just a ship's boy I was then, but I sailed those waters. Home port for Robbie Burns, y'know. And there's—"

He stopped in mid-sentence.

"But what is that?" he asked, looking ahead. The sun, creeping over the horizon behind them, had illuminated the tops of several wide, flat boulders that seemed to float above the Salisbury Plain.

"You've not seen them?" Jane said, smiling. "Now I have one great wonder of the world to introduce you to. 'Tis the great henge. Stonehenge as it's called hereabouts. The finest and grandest stone circle in all of Britain."

"Aye."

As they neared the great stone circle and the sun rose, he could see the scale of the thing, the giant lintels he had first seen supported by massive pillars.

"I've seen standing stones here and there," he said, "but never…"

As the road passed close by the mighty stones, they spent the next while marveling at them. The size. The purpose. Jane recounted some Arthurian legends. Worth wondered about the tools and mechanisms that would be needed to shape and transport such massive stones.

"Even if you had the pieces right there," Jane said, "How would you pick one up and place it atop the others like that?"

"I can't imagine how the ancient ones could've done it," Worth said, "but if it were today and you had a crew from a man o' war, we'd find a way to get the job done."

Jane laughed. "You navy men," she said, smiling at Worth. "And I am sure you would. I am sure you would."

Salisbury lay astern, Bath neared, and Bristol still stood below the horizon when Worth gave a quiet laugh.

"You are amused, sir?" Jane said.

"Just thinking."

"About?"

"A song," he said. "All this time in this two-wheel cart—this chariot—set my mind to thinking of a song."

"You must not leave me in suspense."

"I'm not sure, you see, it's a sailor song and it ain't exactly polite."

"A sailor's song?"

"Aye."

"So, this is a song you sailors would sing when you're off at sea? Weighing anchor and putting up sails. I know a great deal about you navy men. My brothers…"

"Aye, you said. But singing ain't the navy way."

"Navy sailors do not sing?"

"In the fo'c'sle, aye, and ashore. Never on watch."

"I thought all sailors had songs to help them with their pulling and shoving and such. A good, loud song to move the work along."

Worth laughed. "Nay. Not on a man o' war. Any man needs to put in a bit more effort, the bosun or the mate takes a starter to 'em."

"A starter?"

"Aye. A wee whip. The mates use small canes, like riding crops, for starters. A bosun might have a nice bit of a rope, all knotted up neat that he can use to drive the work along. Not quite a cat o' nine tails—more of a wee, scratchy kitten. No songs, though. You don't sing for your supper on a King's ship."

"You are continuing to keep me in suspense, Mr Worth. What of this song that amuses you? And if you have no songs on a navy ship, where do you have it from?"

"I heard it from a black sailor-man in Bristol, right where we're headed. A Yankee he was, but on the run from slavers."

"I am still waiting, sir."

Worth glanced over at her, then looked back at the road.

"If I'm to lead a song, it's you must be the crew."

"I must?"

"You gots to sing it, too."

"Very well, sir. Lead on." And he did.

> *"And we will roll the old chariot along*
> *We'll roll the old chariot along*
> *We'll roll the old chariot along*
> *and we'll all hang on behind"*

He repeated the song thrice—the chorus it was—insisting that Jane sing it with more gusto than decorum. Then he started in with the verses.

> *"A nice bit of cheese won't do us any harm*
> *A nice bit of cheese won't do us any harm*
> *A nice bit of cheese won't do us any harm*
> *And we'll all hang on behind"*

They sang the chorus again. Then Worth offered a new line for the verse, and it continued as they rolled their old chariot along the road to Bristol.

Worth prompted Jane to offer verses.

She thought that "a nice plate of scones" would be harmless. Worth laughed. He countered with "a fine joint of beef."

Jane sang back that "a hearty Irish stew" would not do any harm. Worth took the song into alcoholic waters with "a tankard full of grog." Jane proposed "a hot pot of tea."

Then the song came to a halt after Worth led a verse for "a drop of Nelson's blood."

"A drop of Nelson's blood? Won't do us any harm?" she said, at the end of the verse. "What is that? What sort of thing is that? Drinking blood?"

Worth was laughing again.

"It's not what you think," he said. "Not at all. Nay. Not at all."

He laughed again shaking his head.

"So, Mr Worth, you must elevate my understanding. Why should I not be offended at the idea of taking a sip of Lord Nelson's blood?"

Worth was still smiling. He glanced at Jane and returned his eyes to the road ahead. Not that his eyes were needed. Lady Dalrymple was entirely up to the task herself.

"Trafalgar was fought on 21 October of the year aught five. When Nelson was felled, you knew we wasn't going to roll him up in his hammock with a round shot, sew it up with a stitch in his nose, and send him over the side like a common sailor."

"A stitch in his nose?" Jane said, making a face.

"Aye," worth said. "That's just to be polite. Make sure old Jack's really dead. If he ain't, maybe the stitch'll wake him up."

Jane groaned.

"Lord Nelson was a hero, even before Trafalgar. He had to be brought back home for a proper, hero's burial. Now depending on the winds, a sound ship can take a month to sail from Gibraltar back to Portsmouth. But the old *Victory* was all shot to hell…beg pardon, ma'am. But first, they had to tow her back to Gibraltar for repairs and that would take more time. You canna tuck the old admiral in his bunk and sail back home. You got to take some precautions, so he don't get all—"

"I follow your meaning."

"So, the ship's surgeon, Mr Beatty he was, he come up with a plan. He commandeered a great barrel o' very fine French brandy. He poured some out, tucked Lord Nelson inside, refilled the barrel, and sealed it up."

"What?"

"Stuffed him in a barrel of brandy," Worth said. "He pickled him."

"He…he… He pickled Lord Nelson?"

"Aye. Had to pop out the bung a couple or three times to top him off."

"Top him off?" Jane repeated.

"Aye. Seemed as though His Lordship took a wee dram to ease his travels. Beatty was a clever man. An Irishman, he was. His plan worked. It took more than two months for the *Victory* to bring the admiral home. But when they laid him out in the Painted Hall in Greenwich, people said he never looked better."

Jane leaned back, shaking her head.

"Beatty done good work, you see," Worth continued. "He's the one that took care of m' hand. Most surgeons, they'd a' just lopped it off at the wrist. But Mr Beatty, he did his work real careful like. Saved enough of my fingers so that I can still play the fiddle. Now there you have the story. A drop of Nelson's blood—to a sailor—that'd be a nice sip o' brandy. But o' course, there was a ruckus over it, wouldn't you know. There was them what said Nelson's spiritual journey should'a been made in good English rum."

Jane laughed, and then grew thoughtful.

"Where was it, that he was entombed? Westminster?"

"Nay, it was Saint Paul's."

"Were you in attendance?"

"The likes of me? Nay, I was still on the Rock. They put me ashore to tend m' wounds when the *Victory* put in for repairs. I got shuttled home on a French prize a month later. My last voyage in a man o' war."

"Were you afraid? With the great guns and muskets and all. It all sounds like such a terror."

"You does your duty. Every man has a job, and he sticks to it. The mate is bawling and there's ropes needs hauling. One minute, you're at the great guns and the next, you're trimming sail. After the action, when they're adding up the butcher's bill, that's when you feel the twinges. Maybe it was a near thing. But the fightin', that's your job.

"So, I got m'hand caught on a frog marine's spit. Just the price you pay. I done my duty. And besides, a man's more like to die from some damned disease or an accident or a festering wound than to fall in battle. Ain't no point in worrying. To glory we steer. Why do you ask, Miss Austen? What makes you think on such matters?"

"I worry. For my brothers. Frank and Charles, out at sea, of course. But Henry, too. His illness was so terrible. I feared greatly for him."

"And yourself?"

"Myself?"

"Aye. There's plagues and fevers enough for all of us to have our worries. What is it…what is it that you fear?"

Jane thought about the question as the gig bumped and swayed along the road. At length, she replied:

"I do not believe that I fear death, for death is part of the nature of things and remains a matter of divine providence. I have faith, and I am confident that the faithful will be rewarded in God's Kingdom. If I have a fear, it is of disappearing. I am rather proud of my books. I know, pride.

A sin. I must repent. And yet, I confess, I am proud of my scribblings. They are my children. I should like for them to have a good life.

"I should like, in death, not to disappear without a trace."

❧44❧

"Freddy!"

The woman who opened the door engulfed the dancing master in a hug.

"Isaac. Isaac, come see!" she called back into the house. "It's Freddy!"

Jane felt the glow of the familial affection. A loving brother and sister. A warm welcome home.

"My sister, Sophie Croft," Worth said as he ushered Jane through the door.

"Sophie, let me introduce my...Miss Austen."

Isaac Croft was shaking Worth's left hand vigorously.

"Good day, Miss Austen." He smiled and nodded toward Jane and then back to Worth. "How are ya, lad? What a surprise! Sophie was just saying, we never sees ya. Come, come, sit. Will you have a tot?"

"I have the kettle on," Sophie said. "Please sit down, sit down."

"We're just here for a quick word and a warm up," Worth said. "We've been two days on the road. We'll be off to find an inn for Miss Austen, and then I must find a stable for her horse."

"An inn?" said Sophie. "There's no need of an inn. We've beds enough."

"Aye, lad," Isaac said. "Listen to your sister now."

"I'll be comin' back," Worth said. "Miss Austen requires..."

Jane cringed at the suggestion that his sister's warm, comfortable home was not good enough for this unknown person.

"Well now," Sophie said. "Let's sit down for a nice cuppa tea and see what the lady says."

All eyes were on Jane.

"I should like to think, Mr Worth..."

The instant she spoke, surprise and recognition appeared on Sophie's and Isaac's faces. Miss Austen wasn't just Miss Austen. Miss Austen was a lady.

"I should like to think that if your sister is kind enough to offer the hospitality of her lovely home," Jane continued, "I should think I would be most honored to accept it. Tea would be most agreeable."

Cloaks and coats came off and they settled around a small table half-way between the stove and the hearth.

"Cold, ain't it?" Isaac asked.

"Aye, right cold," Worth said.

A brief exchange concerning the weather followed.

"Your tea is excellent," Jane said. "Is it Pekoe?"

"It's our...it's just the tea from the tea bin at the grocer's. Don't got a name as far as I knows."

"Oh," Jane said. "Well, it is quite good."

"Are you busy in the yards?" Worth asked Isaac. Then he said to Jane, "Isaac's a master craftsman. Turns raw timber into fine ships."

"It's slowed down some. End o' the war," Isaac said. "But that's all right by me. We'll be at work soon. The shipping trade will pick us up."

Bits of conversation spliced with silences continued until the cups were empty.

"Miss Austen," Worth said, donning his coat, "I must see to the gig now. The good Lady Dalrymple needs a warm box and dinner."

"There's a stable just three streets over," Isaac said, rising as quickly as Worth had. "I can take you there. And then maybe I'll stand Freddy a pint at the Arms." He gave Sophie a kiss and put on his coat as he went to the door.

Left alone, the two women looked at each other. Sophie smiled. "Men."

"Indeed," said Jane, smiling back.

"Miss Austen..." Sophie started. "How is it you come to know Freddy?"

"Freddy. Yes, Mr Worth. Your brother was commended to me for his skills as a musician and dancing master. He presided over a—a very...memorable ball recently. You can be sure that, in time, your brother Frederick will achieve great renown for his musical abilities."

"Frederick...?" Sophie said, a large smile creasing her face. "Well, that's all well, I'm sure. But he's always gonna be wee Freddy to me."

Second cups of tea had been poured, and Jane was warmed through.

"How long has it been? Since your parents...?"

"Near to forty years now."

"What happened?"

"It were a plague o' some sort," Sophie said. "A death to the old folks but it spared the wee ones. I were twelve years old and Freddy were six."

"Oh, so young."

"It were hard. It were hard all round. But we were lucky and got to stay together. We was living on a croft up in the Dales. The vicar at Holy Trinity in Wensley took us in. 'Course he had no way to care for us orphans. He could'a sent us to Leeds. Plenty of factory work there for me. And there was orphan homes. But the vicar had family in Hull, and he took us there instead."

"He helped you stay together?"

"A guardian angel, he was. I got a place in service, and they let Freddy stay with me."

"So, you raised him?"

"He were always the independent sort," Sophie said. "But we done all right together."

"And you remain close."

"In a seafaring sort o' way. He were ready to be on his own when he were thirteen. Signed on as a ship's boy. But being at sea, as soon as you haul anchor and set sail, you're on your way back home."

"Frederick told me that most sailors have some special place—a snug harbor."

"Now ain't that the truth."

"When I met Isaac, we were in Hull," Sophie continued. "But he were a Bristol man—so I shifted ports and Freddy shifted his home port with me. So here we be."

"How long have you been married?" Jane asked.

"We just passed twenty-five years. Isaac left the seafarin' life fifteen years ago and we raised our young'uns. It's been a good life."

"Your children?"

"Adam and Theresa. He works down at the harbor. Bits of this and that, still learning. Tessie married a sailor, poor girl," Sophie said with a laugh. "And I'm thinking she'll make me a grandmother soon."

"And Mr Worth?" Jane said. "Freddy?"

"He's not one to settle down," Sophie said. "What with the navy and now this music and dancing, he's always on the move. No time for family but for a bit o' shore leave. Except for the one," she continued with a small smile. "Anne. That were her name. She were a lovely lass. Lived in Hull, and we knowed her a while. Freddy dearly loved that girl."

"What happened?"

"He asked her to marry him, o' course," Sophie said, "and she said 'yes.' But then her family had its say. He's got no means, that's what her mam said. And her da was a sailor and he didn't want his daughter to be marryin' no sailor. Anne were a beautiful girl. Her mother reckoned she could make a better match in town. Poor Freddy. He never had a chance."

"But, did she love him?"

"Makes no matter," Sophie said. "When the people you respect stand against a match, there's no help for it."

"No, I suppose. No, there really is not."

❧ 45 ❧

"**N**ow you can't be visiting a tavern looking like that!" Sophie said.
"Why?" Jane said.

"You'll be the talk of the place. *Oh, look,* they'll all be saying. *She's from a fine house. What's she doing down here?*"

"Oh," Jane said. "Unfortunately, my choices are rather limited."

The men had left the cottage after breakfast. "Inspecting the floating harbor," Isaac said. Opened only six years before, Worth had never had a proper tour of Bristol's new docks, locks, and canals.

The dancing master had proposed to begin the search for Woodman at six bells. Three o'clock in the afternoon, he had translated. *The men will be gone until then,* Jane thought, and she put herself in Sophie's hands.

"We can fix you up to make you less noticeable," Sophie said. "Your hair. A wrap. And I've got a thing or two."

Sophie lifted the lid on a chest, and Jane found herself caught up in her childhood, preparing for a masquerade.

A kerchief looked like it might suit. "With your hair down," Sophie said.

"Hmm," Jane said as she looked at herself in the mirror, not a full-sized glass but big enough. "No, I do not think that looks right."

"An apron?" suggested Sophie.

"A shawl?"

"Your hands are lovely—too nice for a working girl. These gloves? That's better. And here, try this. With this kerchief. Oh, and here's just the right cap. And then me old winter shawl."

Jane looked at herself again in the glass. Her visage was the same but in every other way, she seemed changed. "It is like a theatrical."

"Like being on the stage?"

"Yes, much the same," Jane said. "When I was young, my brothers and sister and I, and others sometimes, we would perform little plays. It was silly and a delightful diversion."

"That's somethin' I thinks all youngsters likes to do. Dress up. Be the mam or the da, like on Twelfth Night."

"Yes, that, too. There is some magic to it, I think." Jane looked at the glass again. "We have two chests at home, filled with costumes and stage properties from our theatrical adventures. My sister and I cannot bear to part with them. You put on a costume—it is all on the outer side—yet it changes you within somehow."

"A new frock will do that."

"Yes. That, too," Jane said. Then she turned once all around. "What do you think?"

Sophie looked Jane up and down and gave her answer consideration.

"I think you're far too pretty a lass to be visiting them sailors' taverns," she said. "But you look the part of the drab, to be sure. They'll not be taking you for a fine lady."

"Very good," Jane said. "Well done, Mrs Croft."

"Until you opens your mouth. If you don't want to be noticed, you'd best be letting Freddy do the talking."

❧46❧

"Ahoy," Worth said, calling to a barkeeper. "Looking for an old shipmate. Have you seen Woodman about? Nate Woodman?"

It had become a routine, an easy line of patter. Jane and Worth had started at the far end of the northern arm of the floating harbor, working their way from one tavern, public house, or inn to the next. They had been inside at least two dozen establishments, Jane thought. *Maybe.* She was not keeping a close count. Worth did the talking. She followed in what seemed like an appropriate, subservient way, though Worth warned her a couple of times to stay back from the counter.

The responses were all negative or cautious. Half the tapsters never heard of the man. The other half had not seen him in days, months, or years.

This place did not appear to have a name, no sign over the door. They only knew it was a tavern because two men stumbled out the door and they heard, more than they saw, the hard drinking within.

"Stay here," Worth had said.

Jane looked at him and rolled her eyes. After all the places she had been that night? Worth had seen the look, sighed, and led the way into the dingy room.

It was the darkest and most poorly finished establishment she had yet seen. Barrels topped with planks served as a bar; barrels, trestles, and boards formed most of the tables. A massive ship's wheel, suspended above the center of the room, provided the only hint of fine woodwork. Candle stubs and wax drippings showed it had once served as a kind of chandelier. *Not now, though. Better to leave the place in the gloom,* she thought, as Worth left her side to speak with the barkeeper.

"Woodman. Nate Woodman," he said. *Loud.* The place was noisy. "Have you seen him?"

The barkeeper started to speak but a man with two pints in hand spoke first.

"It's Woodman you wants? Chips? He's back there," he said, tilting his head toward the darkest corner.

Worth approached a man on a bench, tankard in hand, glaring at the room. Two men in chairs sat around the square table in front of him. As

Worth neared them, he saw the left hand of the man curled around his tankard. The tattoo.

"Woodman?" he said. "Nate Woodman? That you?"

The man narrowed his eyes.

"Nate, it's me, Freddy. Freddy Worth. Just wants to have a chat with you."

The man in the corner still did not speak. He had let go of his pint. His hands were on the edge of the table.

"Do you mind if we has a little sit down?" Worth asked.

"Aye," Woodman said. "I minds."

"It's important. We're just trying to get the name of a fella."

"Go 'way," the man mumbled.

"Nate, it'll just be a tick," Worth said. "I'll stand you another pint."

"Shove off," Woodman said, lowering his eyes and turning back to his drink.

"Listen, Nate, I'm just looking to get the name of a feller," Worth said. "It won't be no matter to him now on account of he's dead." The dancing master continued making a friendly, sort of laughing sound. "A naval sort, I think. A Frenchman."

Woodman shoved back the table and came to his feet. A butcher's knife appeared in his right hand, and he advanced on Worth. The tavern fell quiet. Men cleared out from the middle of the room. They grabbed their pints and formed a gallery as though this was not an uncommon spectacle.

Worth backed away.

"Nate, man. I want no trouble. We just wants to get his name."

Woodman advanced, menacing him with the blade. Worth moved behind a table in the middle of the room. The two men started a dance of sorts, left, then right. Worth kept the table between them, staying a little more than an arm's length away.

"Listen to me, Nate. There is no worry in it for you."

"Damn you," Woodman shouted and slashed his blade in the air over the table.

The two men had completed one time through the dance, one full turn around the table.

"Damn you," Woodman shouted again. He picked up a stool in his free hand and was about to hurl it at Worth when the enormous ship's wheel crashed down from overhead, smashing the table that separated the combatants.

Then…another voice. A strong, decisive voice. A soprano.

"What, pray tell, is wrong with you men?"

Jane stood next to the cleat on the wall where the rope that had tethered the nautical artifact had been secured. Her voice was loud and firm. The sudden assault from a completely unexpected quarter had an effect.

She stepped forward, surveyed the wrecked table, and faced the man called Woodman. She pressed her attack.

"You were a sailor, sir, or so I am told. What do you mean by this?" She gestured toward the knife. Woodman was pointing it at her—at a woman. He lowered his arm. She moved forward one more pace.

"You," she said, pointing at Woodman, "and this man"—pointing at Worth— "were shipmates!"

Her words struck home. Woodman's expression changed, the anger ebbing. More important, the knife had vanished back to wherever it had come from.

"Shipmates," he said, looking back at Worth.

"*Minerve*," Worth said.

"*Minerve*?" Woodman squinted, as if trying to bring the face into focus. "Worth?" he said at length. "Freddy? The *Minerve*? What, that were back in '95?"

"In '96, I think," Worth said. "Hardy was on board then. Lieutenant."

"Aye, and Nelson, too," Woodman said. "Come on her as a commodore."

"Aye."

"That were a long, long time ago."

"Aye."

"Well, how are you now?" Woodman said. "Come to Bristol, eh? Well, come. Sit down, man. Let's have a pint."

Their entertainment ended, the onlookers cleared the debris of the table and stowed the ship's wheel against a wall. Jane and Worth took the places of the men who had been with Woodman. Three pints of dark porter arrived and sat between them. The time the men had spent together on the *Minerve* had been brief; there was not much to recollect. The men spoke more of the war, heartily cursing the Bonaparte.

Jane gave her attention to the beverage. The first taste, a sip, put her in the mind of burned coffee lightened with spoiled milk. Not as horrible to look at but pungent and bitter. A second sip, almost equally as terrible, did provide a hint of small beer which failed to delight yet was familiar.

The men continued their conversation speaking about the state of the navy, as the war had ended. In an effort to be polite, she continued to take modest sips of her porter.

Worth, finally, brought the conversation around to the Frenchman.

"The constable's a fool," Worth said. "There is no inquiry or magistrates involved. It's just Miss Austen here wants to know what were at the bottom of it all."

Woodman was staring at Jane.

"You have our word, Mr Woodman," she said. "It was all so...so strange. It occurred at a party that I had planned. I must know more. Surely you can understand?" She looked at him sincerely. She took another sip of the porter. Waited. "Please."

Woodman drank deeply from his pint and wiped his mouth with his sleeve.

"It were supposed to be some sort o' jest," he said. "That's what we was told. There were no talk of shooting and killing. All the damn guns—beg pardon, ma'am," he said, interrupting himself. "The guns we was carrying didn't have no charges."

"The man in the white uniform?" Jane prompted.

"Aye, the frog," Woodman said. "He planned the whole thing. He come to town and visits a few taverns. Says he's looking for men for a kind of a lark—but he wants real seaman. It's a boarding party, he says."

"Why would you?" Jane said. "It sounds so very...odd. Why?"

"War's over, ma'am. Ships getting condemned and sent to the breakers. Crews paid off. They's no half pay like officers get for us seamen. They's no jobs. The frog offered us money. We took it."

"How much?" Jane asked.

Woodman laughed. "Supposed to be one pound for each man. We got half for signing on. We'd get the other ten shillings at the end. Fools we was. We didn't get paid."

"The Frenchman," Worth asked, "what sort o' man was he?"

"Can't be sure, but my guess, he were an officer. He spoke English. He had airs, though. Some nob...begging your pardon, ma'am."

Forgiving him with a nod, she took another sip.

"But he knew his business. Ordered the men about, braced 'em up, cracked the whip on the horses."

"The horses?" Worth said. "How did you travel?"

"He come for us in a coach. It were a two-day ride and we didn't know where we was at. Then we left the coachman and the coach and boarded a farm wagon. The frog drove us right up to the back of the place. When we got there, it were a complete surprise. Easy it was. Rounded up the servants and stable boys. We just followed his plan. Until it all went to hell...pardon, ma'am...and he got hisself killed."

"And then what happened?" Worth said.

"We withdrew. Rode back on the wagon. We was damn lucky to find the coach. The driver took us to Winchester—the closest harbor so's to speak—and wanted to get paid. There was no money. So, we quarreled, and it were every man for hisself."

"But why take the jewelry?" asked Jane.

"The frog told us to. But that weren't part of the plan and we ain't no thieves, ma'am. We left it."

Worth looked pensive. Woodman, after taking a deep swallow, looked fuzzy again. Jane took another sip and shook her head.

"Mr Woodman," she said, rousing him at the sound of her voice. "Is there anything you can tell us that might help us put a name to the Frenchman?"

Woodman scrunched his face in deliberation, shook his head, and took another long drink. Then the look of someone who might just have remembered something crossed his face.

"Bath," Woodman said. "He might'a come from Bath. First time he come, he were driving a gig. Nobody be takin' a gig for some long trip."

Jane grimaced.

"And I think I saw a mark on the buggy," Woodman continued. "I think it might've been hired outta Bath."

Worth bought Woodman another pint. Jane took another sip, and noted, rather curiously, that it was the last sip in the tankard.

They emerged into a cool, but not uncomfortably cold night. Jane missed her footing slightly, as she stepped onto the cobbles. Worth steadied her. She took his arm and they headed toward Sophie's house. After they rounded the last corner and prepared to knock on the door, Worth turned to face her.

"To Bath?"

"To Bath."

☙ 47 ❧

"Jane? Jane!"

The lady flew out the door and embraced her dear friend.

Was this the lady of the house? A fine house only steps from the Royal Crescent—and she answered her own door?

"Dorothea," Jane said, as the ladies stepped back, holding both hands and smiling at each other.

Worth carried Jane's traveling bag and satchel to the door. The lady indicated he should place them in the vestibule. He complied and left to tend the horse and gig at a mews two blocks away. Upon his return, he was again greeted by the mistress of the house.

"Jane's dancing master?" she said upon opening the door. "Mr Worth, I am told. I am Mrs Jones. How do you do?"

"Ma'am," Worth said, reddening. "I'm just to speak to Miss Austen and then I'll be off to find lodgings."

"Stuff and nonsense, sir," Mrs Jones said. "We have room enough for a regiment right here. Now drop your gear and follow me to the drawing room. We're about to have tea."

A teapot sat on a tray in the center of a rosewood game table. Jane was arranging cups and saucers. She nodded for him to sit, but he refrained.

"I can boil water," Mrs Jones said, making a return trip from the pantry with sugar and milk. "I do hope it hasn't curdled." She dipped a spoon in the milk and tasted it. "It will do. I have just the one girl now, you see, and I gave her the day. You could have let me know, Jane," she said. Her irritation was clearly affectionate. "Since Llewelyn's…well…it has been difficult."

"I do understand," Jane said. "Since Father's passing—"

"Yes, yes. Well, we must carry on. That's what Llewelyn would've said. Even if it is on an empty stomach. I am completely at a loss in the kitchen," she said, turning to Worth. "Boiling water, yes! But that is my limit."

Mrs Jones was a proper lady, Worth saw that, but not pompous or proud. *Neither thick nor thin—solid,* Worth thought. *And with a touch of a Welsh accent.*

"The girl will be back in the morning," Mrs Jones said. "There will be a breakfast so there's that to look forward to."

Smiling, Worth thought he might like Mrs Jones. "I spent some time working in a ship's galley. If I may…?"

"Mr Worth is a man of many talents," Jane said.

"You can cook?" Mrs Jones said. "Then by all means, take a look around and give it a go."

Mrs Jones seated herself and the ladies returned to their conversation. Worth returned later with a serving dish and three small plates.

"Toasted cheese," he said, sliding the teapot to one side and presenting the dish. "Well-loved in the wardroom and the captain's table."

The dish—the simple combination of well-toasted bread with melted cheese—bubbled and even burned just the slightest bit—delighted the ladies.

Worth removed the cozy and poured more tea.

"There is a purpose to our visit," Jane said as Worth, still uncomfortable, resumed his place at the table. "We are looking for a man."

"Well, we're not exactly looking for him," Worth said. "We know right where he is."

"Quite right," Jane said. "We want to identify a man. A man who currently resides in a pauper's grave in Chawton."

Mrs Jones looked more attentively at Jane.

"And it is possible, not at all certain but possible, that he may have been known in Bath."

"In a pauper's grave?" Mrs Jones said. "Why are you interested in the identity of some poor beggar?"

"He was no beggar," Jane said. "He was a Frenchman and by all appearances a gentleman, and possibly a naval officer."

"My. All that. Then how did he come to be buried in a pauper's grave?"

"It's complicated," Worth said. "Miss Austen celebrated her birthday with a ball this year and…"

"Your ball. Oh, yes. You received my reply? I regretted—"

"Dorothea, your note was so kind," Jane said. "You were present in spirit and as it all unfolded, that was surely the best way to attend."

Jane provided the description of the evening, the intrusion, and its fatal consequences. She concluded, "We want to discover the identity of the Frenchman, the intruder who led the invasion. And we have reason to believe he may have connections in Bath. We shall want to make in-quiries. Although now that I think of it, I am not exactly sure where to begin."

"Just asking after an old mate," Worth said. "No need for any more than that."

"That should be easy enough," Mrs Jones said. "Seeking an acquain-tance. By the bye, my friend is searching for an old friend. A French gen-tleman, but he had good English. Blond hair. Rather handsome. Give 'em a little wink. Do you know anyone?"

"That's it exactly," Worth said. "With all these years of war, there can't be too many men fitting that description. A name and we'll be getting somewhere."

"Shall we visit the baths?" Jane said. "A few turns around the Pump Room. You might see people there. The promenades will be empty this time of year, I am afraid."

"No, my dear. We shall gather all the finest gentlefolk of Bath in one place and question them all," Mrs Jones said with a note of triumph in her voice.

Jane and Worth looked at her puzzled.

"Where?" Jane said.

"Aye, and how?" Worth said.

Mrs Jones enjoyed her brilliant plan for a moment longer and then explained. "Tomorrow night. The Advent Assembly. It's the most popu-lar ball of the winter season. Everyone who can dance, and many who cannot, will be there. Your Frenchman sounds like the sort of man who might have been seen at a dance or two, don't you think?"

They looked at each other and nodded.

"So, we shall attend the assembly together."

"But, I cannot," Jane said. "I have nothing appropriate to wear."

"Pish! Jane, we'll find you something from my wardrobe. Maria will be here tomorrow, and she can take in the necessary tucks for you."

"That sounds good for Miss Austen, but…"

"As for you, Mr Worth, your size is not so different from that of my late husband. We shall be able to fit you out splendidly, I am sure."

"But, I'm no gentleman."

"Bother. Neither was Llewelyn, nor are half the men who attend, de-spite their money and titles."

"But I'll be a stranger to 'em."

"Fear not, Mr Worth," Mrs Jones said. "We will polish you up and pass you off as a Polish prince or some such. Oh, Jane. I have been dreading this for so long now. It will be a sort of grand farewell for me. Your presence will be a blessing. This inquiry business will give me purpose. And to be accompanied by a Polish prince!" She laughed. "It will make it ever so much better for me. Please say you will come. Please."

❧ 48 ❧

"Perfect. That is perfect," Mrs Jones said as Jane emerged from behind a screen, wearing a deep blue *robe a l'anglaise*.

Jane nodded and smiled, admiring herself in a long looking glass.

"My blue cloak. Your hair is lovely. A ribbon—matching the gown—I have that. Your hair in a chignon. Miss Jane Austen, you shall be the belle of our ball."

Finding the proper attire for Mr Worth proved more daunting. Mr Jones' closets provided an array of well-fitting jackets, but none seemed to satisfy the ladies, Mrs Jones especially.

"Green," Mrs Jones said as Worth appeared in one jacket. "Green is too sallow. No, that will not do."

"Oh dear, all brown and black, Mr Worth? Will you top it off with a shooting jacket? You are not going to a hunt. It is a ball!"

A light green and buff coat brought howls of laughter from both ladies.

"Llewelyn did attempt to keep up with fashion but this..." Mrs Jones said.

"It has a sporting look about it," Jane said.

"It has a look that says his tailor was sporting with him," Mrs Jones said.

The next outfit provoked even greater laughter. The next? Declared only fit for a funeral.

Mrs Jones took matters into her own hands. Leaving Worth standing in the antechamber wearing his mourning garb, she withdrew into her husband's closets. She emerged a good ten minutes later, with a charcoal jacket and waistcoat of deep burgundy, gold, black, and cream.

The jacket, Worth discovered, fit well, not nearly as loose as the others he had tried. He looked at himself in a long glass and shook his head.

"It," Worth started, "it's a good fit. But, ah, I've never...I mean..."

"It is a perfect fit, Mr Worth," Jane said. "Dorothea, I think it may be the handsomest garment I have ever seen."

"Llewelyn cut a particularly dashing figure in his day. Made the ladies swoon." She nudged Jane gently with her elbow and said softly, "Can you blame me?"

"That will do, sir," Mrs Jones said to Worth, "We have but one item to address—the shoes."

"Your husband's boots are far too small for me," Worth said. "I gave 'em a quick try."

"Then we shall go into town and acquire something appropriate."

"Mrs Jones," Worth started to protest.

"You look so well, sir. You look the part of a prince, I daresay. We cannot have it spoilt."

Worth clicked the heels of the shoes he was wearing and pointed down at them. "I know they're not stylish, but they're not bad looking those," Worth said. "With some blacking and a good rub, they'll do. They're good dancing shoes."

Now it was Jane who nudged Mrs Jones.

"He is correct, Dorothea. With a little attention, his shoes will do well."

Mrs Jones nodded in agreement.

"And to speak the truth," Jane said, "I rather expect no one will be looking at his feet."

❧49❧

"This, of course is the Great Octagon," Mrs Jones said as she ushered Jane and Worth into the Upper Assembly Rooms. "The ladies' cloakroom to the right," she said with a nod, "the Tea Room…"

Mrs Jones continued but Worth was not attending. He looked up at the dome some forty feet above. The massive chandelier. Four white marble fireplaces surrounded a magnificent parquet floor. Four doorways occupied the other walls of the huge, eight-sided chamber.

Worth had been inside all the finest assembly rooms in London and Edinburgh. He had seen elegant ballrooms in great houses and castles across the breadth of Britain. He had never seen a place such as this. He shook his head in wonder.

"Would you like to see the Ball Room?" Mrs Jones said.

Worth nodded.

Mrs Jones guided him into the largest ballroom he had ever seen. His head swiveled and his face went slack as he took in the sight.

One hundred feet in length, nearly fifty feet wide. Five enormous chandeliers above the beautiful oakwood dance floor. To the left, a balcony overlooked a bank of doors. The foot of the hall, the entrance for concerts and theatricals.

To the right, a low stage with musicians tuning and performing the familiar rituals of preparation for a dance.

Jane, who likely had visited these rooms a hundred times or more during her years in Bath, seemed to delight in the dancing master's awe.

After depositing their cloaks, they toured the Tea Room and the Card Room, each as impressive as the next in its own way.

It was not the ornamentation or the fixtures that made the chambers so extraordinary, though all of that was very fine. More than the architectural detail, it was the space. The air. The proportions of the rooms. And as the rooms filled, the place became truly alive. Worth found himself filled with genuine wonder.

He saw Jane and Mrs Jones had returned from the ladies' rooms.

Mrs Jones seems especially lively, Worth thought, as she called out to some people across the Octagon, approaching others as they passed by:

"So good to see you."

"It's been so long."

"How are you?"

"Have you seen ...?" And on she went.

"You remember Miss Austen," she said to one elegantly attired matron. "She resided with us during the aughts."

"Of course," the lady replied, showing not the slightest hint of recognition.

Now Mrs Jones took Worth by the arm.

"And may I present Prince Frederick."

At this, the matron's eyes widened. Worth shot a sideways glance at Mrs Jones.

"Prince, you say." She extended a hand. Worth gave an imperceptible sigh and took her hand and bowed over it in a most gentlemanly manner. "And what is your principality?"

Worth looked at Mrs Jones who smiled and waved her hand.

"He has barely a word in English," she said. "He's from the Continent. Poland, I think. Yes, that must be it. Poland."

"Richard," the lady said. "Richard, come here."

At her command, an elderly gentleman with a halo of white hair, wearing a green velvet coat and breeches, came to her side.

"You must meet Prince Frederick."

Now the gentleman was chuffing at Worth and greeting him with proper courtesy. Worth responded with nods and bows while the elderly gentleman's wife continued. "Some principality in Poland. Does not speak a word of English."

"A Polish prince, eh!" the elderly man said. "And no English? Well now, here is a happy chance. Joseph," he said, waving to another gentleman who had just arrived.

Joseph came at the older man's bidding.

"Joseph, we have one of your countrymen here. It's…ah…"

"Prince Frederick," his wife said.

"Yes, Prince Frederick," the older man said. "But he hasn't a word of English."

Joseph smiled broadly, clicked his heels, and greeted Worth with a bow suitable for royalty.

"Pozdrowienia, wasza wysokość. Witamy w Bath. Gdzie się zatrzymujesz? jest nas tu kilku. Musimy umówić się na obiad."

Worth listened attentively, allowed his mouth a grim smile, and slowly looked at Mrs Jones. For the first time since he had met her, the lady's ebullience seemed to fade, but only for an instant.

"Polish," she said. "Why, you must have misheard me. Or, was it me? Yes, I am sure it was me. I misspoke. Polish, indeed. It is Swedish! Gothenburg or Sölvesborg or someplace like that, eh, Prince Frederick?"

Worth looked at her in wonder and nodded.

"There you are," Mrs Jones said. "My apologies. Now we must find the Andersens, for they have some Swedish." She took Worth by the right arm and Jane by the left. "Or is it Danish? Well, we must go. So nice to see you."

They fled into the Ball Room where they retreated to the warmth of the fire on the far side of the floor for a tête-à-tête. Giggles escaped Jane's lips; her body shook with much more pent-up laughter. Worth was shaking his head and smiling broadly.

"Polish?"

"I apologize, Mr Worth," Mrs Jones said.

"I have the title for a new novel," Jane said. *"Mrs Jones and the Polish Prince."*

"I do beg your pardon," Mrs Jones said. "I know we have inquiries to make, and we shall make them. It is just…it is just that I did so want everything to be gay."

"Dorothea, it shall forever be remembered with delight," Jane said. "We shall rendezvous often in years to come and shake with laughter at the recounting of the tale of Mrs Jones and her Polish Prince."

She had taken Mrs Jones's hand and held it warmly.

"Now, we must be about our business," Mrs Jones said. "Jane and I will mingle with our acquaintances. Mr Worth, we commend you to your own resources."

Worth spent most of the ball on the side of the dance floor, observing.

The music? Acceptable but not inspiring. The man on the pianoforte had trouble with his tempos. The fiddler repeatedly had to slow him down. The wind player lacked the spirit of the invention that Thomas displayed, hewing strictly to the melodies.

The fourth musician seemed familiar, but Worth could not place him. He was the most versatile of the performers. He played the violoncello about half the time, giving the group a strong foundation and helping keep the pianoforte in time. He also had an Irish harp and a lute he used for the quietest pieces. But in such a large hall, filled with dancers, those instruments lacked the voice to carry.

It was with his mandolin that he provided the greatest delight. Either carrying the melody or providing rhythmic energy, he injected wonderful spirit in the more lively pieces. *Well done,* Worth thought.

The dance selection was wanting in the dancing master's estimation, a reflection of popular taste. Minuets and quadrilles for the most part. There was a gavotte which the master of the ceremonies assured the assembly was the newest, most fashionable dance. The occasional country dance was included as a sop, it seemed, to the elders in the crowd.

Worth introduced himself to the master of ceremonies—a man called Colonel Davies. Curiously, Worth thought, the gentleman was elected by the subscribers to the dances in the Upper Assembly Rooms. He served as a sort of official host for the town. And while he may have been well suited for arranging introductions and encouraging attendance, in his artistic role, he seemed unimaginative. Times were changing, to be sure. At many balls and assemblies, including this evening's, ladies in attendance were charged with selecting the music and accompanying dance. But ought not the master of ceremonies lend a guiding hand?

Still, Worth thought with a sigh, *professional courtesy.*

"London, eh?" the colonel asked. "Wilson? Certainly, I know of him. We have put a few of his dances on the programs. Musicians? All in residence here for the season. Well, except for the one at the end, the one with the cello and mandolin. Annoying little instrument that, the mandolin, don't you think? He's from Birmingham or Brighton or somewhere. Filling in. So, you know the dances, eh? Can't let a spare gentleman go to waste."

In a trice, Worth found himself being introduced to a Miss Coopersmith. The music for a dance had just ended. New sets formed for quadrilles.

Assuming his best gentleman's identity, Worth led his partner to the floor. As there was room, he started a new set at the head of the hall, near the musicians.

The master of ceremonies announced Challonier's *Second Set of Favorite French Quadrilles,* a popular arrangement of five figures. He felt a brief pang of desperation when he looked at his partner. She appeared completely lost.

"These are new dances to you?" he inquired.

She nodded. "Perhaps I should sit down?"

"We have our set now," Worth said. "Not the time to withdraw. We must engage. I can prompt you the figures."

She looked up with worry but nodded.

Worth had started a quick description of the first quadrille when he heard a voice from behind.

"Freddy," someone said. "That you, Freddy?"

The mandolin player. Worth paused his tutorial and turned toward the musician. The name came to him.

"Foxwood," Worth said. "Imagine my surprise."

"Looking quite the gentleman there, Freddy."

"It's not a good time," Worth said quietly, darting his eyes toward his partner who was listening attentively to the conversation.

"If you got your fiddle maybe you can sit in?" Foxwood said.

"You are a musician?" the young lady said.

"At the interval," Worth said.

"Foxwood," the leader of the ensemble said. "May we prevail upon you to play with us anytime soon?"

The other three couples in the set had full command of the figures. Worth gave his partner a few prompts. With glances, slight gestures, and the occasional push, the experienced dancers guided the girl through the figures. She had a musician's timing, grace, and a good sense of direction—knew her right from her left. As the fifth figure repeated many elements of the first, the quadrille came to a smooth, flowing, satisfying conclusion. The girl was a very good dancer and the dancing master told her as much.

Worth avoided observation through the next two dances, then the master of ceremonies announced the interval.

"Freddy, old boy. What a surprise. Delighted to see you," Foxwood said, greeting the dancing master like a friend of the longest standing. Worth had worked closely with the man. Once. It was a birthday ball for a nine-year-old girl, memorable because they were paid very well and let off early.

"Good to see you," Foxwood said

"You're looking fit," Worth said. "It's a splendid hall and you're providing music to match."

"Rubbish," Foxwood said. "Unimaginative, either plodding or racing, dreary tune selection, and you cannot actually hear the music when you're at the bottom of the long set. But of course, I thank you for the fine sentiments."

"I'm looking for information," Worth said. "There's a fellow—a Frenchman—and he may be well known in Bath. Uncommonly handsome he was, golden hair. Might have been a sailor."

"I'm just sitting in for a fortnight. If you want information about the dancers here, you'd best speak with the boss."

The leader of the ensemble greeted Worth civilly.

"The young Frenchman, the blond hair. Dashing. Extremely handsome. Yes, I know him to see him. Not a subscriber though. Only comes occasionally. Must be someone's friend." He nodded to Worth and left the stage to speak with the master of ceremonies.

Worth was thanking Foxwood for his assistance when the pianoforte player caught his eye.

"Off to the Tea Room now," Foxwood was saying. "With me for a cuppa?"

Worth shook his head. Foxwood left the stage. He was alone on the stage with the pianoforte player.

"You know something?"

"He is easily recognizable," the young man said. "So, so very handsome."

Up close, Worth realized the man was young. Very young. And slight. Very slight. And painfully shy. He spun back toward Worth on his stool, stood, moved uncomfortably close, and spoke rapidly in a whisper.

"I've seen him here frequently, but more often in the lower rooms. He is so handsome. And when he speaks, his accent…it is just so, so, perfect. Like you, I would like to meet him…"

And then the young man stopped.

"D'ye know anything that might help me?" Worth asked, trying to be encouraging. "I just want his name."

"If you find it out, will you tell me? Please," the young man said.

"Aye, aye, I will. But I need you to help me."

"Ask for him at Mary's," the musician said in a rush. Then he fled the stage.

❧50❧

The Frenchman had been there before, but his identity had not been confirmed.

"Becky Robinson. I have known her for years," Jane said. "She said she had encountered a man just as I described, in lines and sets. She even danced with him as her partner once, but he never gave his name."

"He seems to have been intent on remaining nameless," Worth said.

"He never hid his face," Mrs Jones said. "Several of my friends recognized him, danced with him, and found him most charming and accomplished. But none of them knew his name."

"How could it be? In polite society?" Jane said.

"Oh, Jane, when it is a handsome, charming man in question, the boundaries of polite society become rather indistinct."

"Dorothea," Jane said.

"It's Bath," Mrs Jones said. "Things are changing. You must keep up, you know. And besides, dear Jane, it is only a dance."

"The musicians knew of the Frenchman as well," Worth said. "And one made a suggestion. Mrs Jones, do you know of a place called Mary's?"

Mrs Jones looked thoughtful. Then her eyes widened.

"I suppose…it could be… Well, it is possible…not that I should ever admit to it in polite society. There is, I have heard, a very discreet and very disreputable establishment called Mother Mary's. It's a name that is mentioned only in whispers. Is it possible? Oh, I certainly hope that it is not, but…" Mrs Jones paused. "Jane, Mr Worth, the assembly is ending. I have duties I must attend to. And farewells, more farewells."

Mrs Jones took her leave.

"Dorothea is anxious to see as many of her friends as she can," Jane told Worth. "Her conversations tonight have been rather strange, I think."

"How so?"

"It is as though she is parting company with them forever," Jane said.

"She does appear to be in some financial distress."

"I tried to inquire, discreetly of course, but she completely disregarded me."

"Mrs Jones doesn't seem to be the lady for beatin' around the bush," Worth said.

"You would suggest more direct tactics?"

"Aye."

"Never mind the maneuvers, just go straight at them?"

"Worked for Nelson."

"Perhaps," Jane said. "But we must not be distracted from our mission. How do we locate this Mother Mary's establishment?"

"*We*, Miss Austen? There's to be no we in takin' on a situation like that."

Jane heard the concern in his voice. She expected it.

"You are my employee I shall remind you, Mr Worth. I have trod the sawdust floors of the crudest taverns on the docks of Bristol! What more sinister establishment could there possibly be here in the elegance of Bath?"

"This Mother Mary's will be a most different sort of place," Worth said. "No lady would—"

"Mr Worth! Your first task, Mr Worth, is to discern the location of the establishment. How do you propose to do that?"

Worth opened his mouth, but nothing came out.

"It does not seem to be the sort of establishment Dorothea's friends would know of or admit to knowing of," Jane said. "I could inquire of the master of ceremonies, but that might prove awkward. The young musician who told you of it. Does he know?"

"Nay. Or he won't admit it. I pressed him," Worth said, shaking his head.

"Promenade the streets looking for a sign?" Jane said. They both smiled. Tight smiles.

"You believe him? You think the place truly exists?"

"He believes it exists. Mrs Jones believes it exists."

"We could call on the constable's office."

"If it's the sort of place I'm thinking, they most likely knows all about it. And they know where it is so's they can drop by to grease their fists," Worth said. "But they'll not be telling the likes of us."

They were silent. The music and noise of the dance swirled around them.

"The hacks! Is there anyone who knows a town better than a hackney driver?"

"Aye," Worth said slowly. "Aye."

"We have our course set for the morrow," Jane said. "I will breakfast with Dorothea and pry into her business. You, sir, will hie yourself off to the hackney stands and ply them with your silver tongue."

"There's a different sort of silver what might be more useful," Worth said.

"Yes," Jane said, and sighed. "But make it silver. Not gold."

"Aye," Worth said.

The music for the previous dance had ended. A familiar strain filled the hall, once through as was the custom. Jane recognized it. Almost in unison, they said, "*The Sussex Waltz*."

Glancing up at the musicians, they saw the master of ceremonies in conference with Mrs Jones. When the conversation ended, Mrs Jones remained at the top of the center set in the company of an older gentleman. *A very handsome older gentleman,* Jane thought, wondering if he might be unmarried.

"Dorothea made the music selection," Jane said.

"And she has given Colonel Davies the dance," Worth said.

Mrs Jones, however, seemed not to be interested in her partner. She was watching the dancing master and Jane.

Worth caught her gaze and nodded imperceptibly. He turned to his companion.

"Miss Austen, would you do me the honor?"

Jane blushed. "Mr Worth."

Taken off guard, she looked about. She, too, was caught in Mrs Jones's view. She replied with her eyes and a smile and turned to the dancing master.

"Yes."

❧ 51 ❧

Mr Worth led Miss Austen to the top of the hall to start a new set. Colonel Davies briefed the dancing master; told him what the figures would be. Turn by the right and cast…

The First Change
Miss Austen
As the set assembled below them, Jane recalled the country dances in Steventon. Tune and dance always went together. The entire set danced the first time through. This modern, fashionable dancing with couples below waiting to join in? *Dancing has lost its way in these times*, she thought. But then, she considered the pleasures of couples dancing a waltz.

She glanced at Worth, noting how Mr Jones' suit fit him perfectly. She looked away into the ballroom and then her eyes came back to Mr Worth. *Quite the handsomest gentleman in the hall*, she thought. And yet, he seemed disquieted.

Two bold chords from the musicians. The dance began.

The Second Change
Mr Worth
Rarely limited or self-conscious about his injury, his prosthetic hand felt like a great weight anchored to his wrist when he offered it—his wood and leather apparatus—to Jane. *It provides support, yes, but no feeling,* he thought.

When musicians dance, their timing is routinely perfect. Anticipating, rising on their toes to join hands on the precise sounding of the correct note as they begin a change. Yet, however perfect the timing, the steps and pace, the dance felt wrong. His hand had never felt so large or clumsy or so unfeeling. Circling with neighboring gentlemen caused him no distress.

It was his hand-turn with Jane. His hand.

The Third Change
Miss Austen
Cast, turn away, lose all connection as the others move between. Lost. And found. Yes. *There you are.* Jane loved the simple drama of their progress as it played out each time through the longways dance.

She sensed her partner's disquiet, however, and she believed she understood it. *Never mind the maneuvers*, she thought to her own amusement. *Flout convention.*

As they came together for the turn, she avoided taking the dancing master's hand. Instead she slipped her wrist inside his guard, capturing his wrist with her own.

She noted the surprise in his eyes. She drew her arm back firmly to create a strong connection. No hands or fingers required.

Connected wrist to wrist, the distance between them was lessened. The turn: shorter, smoother, easier. Her partner made a final turn to end facing toward the music, forearms close, wrists connected.

Warm, she thought. *Quite warm.*

THE FOURTH CHANGE
Mr Worth

As they began the change, Jane again slipped her wrist inside his forearm to support herself through the turn. The unusual maneuver had caught him unawares the first time. Now, it seemed the most advantageous manner for executing the turn. He found it a most satisfying way to retain and release the energy of their motion.

Warm, he thought. *Rather warm.*

THE FIFTH CHANGE
Miss Austen

This melody, the *Sussex Waltz,* was said to come from strains borrowed from Amadeus. Jane had no personal knowledge of the origin of the melody, but its beauty led her to believe that it might very well have been touched by master Mozart's hand.

The awkward instant having been resolved, Jane floated through the figures. As when a pebble has been removed from one's shoe, she was left only to think of nothing; nothing but the music, the dance, the flow, the impeccable timing of her partner, and the changes, of course. *What change?* She had lost count. Only the present change mattered.

THE SIXTH CHANGE
Mr Worth

When the dance goes well, it flows gracefully, linked to the music, carrying couples up and down the set in harmony. When the dance is perfect, the entire world ceases to exist. Music takes command of the dancer's body and allows the mind complete peace; complete freedom to be within the music and, if you are truly fortunate, to be with some special person with whom you are sharing precious time.

Turning, casting, crossing, and passing his smiling partner, Worth had lost count of the changes. The music swelled. New couples prepared to join in at the tops. *The last change? Perhaps.*

A beautiful tune and a lovely dance. But, as he led Jane up the set and then separated from her one more time, he imagined how it might feel to capture her in his arms; his right hand supporting her back, hand in hand with his left. He wished that perhaps, instead of this country dance, they might have been a couple for a waltz.

The Last Change

Miss Austen

The music spoke clearly, each instrument adding to the harmonic drama in preparation for the finale. The last change, she was certain.

As they completed the turn, their arms entwined, she drew her partner perhaps one inch closer than ever before and held the connection an instant longer. The dance was ending; she did not want to let it go.

But of course, she must. They must separate, meet, cross, and smile. *Quite the most beautiful melody,* she thought, as Mr Worth and the second lady changed places, then she smiled as she and the second gentleman did the same.

Circle a half and *pas de bas*. A fine dance, she acknowledged, moving first to cross with the second gentlemen. Then the others. Another circle a half, cast, and lead. The music diminuendo to a blissful instant of silence.

As she stood opposite her partner, she dropping a curtsy and he making a proper bow, she imagined how it might have felt, to feel her partner's strong right arm on her back. To trust in her partner's arms. To whirl around the floor. She found herself desiring that perhaps, instead of this country dance, they might have been a couple for a waltz.

❧52❧

"More eggs? No. Then do have some more tea," Mrs Jones said, fussing over Jane.

"Yes, more tea, please," Jane said settling back in her chair.

The breakfast prepared by Mrs Jones' girl, Maria, had been unusual. Toast, eggs, tea, and little else. Mrs Jones had started to ask the girl about bacon or ham but was stopped by the worried shake of the girl's head.

"A warm day and fair weather," Mrs Jones said. "Perhaps we shall take a turn on the Crescent. It's only two streets over. The baths are rather sedate this time of year," she went on. "Would you care to take the waters or at least a few turns around the Pump Room?"

"Dorothea," Jane said, "What is wrong? Please tell me."

Mrs Jones looked at Jane but did not speak.

"Last night, when you spoke to your friends, it was as though you were saying farewell. Forever. What is it? Are you well?"

"My husband died, Jane. My best friend. The man I loved for six and twenty years. Is that not enough?"

"It is cause for great mourning, to be sure, but Llewelyn has been gone these twelve months. Only now you take this turn? No, Dorothea. I know you too well. Something else is at work here. Pray tell me. Please."

"You're too persistent, Jane. There is nothing."

"I do not believe you. I have seen signs of your distress. I can guess. I can imagine. Do you think my imaginings will be less of a burden than the truth?"

"The truth!" Mrs Jones said. "If only we could have the truth." She cradled the warm cup in her hands and looked at Jane. "I am ruined. My life is shattered. I must leave these lodgings. I must leave Bath. I must leave."

At this, the good, brave, joyful woman Jane had known for so many years wept.

Jane poured more tea while Mrs Jones composed herself.

"The mine closed," she said. "The ore ran out. There was no more tin. It'd been a good living, but Llewelyn knew his business. He planned for the eventuality. He saved, planned wisely. Two additional mines were opened, but the ore was poor. They were not profitable. He had invested in a canal company that would link Cardiff with the Rhondda Valley. It was outmaneuvered by the DeWintons, who led another consortium and gained control of the planned route. His investment was lost. Another investment in South America grew splendidly but was undone in that little trade bubble of 1810. His position was secure, but the merchant house in London was bankrupted and that brought him down.

"Llewelyn was left in financial distress. But he remained optimistic. 'Some good will come,' he'd say. 'It'll all work itself round.' He found an opportunity with a syndicate. Sugar from the West Indies. The syndicate was led by a man with a growing reputation as a shrewd man of business. You know the name. Percival Ellicott."

"Ellicott?" Jane started at the news. "Percival?"

Mrs Jones looked at her with a thin smile. "Yes. The same."

"There were numerous investors in Bath," she went on. "Mr Ellicott made only rare appearances. Most of the business were conducted by his associate, a little man with a black mustache."

"Sloat?" Jane said.

"No, no. Another name—short—ah, I have it. Ponts. A Mr Ponts. The business all seemed proper. There were deeds and papers, letters of correspondence. The syndicate paid a handsome dividend at first. Then the money stopped. In a way, the whole business seemed to have vanished. Gone up in smoke.

"We had letters from Mr Ellicott saying he had no knowledge of the syndicate. A deputation of investors was assembled, led by Llewelyn. It traveled to Hampshire.

"Mr Ellicott denied all knowledge of the syndicate. He said they were deluded. Similarly, he denied the existence of a Mr Ponts. The investors provided evidence including deeds with Lord Kellingsford's signature and seal. Percival laughed and dismissed them as forgeries. For most of the investors, their shares amounted to an annoying but trivial loss. For Llewelyn, it represented the remainder of his capital. So, he undertook the mission to the Indies to rescue the investment."

Mrs Jones stopped again to compose herself.

"You know how his mission ended with a tropical fever on a faraway shore. I am a woman," she continued. "I have no man of business. I have no family. I have no funds."

She took more tea.

"I have considered taking a voyage, out to sea. Far away."

She sipped her tea.

"I have had a very good life. I know this. I do not propose to end in a debtor's tomb. Or in the tombs with debtors."

Percival Ellicott? Sloat? Ponts? The Frenchman? Jane thought of the puzzle pieces.

"Dorothea, there is more to this. Much more. I do not know what, but you must not despair."

"Despair? Oh no, Jane. I am past despair. The business is simple. I have reached the endgame and I must resign."

"No. The business is not at all simple," Jane said. "We must look at the papers and deeds you have. Myself. Mr Worth. We will look at them with fresh eyes. My brother Henry can serve as your man of business. He understands these financial maneuverings and he knows many of the leading bankers in Bath. There is an evil web here, woven through with deaths and deceit. I am determined it shall be untangled."

☙ 53 ❧

Worth returned to the lodgings at ten o'clock that morning. "Four bells of the forenoon watch," Jane said, welcoming him to the table for toast and tea.

Worth laughed.

"You're getting good at telling time the proper way," he said and began his report. "I talked to six or eight drivers who swore they'd never heard o' such a place. Mother Mary's? What's that? Girls' school? A nunnery? The Sisters of Saint Mary? Finally, I found one who said he might have heard of a place called Mother Mary's which, he said, was known to be a very secret sort of establishment."

"Did he know its location?" Jane said.

"Nay, he just thought it were by the river, near the quay."

"A very seedy quarter," Mrs Jones said. "Extremely dangerous."

"I queried several other hacks. Two had heard of Mother Mary's, but they dinna know where it was, or at least they weren't telling me."

"So, we do not know where it is?" Jane said.

"I'm getting to it. I moved along and was talking to the hacks in front of Amery's Hotel with more silver showing. With a couple of 'em, it seemed like certain they knew, but they weren't talking. But I seen the porter at the hotel. He was watching me with great interest. I walked away, down the street, talking to some other hacks, and let the ones at the hotel move on. Then I went back to the porter. Ten shillings it took, but he give me the whole way of it."

"The address?" Mrs Jones asked.

"Nay. No address. Just a backways alley and door. Down by the river like the one hack said. Between Back Street and Corn, off Little Corn Street."

"Are you confident of the location?"

"At ten shillings? I looked straight away. The alley? The door? They're real. The rest of it, I'll have to see."

"The rest of it?" asked Jane.

"The place ain't open until eight o'clock—eight in the evening," Worth said, then added, "that's—"

"Eight bells," Jane said. "The end of the first dog watch."

"And there's a code," Worth said. "A special knock you gotta give for 'em to let you in. I'm thinking I'll be going about ten o'clock. Back by midnight. Let you know what I find."

"We shall return, Dorothea, by midnight, to let you know what we discover," Jane said.

"Miss Austen, these are terrible places. No lady should—"

"Mr Worth, am I not your employer—"

"Mrs Jones," Worth started, turning to that lady.

"Who provided you with the silver to pay for the information you obtained?" Jane continued.

Mrs Jones returned Worth's look and sighed. She wore a tight smile, shrugging her shoulders.

"Remember Bristol, Mr Worth," Jane said. "I am no shrinking violet."

"Nay, but Miss Austen, this kind o' place is different!"

"Quite different, I am sure. Quite different. And this authoress relishes the opportunity to see this netherworld for herself."

"Miss Austen—"

"Mr Worth, would you have me discharge you and undertake the quest by myself?"

Silence.

"Good."

"Now, Dorothea, as I have learned, I must dress my part so as not to stand out."

"My wardrobe is at your disposal."

"Perhaps, with the right trimmings? We must look for something flagrantly disrespectable. I believe that for this night, I must look the part of a trollop."

❧ 54 ❦

The hack left its passengers off on Corn Street. Worth and his companion, a woman who in no outward way resembled Jane Austen, turned down Little Corn Street and entered the unnamed alley. The cold, damp atmosphere penetrated her cloak and she shivered. The rank odors caused her stomach to clench.

Jane swallowed hard as they approached. In the darkness of the alley, a thin line of light at the bottom of the door shone like a lighthouse beacon.

As Worth prepared to knock, he chuckled. "Here you are," he said quietly. "Having a nice wooden hand is good for something."

They heard faint voices from the other side of the door. And music.

Worth knocked. One, two, three. A pause. One knock. Another pause. One, two.

Then they waited. And waited.

"Perhaps a change in the code," Jane said. She shivered.

"Maybe. Maybe they dinna hear?"

Worth started to raise his hand to knock again when the door swung open.

❧55❧

"A *sonotina*," Jane said absentmindedly as she looked around the elegant chamber. "I do believe it is by Plyel. I have it in my music collection."

Gleaming brass sconces illuminated the small vestibule. The great room glittered with crystal and silver. Lace and linen covered the tables. Large mirrors hung on the walls, adding to the chamber's impression of spaciousness.

The liveried man holding the door cleared his throat and gestured them into the room. Upon locking the door behind them, he faced the newcomers.

"The dinner seating has passed," he said. "But our small plates remain. You wish to be seated?"

While treating them cordially, the man stared at Worth and Jane, with a bewildered air. He held out his hands. Jane and Worth looked at each other before Worth responded.

"Ah. Aye. Your wrap," he said to Jane.

"Oh, no," she said, drawing her shawl around herself more snugly.

The footman led them to a small table at the farthest end of the room, and they felt the eyes of two dozen patrons, mostly men—gentlemen—all fastidiously dressed. There were, Jane noted, two ladies as well. Two tall ladies, elegantly attired with splendid hair that must be wigged.

The music stopped. The room quieted.

Two gentlemen at a nearby table rose. Two more men from the bar joined them, as did the man who had been playing the pianoforte.

Jane and Worth found themselves hemmed in by a wall of forbidding faces.

Worth whispered to Jane, "'Tis a molly house."

"What's that?" said the first man who had arrived at the table. "We can't hear you."

"I think he said this is a 'molly house'," the second man said.

"A molly house!" said the first.

The man from the pianoforte leaned over the table. "A molly house? Was that what you were saying? You went out for a stroll and stumbled into a den of he-strumpet, molly men?"

"Who are you?" a man from the bar asked. "And just what are you about?"

"You'll not be abusing this lady," Worth said, standing.

"This lady?" the musician asked. "Some tarted up little wench? In this here molly house? She does not look like a genteel lady. Are you sure?"

Worth's fists balled as he readied his reply, but another voice roared, dominating the din and silencing the room.

"The hell you say!" The newcomer's bellow was followed by a series of profanities along with commands to "behave yourselves."

The men who had surrounded the table moved away and left Jane staring at a very large, handsome man wearing a lavender gown trimmed with lace and blue silk ribbons. He wore a plum-colored satin spencer over his gown. His hair, brown but nearly rowan, and shoulder length, tumbled back from under a plum-coloured bandeau while his face was framed in delicate ringlets. His natural hair or a wig? Jane could not say.

"New arrivals, eh?" he said, his voice *basso profundo*. "Now, there's no cause for alarm. Or disputes or fisticuffs! Let us be more welcoming." He chivvied the angry men back towards their tables, then snapped his fingers. "Aha! I have it. Something from the cellar—a very nice Madeira, just arrived from a dear friend in Cornwall. Shall we try it?"

He...? Or she? Jane wondered. Perhaps, as in the theatre, the outward appearance expresses the inner truth.

She, Jane decided.

The newcomer—the peacemaker—waved to a serving man.

"The case is still in the cellar," she said. "It has not been racked yet. Bring two...no...make it three bottles."

Pacified by the promised wine, the concerned customers continued to withdraw and with a few smiles and murmurs of approval. The waiter bustled toward the cellar, and calm was restored.

"Good evening," the newcomer said, addressing Jane and Worth and dropping a very proper curtsy. "You have my apologies for that little bit of confusion. You can appreciate, I am sure, the concern that the discovery of...strangers in our midst might raise. But that cannot be an excuse for rudeness. Welcome to Mother Mary's," she said, most graciously. She signaled to another waiter who came to her side.

"We shall want refreshment," she said. "A glass of burgundy for the gentleman?" she asked, looking at Worth who nodded assent. "And, we have an excellent German hock, light as air."

Jane shook her head. Then, almost unbidden, she added, "Perchance...? I have acquired a little taste for some...porter?"

The lady, their host, smiled broadly.

"Two pints," she said, and the serving man left. "May I," she asked, touching the back of the chair. Jane and Worth nodded in assent. She looked expectantly at the dancing master.

Worth sat still, puzzled at first. Then it came to him. "Ah," he said as he rose and moved to hold her chair.

"Good evening," she said as she adjusted her skirts and settled herself. "Welcome. It is such a pleasure to make new acquaintances. I am Mother Mary."

❧ 56 ❦

"Dead?" Mary's exclamation quieted the room. "Dead, you say? No, it cannot be. Just this month, a week ago, it may it have been, he was here."

Mary had immediately recognized the man from Worth's description.

"Lavelle," she said. "Maurice Lavelle. Simply the sweetest young man you ever would want to meet. He is…was, you say…a lovely young fellow. A French naval officer to be sure, but he despised Napoleon. He was a gentleman. His ship was captured and taken to Portsmouth. He gave his parole and has been here ever since."

"Parole?" Jane asked.

"Customary courtesy for gentlemen at war," Worth said. "If an officer gives quarter and is taken prisoner, he can just say he promises not to fight anymore, and they lets him go."

"'Tis the proper thing for gentlemen to do," Mary said. "Honorable."

"Sailors. Soldiers. Your lower deck fighting men of course, they've got no honor. So, they gets pressed or put in prison. Sometimes they just gets shot for their want of honor."

Then Worth related the complete story of the Frenchman's demise.

"But, this shooting," Mary said, "Maurice hated violence. He would never do such a thing."

"Did he know how to shoot?" Worth asked.

"Oh, yes, that he did." Mary replied. "He accompanied some of the lads here on hunts. Kendall, or was it Phillips—no matter—said he was a dab hand at it. Could shoot a bird on the wing with a pistol, they said."

Worth and Jane exchanged glances.

"Do you know where he lived?" Jane asked.

"Here? In Bath? I do not," Mary said.

"And he kept lodgings elsewhere, in Portsmouth, I presume. He would be here for a few weeks, then go away for a while, then be back. He must've had lodgings somewhere here in town, but…?"

"What about his friends?" Jane asked, putting down her tankard and taking up the questioning. "Would they know?" She looked around the room. "Would anyone know? Might someone have gone home with him?"

"Maurice was well-known and well-liked," Mary said. "And discreet. When he spent time with his friends, it was always as a guest at their abode. He was so sweet. I took him home a few times myself."

"He did not have a...a special friend?" Jane asked.

"Maurice was very cautious. Although— There was one time," she went on, "someone he wanted to introduce. They barely stepped past the vestibule. He was a soldier, I think. Given the punishments for...us, it is completely understandable that he might be extremely shy. Disclosure? Disclosure would cost him his life."

"Don't stop the ones that has tender feelings," Worth said.

"But forces them to be so very circumspect," Mary continued. "I only saw Maurice's friend that once, at most for a minute."

"A soldier?" Worth said.

"Yes, and an officer to be sure," Mary said. "Dragoon, I thought, but cavalry of some sort certainly—he had a crop and spurs. So handsome. More than a few of the boys in here would have liked for him to give them a ride. But, a name? No, I asked. Maurice never revealed it, but recently, it might have been the last time I saw him, Maurice spoke of"— looking at Jane— "his special someone. I thought it likely to be the same man. Maurice simply referred to him as: *mon capitaine*."

⬿ 57 ⬾

"My stomach is aching, groaning, and complaining. Please feed me, it is saying."

"You're on a mission, Miss Austen. You volunteered."

"How did I let you convince me?"

Worth laughed and made no effort to correct her. He did, however, tear another chunk off the loaf of bread he was carrying.

"Mmm. And the scent," she said, holding the crust close. "Roses and lilacs and lavender are fine. The delicate scents of powders and perfumes offer great pleasures. The aroma of a blazing fire when one enters a cottage on a snowy day delivers comfort." She bit into her bread. After swallowing, she continued. "But there is nothing quite so pleasing to all the senses, nothing as luscious as the air of the bakery when the morning loaves appear."

"Especially when you're up and about without your breakfast."

"So true," Jane said and took another bite.

The logic, Jane thought, *was sound. Lavelle was a single gentleman. There was no suggestion that he had a servant. He was a Frenchman.*

If he was French, she asserted to Worth, he would need *le pain quotidian*—his daily bread.

"If we find his bakery, we will be close to where he lives," she said. Worth agreed.

At seven the next morning—six bells on the morning watch—they visited Bath's bakeries as they opened for business.

Now, as they entered a third establishment filled with delicious baking scents, Jane took the lead.

"Good sir," she said, addressing the baker as he emerged from the back of the shop with a tray laden with scones.

"Oh," she said, scenting his cargo. "Good sir, I am in need of one of your scones."

He plucked one from the tray with a spatula as she found her coin purse. She glanced at Worth. He smiled and shook his head. She exchanged a coin for the scone and continued her inquisition.

"I am looking for a friend," she said. "He is expecting my visit, but I have lost his address."

The baker looked perplexed.

"I thought he might be a customer," she said. "He is easily recognized."

The baker moved the pan to one side and rearranged his wares.

"Tall." She held her hand up above Worth's height. "About thirty years in age. Handsome with long blond hair and—he is French."

The last word caught the baker's ears.

"Frenchy, you say."

Jane nodded.

"Not many frogs, ah, Frenchmen around these days. There is one, comes in every day for a while, then vanishes, and then he's back. A gentleman and cuts a fine figure, like you says. Not many ladies and gentlemen buys they's own bread, you know. Mostly it's the cooks and maids."

Jane caught Worth's eye. He nodded.

"He might be your lad, but I don't know where he lives," the baker said. "Somewhere near abouts though, I reckon."

"Is there anyone you think we might speak to?" Jane asked, smiling broadly at the man.

"Monsieur Pierre," the baker said, then laughed. "That ain't his name, but I calls him that and he laughs. He's a Frenchman. He's got the red brick house on Birdwell Street. It's just one door up from Westgate. He lives there and he takes in lodgers."

As they trod up Birdwell, Jane popped the last bit of her scone in her mouth and gave an approving "mmm."

Worth glanced over at her as she proceeded, in the most inelegant fashion, to nibble the last crumbs from her fingers.

A knock at the door of the house roused the landlord. As it was not yet eight o'clock, they met an extremely angry man who apparently did not speak a word of English.

"Monsieur Lavelle?" Jane started. "Is he your lodger? Monsieur Maurice Lavelle?"

The man was shaking his head.

"Non, non, je ne parle anglaise," he said.

"C'est tres important. Connaisez vous…"

"Non, non, non," the man insisted. *"Pardon. Pas d'anglaise."*

"S'il vous plait," Jane said.

"Non!" he repeated and tried to close the door. Worth reached out to catch it.

"Aagh." The landlord's effort to close the door left the wooden fingers of Worth's right hand jammed in the crack. The dancing master feigned another cry of pain.

"Pardon, pardon, monsieur," the landlord said as he quickly opened the door again. "I didn't mean to…your hand…" The shock of smashing a poor man's hand in his door jolted his comprehension *de l'anglaise,* it seemed.

"No, no, nothing broken," Worth said, cradling his prosthetic with his left hand. Jane noticed he had moved a half pace forward and was well-positioned to block any further attempts to shut them out.

"It's about Monsieur Lavelle," Worth said, taking the most direct route to getting the landlord's attention. "He's dead."

"Mon dieu," the landlord said.

Now they had his interest.

Five minutes later they were seated with their shocked host at a small breakfast table in the back of the house. They recounted their story about the mysterious Frenchman, now interred in Alton. Monsieur Cartier, the landlord, allowed that it seemed possible that the man was his boarder, Monsieur Lavelle.

"He had no papers?" The landlord asked, "No purse?"

"Nothing with his name."

"He was wearing a uniform," Jane said. "It was white. Excellent fit. But it bore no ribbons, medals, or insignia."

"The young man had such a uniform," the landlord allowed. "He was, how you say it, a man about town. But he was always polite, so courteous, and never had a complaint. He loved being in your country. And he shared our loathing of Bonaparte."

Cartier served them coffee. Worth set out the bread and chided Jane for breaking it earlier. Cartier supplied butter and strawberry jam. Surrounded as he was by tea drinkers, Worth expressed great satisfaction in the dark brew the landlord served.

"Your hand," Cartier said, suddenly recalling the incident at the door.

"Nothing," Worth said truthfully.

"Monsieur Cartier," Jane said, "Would it be possible for us to see Monsieur Lavelle's rooms? There may be something that will help us confirm our shared suspicions."

The landlord appeared reluctant, as though he still held out some hope.

"You shall come with us, of course," Jane continued. "We will not take anything. Just look?" She pleaded with her eyes. *S'il vous plaît?*"

Cartier took a key from a drawer and led them up the stairs to a room at the back of the house.

The bed was made, the floors swept perfectly clean, the chamber pot dry; the place was immaculate.

"Did Monsieur Lavelle have any friends? Visitors?" Jane said.

"Occasionally," Cartier said. "Maurice was always so discreet, as you say. A perfect gentleman and one does not—put one's nose—in the affairs of a gentleman. There was one special friend. A man. A soldier, I believe. But I do not know any more."

"What is this?" Jane said.

A small dish on the bureau held a piece of embroidered cloth, a black rectangle decorated in gold embroidery with a crown and stars. Some loose threads remained around its edges.

The landlord shrugged. Worth examined it.

"A shoulder board," Worth said. "Shows an officer's rank. Goes just here," he said, gesturing with it. "If it were a marine, it would be for a lieutenant."

"So, this would have belonged to Monsieur Lavelle," Jane said. "Lieutenant Lavelle."

"Nay," Worth said. "French uniforms don't have shoulder boards. 'Tis English."

They continued their examination of the room. Worth pointed to a leather case on the chamber's writing desk.

"May I?"

The landlord nodded. Worth lifted the lid. The velvet contours of the interior were designed to cradle a pair of pistols. One weapon, a beautifully engraved, two-barreled flintlock, rested within. The matching space designed to hold a second weapon was empty.

"I canna be sure without holding the other alongside this one," Worth said, "but I'll swear on the Immortal Memory that I've seen and held this pistol's twin."

They completed their examination of the room and found nothing else of interest. Worth made a show of adjusting the articles on the bureau just as he had found them. In the process, he palmed and pocketed the shoulder board.

On their departure, Worth asked Cartier for directions to the nearest stable. There was one more thread left to be pulled upon in Bath.

Less than a block away, they found a bustling establishment with carriages, phaetons, and gigs for hire.

A large, burly man in a leather apron stopped shoeing a horse to speak with them. He recognized Maurice Lavelle by Worth's description. And yes, the Frenchman rented a gig about two weeks ago, he thought.

"What about a carriage?" Worth said.

"Nay, he never hired carriage nor coach. Just the little gig."

"Have you hired out any large vehicles recently that were not returned properly?" Jane asked. "Or at all?"

This question provoked a short burst of profanity. "Beggin' your pardon, ma'am, but you brung it up. I've had one damnable incident. Bloody cove, a gentleman he was, hired me biggest coach about ten days ago. Supposed to have it back in four days, he was. Time come and I'm waiting and waiting, and my coach ain't come back. Then yesterday, just yesterday, I gets word from a hostler that he's got me rig, horses and all. And he's in Winchester. Can you imagine it? That's seventy bloody miles away! Pardon, ma'am, but you understand. Now, I gots to get it back here. It's a load..., ah, it's troublesome, you know."

Jane nodded. "And the man who hired the coach—it was not the Frenchman?"

"Nay. English as old roast beef he was."

"A soldier?" Worth said.

"Nay. He were some fancy gent, all dressed in black, and he were wearing a bright red cloth around his neck."

"A red cravat?" Jane asked.

The hostler shrugged. "I don't know what you call them things. I just knows that real gentlemen put things back where they belongs."

❧58❧

The travelers rose at dawn for the long journey back to Chawton.

"There is hope for you to recover your capital and income," Jane said to Mrs Jones as she prepared to leave. "It is a knotty business, this syndicate, but we are working the cords to loosen the bonds and untangle it."

Jane had spent three hours the previous evening looking at letters and other documents and had copied the names and addresses of the investors, solicitors, and agents.

"I shall enlist Henry in your cause. You must not be bereft."

Mrs Jones appeared reinvigorated as the ladies parted with affection.

Worth brought the gig around from the stable. Under Jane's tutelage, he had raised his driving skills to something approaching passable, she had said, but with the amiable Lady Dalrymple in the hitch, there was little that could go wrong.

Baggage stowed, adieus said, they bade Bath farewell.

"What do you think, Mr Worth?"

"I think we have a long road ahead, Miss Austen."

"On our findings, sir. On our discoveries. On the identity of the Frenchman."

"It is clear that the whole of this business is not clear," Worth said. "I see the pieces, but I canna make out the puzzle."

"Do you think Captain Wembley is the Frenchman's discreet friend?"

"He might be. He might not."

"What about Percival?" Jane said. "Why would he be involved? Hiring the coach."

"If he's a part of the plot, it truly is a rum business, with him getting caught in his own ambush."

"The syndicate? Do you think that Lavelle was involved in that? He and Wembley were…intimates."

"I canna say."

"And Hinch," Jane said. "Did I tell you? I saw Hinch, the Kellingsford gamekeeper, moments before the ball began. He seems an evil man."

"Not just *seems*, Miss Austen. He's evil right through."

"What shall we do?" Jane said.

"Do?"

"Yes. Do. Take action. What action shall we take?"

"Miss Austen, I'm just a poor sailin' man and a fiddler. And if you be wanting it, I can teach you the steps to some dances. This business with the Frenchman and shooting and all, that's work for constables or magistrates and such."

"But now we know—"

"There's but one thing we know. We know the Frenchman were a navy lieutenant on parole and his name was Maurice Lavelle. We knows that on account of what the landlord, the Cartier fella said. And the pistol. I'm sure that it were the mate of the one he had when he died. That's all we know."

Another long silence.

"We can go to the constable and tell him," Worth said. "Identify the Frenchman. The constable's the law. Maybe he'll take it to the magistrate. Have an inquiry. They'll know about it for the Assizes. That's all we can do."

"But why? It was not a robbery," Jane said. "You agree with me on that point?"

"If it were a robbery, it were a damned— Pardon. It were a badly done piece of work. Nay. I don't think it was robbery."

"Therefore, it must have been…?"

The question hung between them.

"Aye. Murder," Worth finally said. "And now the murderer is dead. We know his name and we can tell it to the constable. That's all we can do."

Silence.

"Percival was involved in the syndicate that cheated Mrs Jones. It led to her husband's death. How does that fit?"

"Oh, Miss Austen." Worth groaned. "It don't fit."

"It must be set right," she said, but mostly to herself.

"Your brother. Like you told Mrs Jones, you'll have him write letters and do the business what men of business do. Your brother Henry. He'll sort it out," Worth said but without much conviction.

"Hinch," Jane said. "What about him?"

"You stay away from him. Don't do anything to cross his tracks."

"So, we are to do nothing?"

"We'll talk to the constable. Tell him what we know. About Lavelle."

Jane sighed.

"We'll do nothing."

❧ 59 ❧

"Constable Claypoole, now here you are," Worth said as he entered the bakery. Having been to the inn and the grocers, he was about to end his search for the man.

"Harrumph." The constable returned to his business with the baker.

"I was hoping to have a word with you," Worth said. "A matter of some interest."

Claypoole squinted towards Worth and harrumphed again.

"The dancing fellow, what's your name?"

"Worth."

"Worth-less, I'll say it," the constable said. "Trouble me with your survey of my rooms, and then you put me off."

The constable advanced on Worth, his jowls quivering.

"Not such a bad thing one supposes when one sees all of the trouble you made with your blasted ball. Killings and blood, and to top it off, a damned pauper to bury—at the constable's expense! You shall have no words with me, you meddlesome… Begone," Claypoole said as he barged past Worth, through the door and into the street. He was entering his inn when Worth caught up with him.

"Mr Claypoole, sir. Constable—"

"I'll be hiring no rooms to you, sir. No indeed. No, not unless"—turning back to face the dancing master—"if you want to hire the finest rooms in Hampshire, you will pay six pounds. Double the usual and not a penny less."

"Constable, sir."

"You will pay all expenses. Hall, service, food, all expenses."

"It's about your pauper, sir," Worth said.

Claypoole puffed his cheeks and squinted at Worth.

"I have his name," Worth said.

The constable's visage brightened.

"Do you now? His name? Well, that is a development. We can find the poor man's family. They will want to honor him properly. Make up for our outlay."

He nodded and a smile appeared.

"They may be in want of a proper gravestone." Claypoole laid a pudgy finger on the side of his nose. "Let us repair to the inn. You can give me the details."

Ten minutes later, Worth was walking down the High Street toward the river. Claypoole's foul mood had returned when he learned Lavelle had no known relatives in England. Worth, however, felt lighter.

Holly branches and evergreen wreaths adorned some of the shops. Christmas approached. His work for Jane had been completed. He had unburdened himself to the constable. He had fulfilled all his obligations. His involvement—his time in Hampshire—was over.

❧60❧

"Your Mr Worth was perfectly correct," Cassandra said. "You had no business going on such an escapade, of course. Your behavior was abominable."

Jane sat on the bench of the pianoforte, facing into the parlor. Her mother sat on the settee, at her needlework, occasionally looking up at Jane and issuing a disappointed sigh. Cassandra paced back and forth, ticking off Jane's transgressions on her fingers.

"Taking Edward's equipage without his permission, traveling without a proper chaperone…"

Jane had given an account of her travels when she returned on the previous day. She had felt some true remorse as she endured her sister's and her mother's disapprobation.

During a second scolding, following a late dinner, Jane wondered, with a slight trace of amusement, what their reactions might have been had she told them what had actually transpired. Her costumes? Mother Mary? Her growing taste for porter? She kept those and many other details to herself.

As she endured her third excoriation, Jane found it tiresome.

"This dancing master fellow is a reprobate," Cassandra said. "We should never have allowed him to accompany you to Bristol. He is a scoundrel. If any word of this should reach society, we will be ostracized."

Jane wondered if Worth had informed the constable yet, and how the constable responded. She feared Claypoole would do nothing.

"Of course, he is correct on one account," Cass said. "He will inform the constable of the Frenchman's identity. The case will be heard at the next Assizes and that will put an end to it."

Her mother nodded vigorously.

"Oh lord, what will Edward say when he returns?" Cassandra said. "He will undoubtedly hear about the borrowing of his gig and horse. You must say nothing of this to our brothers. Henry will be scandalized, I fear."

"And Frank? And Charles?" Jane said, from beneath lowered brows.

"The danger with them is that they may take it for a lark. Some great adventure. A naval action. Oh!" Cassandra, her outrage spent, collapsed on the settee next to her mother.

Jane allowed silence to settle on the room. She thought about playing the pianoforte. She thought about writing—she had several fresh thoughts for her next novel. But concern about the constable's reaction to the new information exceeded all her other interests.

The scolding had ended. Time to seize the opportunity.

"I must take some air," she said. She took up her cloak and was out the door.

The weather was fair, not too cold. The holidays neared. It would be a good day for a walk. Perhaps toward Alton?

❧61❧

The mirrors his father placed all throughout Kellingsford constantly surprised Aloysius. Each time he spied himself, he was stunned for an instant. *Lord Kellingsford,* he thought, wondering at his destiny. Then he shook his head. *Lord, but to what end?* He sighed.

Gloom shrouded the house. The sadness at his father's loss of wit, the sorrow at his brother's sudden death. Or was it remorse? Or shame?

Kellingsford felt vacant. For all his ill humor and peevish ways, his parsimony and extraordinary irritability, Percival had filled up the place. Now, as the heir, Aloysius thought he ought to oversee the establishment. But Miss Ellicott had taken Sloat in hand and they were managing the estate with no need of his assistance.

Wembley, Aloysius thought. *Where was Wembley?* His visits had become infrequent, and the man seemed distracted—as though in mourning too. But of course, they were all in mourning. *Poor, dear, Percival.* Aloysius felt his chest tightening. *Air,* he thought to himself. *I need air.*

He commanded Jerome to call for the curricle. He would take a drive. He donned his great coat and gloves and was shortly on the Winchester Road toward Alton.

He noted the signs of the season. A wreath on a door. Holly and ivy entwined on a post.

Thoughts of Christmastide led to thoughts of Saint Stephen's Day, when a proper lord made life merry for servants and others.

A proper lord, he thought. *Am I not a proper lord?*

As he drove on toward Alton, a plan emerged that stirred his imagination, a plan worthy of a proper lord.

❧ 62 ❧

"Miss Austen! On your way into town. What luck. You must ride with me." Aloysius had already offered Jane a hand up to the seat. "A splendid day, is it not?" he said. "Not so cold. Quite pleasant."

As difficult as it was to refuse the impetuous young man, Jane did resist.

"I am en route to Alton, seeking Mr Worth," she said. "He had some business there and I must know the outcome."

"All the more reason to join me," he said. "I, too, am in search of the dancing master. We must combine our forces."

Jane sighed and accepted his hand to step up into the curricle.

"I have had a thought—a wonderful thought," Aloysius said. "As the heir of Kellingsford—the future Lord Kellingsford—it is essential that I have a thought. A great number of thoughts, even."

"A proper lord must be thought—full."

Aloysius was, indeed, a sweetly irresistible, amiable young man.

"My thoughts have run to the holidays, Miss Austen. The holidays are expected to be happy occasions, mirth and merriment and pleasant hubbub. Is that not so?"

"Quite so," she said. "And a time for receiving visits and welcoming family and friends."

"We are in agreement then," Aloysius said. "And yet, as I ramble about Kellingsford, I have found it not to be festive. In truth, Miss Austen, it is quite the opposite, dressed for mourning and echoing with recent terrible events. Oh, I should apologize for raising those specters."

"That is unnecessary," Jane said. "I only suffered an inconvenience. You suffered a great loss."

"Yes, a great loss," Aloysius agreed, "and a great increase in responsibility. And this brings me around to the holidays again. As lord—future lord—must I not see to holiday traditions?"

"Perhaps," Jane said. "But the house is still in mourning."

"Yes, that. I have been thinking a great deal on that. But, aha, tally-ho! Here's our dancing master!"

They met Worth on the bridge across the Wey. Aloysius negotiated terms for a swift rendezvous at the Rose and Crown where he promised to reveal all.

❧ 63 ❦

Seated around a pot of tea and a coffee for the dancing master, Aloysius unfolded his scheme.

"A house party! We must have a house party on Saint Stephen's Day," he said. "For the service, for our tenants, and their families, and for all our dear friends. We shall distribute our boxes as any good family should. We shall offer food and drink. And there must be dancing, music, and merriment."

"But," Jane started to object.

"We shall not be in the ballroom. The memories." Aloysius sighed. "Too soon. We shall instead throw open the drawing rooms. A grand salon for the gathering."

"Aloysius, you are forgetting—"

"Mourning, Miss Austen? Am I forgetting that we are in mourning? No, I am not. I am not forgetting Percival, dear Percy. He was such a warm, caring, and thoughtful person that he...he would've wanted us to have a festive time in his absence."

Worth and Jane stared at Aloysius.

"Come now," Aloysius said. "We know the mourning at Kellingsford is a sham. Percival is missed—truly missed—by no one with the exceptions of his business agent, Sloat, and the gamekeeper. And I am not even sure about them. Miss Austen, you knew my father in years past. You recall his warmth and hospitality?"

Jane nodded.

"So, we shall recapture a bit of that spirit. That would be a good thing, would it not?"

Jane smiled. She thought about the Lord Kellingsford she had first met. She had to nod in agreement.

"And what of the enmity Percival engendered with our tenants. As the future Lord Kellingsford, would it not be wise for me to repair some of the damage Percival did? My big brother's grand design for the estate seems to have passed on along with its author. We need our tenants to be successful to keep the estate solvent. I believe this gathering will start us on a new and better path."

The table was quiet for a moment. Jane considered the young lord's words.

"I find your reasoning to be most sensible," Jane finally said. "You have indeed been thinking earnestly on your responsibilities."

Worth nodded as well. "Aye, well done."

"Then we are agreed," Aloysius said. "We shall have a house party at Kellingsford on Saint Stephen's Day!"

The plan was made. The dancing master, as a guest at Kellingsford, agreed to provide music and lead some capers. Jane said she would join in the music making. Aloysius promised food and sweets and drink.

Insisting that it would be no effort at all, Jane said she would arrange some sort of theatrical. A Punch and Judy or, possibly, a pantomime.

"'Tis but in three days," Worth said.

"We will have to hurry with the invitations. But we have a great store of costumes, masks, puppets, and theatrical devices in the attic of our cottage," she said. "We can make up a wonderful show."

"Costumes? Masks? Puppets?" Aloysius said. "That sounds delightful but certainly, it is far too much to ask."

"I insist," Jane replied. "I insist."

❧64❧

"I may be a poorly educated sailor man, Miss Austen, but I have read many of the works by Mr William Shakespeare. Furthermore, I personally attended one of Mr Kean's performances of the play *Hamlet* at the Drury Lane."

Worth addressed Jane over the ever-present pot of tea at the Rose and Crown. Twenty and four hours earlier, he had agreed to the plan for a house party at Kellingsford. He was perusing Jane's proposition for a pantomime.

"I look at this, Miss Austen," he said, leafing through the foolscap sheets in front of him, "and I see a plot."

Jane listened attentively.

"Here, in the action of your pantomime, you have Harlequin as a spirited, devil-may-care fellow. Lively and full of wit. And now, Pantaloon, all dressed in black, grabbing the purse of every man who walks by. And along comes a dashing white knight. And here in the last scene, the white knight comes to bash Harlequin, and the clown bends down, so the knight strikes Pantaloon instead."

"It is just the sort of humor that children love," Jane said.

"And he does it again," Worth said. "And again."

"Like a Punch and Judy," Jane said. "It will have a delightful comic effect that everyone will understand."

"Understand, is it?" Worth said. "If it's understanding you wants, why not have your Pantaloon wear a red cravat and bring your knight in carrying a French flag? What are you thinkin', Miss Austen? Do you believe you can catch Captain Wembley in this silly mousetrap of yours? D'ye think he'll jump out of his seat and call to light all the candles?"

"No, I do not," Jane said, "for we will have all the candles lit. I want to see his face. I want to see what it betrays."

"I can tell you what you'll see, Miss Austen. You'll see he's a dangerous man. And you want to poke him with your sharpened quill?"

"I want to see how he reacts."

"We agreed," Worth said. "Tell the constable what's what and that's an end to it."

"We agreed that the constable's a fool."

"That may be, and it may be a poor ending to the story, but there's times when even the boldest action canna save the day."

"Nothing will happen, Mr Worth. This is not some great fleet action. It is a silly, farcical pantomime."

"You're proposing to poke a bear with a stick."

"At most, the bear may grumble and growl a little bit. I just want to see his face."

"There is danger in your plan."

"Are you assuming the role of *my sister*, now? Beware! Beware!"

"Would you make a fool o' me, too?"

Jane stopped.

"No. No, Mr Worth. Never. But truly, I see no great harm in this. It's an entertainment. A farce. Everyone will be laughing. It is possible, even likely, the captain will not be in attendance. If so, he may never catch the drift. If he does twig to it, then possibly there will be a grimace or a wince. Nothing more, you can be sure."

"Miss Austen…"

"A tiny tweak in a room full of laughing people. Let us see if he betrays himself."

"Miss Austen…Miss Austen, you're the captain of this ship. I'm just a sailor man. 'Tis my duty to speak my mind—with permission, of course—and then carry out the captain's orders. Now, you've heard what I think of your scheme. I've spoken my mind. But remember, there's many who's got their fingers snapped when setting out a mousetrap."

❧ 65 ❧

The dancing master crept into Saint Nicholas Church under the cover of *Adeste, Fideles*. Christmas Eve exerts a powerful attraction, even for a wayward old soul. And the music—one can always count on the old hymns.

The sanctuary appeared full but not packed. The parishioners gave good account of themselves as the hymn entered the final change, the Latin verse, the one Worth liked best. He was never all that certain about the words for the middle verses. What he wanted in knowing them though, he made up for in the refrains.

But the Latin? He knew and loved the Latin verse.

"Venite adoremus
Venite adoremus
Venite adoremus
Do-o-minum"

Worth shifted to the left, along the back wall of the sanctuary, all the way over on the Gospel side. The church was small but not tiny. Ten rows of pews that would each seat four comfortably flanked the center aisle. From the corner where he stood, a second aisle led to the front of the church. He moved up the side aisle a few steps and saw the Austens seated in the front rows on the Epistle side.

Right and left; that was for dancing, of course. But the theater folk, they turned it all around. Stage left was right, and right was left. Actors. What do they know? Aboard ship: starboard and port. Being in a church, he thought of the Epistle side and the Gospel side. He had attended services faithfully as a boy, which was Sophie's doing. They always preferred the preaching on the Gospel side of the aisle.

The navy had its religion, too, but it was nothing like church on dry land. The ship's captain led services on a man o' war. He read the Prayer Book and he preached the Articles of War; thirty-five articles, a hundred causes for flogging, and thirteen threats of punishment by death. It made the parish parson's promises of hell-fire and damnation look like a lovely stroll in the park.

Ah. *Hark the Herald Angels*. Mr Wesley wrote that one. Nice lyrics. Full of hope.

> *"Joyful all ye nations rise,*
> *join the triumph of the skies"*

Soaring words but a somber tune; the Easter Hymn it was. The words fit well enough but not really the right spirit for Christmas. *There's a hymn truly in want of new music.*

The fellow playing the pianoforte tried heartily to pull the congregation along, but it was, Worth thought, *somewhat dull and listless.*

The church was too small to have room for or need of an organ. That was a good thing, in Worth's mind. *If there's anything that will sink the raised voices of choir and congregation, it's a broadside from a blasted organ.*

Oh, it's one thing in a grand cathedral, he would allow. Give it a hundred-foot ceiling and a hundred voices in the choir and a thousand folks in the seats; that's one thing. The music grows hazy in those great stone caverns, but it has a special power as it makes the ground beneath you tremble. And there was Bach. He was an organ grinder by trade. And he wrote some very fine ditties for the organ. Otherwise, Worth decided long ago he had little use for the instrument.

The pianoforte caught his ear. A different touch, he noticed.

Miss Austen!

He almost said it out loud. He moved a little further down the aisle and found a spot where he could see her, seated at the pianoforte, facing the pulpit, her profile toward the congregation.

"Christians, awake."

Yes, and she's giving the old tune some life. With an organ grinder in charge, he'd plod along at half the pace, somewhere between *lento* and *largo.* Jane had the old hymn trotting along in *adagio.* Truly, it brought the old song to life.

When the congregation rose to sing, Worth was forced to shift his position to keep sight of her. She had a most admirable countenance, he decided. She had eyes for the music in front of her, but she was not depending on it. She looked up frequently, glanced at the rector and around at the parishioners. She was in the music, smiling, and warmed by it.

The congregation warmed to her touch. The church rang with the hymn.

> *"Christians, awake!*
> *Salute the happy morn,*
> *Whereon the Saviour*
> *of the world was born"*

As the last change came round, Worth could not help himself. He moved next to a woman at the end of the nearest pew and gestured: Might he look on the hymn book with her?

She smiled and shared the book between them.

The dancing master added his voice to the congregation. It was not a well-trained voice. For all his musicality, he never mastered vocal harmonies. He sang like a common sailor man; here's the melody lad, give it a good shout.

When the hymn ended, he smiled warmly at his choir mate and slipped back into the shadows.

If religion were music, he thought he might be a truly religious man. But, was not music a religion? Where did that which was sacred end and perfect harmony begin? For all the preaching and chanting, the reciting and praying, was it not when the churchgoers were singing that they came together as one, transcended their daily cares and reached some better place?

Worth left the church as stealthily as he had arrived, under the cover of a benediction. As he made the turn onto the private road away from Chawton House, he heard the final hymn of the service. It was always the final hymn on a proper Christmas Eve.

He turned onto the Winchester Road, on his way back to Kellingsford, singing quietly to himself.

"Joy to the world…"

৵66৵

L aughter and holiday cheer filled Kellingsford on Saint Stephen's Day. Guests cleared a groaning board; mugs and glasses were filled and refilled.

Aloysius proved to be a charming host, making merry with children, greeting tenants and neighbors, and listening to them with care. He seemed more settled, less of a dandy, Jane thought as she observed him through the day.

Captain Wembley was in attendance. The Austens came, including Captain Frank Austen. With Admiral Harwell on board, it made for a striking military presence.

Mr Worth led the gathering in *Heart of Oak* to a great, exuberant chorus.

The music proved to be a wonderful success. Mr Worth accompanied Jane as she sang two delightful songs. And then, to quell the enthusiastic response, she was forced to sing two more.

The pantomime provided a marvelous finale to the entertainment. Tremendous laughs, great applause, more laughter. *A hit, a palpable hit,* Jane thought.

Yet, in her private observation of Wembley, there was nothing for Jane to see. He laughed and applauded in step with everyone else. Not one grimace nor any sign of provocation.

A miss. A palpable miss. Perhaps she was entirely wrong.

Mr Worth had been correct. And he would certainly tell her so when they met on the morrow at the Rose and Crown. *Six bells on the afternoon watch,* she mused. *Three o'clock.* They would settle their business accounts, and she would bid him adieu. With a letter, to be sure. She would certainly provide him with a letter.

❧67❧

"He knows too much," Wembley said. "Party tricks and provocations. And you joined in on it! You! He presents a real danger, Aloysius. This dancing master must be dealt with."

Captain Wembley's anger erupted the instant they were alone. Aloysius tried to calm him.

"He's nothing but a caper merchant, Reggie. He's no harm."

"Are you blind? You fool!"

"Reggie, I never—"

"The pantomime was a trap," Wembley said.

"Reggie, it was a Punch and Judy. A silly exercise in knocking characters about with pillow swords and clubs. Nothing more."

"Ally, your Mr Worth is a dangerous man. He has been to war, seen men fight and die."

"Surely you didn't believe that story? All that nonsense about Trafalgar? I spoke to him on it—it was nothing but a tale. He injured his hand in some shipboard accident."

"Oh, Aloysius. My dear sweet Ally. You, you…" Wembley seemed calmer. "However, you spoke to him, he told you what you wanted to believe. I have more intelligence of him. Hinch, your gamekeeper, we have an alliance of a sort. The dancing man is no dandy, Ally. He is a damned capable former navy man. He identified the Frenchman I regrettably recruited for our little charade. Oh, Ally, you know how sorry I am about—"

"No, no, Reggie. I understand. It was all a mistake. There's nothing to be done now."

"Yet, this dancing man poses a threat."

"But he is such a talented fellow. Surely, he'll just hie himself back to London and play his music and prance about?"

"If he ships out tomorrow morning, you may be right. If not…"

"Reggie, surely you're not—"

"Nothing fatal, Ally. A sea voyage. He is, after all, a sailor. Perhaps there is a want of fiddlers in, let us say, Australia?"

❧68❧

"Will you have a coffee?" Jane asked. "I know it is your preference."

"Nay, the coffee here is horrible. I'm thinking it's not coffee at all—just some corn husks or wheat chaff that they burn and brew," Worth said. "To my mind, tea is a lady's drink. But say this for it, it's dependable."

"Dependability is such a wonderful virtue. The world is filled with so much uncertainty."

The pot of tea arrived, and Jane poured.

"Where is it you will travel next?"

"Back to Town. Then up north."

"Oh, yes, I recall. Dancing master for a great house, was it not?"

"Maybe. Maybe not. So much uncertainty."

"What is it you want, Mr Worth? Your talents as a dancing master are great. Look here, I have prepared a letter for you, singing your praises."

She passed the folded letter to him. He shook his head.

"Nay, you shouldn't've. It were such a—"

"Everything that you did was perfect, in my opinion. As your employer, sir, mine is the only opinion that matters. Do you not wish to continue to present dances in Town? I should very much enjoy attending balls led by Mr Worth with music by The Hirelings."

"'Tis a hard life for music makers, Miss Austen. The gentlemen who hire you complain every time. Why does it cost so much? They don't know or they forget. It's hard work that requires practice, late nights. We got to travel to get places, and we only get work six months of the year at best."

"You might follow Mr Wilson's path. Create your own balls and assemblies."

"That's not so easy," he said.

"No, I know it is not."

They sipped their tea.

"Well now, we must settle our accounts." She withdrew a piece of folded paper from her satchel and passed it to him. "Our agreed sum."

He unfolded the sheet and withdrew fifteen one-pound notes drawn on Henry's London bank. He nodded to her, counted off eleven of the notes, and placed them in the little book he carried. He put the remaining notes back in the packet, slipped the folded flap closed, and pushed it back across the table to her.

"Mr Worth?"

"I am whole, Miss Austen. You have paid the musicians and me for our time and travel. The free use of the ballroom was a great savings. Whether it was a boon...?" He shook his head.

"Mr Worth—"

"Now what will your noble society friends be saying if they see a lady provoking an argument with a gentleman?"

"You are not a gentleman."

"True, very true. But you are a lady."

The packet rested on her side of the table.

"You can hire me again sometime, and I'll do a proper job of it," he said. "And another thing. You can give me a copy of your next book. With an inscription if you please."

She smiled.

"You will like it, I think. A story about a headstrong young woman."

At those words, Worth laughed.

Jane blushed, just the faintest.

"A girl, really, who meddles in the lives of everyone around her and leaves chaos in her wake." She sighed. "I suppose I have been a little like that girl, have I not? Hieing off to Bristol and Bath. Was it terribly awkward for you?"

Worth smiled and shook his head. "Nay. It were a great adventure. You've got a bit of Lord Nelson in you, lass. Never mind the maneuvers—"

"Just go straight at them. You were entirely correct about it all in the end," she said. "I apologize for my insistence on the theme of the pantomime. The captain did not display the slightest trace of emotion."

"Perhaps a mousetrap like that only works in a play?"

"Perhaps."

"You must keep me advised of your address," she said, "that I may hire you again sometime or provide someone with a reference."

"That'd be most kind. How can I write you?"

"Jane Austen. Chawton. The post is very dependable."

"Yes," he said. "Dependable. A fine virtue. Dependability."

"I must be gone now. Cassandra and Mama will be waiting their afternoon tea."

Worth rose.

"You'll give them my regards?"

"I shall."

He wanted to accompany her on the walk back to Chawton. But to what end? More difficult conversation? Another awkward parting?

No. It was done.

Worth remained at the table another hour, took another pot of tea, and drank none of it.

His thoughts wandered along roadways leading past Chawton to Bath and Bristol and beyond. He wondered about ladies and girls…and even Anne. That lovely lass. Was she still in Hull? Was she married? Surely, she would be married. Such a lovely young woman would be married. Would she not?

It was almost dark when he set out for Kellingsford. A light snow fell. The road was empty.

❧ 69 ❧

Three dragoons seized the dancing master as he entered the servants' door. With one trooper on each arm and a corporal leading the way, they marched him around to the portico, up the steps, and into the vestibule where four more soldiers waited.

"We have him, sir," the corporal announced, directing his words toward the drawing room.

Captain Wembley emerged. "Yes indeed, you have him. Yes indeed. Come now, Constable Claypoole," he continued, directing his words back into the drawing room. "Let us see what mischief this rascal has been up to. No good, I'll warrant."

There was a wait—a long wait—and Constable Claypoole appeared in the doorway.

"Jerome, will you lead the constable to the rooms this man is occupying," Wembley said. He nodded to the butler, then glared at Worth.

Jerome gave a nod in return and led the group up the grand staircase. The constable moved toward the foot of the stairs, sighed heavily, and began his ponderous climb. Worth, surrounded by dragoons, followed, step by torturous step.

The party waited at the top of the stairs while the constable recovered. He took two pinches from his snuff box. In his winded state, he was careless, resulting in a huge, uncontrolled sneeze. The constable's soggy kerchief was put to use. Then the march continued.

A small door at the end of a long corridor opened to the servants' quarters. Jerome held the door while the constable considered his best course. Finally, he slid his body into the opening and with some inhaling and pressing on his belly, managed to squeeze through. The company navigated more passages and another flight of stairs—the constable stopping nearly a minute on a landing to recover his strength—and finally arrived at the rooms Worth occupied.

"Now, we must see what's what," Wembley said. "I have heard of this matter on good authority, but you must see for yourself, Constable."

Wembley opened the door. The constable again had to squeeze through the opening, followed by the others.

"Corporal, open it," Wembley ordered, pointing to a wooden crate on the floor next to the writing table.

The constable, breathing heavily, held the back of a chair for support. The corporal prised the lid off the box easily and removed its contents, bottles of wine, and placed them on the table.

"Now, what's this?" Wembley said, taking a bottle. "Wine. French wine, I see."

He held the bottle for the constable to see. Claypoole, still breathing heavily, squinted.

"Yes, yes indeed, French wine," the constable agreed.

"And yet, is it stamped? Has the proper tax been paid?" Wembley said.

He handed the bottle to the constable who took it with both hands.

"I am not...ah," Claypoole started. He rotated the bottle, looking at the bottom. "No, there is not a stamp."

He swayed.

"Smuggled goods then?" Wembley said.

"You must inspect the box as well, and the other bottles," the constable said, handing the bottle back to Wembley and regaining his grip on of the chair. His experience as a shopkeeper had taught him that bureaucrats and their lackeys often cut corners. He'd seen it more than once, when a taxman did not take the time to affix the proper stamp on each bottle. "Inspect the bottom of the box, too," he said. "You never know."

"There is nothing..." Wembley started to say, then stopped.

"Corporal," Wembley said, "inspect the box carefully, as the constable suggests."

Claypoole rounded the chair and eased himself down.

Worth, seeing the scheme unfolding, edged away from the dragoons. Only a pace, but it might serve. As Claypoole's bulk settled into the chair, it twisted. A brace shattered. One leg collapsed. Claypoole waved his arms, but there was nothing to grasp. A dragoon standing behind the constable was felled. Claypoole's feet flew up, hitting the table and sending the case of wine bottles onto the floor. Claypoole howled in shock and some pain. Wembley cursed.

Worth took one step to the side and slipped into the inner sleeping chamber. There was no lock on the door, not even a strong latch. Worth seized the small chair in the chamber and wedged it as tightly as he could between the door handle and the floor. It would not bear more than one assault from the dragoons, but it *might* serve, give him enough time.

He heard shouts and the door rattled as he raised the window. The first assault on the door came as he swung out the window clinging to the thick ivy vines that covered the back walls of Kellingsford like the ropes of a ship's rigging.

He heard another crash against the door.

As he gained purchase on the living ratlines, his mind cleared. Snow whipped around him. The ground, already white, seemed inhospitable. Another crash and splintering sounds.

The old sailor started climbing upward to the roof.

❧ 70 ❧

Freddy Worth had spent two decades at sea laying out on spars, reefing sails, hauling up masts, splicing ropes, and repairing rigging damaged by shot and gale. All of that while clinging to lines twenty, fifty, sometimes a hundred feet and more above oak planks and the bottomless deep, swaying port and starboard, fore and aft, buffeted by the wind, and rolling with the sea.

The route to the roof of the house would not have troubled a ship's boy.

By the time he heard the voices of the searchers below, Worth had found a niche behind a chimney, invisible from the ground. The bricks even offered warmth.

He heard Wembley shouting over the confusion below.

"You idiots," the captain said. "You've gone and walked over all his tracks. Form a perimeter. A careful search. Find his trail."

The snow was still falling, and it would cover footprints quick enough. There was a bit of wind blowing. It was dark. They would never find his trail. They would never find his trail because he had not left one.

Hours later, Worth heard the faint tolling of a long-case clock from somewhere within the great house. Four o'clock. Eight bells on the morning watch. The snow had stopped; the searchers retired. Worth swung down from the roof and made his way back to his former bed-chamber window. It had a latch, but the pieces were ill fitted. Hooking his prosthetic hand into the vines, he was able to coax the window open and creep back into the room.

With great care he stepped over some of the wreckage of the door and made his way into the front room, searching the table and coat hooks. He did not see the broken chair leg until he accidentally caught it with his toe and sent it rolling toward the hearth. He stilled. It sounded like a coach and four passing on cobbles.

Frozen in place, Worth heard a loud voice directly beyond the door to the rooms.

"Nay, nay, lass. You'll not be laying no fires here for a while," came a familiar raspy voice. "I'm to stand watch, the constable says. No one in or out."

Worth could not make out the murmured reply.

"Ha, it's good luck for you," Marryat said. "It'll save you many a trip up the stairs with a scuttle o' coal."

Footsteps, then the hall grew quiet. Worth went to the cloak closet and lifted the latch with a quiet click.

The door opened a crack.

"It's in the wardrobe in the sleeping room," Marryat said. "Your fiddle. And there's a good warm greatcoat. Gets 'em, lad. And come back here."

Worth shook his head. Sometimes you just give a whistle and find a fair wind. He found his fiddle and the promised coat and returned to the door.

"How'd you know I'd be back?" he whispered.

"I just thunk like a sailor," the old man said. "'The lad's likely to find a safe harbor, reef his sails, drop anchor, and wait out the blow.' That's what I reckoned. Did you shut the window?"

"Aye."

"Come on then. We've got a safe passage. And there's room in the stable for one more stinkin' old dog, or so I hear."

228 ❖ RIDGWAY KENNEDY

❧ 71 ❦

"We got to search the place again," the voice said. "Captain's orders."

"You done it before. Nothin' gonna change," came the reply. *That was Marryat,* Worth thought, as he came out of a deep sleep.

"Orders is orders," came the other voice. Worth recognized it—the corporal of the dragoons.

From his hiding place buried under a tarpaulin and hay, the voices were muffled but clear enough.

"Go on about it," Marryat said. "I'll just be keeping on with my business."

Worth felt the pile of fodder move. *The tines of a pitchfork,* he presumed.

"Be about it, lads," the corporal called out to his troops.

"No sign of 'im, eh?" Marryat asked.

"Nah. Done a right good scamper. Vanished. You ain't got him hidin' in your straw pile there," the corporal said, laughing.

Marryat joined with his laughter.

"Aye, and I'll be turning 'im right over for ye." Worth felt the pile shake as Marryat drove the fork into it. "Here now, what we got?" This time the fork slid under Worth, under and out. "Let's give it a good shake," Marryat said, guiding the fork right into the middle of the pile.

The tarpaulin cushioned the thrust when it struck Worth's hip and buttocks. Probably didn't draw blood, he thought, but damned painful. He managed to remain silent.

"I reckon he's gone to ground," the corporal said. "Found hisself a hidey hole and he's laying low. Maybe even has some folks looking out for him."

"That's not so likely," Marryat said. "He's a stranger. Ain't got friends around here."

"There's the scribbler," the corporal said. "That's what the captain calls her. He's got a lookout posted on her cottage. He best not be knocking on her door."

"What can a lady do?" Marryat said.

"Don't know, but Wembley's got a watch posted right across the road. That's on top of all the patrolling."

"We done more patrolling in the last day than we done in a fortnight," the corporal said. "All about this estate, and all around the place across the way."

"Chawton House?" Marryat said.

"Aye, that's it. Up and down every damn street. Alton, too."

"On foot?" Marryat said.

"Mostly on horse. Captain says we cover more ground that way. He's having a bloody fit about it, Wembley is. Never seen him in such a state. And the man we're chasing, he's supposed to be a smuggler, which he ain't."

"He ain't?" Marryat said.

"Ah," the corporal gave a deep sigh. "Never you mind."

"So, your captain, he's on a tear?"

"Captain Wembley's a right martinet all the time, but now—"

"He's hard?" Marryat said.

"He believes in…discipline. It's not so bad now. Only one flogging since we come back from France. But back then, he were free with a lash. We had a runner back in Belgium, just afore Waterloo. A Johnny Newcomb, only a lad. Wembley, he were a lieutenant then, he disciplined the boy. Gave him three hundred strokes. Gave the first hundred to the boy hisself."

"Hard," Marryat said.

"Here's the thing, though," the corporal said. "The punishment for running is hangin'. When Wembley got done flogging the poor lad, he hung 'im."

They were quiet.

"Discipline," the corporal said. "That's the thing with 'im. Discipline."

❧72❧

Three broad planks laid across the stable's rafters created a kind of crow's nest. It wasn't as warm as hunkering down in the hay, but it was less exposed. If the soldiers came back, they'd likely not even notice it; some old tack likely, covered by a tarpaulin. It was even more unlikely that a landsman in cavalry boots would venture to take the perilous walk along the rafters to investigate more closely.

From his perch, Worth had a full view of the stable, the comings and goings of horses, grooms, and drivers, and, near dusk, the arrival of Hinch.

"Where is he?" Hinch peered down at Marryat. "Where is he, you bloody fool! I been keeping an eye on you."

Hinch seized a pitchfork and walked over to the loose box where Worth had been hiding that morning.

"I seen you tossing bits of hay around this here pile. Is this where he's at?"

Hinch tore into the fodder, driving the pitchfork into it, scattering the feed around in front of the bin, wading into it, kicking around, and stabbing for a minute or more.

"Not here, eh?" Hinch finally admitted, panting. "But he's somewheres about. Where is he? You're a bloody house servant, Mr Marryat. Now, what's a house servant doing in the stable? Eh? Where is he?"

Marryat held his ground. "Who?" he said. "What the bloody hell are you yapping about?"

Hinch bellowed. "The prancing man! Mr Fiddle Dee. Your pal, the sailor!"

"I can't say where he is." He shrugged his shoulders. "You sure he's not still in his chambers?"

"I knows you's helping 'im," Hinch snarled. "And you're gonna pay!"

"You can take it up with His Lordship," Marryat said.

"His Lordship is barmy. He's most gone. And when he's gone, you're gone."

Hinch's wrath had subsided. Now he approached Marryat closely again.

"You're hiding him, you stupid old man. Your sailin' pal. The jolly tar. You're hidin' him. And I am gonna find 'im."

"Not in here," Marryat said, looking steadily at Hinch. The old man shrugged his shoulders and left.

Even though the light was failing, Hinch searched the stable. He was systematic, peering, and poking into every corner. He moved horses and inspected each loose box.

As it grew darker, Hinch found a lantern. He had moved to the loft and was again, slowly and methodically, searching. Probing bales of hay. Shifting bundles. Knocking on walls and searching for hollows.

The lantern dimmed and then went out. Worth heard Hinch descend to the stable floor. He heard a clatter. The lantern? Rattling sounds. Creaking. The stable door? Hinges?

A slash of pale moonlight spread into a wide pool on the stable floor. The black shadow on the floor mirrored the gamekeeper's figure as he started to walk away from the stable. Then the figure stopped and stood in the open doorway.

"I'm gonna find you, Mr Dancey Man," Hinch said in almost a whisper.

Then a shout:

"I'm gonna find you!"

❧73❧

Worth rapped on the door again, a little harder, reminded once more of the advantages of hardwood knuckles. The parlor remained dark.

Finally, the maid Flora, holding a candle, cracked open the door.

"Mr Worth!" she said, frozen.

"I need to speak with Miss Austen, please," he said. "Miss Jane. Can you ask her to come speak with me?"

Less than a minute later, Jane was at the door bidding Worth inside.

"Mr Worth, I have been so worried—"

"If there's one thing a lazy man such as m'self is good at, it's laying low and keeping out the way."

"We must be careful. They have a watchman."

"I know. I heard about it today. I took to the woods and came around the back. I don't think they could've seen me."

"Mr Worth," she said, then stopped and gave him a small smile. "I apologize, sir. I do so apologize—I lit the fuse. My foolish pantomime. I am so filled with remorse—"

"Calm yourself, lass. You can't know for sure what moved the man. I did hear more about him though, our Captain Wembley. He's a hard man, maybe even twisted. He's just following his nature."

"I have gone over and over it since the party," she said. "I am sure my little theatrical set him off."

Cassandra had come down the stairs. Flora continued to hover, and she started to light another candle.

"No," Jane said. "We must not arouse the suspicions of our watchman."

"Are you sure you have not been observed, Mr Worth?" Cassandra said. "The constable has raised the hue and cry. We have been visited and inspected by dragoons, most thoroughly, on two occasions. You are, I collect, the most infamous rogue in all of Hampshire."

Worth sighed.

"It's all a charade. You know that, don't you? I never smuggled any French wine," he said. "Now, a drop of a good Scotch whisky? That might be worth the risk. But frog wine?"

He could make out at least one smile in the dim candlelight. He heard one of the Miss Austens chuckle.

"Ladies," he said, "I was hoping to trouble you for some help. My prospects appear bleak right now. A hanging or a flogging or a trip to Australia appear to be close at hand. And the hunt ain't dying down. Could you assist me with the loan of a horse? Help me put some miles between me and the good Captain Wembley?"

"Mr Worth, we have the greatest confidence in your innocence and the greatest sympathy for your situation, but—" Cassandra started.

"Yes," Jane said.

"Jane!"

"Yes, you certainly shall have a horse, with a guide to help you navigate through our nearby countryside."

"Jane!" Cassandra exclaimed again. "You are a lady. You are not—"

"I have been thinking of nothing other than this since the alarm was first raised, Cassandra. I have placed Mr Worth in peril."

"You are a lady, Miss Jane," Worth started. "You have no business—"

"Not my business?" Jane said, cutting him off. "I believe I'll be the one to decide about that. Yes, Cass, I am a lady—a lady who takes her debts seriously. And you, Mr Worth, are no horseman. Nor do you know the trails and landscape hereabouts."

"Jane, you are being impossible."

"Yes, my dear sister. Yes, I am," Jane said and embraced her sister warmly. "Please forgive me and cleanse me of my sins for posterity."

Jane ended her embrace, but keeping her hands on her sister's shoulders, she kept her close.

"I am not a young lady anymore, Cass. I am a hireling. I know so much more of the world than that frivolous girl who grew up in Steventon and frolicked in Bath. I have work to do. A great deal of work. And right now, I have a debt to repay."

Jane hurried up the stairs leaving Worth and Cassandra staring at each other in an awkward silence. Worth broke it.

"Another favor?"

Cassandra sighed. "Yes."

"My fiddle," he said. "I'm thinking my travels may be rough. I canna be sure how I'll get about. And, if someone is seeking me…a man going around with a fiddle case? Now that stands out a wee bit, don't you think?"

Cassandra held out her arms. Worth placed his instrument in them.

"Keep her warm but not hot. Nowhere near a fire," Cassandra said. "Keep her properly watered. Perhaps when you return for her, she will have got seeds, sprouted, and blossomed with baby violins."

Worth smiled.

"I will keep your Mirabella safe for you."

Cassandra was placing the fiddle on the settee when a lad in riding breeches and boots came back down the stairs. The person wore a small farmer's coat with a satchel slung over it.

"Jane?" Cassandra said. "Jane?"

"Mr Worth's appearance at our door was an obvious twist for this plot. Our watchman across the way proves that point. I have been preparing in the event the tale took this turn. I have some food," Jane said to Worth, patting the satchel. "We are best served by the cover of darkness for the beginning of our journey, I think. Do you agree?"

Worth, still startled by Jane's appearance, found his voice.

"Aye."

Jane swept her hair up and under a loose-fitting, round wool cap.

"What is your destination?" Jane said.

"Well, I've been thinking—" He fell silent.

"Good. Keep working on that part. It will be important. I shall only be gone a day or two," Jane said embracing her sister. "I am on a mission. That is what you must tell Frank and Mama. A matter of honor. I pray they will understand."

Jane was not waiting for responses. She faced the dancing master.

"Now, Mr Worth. Let us be gone."

☙74❧

Jane knocked on the door of the stable master's living quarters, a tiny room connected to one end of the stable. No answer. She knocked again. It was late. The usual ten-minute walk from the cottage to Chawton House had taken nearer to a half an hour as she and Worth had detoured through fields and woods to avoid the watchman.

She knocked again.

"What's this about?"

The voice came from behind them.

"Hotchkiss," Jane said. "Just trying to raise you, old man."

"And now you done it, lass. But what's this you're wearin'?

"And here's the fiddling feller, too," the stable master said, peering at Worth.

"That's quite a jig you've got them folks a dancing. There's searchers coming and going, looking all around for you."

"Have they been here today?" Jane said.

"Not more than twenty minutes ago," Hotchkiss said, "a troop o' dragoons, no less. And the gamekeeper from Kellingsford—he was here, too, saying he's a deputy to the constable. He's looking for you too."

Worth grimaced and nodded.

"Horses," Jane said. "I need to borrow two of Edward's horses."

"I told you, Miss Austen, Mr Edward won't allow it. Captain Austen wrote to him about the gig, and he said no, never, I should'na done it."

"That was the gig," Jane said, "and I did take it for several days—much too long. I will make amends to Edward, I promise. But I do need two horses."

"Miss Austen—"

"It can be like our riding lessons," Jane said. "No one needs to know. I'll be back in a day. I promise. Hotchkiss, you've been such a dear."

"Nay. What do you think your brothers will say if I let you go riding off with all them dragoons out searching?"

"This is all wrong, you know," Jane said. "These accusations against Mr Worth."

"No," Worth said, taking up the argument. "He's right. The idea of allowin' you to go out. That's what's wrong here. I must be mad."

"Frederick!"

"Freddy, Miss Austen. My name is Freddy!"

"Mr Worth! Hotchkiss!" Jane hissed. "Into the stable. Now!"

The men complied. Worth closed the stable door while Hotchkiss lit a lantern. Jane bore down on them.

"You sir, Mr Hotchkiss, are in the service of my family, are you not?" She did not wait for a reply. "As a lady of this family, I should think that an honorable man in service would respect a lady's request. And as to you, Mr Worth, you are my hireling. I am your employer, am I not? And we have this unfortunate predicament in which I have placed your liberty and possibly your life at risk. My honor and the honor of my family are at stake, gentlemen. I shall brook no objections from you. My course is set.

"Hotchkiss," she said, "I require the use of two horses. Caesar will do for me. A young man's saddle will do nicely. Mr Worth needs an even-tempered mount. I think Daisy will be the best."

She drew a breath.

"What about m' dear Lady Dalrymple?" Worth said, resigned it seemed, to follow instructions. "At least I know her."

"She's a draft horse, Mr Worth. We need mounts that are broken with saddles."

"Daisy?" the dancing master said. "You will take the noble Caesar and I'll get Daisy?"

He balked, Jane saw, but did not refuse.

"Hotchkiss," she said, coming back to the old man. "I will take all responsibility for this. You may report that I overpowered you with my insistence, charm, and tears. When I return, I will throw myself on my brothers' mercies. I will not permit you any portion of the blame. Horses, sir. I need two horses."

The old man looked at her. He nodded.

"Let's be about it, then," she said.

Ten minutes later, the horses Jane selected were saddled. Jane had found two extra cloaks and rolled them up with blankets and tied the bundle behind her saddle.

As Jane and Worth made their final preparations to mount, Hotchkiss came over with a pair of saddlebags.

"Groats," he said, as he tied them onto Daisy's back. "Feed the horses. Keep yourselves from starving in a pinch."

Just before mounting her horse, Jane found Hotchkiss and embraced him.

"Thank you, old man," she said.

They mounted.

Hotchkiss doused the lantern and opened the stable door. The horses walked slowly into the moonlight.

The stable master followed them out and pushed the door closed silently behind him, watching the riders. The small cross atop Saint Nicholas, profiled against the starry sky, caught his eye. He lifted his head and nodded.

"Aye," he said to himself.

He bowed his head.

❧ 75 ❧

In the nighttime stillness, horseshoes rang like alarm bells on the cob-blestone drive. Both riders cringed at the noise.

The Winchester Road toward London, then south on the Selborne Road, would lead them away from Kellingsford and the dragoons' camp. That was the plan.

Less than one hundred yards from the road, they heard other horses. They stopped on the bridleway and remained as quiet as possible.

The sliver of the moon gave just enough light to make out the shapes of several riders, five or six or more. The dragoons.

Jane patted Caesar gently on the neck. The only noise, horses and rid-ers breathing, until Caesar, perhaps scenting the other horses, perhaps anticipating the start of a hunt, *perhaps, perhaps, perhaps,* gave a small snort.

Not loud. Not agitated. Perhaps not noticeable at a distance of one hundred yards.

Out on the roadway, a spark flared. It made some small movements, giving just enough light to pick out a mounted soldier. Then, like a tiny shooting star, the spark arced into the air, curved, and dropped. Its fall stopped abruptly when it hit the ground, but it still moved, rolling.

Then the shooting star burst into a glowing ball of fire, a tiny sun, turning night into day.

"Riders!" came a shout.

"Halt" and "stop" and the sounds of riders wheeling about and turn-ing up the drive could be heard.

Jane had already turned Caesar. "Follow me."

Worth gave a tentative tug on the reins, but Daisy had already wheeled and trailed close behind. Jane rode through a narrow passage next to the stable, then through a gate, a paddock area, and another gate onto a small lawn alongside a fence.

The dragoons, clattering up the drive, followed the riders. *No more than fifty yards,* Worth thought. Even less. *A stern chase. A superior force. Hopeless.*

"Horses is out!" came a loud shout. *Hotchkiss.*

"Open the gate," roared a voice.

"Nay, gots to close the paddock. Horses is out."

"Stop it, you fool. They're getting away."

Jane cornered the end of the fence and entered an open pasture.

"Give Daisy her head now," Jane shouted as Caesar accelerated. "Let her run."

Worth clung to the saddle with his left hand and gripped the horse as best he could with his knees. With his right hand, he retained a loose grip on the reins. He settled into the rhythm of her pace, like a sailor moving about the deck on a rough sea, getting the feel of the ocean and the sway of the deck, and rolling with the waves and swell. The sudden burst of the blue light, the soldiers' flare, had blinded the riders. As his vision cleared, Worth could see Jane and Caesar, charging forward. Daisy, a strong and willing lassie, eagerly took up the chase.

Worth looked back. The dragoons were not yet in the meadow. *Hotchkiss.* His delaying action had given them a chance.

Jane drove forward, her pace undiminished. Farther ahead, approaching quickly, he saw a fence.

"Miss Austen," he shouted. "I don't know how to jump."

"It's all right," she called back. "Your horse knows what to do. Just hold fast!"

So, he did.

The extraordinary animal under Worth gathered herself ten paces from the rails. She cut her stride slightly. Worth felt himself drop and rock back and then—they were flying. Lifted from the saddle, his right leg lost a stirrup, but he clung to the pommel with his left hand as though his life depended on it, which it did.

As Daisy's front hooves touched down, he was thrown forward over her neck, but he held on, by God, he held on.

As the horses continued their flight across a second meadow, Worth regained his stirrup. Now he settled into Daisy's gait, feeling himself riding more in harmony with the beast. Not perfect but getting the feel of it.

A second set of rails appeared on the horizon and, in an instant, it seemed, the horses were upon them.

Worth felt his mount's approach, gathering, and leap, and he moved with her. He kept his seat for the flight and rocked back in anticipation of the landing.

The meadow ended. The horses slowed as Jane guided Caesar onto a woodland track. Just before they entered the shadows, Worth looked back.

The dragoons were halfway across the first meadow. They were coming. But Jane had piloted this countryside before. She had charts and
soundings. With this lady as his navigator, he had a chance.

❧ 76 ❧

"A minor abbey," Jane said, answering Worth's unspoken query. The moon, almost directly overhead, illuminated the remains of a tower. "After the Normans burned it, the people here relied upon it as a quarry. Ready cut building stone for the taking. And here we shall rest."

"It's safe?"

"The ruin is not well known. 'Tis a ghost in a wood that is owned, but untended, by Edward. Its chief advantage is the promontory."

They dismounted their horses, and Jane unstrapped two saddle blankets and one of the bags Hotchkiss had packed.

"Spread it out for Daisy, smooth side up," she said, handing one blanket to Worth. "Three hands full of groats. 'Feeds 'em just a lil' bit and often,' as Hotchkiss says. They will want to be watered the next stream we pass."

After hobbling the horses, Jane led Worth through the center of the derelict abbey to a low wall. Worth had been aware they were climbing for the last part of their flight. Jane had an intimate knowledge of the trails. She led him right and left from one path to another, and then guided them for a while through a shallow burn. The scant water barely wetted the horses' hooves, but the rocky bed would not reveal their path if the dragoons returned to search in daylight.

From there they turned onto a trail that led back and forth to this higher ground.

"The Winchester Road," she said, pointing. "The bell tower of Saint Nicholas."

"You've led us right up to the crow's nest. Now what?" he said to her and to himself.

"We wait while you decide which direction to take."

"Aye, which way indeed."

"We can strike out to the north and west," Jane said. "Take the road for Bristol. Your sister."

"That takes us nearer the dragoons. And then a long, long road."

"East. Go to London? An easy place to hide."

"Aye, or west to Cornwall, where every man with a boat is a smuggler. Get lost in another sort o' crowd."

"South?"

"The coast. A place where a sailor don't stand out. Even an old, one-handed sailor might find a berth on a ship bound for…somewheres."

"What do you think?"

"Horsemen," Worth said, pointing toward the Winchester Road. "Wembley's dragoons."

"Possibly they have given up their search?"

"Or they're heading back to camp to get fresh mounts."

"They will have to be passed if you were to travel north."

"Or east or west," Worth said.

"So, it is to the south. To Portsmouth? Southampton?"

"Someplace a wee bit quieter. Fewer naval forces, lest the alarm be raised in those quarters."

"You have a destination in mind?"

"A fishin' village. I spent a while there. Langstone."

Caesar caught their attention with a snort. Daisy, even more disturbed, whinnied. Both horses danced in place. Jane and Worth hurried back to calm them.

The horses quieted but remained agitated. They had eaten. The riders rolled up the blankets, but before remounting Worth said "shh." He stared into the dark woods beside the trail, then moved past the horses to the edge of the darkness.

Jane waited. "What it is it?" she asked when Worth returned.

"I canna see it, but… It's like something—someone's—watching."

❧ 77 ❧

"We have made very good time," Jane said. "We are nearly halfway and, let's see, four bells? Still the morning watch?"

Petersfield offered food and water for both the horses and the travelers. The inn's ostler was waiting for them, holding their horses, when they left the public room.

"You have no fear of him," Worth said as she remounted Caesar. "He's a big beastie."

"I loved horses as a child. I did so want to have riding lessons. But with six children…well…only the eldest, James and Edward, were afforded the opportunity. Coming to Chawton—meeting Hotchkiss—allowed me to pursue my childish fancies."

Worth mounted Daisy. With the fair weather and their early start, they would easily reach Langstone by nightfall. Still, there were miles to go. They chatted amiably.

After ascending a steep hill, their talk returned to Wembley and his attempt to detain the dancing master.

"How did you slip his noose?" Jane asked. "Some fancy footwork, I shall warrant."

"Luck," Worth replied. "Luck and some help from the footman you met—the old sailor, Marryat."

Jane listened intently as Worth related the tale of his escape.

"And now, we have all this," she said when the story was done. "Another chapter in the novel. It is growing into quite an adventure."

"Oh, I do so apologize for provoking the captain—"

"Nay, nay, Miss Austen," Worth said. "You canna be sure the pantomime was the cause and—"

"And what?"

"Well, if it was the case, then you can congratulate yourself on setting a very fine mousetrap."

They shared in a moment of quiet laughter. Then Jane laughed again.

"And what's that about?" Worth said.

"Thinking. Remembering."

"Yes," Worth prompted. "Go on."

"My cousin. My sister. Eliza."

"Your cousin? Or sister? Now which is it," he said.

"Both, actually. First my cousin. She had precedence as she was my elder. When I was born, I became her cousin."

"And your sister?"

"Properly, my sister-in-law. She married Henry. She was truly everything to him. She transformed him and he has not been the same since she died."

"What brings her to your mind as you go travelling in the company of a fugitive pursued by a squad of dragoons and lord knows who else?"

"Eliza would have been delighted when we sat with her to recount our tale," Jane said. "She was truly the most extraordinary woman. Beautiful and a brilliant wit. She could ride and she could shoot. She married a French count who was not actually a count. But then she was not actually the heiress that she led him to believe, so they were an excellent match."

"But you said she married Henry."

"Ah, yes. Her count, Jean François Capot de Feuillide, might not have been a true count but he was somewhat royal and very loyal to the crown."

"The Revolution?"

"He escaped the first wave of executions. But when the revolutionary fervor cooled, he decided to return to France that he might pursue some agricultural project. Madame de Feuillide, my cousin Eliza, sensibly remained in England. Le Comte was mistaken in his confidence. On his return, he was greeted by Monsieur Le Guillotine. The result was unsurprisingly foreseeable."

"Your cousin was left in mourning?"

"Eliza was indomitable. She lived a life worthy of her namesake queen. As a child, I reviled our former monarch, Elizabeth, for her despicable treatment of her cousin, the rightful and righteous Queen Mary. I am an Anglican to be sure, but I have always felt that Mary and all Catholics were treated most cruelly in those times. But as I consider her today—"

"Queen Elizabeth?"

"Queen Elizabeth. She may well have been a tyrant and betrayer of trust, but she held onto power in a royal snake pit for nearly forty-five years. She waged war, took vengeance on her enemies, and lopped off heads whenever necessity arose. Now, Mr Worth, with that sort of monarch in our history, why is it that society treats ladies as frail and fainting and always in need of a man to conduct business or manage property or to do…anything?"

"Why is it?"

"After experiencing the reign of Elizabeth, the men regained power and never wanted a woman, any woman, in power again. So, you see, the powerless state of women today is all Queen Elizabeth's fault. It is, I suppose, all the more reason to despise her."

"Back to *your* history, Miss Austen. To Eliza, your cousin, Elizabeth, who it seems you did not despise. Eliza was then, a widow. And Henry courted her?"

Jane laughed. "Henry, I am sure, thought he was courting her. He gave all indications. That certainly was what the family thought. In fact, Eliza looked about, spotted my dear sweet brother, cast her line, set the hook, and reeled him in. He never had a chance."

Worth laughed, but then grew serious. "Yet, you still admired Eliza."

"I loved her. She was certainly the best thing that ever happened to Henry. He was never made to be a great man of business. He is thoughtful, generous, kind, and sympathetic, hardly the qualities of a successful banker.

"Eliza encouraged him, guided him, and stood by his side in society where so much business is done. He achieved great success because she was his right hand. And since her death, left to his own nature, his business arrangements have not fared well. I fear for his prospects. Oh, Eliza. How she completed him. How she inspired me. And, I assure you, she would have approved of all of this and laughed. My appearances in Bristol and in Bath, and now our flight. On horseback. Oh, how she would have laughed."

↝78↜

"It's here I found out I were a sailor and not any kind of fishermen," Worth said. "Seems like it's the same sorta life, ships and sea and sails and such, but it's not."

"And why is that?"

They had stabled the horses and were walking down the main road of Langstone toward the harbor where Worth hoped there might be a respectable inn.

"Well now, a fisherman is in and out with the tides, day after day. Real sailors get out on the sea and go somewheres."

"You told me sailors have a wish to be home. A snug harbor every night? Would that not be agreeable?"

"Maybe for some. But there's more to this fishing business. A fisherman makes sail, hauls and tacks, and hauls and tacks. And then you gets your nets out and you sets 'em out, and hauls 'em in and sets 'em out, and hauls 'em in. It ain't sailing. It's just more tackin' and more haulin' and more haulin' and more tackin'. Then, if you're lucky, you end up knee-deep in stinking fish. Real sailors set sail and off you go. Reef the sails now and then. Set about to tack or wear after some great long reach and feel the wind blow."

"Fishing is hard work then," Jane said.

"Bloody hard work," Worth said. "And come a blow, you're in a tiny barkey what gets tossed about by the waves and flattened by the wind. Nay, give me a real ship what can drive through a swell and stand up to a blow. I spent a month here, working on fishing boats. I come away knowing I'd rather face the hot terror of a boarding action then another bloody boatload of mackerel. It's no kinda life for a sailor."

Jane laughed.

They were nearing the docks when they heard a clatter of horseshoes on cobbles. Horses. Several horses. But not the creaks and groans that might signal a wagon or carriage.

Worth gestured toward a side passage ahead of them. From the dark recess, they watched the parade pass by: Wembley and his dragoons.

"What the hell," Worth said. "Begging your pardon, ma'am, but...how?"

"Back to the stable? Reverse course?"

"Our horses are weary. They've got fresher mounts. Nay, I'd best make for the harbor. Wembley's not after you," Worth said. "You'll be safe."

"Are you certain? If he thinks I helped you escape?"

Worth thought about what she said and what he knew about Wembley.

"Miss Austen," he said, sighing. "This is a miserable predicament we're in."

"Do you believe Captain Wembley is an honorable gentleman?"

Worth looked at her. She held his eyes. He briefly bowed his head with his eyes closed, then raised his head and looked at Jane again.

"May God forgive me. Come on, Miss Austen. We needs to find us a boat."

❧ 79 ❧

The decision was easy. Thirty or more vessels of various sizes floated at anchor in the bay but only two were tied up to the pier.

The two masted schooner would take a dozen men to handle. The single stick boat in front of her—a smack, as this kind of small fishing boat was called—would have to serve. They boarded her.

Even with only one good hand, Worth raised the jib easily. As he worked on the mainsail, they heard the gunshot.

They turned their heads toward the village. Worth pointed. They saw the red jacket, even in the growing gloom.

"A lookout. They've found us," Worth said. "Wembley knows his craft."

Worth loosed the reefing lines on the mainsail, ran the mainsail halyard around a belaying pin, and gave the end of it to Jane.

"As I pull down on it, take in the slack. It'll come easy, and the turn round the pin will hold it for you."

With a dozen long pulls the sail was up. Worth jumped to the pier and freed the stern line, tossing it to Jane. After loosing the bow line, he jumped down into the boat and shoved the bow away from the dock. The light breeze caught the sails as the little boat drifted out to clear the bulk of the schooner. Worth moved to the stern and took the tiller. Jane moved forward. They were away.

"Ready now in ranks!" Wembley's voice floated over them.

"Sir, there's a lady—"

"Corporal, your pistol, if you please." The fishing smack was passing the schooner. Worth could not see what was happening on the pier.

A stronger breath of wind, and the smack gathered speed. As it cleared the stern of the schooner, they saw a row of redcoats in line, muskets ready.

"Down," Worth said. "As long as you're below the gunnel, you've not a thing to fear."

Jane complied.

"Aim!"

Now Worth lowered himself as far as possible while keeping a hand on the tiller.

"Musket balls bounce off a sturdy hull," Worth said, as he hunkered down. "Like as not, they won't even punch through the canvas."

"Fire," Wembley commanded.

The noise was impressive and at least two balls rattled against the side of the little boat.

Worth stood and took hold of the main sheet, the line that controls the angle of the sail, and tightened it.

"They'll be about twenty seconds to reload and fire a second volley," he said, "if they're any good."

He was lying next to the gunnel when the second volley roared.

"More like thirty seconds. Keep down. They'll have one more shot before we're well out of range. The wind's against us," Worth said. "Dead out of the South. We'll have to tack our way to the channel. You can breathe easy, Miss Austen. You've nothing to fear from muskets."

"I appreciate your confidence," she replied. "I hope you will forgive me for having just a sliver of doubt."

"Muskets. Blunderbusses. They's dangerous to men running about on an open deck or up in the rigging. But a wooden wall, even this wee barkey, it'll keep you safe."

"It has been more than thirty seconds," Jane said.

"Aye, so it has."

Worth raised his head.

"Damn," he said. "Oh…pardon. The shit…oh, no, I do beg your pardon. Miss Austen, you can sit up for a while."

"What is going on?"

"He's following us. Takin' a lifeboat. Damn fool landsmen. Gonna get themselves drowned."

Jane looked back at the shore where the dragoons had launched a broad beamed rowing boat. With three men on each side, pulling long oars, it was slicing through the bay.

"Mr Worth!" Her alarm was apparent.

"You've naught to worry about, lass. They's landsmen. Just look there. One of them's caught a crab."

Jane looked back and saw that the oarsmen had fallen into disarray.

"They got muskets which are not dependable at any time. But flint-locks in an open boat at sea? It's foolishness."

"They are rowing again. In unison," Jane said.

"Aye, the fellow in the stern, I think it's the corporal. He's steadying 'em."

"Are they going to catch us?"

"Now that's a good question, ain't it," Worth said. "We've got the wind coming at us so, we'll be tacking back and forth, five or six long reaches. They've got oars, and they can steer a straight line to the channel. But they got the wind in their faces and oarsmen get tired and landsmen gets blisters."

"Are they going to catch us, Mr Worth?"

"Ready to come about," Worth said. "Watch your head now. Comin' around."

The big boom that anchored the bottom of the sail swung over their heads. The jib snapped to attention, billowing in the opposite direction. Worth tightened the jib and adjusted the main sheet, and the little boat settled on its new course. Rocking a little more, diving and rising a little more, as they settled on their new course.

Worth looked back. The dragoons stroked steadily. Not as deep or strong as sailors but steady.

"It'll be a near thing, Miss Austen. It'll be a near thing."

❧80❧

The pursuit lasted nearly an hour. Darkness fell but moonlight kept the adversaries in sight.

Worth reassured Jane with information about the real perils of naval warfare.

Muskets were useless, except in a melee, like a boarding party. Rifles posed a greater danger, more range and greater accuracy, but they took longer to load.

"You look at a man o' war and you see the great guns flinging a great weight o' metal. There's danger there, but round shot is the least of it. It's the splinters that go flyin' when hot iron smashes into a hull, spikes of wood everywhere, one ball and a thousand splinters. Or let a shot burst a gun port and tear away the breechings—the ropes and pulleys what keeps a gun in place—then you got some real trouble. Every great gun is on wheels, you see. Imagine you got six thousand pounds of iron, oak and brass rollin' across the deck every time a ship rocks. A loose cannon. Now, there's adventure for you."

"Thank you, Mr Worth," Jane said. "I believe that musket balls provide sufficient excitement for me."

"We're on our last reach now," Worth said. "One more tack and we're sailing out the channel and into the Solent, open sea. They'll not be chasing us there."

"They are almost upon us, Mr Worth."

"Aye. But what is there for 'em to do?"

He spoke more confidently than he felt. He knew what he would do. Take Nelson's approach. Go straight at 'em. A boarding party. It would be risky, but the chance of success would be good.

"Damn." There was one other thing they could do. "Beg pardon. Get ready to lie low."

The lifeboat was only three lengths off their starboard beam. He could hear Wembley giving orders and he saw movement.

"You can't, sir," the corporal shouted.

"Make ready, men. Corporal, this is naval war. It calls for a broadside."

On their current courses the boats would pass within a length—or less. Worth was preparing to change course, to try to open up more water.

Now Wembley had taken the helm of the lifeboat.

"Prepare to a form a rank," he barked. "You will stand and fire on my command. You can shoot straight down at them."

Worth shook his head. The man was insane. Worth devised another plan. Never mind the maneuvers.

"Forward," he said to Jane. "Curl up in the bow. Stay down."

He pushed the tiller hard to port. The smack turned to starboard, heading straight at the lifeboat.

Taking a light line that was tied to one side of the boat, he double looped it around the tiller handle and belayed it on a pin on the other side. With the tiller lashed in place, he stood and loosened the main sheet. With the mast, sails, and boom lined up in front of him, he did not offer a target. The main sheet was completely slack, and the boom could swing freely. It would not do for sailing, but that was not what he had in mind.

"Prepare to fire," Wembley shouted.

The fishing smack was only a length from the lifeboat when Worth untied the tiller and turned it hard to starboard. Worth pushed on the boom. The sail caught the wind.

From afar, the rigging on a sailboat looks graceful and delicate, but looks are deceiving. The mast, even on an insignificant fishing smack, is a tree trunk, near to a foot thick at its base. The boom, swinging around the mast and lashed to the bottom of the mainsail, is the biggest, strongest limb on that tree. A massive piece of timber.

When the smack turned, the sail caught the full force of the wind and began a mighty swing. It arced out over the water. With the heeling of the little boat, leaning with the wind, the boom was low, only a few feet of clearance above the waves and nearly level with the gunwales of the lifeboat.

As the fishing boat swept alongside the pursuers, the boom reached all the way across the lifeboat and swept the cockpit clean.

"Miss Austen, you can get up. They'll not be bothering us now."

Worth handed in the main sheet, pulling with his left, and dogging it with his right. The little boat, powered by the freshening wind, leapt forward.

"One more tack and we're out the channel."

"What happened to them?"

Worth looked back. They both heard the voices.

Lifeboats are built to take abuse and stay afloat. They are built with broad beams and heavy bottoms so the occupants can drag swimmers and sailors up over the sides. But they are not built to support eight men trying to stand and move about, suddenly caught up in a fright, with waves coming at them from the side.

"She's turned turtle," Worth said. "Capsized."

They both heard the voices, the cries for help.

"What's going to happen to them?"

Worth was silent.

"What is going to happen to those men?"

More silence.

"Mr Worth?"

"They'll be getting their rewards," he said. "Waging war on a lady. There's your justice. Ready to come about. Watch your head."

"Frederick!"

"Freddy," he said, with some heat.

"What is going to happen to those men?"

"Watch your head." Worth swung the tiller starboard. The boat veered to port and centered on the channel.

"Mr Worth," she said, calmly but firmly. "We must go back."

"Miss Austen, may I have leave to remind you that those are the men who were firing muskets at you?"

"I know."

"And me?"

"I know. But with their boots and uniforms in a cold sea?"

"It's not so cold," Worth said. "The tropic current warms these waters."

"Mr Worth, we...I...cannot allow those men to drown. They were only following orders."

"Bad orders."

"Yes."

"Maybe they have learned a lesson."

"Miss Austen—"

"They are in the water. We are in no danger from their muskets or pistols."

"They have sabers, knives and ill will—"

"They are pleading for help."

Worth said nothing.

"Turn us around, Mr Worth. I am your employer. That is an order."

Worth resorted to profanity. He swore like a sailor. But Jane did not flinch.

"Mr Worth. Freddy. Please. Turn us around."

"We'll not be taking them on board this boat. There's no room and I don't trust 'em."

"You will think of something to do," Jane said. "You are extremely resourceful."

"Aye, aye, sir. Ma'am." He swung the boat around.

❧81❦

R unning with the wind, the smack made a swift return to Langstone.
The trip lasted only a half an hour, despite the drag of a fishing net
serving as a lifeline for a complement of waterlogged dragoons.

Worth did not try to dock the craft. He drove through the anchored
boats toward the muddy beach where dozens of tenders and skiffs were
drawn up. The tide was ebbing. The little boat would be high and dry for
its owner to re-float on the next tide.

"Take hold," Worth warned Jane. "You'll be thrown forward. Brace
yourself."

The boat struck the beach with a lurch and a grinding sound.

"Up and off at the bow," he said. "Let's keep you dry."

He was over the side and knee-deep in the water.

"Mr Worth, I am damp from head to toe."

"Damp, as you say. Not soaked through. Let's keep it that way."

In her riding gear, Jane was quite nimble. She went over the side at the
bow. Worth made a step for her with his hands, and she was able to
spring onto the beach.

"Oh, how diverting," she said. "Shall we do it again?"

They both laughed. Then quickly stopped.

The dragoons began emerging from the sea on the other side of the
boat.

When they circled back to the lifeboat and cast the net overboard, the
corporal had given parole for himself and his men. The dragoons were
not prisoners, of course, but they had been in a sort of war. The rescue,
at Jane's insistence, was certainly an honorable action. A promise to cease
all hostilities made sense. It especially made sense to men struggling simply to stay afloat, clinging to an overturned lifeboat in the middle of a
rolling sea at night.

Once they had come ashore, Worth and Jane would find out if the
truce would hold.

The corporal had spoken for the men, not Wembley, and they soon
discovered why. The last man to make it out of the water, a large dragoon, had hold of a rope. Two more men joined him and hauled it. The

other end was tied around two black boots, spurs still affixed, and the remains of Captain Reginald Wembley.

"Army don't have burials at sea, you know," the corporal said as he came over to Worth and Jane. "Leave no man behind. That's what we says. Even when it's nothin' but a poor officer's damned corpse."

A blast of wind hit them, stronger and colder; they all needed shelter.

The beach sloped upward. A jumble of boulders and rocks served as a wall, only a few feet high, supporting the harbor road where Worth saw signs of life beckoning.

"Shall we seek refuge," Jane said, following his gaze.

"Aye," he said.

They set off directly toward the glow from some harborside establishment—an inn or a tavern—it did not matter as long as it was warm.

The dragoons, carrying Wembley's body, followed them.

Jane clambered over the rocks and ascended a small boulder.

"Have a care," Worth said.

He hurried up next to her, stepping on a higher stone to assist her.

Sailors have a fear of falling. To go overboard and be lost meant inevitably to drown. A fall from a spar onto an oak deck could be harder still; death might prove kinder than the crippling injury you survived. A landsman—this landswoman—a creature of fields, pastures, lawn, home, and hearth. *She lacks the sailor's fear. She does not know the peril.*

Jane placed one foot on a small, round rock wedged between larger stones, tried it, and found it steady. It would be an easy step to the boulder above it and then the road.

As she placed her full weight on it, the rock slipped, turned, and she began to topple.

Worth reached out with his right hand and caught her wrist. His damaged hand was still strong enough for most jobs. Strong enough to handle a sea chest or wield a cook pan or to make a fiddle bow dance. But not strong enough to hold a falling lady.

Among the fears of falling, height is the greatest, the fear you feel in your groin. How long would it take from the moment you lost your grip? But most falls only take an instant. Most falls end with a caution, a care, and a helping hand up. Most falls.

Jane fell sideways. She reached out to break her fall, caught a rock with her hand. Her shoulders twisted sharply. Her back struck the side of the boulder. Then, with a sound like that of one stone hitting another, she struck the back of her head.

She did not move.

The dancing master did not breathe.

❧ 82 ❦

With extra hands, gentle hands, the dragoons helped Worth carry the lady up to the roadway. A small inn provided a refuge.

The innkeeper's wife, Mrs Bailey, led Worth, carrying Jane, to a chamber on the second floor.

"It's above the hearth," she said. "Warmest room in the house. What happened?"

"The lady slipped. Fell. Coming up from the beach. She struck her head."

He examined her again, moving Jane's head to the side. No blood. No fracture, he hoped.

"This is woman's work, now," the good lady said. "Let me tend to her. You and the rest of your friends need to dry out."

Friends, Worth thought. Earlier they had been firing muskets at him, but he did not correct her.

"How's your lady," the corporal said when Worth came down the stairs.

It was all so complicated. Worth did not correct him either.

"Abed. The innkeeper's good wife is tending to her."

"She's had a bad knock is all. She'll come around. Doggett," the corporal said, offering a hand.

"Worth," the dancing master said, taking it.

"There's no forgiving us, for all of this," Doggett said. "Officers gives orders. Soldiers gotta follow 'em. Even if…"

"Even if?"

"War is a brutal business," Doggett said. "Makes a man hard. Makes him angry. Makes him fearful at times, waking up in the middle of the night in a sweat."

Worth nodded. Doggett could see that he understood.

"But war don't make a man cruel. Ain't but one man I ever served with what enjoyed the sight o' blood. Two o' the lads found a barrow out back. They're carting him up from the beach. There's a shed out back. Cold as it is, he'll keep well enough."

A few minutes later, the men were back. Worth went out with the corporal and looked at the corpse in the glow of the light from the inn.

Worth had seen too many wounds from accidents and battles. The captain's head had been struck hard, bruised. The boom of the fishing smack might have done that. But there was another wound on the right side of his head that likely killed him, that, and the seawater. The butt of a musket? The hilt of a saber? It was hard to know what had done it, but the man's skull had been smashed.

"Terrible wound," Worth said.

"Terrible, indeed," Doggett said. "When that sail swung around it knocked him down. Must've hit his head on the edge of the boat or something."

"Bad luck, that."

"Terrible bad luck," Doggett said. "Take 'im into the shed out back," he said to his men. "Lay him out nice and straight. Make it easier to manage him when he stiffens up."

Worth and the soldiers began a friendly occupation of the inn. Jackets and other gear were spread out to dry everywhere. The innkeeper, a jovial, portly man, provided a stew, bread, small beer, and a few tots of rum to ward off the chills.

The lady of the house and the dancing master took turns attending Jane.

The author could not be roused, but she showed signs of dreams in her fretful sleep. She would make small sounds and Worth thought she was about to awaken. He would say her name, but she did not hear.

Then he would return to his counting of the ways he cursed himself for allowing all of this to happen.

Worth and the corporal took the two small chambers that remained for guests at the inn while the troops made do around the public room.

The night passed peacefully. At daybreak, the innkeepers made a pot of porridge to go with eggs and fried ham. The soldiers swore oaths of loyalty to the good couple, declaring they had never been so well fed since signing on to serve the King.

Jane remained asleep.

"She will wake up soon now," Mrs Bailey said. "I know. I have prayed for her."

Pray, Worth thought, as he sat watching over the lady.

The sun was well up, touching the window of the room. The day was freezing cold and bright. A patch of sunlight moved across the wall to the lady's bed.

Pray, Worth thought.

He bowed his head and closed his eyes.

❧83❧

"Mr Worth. Mr Worth."
The voice was barely audible.

He had dozed off. He roused and looked at the lady.

"Frederick," Jane said, still just a whisper.

"Freddy," he replied automatically. "You're awake."

"Yes, yes, I am awake, and you were asleep."

"You were asleep," Worth said. "You were concussed. And now, you're awake."

"Stop talking, sir. My head hurts. I am in pain. And I am dry. I need water."

"Ah, there you are, miss," Mrs Bailey said as she entered the room. "I told you she'd be up soon. Now leave us be. Us ladies must tend to ladies' business."

Worth gladly gave way to ladies' business, and the slightest portion of the guilt and fear he carried, fell away as he descended the stairs.

Dried out, kitted up, conversing, and playing whist, the occupying troops filled the public room with a warm glow.

"Miss Austen is awake," he announced. Murmurs of approval all around. "She'll be needing rest now," Worth said to Doggett as the corporal came over to speak with him.

"That's certain," the corporal said.

"So, if you and your men want to push on?"

"We can't do that," Doggett said.

"Can't?"

"Nay. We have our duty to perform."

Worth stared at him.

"The captain's corpse. And the return of a notorious smuggler," the corporal continued.

He looked serious, yet friendly.

"There's a warrant issued for you, Mr Worth. Now, it's unfortunate that our patrol has taken casualties, but it's a soldier's duty to carry out his mission. That's the way you navy men do things, ain't it?"

"So, what's the plan?" Worth said.

"Seems as though we have located the notorious smuggler," Doggett said. "We have him trapped and are laying siege."

"Laying siege?" Worth said.

"Aye. Rough business. When an enemy is holed up in some kind of fortress, you've got to blast 'em out or starve 'em out. It might take some time. So, my plan is to wait you out, as long as it takes, and escort you back to barracks as our prisoner."

"I see."

"And I will explain to my superior officers that there was a serious mistake. That somehow, a case of wine from the officers' mess found its way to a great house near Chawton. I saw the case and recognized it. I can swear to it. And I know where they can find several more cases just like it."

Worth nodded. Both men wore grim smiles.

"D'ya have confidence? D'ye think the other officers will listen to you?"

"They had no love for Wembley," Doggett said. "They knew him well enough. They'll listen."

Worth felt more of the weight begin to lift.

"Then it appears that I'm going to be in debt to a poor, ground pounding, swaddy," Worth said.

"Mind your tongue, sailor." The corporal laughed. "Lads," Doggett said, rousting the two dragoons who were not at the card table. "It looks like we're in for a hell of a siege here. We need to lay in more supplies."

He handed one of them a coin.

"Go scout out yon tavern. See if they have any spare mortars or artillery so we can blast these beggars out."

"But" and "Cannon, sir?" the young soldiers were saying.

"If you can't find any artillery then bring back four flagons of their best ale. We're just gonna have to mount a blockade and wait for 'em to surrender."

To Worth, he said, "I reckon we can keep you bottled up for two or three days, if needs be."

"What about...?" Worth nodded toward the back of the inn, in the direction of the shed.

"Long as it stays this cold, he'll be fine."

Worth sighed again, relieved of a little more of the weight he had been carrying. A deep sigh.

"I'm going out for a turn," he said. "Get some air."

He nodded an invitation to the corporal to join him.

"Must be something about a freezing wind that loves a navy man," Doggett said. "I am staying here where 'tis warm and there's the promise of a pint of good ale."

The men looked at each other, nodded, and smiled.

Worth, still smiling as he left the inn, turned onto the road.

The day was clear and crisp; as expected, the westerly breeze came strong and cold. Worth glanced up at the inn and saw the profile of Mrs Bailey in the window of Jane's room. She was bending over the author's bed.

He swallowed hard and began walking. He was facing into the wind; the cold biting his face caused him to squint. He felt something wet on his cheek.

The wind, he thought as he brushed away a few salty drops. *Must be the wind.* A cold wind will do that.

❧84❧

"A coach?" Worth asked.

"Aye, aye, sir," Doggett said, smiling.

"It would be…but, how can you?"

"Captain Wembley, being in the state he is in, requires a conveyance to return to base. Since he's much too dignified a gentleman to return strapped over a saddle, some sort of coach is required."

"What about the expense?" Worth said. "It will be—"

"And, since the captain had more than a few gold coins about his person upon his demise, I'm thinking he would definitely want us to procure a vehicle that befitted a man of his stature."

"Corporal Doggett, d'ye think it wise?"

"Indeed, I do sir. I can assure you that not a penny will be pilfered from the captain's purse," the corporal said. "We shall maintain a strict accounting. But it is well known that officers frequently contribute from their own pocket to the good of the service. I am certain Captain Wembley will be respected and well-remembered for his generosity."

Less than four and twenty hours after her revival, Jane was on her way home.

On the day of her recovery, the innkeeper's wife plied her with willow bark tea, helped her bathe, fed her, and fitted her in a proper lady's frock. Jane's head still ached, but the pain was receding. At dinner, she descended to the public room and was received with kindness.

Worth met her with relief; the dragoons with warm acknowledgement of her part in their rescue; the innkeepers with the pleasure of bestowing kindness on another.

An express was sent to Cassandra during the day, but Jane insisted they must return to Chawton on the morrow. She was prepared to ride, but Corporal Doggett had made other arrangements.

The weather remained cold, but the wind had abated, and the sun shone bright. Captain Wembley rested comfortably on the gate of a neat two-horse carriage. Corporal Doggett sat atop the coach with the driver. The remaining dragoons were on horseback, leading the spare mounts including Caesar and the deceased captain's gelding.

"What a strange parade," Jane said to Worth as the group assembled in front of the inn. "It is a sort of funeral cortège. The return of a fallen soldier. But with the air of a country fair."

"The captain is much better loved now than when he was in life," Worth said. "I have more of it from Doggett."

The Baileys appeared bearing parcels and a large jug. Captain Wembley had been a generous patron of the establishment, it seemed, and the innkeeper and his wife genuinely liked their guests. The soldiers gratefully accepted the bundles.

Jane embraced Mrs Bailey. In the plain frock the good lady had given her, the two could be mistaken for mother and daughter, and the warmth Jane felt for the lady was not far from that mark.

"They saddled up Daisy," Worth said, as he prepared to hand Jane into the coach. "I'll be close behind. Wave a hand if you've any needs."

Jane stopped. She removed her foot from the coach step and faced the dancing master. "Must we go through this again?"

"Miss Austen, as a respectable lady—"

"Mr Worth, respectable ladies do not gad about on horseback—riding astride—nor go sailing off in fishing boats. Nor visit sailor's taverns nor call on Molly houses. I am weary, and my head continues to ache. I require accompaniment and distraction."

"But…"

Jane shook her head, drew a large breath, and sighed deeply. She winced with some pain and cupped her forehead in her hands for a moment, then she looked up at him again.

"For goodness' sake, Freddy, be a good boy and do as you are told."

She climbed, unassisted, into the carriage.

The dancing master, after recovering his dignity, did as he was told.

❧85❧

A s the party traveled north, Worth pointed at a few landmarks: signal towers, relay stations, and other navy outposts.

"When Wembley was searching, maybe they helped?"

"How did he know where we were going? So soon? What does the corporal say?"

"Doggett don't know. He says the captain rode out early, come back, and then set off on the road south. He seemed to ken right where we was headed."

The convoy stopped in Petersfield to change out the horses and partake of the innkeepers' fare: bread, ham, and good cheese with small beer.

"King Billy," Worth said, pointing at the equestrian statue in the town square.

"William the Third is the preferred name around here," Jane said. "I think of him as the lesser half of William and Mary. She, at least, was English."

"Now, Miss Austen, Billy Boy was a battler—a great military leader."

"William famously succeeded in routing a much smaller force, composed of raw recruits that was led by an inept commander at the Battle of the Boyne," Jane said. "Whilst Mary, the Queen Regent—not a mere consort—ran the shop while he was away and handled matters firmly and fairly."

"I think you're too hard on the laddie."

"I think, on the whole, England has been much better served when women were on the throne."

"Even Elizabeth?" he asked.

"Oh bother, bloody Elizabeth. She was a dishonorable wretch for the way she treated her cousin, but she ran a tight ship of state."

"You have strong opinions on these matters, Miss Austen."

"Yes. Yes, I do. And more important, my opinions are well-informed, astute, and always correct."

"I believe you have all the makings of a queen."

"I agree," she said. They both smiled. Then, she grew thoughtful.

"My *History of England*," she said. "It is a clever conceit. If I wrote it again, properly, and extended it to our modern day—in a single volume—a humorous history? Something like that might sell. What think you, Mr Worth?"

"I think that whatever you set your mind to do is most likely to succeed."

He did not answer her question, of course, but she was satisfied with his response.

With the food and drink and fresh air, Jane's headache continued to recede. The familiar sounds and motions of the carriage proved calming. The stress of the escape and of the encounter at sea eased. In the sunlight and wrapped in a warm cloak and with a blanket across her lap, she fell asleep. As the carriage rocked her gently, she nestled against Worth's shoulder.

He found himself slightly alarmed, but truly quite pleased. Here was a lady of wit and grace, a lady who could dance and sing, who could ride, and stand up for herself to any man, and he admired her for that.

He looked down at her. A lovely face. Her hair, freshly washed by the innkeeper's wife, scented with some fragrance. *Lavender?*

The carriage lurched. Jane shifted and put more weight on his shoulder and side.

He bent his head down until his cheek nearly brushed against her hair and gathered in the scent.

Yes, lavender.

❧ 86 ❧

The carriage struck an especially deep rut at the turnoff for the Worldhams. Jane was thrown away from Worth toward the side of the carriage. He reached around and captured her shoulder before it, and more important, her head, might meet the hard wood paneling.

Worth quickly withdrew his support as she righted herself.

"Our progress?" she asked, blinking sleep away and yawning, looking for all the world like a small child just awakened from a nap.

"Through Selborne, near the Worldhams."

"An easy journey," she said.

"Fair skies, calm seas, and a following wind."

"You deserve an easy voyage, Mr Worth. I have put you out so badly."

"Nay, Miss Austen. 'Tis I who placed you in peril. The good Lord spared me a lifetime o' regret, keepin' you safe in the palm of His hand."

"Your fears were unfounded, I am sure," Jane said. "As any of my family will tell you, I have a very hard head."

They smiled.

"And how is your head?"

Jane looked thoughtful, then touched the back of her head with her left hand.

"Oh. The knot where my head struck is still rather tender, but the headache and fog have vanished. And I am hungry. And thirsty. Symptoms, I believe of a complete recovery."

"Healthy signs, indeed. There's a bit left from the innkeepers' larder," he said, picking up the basket that was on the floor.

She fell on the cheese eagerly. It was, after all, very good cheese. She left the bread. It had grown hard. It would be consigned to be eaten with soup or stew.

After drinking the last of the small beer, she sat back, feeling some satisfaction if not contentment.

"We have all the pieces of the puzzle, I think," Jane said. "Wembley in the center. The Frenchman, Lieutenant Lavelle. It seems Aloysius must be involved somehow. Percival and Percival's involvement in the syndicate. But how do they all fit together?"

"Wembley had a secret. He dinna want the world to know," Worth said. "Him being a…friend of a person what makes visits to a molly house. That's dangerous. In the navy, death by hanging. In the army, they may just shoot you. In either service, it's a mortal peril."

"And Aloysius? He seemed to have been very good friends with the captain."

"Aye, very good friends. But he's not in the service. The danger's not quite so great. The punishment's still death, but amongst the rich and powerful and even the ordinary, it's not so eagerly enforced."

"The Frenchman's attack on the night of my ball? It had nothing to do with robbery. It was a murder plot, was it not?"

"That'd be what I'd say."

"And it appears that Percival was involved—he was the man who hired the coach used by the raiders."

"Aye."

"Aloysius was the intended victim?"

"It appears that could be the case," Worth said.

"It makes no sense. Pieces. But how do they fit together? It's making my head hurt again."

"Then stop thinking on it."

She rejected his suggestion with a "harrumph" and looked at him directly.

"There is one more puzzle piece rattling around, and I am certain you can help put it in its place," Jane said.

"And what'd that be?"

"The manuscript and copyright for *Susan*. What did you do?"

"Miss Austen, I dinna—"

"You were involved."

"It was your brother's doing. Henry."

"Ah yes, Henry," Jane said. "I have discussed the matter with Henry, and I have most of the story. You, it appears, arranged a private negotiation with Mr Crosby."

"He wasn't supposed to tell you—"

"It's not Henry's fault," she insisted. "I can be very persuasive when I set my mind to it. Don't you agree?"

"Aye," he said with a sigh.

"So, you did have a private meeting with the younger Mr Crosby after he raised the price to more than two hundred pounds?"

"Aye."

"What did you do? What did you say to get him to sell it back to Henry for the original ten pounds?"

Inwardly, Worth sighed. Henry had not told her everything.

"Come, come, Mr Worth. Out with it."

"I dinna do anything. I just made him a proposal for a book. Maybe it could take the place of your *Susan*, I said. That's all."

"And what sort of book did you propose?" she said, smiling and genuinely curious.

"A nautical theme," he said. "You must write about the things you knows about, right? That's for the best."

"And what sort of nautical theme," she persisted.

"War at sea. The fightin' navy. Fleet actions. Tactics."

"Fighting? Tactics?" Jane asked. "What was the title of your proposed book?"

Worth looked out the coach window for a moment, then turned back to confess.

"The Fire Ship."

Jane could not help herself. She started to laugh.

"Oh, Mr Worth. Oh my. I know about fire ships. My brother Charles has told me all about their use. So, sitting in a commercial house, filled with books and paper, you made this novel proposition."

"The man was being most unreasonable. I thought that a fiery adventure story might bring him round."

"Fiery adventure indeed."

❧ 87 ❦

The colonel listened to Corporal Doggett's report without interrupting him. A pursuit undertaken due to an unfortunate error. A case of the officers' wine misplaced. A tragic accident while making a short trip by boat. The warrant? All a mistake, of course.

"The feller's right here, sir. He's a dancing master—a caper merchant—hardly a smuggler."

The corporal gave his commander Wembley's purse, still heavy with coin, though with a little more copper and silver now than gold.

The major bade them deliver the corpse to the quartermaster for disposition to the family. He seemed disinclined to summon up the battalion to honor their fallen comrade. It was after all, just an unfortunate accident, hardly suitable for military honors.

The quartermaster asked Doggett to provide him with a fresh uniform for the captain, so that Captain Wembley would be suitably presentable in his final repose. The salt-crusted, disheveled red coat and breeches would not do.

Doggett went to the captain's quarters, and Worth followed him. He had not been forbidden.

Wembley's rooms proved to be neat and orderly.

While Doggett assembled a full-dress kit for the captain, Worth looked through the other uniforms and clothing that hung in the wardrobe.

He came across a black coat. *Unusual,* Worth thought. Even more unusual, there was a red cravat looped around the hanger under the jacket.

Worth examined all the pockets of the jacket and found two items: a sheaf of folded papers and a small book.

Doggett had found a pair of boots that went with the dress kit. He was busy blacking and buffing them.

Worth pocketed the papers and book.

❧88❧

"The names. Some are familiar. Jones, of course, and here is Bellingham. His wife frequented the Pump Room daily." Cassandra turned the pages of the notebook. "Stevens, or possibly his son, present at every ball."

Jane read the letters a third or fourth time. The dancing master sipped a cup of tea.

"They are copies, of course," Jane said, "but not fair copies. Two writers, one hand. This is most perplexing."

Jane and Cassandra exchanged documents again.

"And you found them in the captain's wardrobe?" Jane asked Worth.

"Aye. In an inner pocket of a black jacket."

"Along with the red cravat?" Cassandra said.

"Aye."

"And therefore," Cassandra continued, "you have concluded that Captain Wembley impersonated Percival Ellicott? The idea is…preposterous. The Ellicotts own significant properties in Bath. They must be well known there. An impersonator?"

"Lord Kellingsford is well known, yes. Aloysius, certainly," Jane said. "But Percival? As a child, yes, he was seen in Bath. But when he reached maturity? Do you ever recall meeting him in Bath? Seeing him at an assembly?"

Cassandra was quiet.

"I only remember being introduced to him after we shifted our lodgings to Chawton," Jane said.

"Mrs Jones believes her husband was caught in a scheme. A scheme orchestrated by Percival," Jane said. "Yet when confronted, she said Percival denied all knowledge. Perhaps he was entirely innocent of the truth."

"But Jane, these are gentlemen experienced in the ways of business," Cassandra said.

"Gentlemen, indeed. Trusting other gentlemen, as Henry trusted Mr Gray at the bank in Alton."

"At least twenty men are listed in your notes," Cassandra said. "How could they all be seduced?"

"They seduced one another," Jane said. "The withdrawals suggest they received good dividends. There are assets—the deeds—but no income. The dividends came from money deposited by new investors."

"And Llewelyn?" Cassandra said.

"He came in at the end," Jane said. "Many gentlemen of Bath were investors. Most of the investments were smaller sums, but the scheme was collapsing. His money kept it alive a little longer. And then he died."

"But...the charade? What makes you believe Wembley was actually impersonating Percival in Bath?"

"The carriage hire," Worth said. "A gentleman in a black jacket and red cravat hired the coach used by the Frenchman and his lot. That never was Percival. The clothing in Wembley's wardrobe cries out that it was him."

"Then what of these letters," Cassandra said. "What is their import?"

"'Dearest Reggie,' 'My Dear Reggie,' and one 'Dear Ally,'" Jane said as she leafed through the pages. "With what we learned of the captain and Lieutenant Lavelle, the meaning is perfectly clear."

"Of course, I understand that part," Cassandra said. "The letters suggest Aloysius and the captain...I see that part. But they are not actual letters, are they? They were not creased and folded for the post. Some are incomplete. What of that?"

"Some kind o' false flag operation?" Worth said. "Counterfeits? A *ruse de guerre*? That's possible."

"Possibly," Jane said. "Or, possibly, they are copies of true letters."

"They are all in the same hand," Cassandra said.

"Real or imagined? Written by whom?" Jane said. "I think we must have answers."

"There's only one person left to ask," Worth said. "I'm returning to Kellingsford to collect my chest. I can talk to—"

"Not without me," Jane said sharply.

"It is too late to do it today," Cassandra said.

Jane looked at her sister thoughtfully, then nodded. "Too late."

"Tomorrow, then?" Worth said.

"Tomorrow," Jane said.

All was agreed.

Worth would go to Kellingsford and shift his lodgings to Alton. Cassandra would tend to Mirabella for one more night. On the morrow, the author and the dancing master would confront the heir of Kellingsford: Aloysius Ellicott.

❧89❧

"Four bells on the forenoon watch," Jane said.

Worth smiled.

"You have shifted your lodgings?"

"Aye."

"It went well?"

"Marryat conjured up a wagon from the stables and lent me a hand," Worth said. "Smooth sailing."

"Aloysius. Mr Ellicott?"

"He's about. That's what Marryat told me last night. I dinna see the young man myself but I wasn't seeking him."

The cold abated; the roadway clear; the walk to Kellingsford proved quite pleasant for midwinter.

"Tomorrow being Twelfth Night, will you stay another day?" Jane said. "Dine with us. We could play some music. It would be merry."

"Would that I could," Worth said. "I must get m'self back to Town."

"You have an engagement?"

"Aye."

"What sort? A ball? Something with Mr Wilson?"

"There is a…gathering at the Quinns. A small thing…but it's—"

"You must give my fond regards to Sarah, then. And I must have a report on how her patroness received my inscription."

"Aye," Worth said. "Aye."

They began speaking about the weather.

"Do you think Aloysius will receive us?" Jane said as they approached the portico at Kellingsford.

"It's his nature—"

Hinch, in his greatcoat, waxed cap, and long boots, stepped from behind the garden hedge and stood in front of them.

Their eyes were not drawn to the man's grubby clothing, pinched face, or greasy black hair. They focused instead on the black pistol in the gamekeeper's hand.

"Now here you are," Hinch said. He was smiling, revealing several missing teeth. "And I thought I was going to have to get m'self to Alton to take you, Mr Worth."

"What business do you have here, Mr Hinch?" Jane asked.

"Constable Hinch," the man said waving the barrel of the pistol at them. "And the law says that Worth here must be detained. There's a warrant for him. Smuggler."

"That is not true," she said. "And it is not your business."

"Captain Wembley made it my business, ma'am. Said I was to keep an eye on him. And then the constable, he deputized me. So, I'm his assistant now, y'see. You thinks you're so smart, hiding from the dragoons. Right clever, you was. But you can't hide from a proper gamekeeper, I'll have ya know. You won't get by old Hinch."

The gamekeeper advanced on them, keeping his pistol aimed at Worth.

"I put the captain to rights when you run off on the Selborne Road. Now, you kneel down, Mr Dancing Man, 'cause I'm going to truss you up for the captain."

"The captain? Captain Wembley—"

"Hush, Miss Austen," Worth said. "Hinch here has his duty."

Worth had started shifting to the right, away from Jane.

"You shouldna' be pointing a weapon in the direction of a lady, Hinch. What kind of man are you?"

Hinch kept his pistol aimed at Worth.

"Get on your knees. Now."

"Nay, Mr Hinch. We're both men of our word, are we not? Men of honor?" Worth said. He had moved well clear of Jane. "Come on now, Mr Hinch. Here I am. Ain't you comin' to take me?"

He stood still, feet slightly spread, at ease with his hands linked behind his back. He worked the fastenings on his prosthetic right hand with the fingers of his left.

"Miss Austen. What was it? The words Lord Nelson said. Never mind the maneuvers. It's your turn now, Hinch," he said, squaring up to the gamekeeper. "Time to take your best shot."

Worth's right arm whirled around, and he threw the prosthetic hand at the gamekeeper.

Something the size of a glove—bits of wood and cloth and leather—would never hurt a man nor halt an attacker. But some human responses are involuntary and unstoppable. Nor was Hinch, for all his skill at stalking, trapping, and killing, accustomed to confrontations with creatures that fought back.

Worth deviated from Nelson's advice slightly. He moved forward, then ducked, dove, and rolled.

A flintlock, whether it is a long gun or a pistol, operates like a miniature cannon. The trigger releases the hammer causing flint to strike steel. The spark ignites powder that functions as a fuse. The burning powder must pass through a narrow hole bored in the breech of the weapon. There it ignites the primary charge causing the explosion that fires the ball out the barrel. All of that takes time.

That pause, between the pull of the trigger and the firing of the ball, makes it extraordinarily difficult to strike a moving target. Hinch, distracted by the object Worth threw at him, tried to bring his gun to bear.

He tried.

As the dancing master had suggested, he took his best shot.

❧ 90 ❧

Five seconds later, Worth had Hinch pinned face down in the gravel. Ten seconds later, summoned by the sound of the gunshot, several servants were present.

"Marryat," Worth said, seeing the old man. "The stable. Get some lashings."

One minute later, Aloysius Ellicott appeared at the top of the portico.

"Mr Ellicott," Jane called. "We need to speak with you."

Aloysius remained at the top of the steps, observing the activity below.

Marryat returned, cordage in hand. Worth bound the gamekeeper's hands behind his back and added a hobbling rope to his ankles.

Just as the task was completed, the dull black carriage with barred windows arrived. The constable's wagon with the constable's deputy, Turkle, on the box, came to a halt near the portico.

"Now you'll see," Hinch growled. "The constable's got your warrant. You'll be paying for laying hands on his deputy. You'll see."

Turkle jumped down and opened the carriage door straight away. Admiral Harwell emerged.

"Mr Claypoole passed me a word," the admiral said. "The constable was needed at Kellingsford."

"I sent for the constable!" Hinch shouted. "We needs the constable here. There's a smuggler."

"You have the constable here, Mr Hinch," the admiral said, staring at the trussed-up gamekeeper.

"Claypoole," Hinch shouted. "We needs the constable. Mr Claypoole."

The admiral bent to get the gamekeeper's eyes. "Mr Claypoole has retired, Mr Hinch. He has served his term as constable."

Turning to Worth, Jane, and the others, he continued. "Rarely, if ever, have I met an officer so grateful to be relieved of his command. The rector has selected me as the next unfortunate to occupy the office of parish constable. Now, I have been summoned. What is the matter?"

"Hinch, here, committed an assault on Miss Austen and myself. Armed assault. With a pistol," Worth said, taking the black weapon from Marryat and handing it to the admiral.

"I was detaining 'im," Hinch said. "The smuggler. We has a warrant."

"As constable, there's another bit of business you may want to attend to," Worth said. "The death of one of your tenants, Mr Robert Morgan."

"Yes, dreadful business. What of it?"

"You saw the injuries," Worth said.

"Yes."

"A fall from a roof?" Worth shook his head and said to Jane, "What was that thing you was telling me about?"

"A mantrap," Jane said. "A large device, maybe three feet across, with a very strong spring. The jaws are powerful enough to crush the leg of any unfortunate creature that steps on one."

"Think on the wounds you saw, Admiral," Worth said. "The man's leg was crushed, was it not?"

"Your point is taken," the admiral said.

"Mantraps were used by gamekeepers in some centuries past to deter poachers," Jane said.

"Gamekeepers," Worth said. "You might want to detain Mr Hinch while you search the sheds and grounds. See if Mr Hinch has any such devices?"

The admiral looked at Hinch with even greater interest.

"Yes, yes, I think the matter bears further examination. Mr Hinch, I shall arrange accommodation for you in Alton for a while. Help him up now," the admiral said. Turkle and Marryat obliged. Hinch, still bound, was loaded into the carriage. The admiral took a place on the box, next to Turkle.

"Mr Worth, Miss Austen. Please remain at hand. I'll have more questions for you presently," the new constable said. Then he prodded Turkle, and the vehicle was on its way.

Jane and the dancing master looked up to the portico for Aloysius. He was gone.

☙91☙

"Mr Ellicott," Jane called out from the vestibule. "Aloysius!" Jerome appeared. "Mr Ellicott is indisposed."

"We must speak with him," she said. "We must."

"But—"

"Mr Ellicott " Worth called out. "Mr Ellicott! We needs to speak with you. About your friend, Captain Wembley."

"Mr Ellicott left instructions—"

"Allow them to enter." The words came from the library.

Aloysius sat in his brother's old chair, behind the writing desk. His sister sat in the upholstered chair in the corner—the one Aloysius had occupied in the past. The young man looked pale. Serious. His sister also seemed unusually somber.

Aloysius stood and came around to greet Jane and Worth.

"You have news of Captain Wembley," Aloysius said.

"We are in possession of some information," Jane said. "It seems part of the puzzle. We are trying to see where it fits."

"You said you had news of Captain Wembley," Aloysius said. "He has been on a mission of late. Searching, I have been told, for none other than you, Mr Worth."

Worth looked at Jane.

"We have been made…quite aware of his exertions," she said after a brief pause.

"The constable's wagon has departed," Aloysius said. "And yet, here you stand? You speak of puzzles, Miss Austen. I must say, I find myself most confounded."

Aloysius turned away and paced in front of the fire. Worth noted that he had taken an object from his waistcoat pocket. He held it gently in two hands.

"You said you wanted to speak to me about Captain Wembley?"

"Some letters have come into our possession," Jane said.

Worth withdrew them from his coat and handed them to Aloysius. The young man put the object on the writing desk as he looked through the papers. A black rectangle. Gold embroidery.

"Yes, yes," he said, leafing through the papers and shaking his head. "Yes, I know—" Then, he was struck. He clenched his fists, crushed the papers, and shouted, "How did you obtain these? How? Where?" The young man appeared prepared to fling himself on Worth.

"Easy, man. We have no quarrel," Worth said, backing away.

"We have brought them to you," Jane said. "To you. For you only."

"I know all about these damn papers, don't I, Letitia, dear?"

He glared at his sister and slapped them down on the writing desk.

"They were in Reggie's possession. How did you get them? How?"

Jane moved between the two men. She spoke calmly. "At his barracks. Mr Worth found them at his barracks along with certain other items of great concern."

"What were you...? He allowed you?"

Jane looked at the dancing master. Of course, there was no reason for Aloysius to be informed. He did not yet know of his lover's death.

"Sir," she said, "your very good friend, the captain..." She touched his shoulder as she looked at him. She told him first with her eyes. "Captain Wembley is dead."

Aloysius stood speechless. Stunned.

"An accident," Worth said. "An emergency ferry crossing. At Langstone. You can ask his man, Corporal Doggett. He was there. We brought him...his body...back to the camp. Doggett was obtaining a uniform for the captain. I accompanied him. The letters...turned up."

Aloysius calmed himself. He swallowed his emotion. He grew cold. He picked up the small object from the desk again.

"How dare you? To prowl amongst his things. To besmirch his honor. A man of dignity. Integrity. Action. You, a fraud. Telling your lies about Trafalgar."

He held the object cupped in both hands.

"Reginald was a man. He stood face to face with England's enemies. He never wavered in the face of danger. He was no coward."

Worth knew the young man was vulnerable, but his provocations struck home.

"There's more, sir," Worth said. "There's evidence that your Reginald was part of a deceitful financial scheme. That he swindled people."

"No, he would never have done such a thing. You are mistaken. You are lying."

"There's evidence that he participated in the plot that brought the Frenchman and his raiders to Kellingsford," Worth said, bearing down on the young man.

Aloysius stood still, clutching the little object in his hands, shaking.

"There is evidence he plotted your own brother's murder."

"No," Aloysius said in barely a whisper. "No, no, no, no… It was an accident."

"But at least you can rest assured that he cared for you, boy," Worth said. "You were never the assassin's target. It was Percival all along. And then your fine captain murdered his French lover and spared you."

The flames of the young man's anger reignited. "How dare you!"

"That shoulder board in your hands," Worth said. "It's a lieutenant's board. That's a prize many an officer treasures. That one belonged to Captain Wembley, didn't it?"

Aloysius looked at the gold-trimmed rectangle, at the gold stripes and pips. He said nothing.

"Something to remember him by. And, now, here's it's mate," Worth continued, taking an identical shoulder board out of his pocket and offering it to Aloysius.

"We found it in the Frenchman's—Lieutenant Lavelle's—lodgings in Bath."

"In his…?"

Aloysius reached out, then stopped.

He let the shoulder board in his hands fall to the floor.

Wounded, dying animals sometimes make a sound, a cry of pain and anguish as their lives escape; they keen for themselves as there will be no one to mourn for them later.

Aloysius Ellicott, the young heir of Kellingsford, made such a sound.

He staggered and grasped the edge of the writing desk to steady himself. Swaying just a little, he raised his chin, released his grip, and left the room.

❧92❧

L etitia Ellicott stood behind the writing table, gathering up the papers. "They are letters, as you can see," Jane said. "Deeply personal letters."

"Oh my, yes, so I see," Letitia said in her odd, babbling way.

"They're not to be exposed," Worth said. "We assured your brother."

"Four, five, and six… Quite right. Thank you," she said, smiling at the author and the dancing master. Letitia tore the papers in half and put them in the fire. In the heat of the glowing coals, they instantly flared up, illuminating her figure in a golden glow. She pulled the bell cord.

Jane recovered her voice first. "Miss Ellicott, those letters were—"

"Nothing," Letitia said, decisively. "They were nothing." Letitia circled to face Jane.

"They were evidence—"

"Of nothing," Letitia said. "Some nonsense. Copies of something in a woman's hand. They might possibly serve to convince someone that original letters existed, but I know nothing of the matter. Of course, if any such letters did exist, they would be ever so helpful in persuading the young man to behave properly, don't you think?"

"But?" Jane gasped. The board had shifted; the pieces knocked askew. Once again, she was trying to work out the puzzle. "Why? Your brother—your brother inherits."

"Oh, no. Aloysius has behaved most properly toward his loving, elder sister, you see. The entail is removed. Darling Ally has agreed. And of course, my dear Papa agrees any time I bring him documents. Oh, Simon, here you are," Letitia said as Sloat entered the library. "I have such good news for you. Our accounts all appear to be settled. Miss Austen"—turning back to the author—"I believe a lady ought to have an income and property. I am certain you agree. Like the lovely Lady Catherine de Bourgh in your novel. Which one was that?"

"*Pride and Prejudice*," Worth answered numbly, stunned by the change in Letitia.

"Oh, yes, that one. Now, Simon, we must—"

"You want to be careful with that man," Worth said, loud enough to stop her conversation. "He's a thief."

"He is a conniving thief *and a rogue*," Jane said.

Letitia smiled at the author.

"Yes, Miss Austen, I know. And now"—giggling, she took Sloat's hand in both of her hands and clasped it warmly to her breast— "he is my conniving thief and rogue."

Letitia took Simon Sloat's arm and walked to the library door.

❧93❧

"Avast!"

With the experience gained in a tavern, in a stable, and in small fishing boat entering a harbor channel, Jane had discovered the ability to command with a word.

Letitia and Sloat stopped. They looked as if they were trying to find some other woman who might have spoken to them so forcefully.

Jane walked up to Sloat. She stared at him, her eyes level with those of the little man. She spoke so softly that it amplified her rage.

"Miss Ellicott, your man of business"—turning her glare on Letitia—"your conniving thief and rogue—has caused irreparable harm to my friend Mrs Dorothea Jones."

She advanced. Sloat and Letitia retreated in the face of her quiet fury.

"Whilst you and your Mr Sloat cannot bring her husband back from his tomb in the West Indies, you shall make her whole in capital and income." Turning to Letitia, Jane said, "You. Shall."

Letitia began one of her well-practiced, "oh what a silly girl I am," tittering laughs. With her curls bouncing, she fluttered her skirts and flounced past Jane, back into the middle of the library. She smiled and spoke with laughter in her voice:

"Whatever are you going on about, Miss Austen? I am sure I know nothing of these matters."

"As you say, Miss Ellicott. I doubt you, but you are of course, only a woman. Your man Mr Sloat, however, he knows the entire scheme, and he can be summoned."

With this, Sloat hurried around Jane to Letitia's side for a whispered conference.

"You shall make Mrs Jones whole," Jane repeated. "Upon your peril."

"Peril?" Letitia exclaimed. "What peril? Miss Austen, your storytelling skills are most remarkable. You've conjured up a delightful fantasy."

"No, Miss Ellicott. The peril is real. You face the peril of the ruin of your family name. You face the peril of the court room, of lawsuits and bankruptcy."

Another whispered conference.

"Evidence?" Letitia said. "This is all supposition. You have no proof. There is no peril."

"Mr Worth," Jane said, "you might share a few entries from the late Captain Wembley's diary."

"With pleasure." Worth withdrew the notebook from his pocket and opened it.

"Lord Ramsey, 12 Abbey Green, Bath. 200 pounds, 12 May 1813. Baron von Rosskoff, 17 The Circus, 17 May 1813 350. Deposit from Hallam's Bank—"

"Nonsense. A silly book with some names." Letitia said to Sloat, "Simon, would you explain why this is so much rubbish?"

"Ah, yes," Jane said. "And your man, Mr Sloat—or should I say—Mr Ponts, the only known, living perpetrator of the scheme. He will face the peril of many years in prison—if he escapes the gallows. Oh, yes, Letitia, I am confident your man will be identified. Is not all of this sufficient peril to merit your concern?"

Sloat was not prepared to speak; he recognized the peril.

"Mr Worth, I have an idea for a new book," Jane said. "A brief novel, only one volume. A sort of satire, I suppose. It will describe a scheme, conducted by a terribly compromised man who dishonored his military uniform. And he is abetted by a conniving thief, a rogue. They may have had accomplices. We shall weave the possibilities into the plot, just to keep our readers interested. Perhaps *some lady* of noble birth? The story will prove most engaging to a very select audience, I think. Merely a few dozen or so men—powerful men—who reside at times in Bath. Men who were taken in by the scheme. Mr Worth, I believe you have some of their names?"

She looked at Worth. He smiled, tapped the notebook he held, and nodded.

"I can present it as a comic novel, I suppose. Perhaps the gentlemen will view all this as an entertaining amusement. Have a good laugh about their silly little losses? Or might they take it more seriously? Could this tale take a tragic turn? It will be interesting to see how the story goes. What shall we call it? Can you think of a title, Mr Worth? Something like *The Gallows Walk*?"

"That catches the sense of the tale, but it seems so gloomy. Maybe something with a nautical theme?" Worth said. "Gentlemen like books about ships and the sea."

"*The Fire Ship?*"

"Nay, that title's been taken," Worth said. "But along that line, you could consider *The Prison Hulk*. A story about life in a floatin' jail. Hell on water, 'tis said."

"A most interesting possibility. Miss Ellicott, Mr Sloat, what think you on that title?" Jane asked, walking up to them, smiling. The two retreated to the farthest corner of the library.

"You've driven your attack home, Miss Austen," Worth said as he joined her. "You're about to carry the day."

"It is a perversion of justice, sir. My game makes me now no better than Miss Ellicott in her blackmail. But if it makes Mrs Jones whole then..."

"Call it a victory. Justice in the end."

"It is a most unsatisfactory conclusion, I think. Yet, as matters stand, it is the best I can imagine," Jane said.

"'Tis a hard business, this writing of a life story."

"Indeed. Yes, indeed."

They fell silent. The clatter of hooves, the scrape of wheels, and the sound of servants' footsteps in the vestibule announced the arrival of a carriage. Miss Ellicott and Sloat ended their conversation.

"Miss Austen," said Letitia, assuming the manner of a grand lady. "I shall require some time to consider this matter. I shall speak to you in three days."

Jane smiled, moved to within inches of the lady, and spoke.

"Miss Ellicott, you will draw up papers and make Mrs Jones whole today. You will do that or, when next we see the new constable, Admiral Harwell, we will provide him with the deceased captain's records of the scheme, and I will begin work on my new book."

Letitia's energy flagged in the face of Jane's fierce rebuff. Her curls bounced as she returned to Sloat, perhaps to contemplate another move in the game.

Sloat, however, was staring at the doorway into the vestibule.

"Admiral Harwell," Jerome announced.

"Well, there you are," Jane said quietly to Letitia. "Decide."

❧94❧

"Not too cold. Never near the fires. And I watered her every day," Cassandra said, putting the fiddle case in Worth's hands.

He opened it briefly, smiled at the sight, closed the case, and placed it on the floor next to his chair.

"The nature of the conspiracy remains unclear to me," Mrs Austen said. "Who was behind the scheme?"

Worth picked up a teacup and nodded to Jane.

"We cannot be sure," Jane said. "Sloat was certainly the most active participant, but he did not admit Miss Ellicott's involvement."

"Wembley was a principal actor. He undoubtedly used proceeds from the scheme to purchase his captain's commission."

"What about Mr Aloysius Ellicott?" Cassandra said. "Was he aware of it?"

Jane shook her head slowly. "We do not know."

"Did Mr Ellicott know about the attack? His brother's murder?" Cassandra said.

Jane continued to shake her head. "We do not know."

"He acted on Wembley's orders," Worth said. "He helped make sure of the time. But, did he know what was going to happen or was he an unwitting fool? Only the young man can say."

"What do you think, sir?" Mrs Austen pressed.

Worth cast a questioning look at Jane. She looked his question back to him.

"I think he's an almost innocent fool," Worth said. "He should have been aware. He shoulda asked questions but he dinna."

"He was infatuated," Jane said.

"With a man?" Mrs Austen said, making a very unhappy face.

"It is the world as it is," Jane said. "Not as society would wish it might be."

"Well," Mrs Austen huffed, "I find it quite…quite…"

"Uncomfortable," Jane suggested. "Yes, that is as society has dictated. A crime. Punishable by death. That is the real abomination."

"Jane…" Mrs Austen said, shocked but only a little.

Cassandra looked inquiringly at her younger sister, expressing neither disapproval nor approbation.

"I have seen a little more of the world this fortnight," Jane went on. "I have drunk porter, masqueraded as a wench, and visited a Molly house." There was a note of triumph in her words.

"My, my," Cassandra said, shaking her head but smiling. "Where, oh where has my dearest, sweetest, most innocent sister gone?"

"She is returned to her childhood, I fear," Mrs Austen said. "She is once again, as you frequently complained, your abominable little sister."

"Why, I never—"

"Oh yes, you did," her mother replied.

Worth smiled. They might be fine ladies, but they played familiar family roles first.

"If we are to speak of abominations, what is to become of the horrible gamekeeper? What is his name?" Cassandra said.

"Hinch," Worth said.

"Another unanswered question," Jane said.

"It'll be up to the constable, the admiral," Worth said. "He's a good man but Hinch is a slippery devil."

"If he has a mantrap..." Jane said.

"If he has such a device, and if the constable finds it, then justice may possibly be done," Worth said. "But there's no witnesses. No proof. Poor Mr Morgan has been underground for weeks."

"Hinch did us wrong with his spying," Jane said. "He placed the contraband in Mr Worth's chamber, as well. Marryat told us that."

"But Wembley's dead. His crimes die with him," Worth said. "Hinch will lose his place at Kellingsford. You'll not be seeing him about. There's a bit of justice in that for you."

"Just a bit of justice, sir," Mrs Austen said. "That would seem to be the entire story as you and my daughter tell it. Bits and pieces of justice. People wreathed in suspicion who pay no price."

"We have made Mrs Jones whole," Jane said. "Sloat prepared the papers under our gaze today and Lord Kellingsford signed them. One person, at least, is whole."

"As long as you do not merit the loss of a husband," Mrs Austen said.

"You must confess, dear sister, your tale arrives at a most unsatisfactory conclusion," Cassandra said

"It is not a novel," Jane said with some heat. "It is life as we live it."

"Which is why life, as we live it, is a most unsatisfactory subject for a novel," Cassandra said.

"You are cruel. Most cruel. I am in despair," Jane said, assuming the role of the younger child she once was. She frowned but it was a playful frown contrived to distract the other ladies.

"That is why we have our music, Miss Jane," Worth said. "Music. A song or a dance, the way Mr Shakespeare ended so many of his plays. That's a proper end for everything."

Worth placed his fiddle case on his chair, removed his prosthetic, and prepared to play. Soon, he was standing at the end of the pianoforte by Jane's left hand. They tested the fiddle against the instrument's tuning. Then Jane turned back to her mother and sister.

"What shall we have?"

"*Yellow Stockings*," Cassandra said.

"*The Comical Fellow*," Mrs Austen suggested.

The music began. *Yellow Stockings*, indeed, at a lively clip for three changes.

"A good warm up, I think," Worth said.

"*D*," Worth said at the end of the third change, signaling the shift to *The Comical Fellow*, and Jane picked it up perfectly; it was her turn.

"*F*," she said, seizing the melody and setting the pace for *The Physical Snob*.

The music was grand. They played on, rarely pausing. Cassandra offered occasional suggestions and was always rewarded. Mrs Austen appeared content to listen and attend to her needlework.

At length, Worth and Jane revisited *The Sussex Waltz*.

"It's borrowed from the work of Mozart, I'm told," Worth said.

"Is that so? I should not be at all surprised," she said politely as she played a short introduction to the melody.

As the last chord faded, Jane looked at him and smiled.

"One more, shall we? *Knole Park*? That was our first collaboration."

"That would be nice," he said, "or might you like to hear something new? 'Tis a special tune that's been locked within for some time. Now's a chance to set it free."

Cassandra was first to reply. "We must hear it, Mr Worth. How auspicious. A new tune. We must hear it this instant."

He looked at Jane.

"Yes," she agreed. "We must."

Worth took fiddle and bow in hand and played the tune once through. The tempo—not fast, not slow—stately might be the word.

The first strain in D major seemed a kind of fanfare. It had a noble air about it. The second strain echoed but did not precisely repeat the first.

As the passage concluded, it took a quick rise and then a dip, preparing the ear for what came next. A lament of a sort as the third strain dipped into a minor key. This strain captured an entirely different feeling. While having the contours of the first parts of the tune, it visited another set of emotions.

Now the fourth strain; starting in the minor key but then rising, building, preparing to soar into the next change.

As the final notes died out, Jane cocked her head.

"Again," she said.

Worth played through the tune again and this time, as he ended the final strain, the three ladies showered him with approval. Applause, of course, and words.

"Wonderful."

"Lovely."

"Brilliant."

"We must have a dance for it."

"How clever."

In front of all the praise, he heard Jane say, "I must have it."

Worth flushed, surprised by the ladies' warmth, surprised at his own warmth.

"Do you have it on paper?" Jane said. "Do you have it written out?"

"Nay, it's just been in my head. First a wee melody, then a strain, and then the answering strains. This is the first time I've heard it m'self."

Jane had that look in her eyes. "Well, I must have it."

She stood and took quill, ink, and music paper from her writing table, and arranged her tools, then dipped her quill.

"Now give me the first measure."

Within ten minutes, she had written out the music. Worth tested it. She made some small corrections and additions. When they were both satisfied, she set the paper on the pianoforte's music stand.

"Now, sir," she said. "Let us give this new music a proper debut."

They played the tune magnificently, trading leads, exploring it with more volume, with less. It went around five or possibly six times, one loses track when caught in the flow.

The music ended.

The response from the ladies this time was more sedate, yet, even warmer. Worth found himself caught in the glow when Jane spoke to him. She had taken the music from the stand and placed it on her writing table, her pen poised.

"What is it called?" she said. "A tune that is so wonderful, it must have a name."

Worth opened his mouth, stopped, then put his fiddle away, and said, "I was thinking…"

"Yes, Mr Worth, you were thinking," Cassandra said, teasing him. "So, what is the name of this new tune?"

"I was thinking of a lady," Worth said.

"A lady?" Jane and Cassandra said, almost in unison.

"Miss Jane has spoken so very warmly of her, your cousin, your sister, Miss Eliza. A very superior lady." He smiled at Jane. "A woman of great spirit. What was it you said? She'd be the one after dinner to go drink brandy and smoke cigars with the gents?"

"Jane!" Mrs Austen said. "You did not say such a thing."

"Of course, she did, Mama," Cassandra said. "Because it is true. Our Eliza was defiantly unconventional, and we loved her for it."

"And you miss her," Worth said. "That's where the sad strain comes from. You can never be…together…again."

"For the title?" Jane said. "*Lament for Eliza*—no—it's not a lament. *The Farewell?*

"*Planxty Eliza*—that's what the old Irish harper might'a called it," Worth said

"*Eliza's Song*," Cassandra said.

"*Dear Cousin Eliza*," Mrs Austen said. "Or should it be sister…oh, I am completely useless in these things."

"Just the name," Worth said. "*Eliza*."

And that was what Jane wrote.

Later that evening, after Mr Worth had departed and Mrs Austen retired, Jane and Cassandra sat reading in companionable silence. It was past time for bed, but sleep seemed too far away. The music of the evening still echoed in the room.

Jane marked and closed her book and went to the pianoforte. The music for *Eliza* now rested on the music stand, but Jane did not need it. She played the tune softly, one time through.

"It was so very kind of Mr Worth," she said, "to create such a lovely piece of music for our dear Eliza. Do you not agree?"

Cassandra looked at her sister and sighed.

"Oh, Jane. Your dancing master did not create that melody for Eliza," she said, marking and closing her book.

"He intends it entirely for you."

❧95❧

"M r Worth!"

The dancing master started.

"I am so glad I have arrived in time."

"Miss Austen. You have seized the advantage, taken me completely by surprise."

"I have something for you," she said, producing a half sheet of foolscap.

"It is your new tune. A fair copy."

Worth took the paper, unfolded, and looked at it. The music in full. But no title. He nodded.

"Many thanks."

Worth was waiting in front of the Rose and Crown, his sea chest packed and fiddle slung over his shoulder. He put the fiddle case on the chest and slipped the sheet of music under the body of the instrument.

"Are you keeping her well-watered?" Jane asked. "I wonder that some-day she may grow into a viola."

Worth smiled.

"What is your destination today?"

"Just to Town. A visit with the Quinns."

"Will you be staying in Town long?"

"Just a day or two. Then off to the north."

"Do you have any engagements?"

"Nay, but I'm hoping for something. The great house I told you of. That might work out. Maybe teach them a bit of music. Teach 'em some dancing."

"Sailors keep a home in their hearts, you said. Will you pass by on your way to Bristol soon?"

"Nay, I'm shifting back to Hull. I still have a few shipmates there."

"But...your sister will certainly miss you. She is such a good lady. You must not neglect her."

"You're right. Sophie is a dear. I'll be a good boy."

"The coach is delayed," Jane said. "We must take a turn. They will have to change horses. There is time."

"Aye. As you wish."

They walked down the High Street toward the bridge. Jane stopped and addressed him sharply.

"Today is Twelfth Night. We must set the world out of order. Here Mr Worth, I shall be your beast of burden—even though it's a very slight burden. Let me carry your fiddle."

They laughed. He gave her the instrument case which she carried, her arms wrapped around it, in front of her.

"So how is the author of *Sense and Sensibility* faring? Where are you in your literary travails?"

"I am in a state of disarray," she said quietly. "The events of the past fortnight have knocked me off my stride. But I am determined to set things to right."

"What shall I look for next?"

"One word only. *Emma*."

"Is this the 'headstrong young woman' you spoke of? Mind, you've already promised me the volumes," he said.

"The same, but—"

"With an inscription," he added.

"But I am not sure you will like it."

"Why wouldn't I?"

"Emma is a silly, flighty girl who minds the business of others while ignoring what is right before her nose. As serious as you are, Mr Worth, I fear you may find the whole of it too frivolous."

"Like Marianne, your younger Dashwood lady. Unlike your more serious Elinor?"

"Yes."

"But you bring Marianne around in time. Does your Emma come to her senses? I'll wager there's a well-respected gentleman who may offer a kindly, guiding hand?"

"Ah! You have found me out. Yes, Mr Knightley plays a major role."

"He guides her," Worth said, "but he does not break her spirit?"

"He is a fine gentleman who has long cared for her with all her faults. And no, he does not injure her spirit."

"And they live happily ever after."

"Mr Worth, you presume too much," Jane said, laughing. "Yes, yes, of course they do."

"Then I'll love the lady well and enjoy her story. But what new stories have you?"

"There is *Susan*. You know all about *Susan*. It must be revised, revised, and revised again. Still, I think it may have some merit."

"Ah, that's just an old hull. You're putting her up on timbers for a refit. You can do that with your *History of England*, too. From what you've said, it would be a very amusing volume."

"It might send me to the gallows. If my thoughts on the old monarchy reached Royal ears, I'd be condemned in a trice. If I were fortunate, I would soon take up residence in Australia."

"So, tell me then, what new stories do you have?"

They were standing on the bridge, looking down the little stream.

"I have one thought. A girl—a woman really—as she is older. She has seen more of life than most of my ladies."

"What is her name?"

"Anne, I think."

"'Tis a good name," he said. "I like it."

"She falls in love, of course, and she agrees to marry. But then she is dissuaded. The man is neither noble nor has he great means. It's a bad match—her family, or some older, much respected friend, convince her of that. Reluctantly she agrees to break off the engagement.

"She lives with regret, but later, and this is the main theme of the story I think, she has a second chance."

"She meets this man again?"

"Yes. But he is unsure, and she is unsure. As ever, there is adversity. But I will not spoil the story for you if I say that she has never stopped loving him. And he...of that, I am not yet quite sure. You realize, Mr Worth, second chances are rare in this world. They are so difficult to find. But when one has an income and independence, then perhaps they may be more easily attained."

"It sounds like a very worthy story," he said.

Her eyes sparkled as she looked up at him.

"Yes. Yes, indeed."

Then Jane shook her head abruptly. "I had almost forgotten. I have an engagement for you. Have you a calendar?"

"I have my book," he said, retrieving it from his inner coat pocket.

"On 16 December, in the year 1825, your services shall be required to arrange music and serve as master of ceremonies for a ball to honor the fiftieth birthday of Miss Jane Austen. Do you have any engagements for that date? Is your calendar free?"

Worth laughed.

"You want to plan ten years ahead? I will be sure I'm free."

"And we must have the Quinns and Mr Thomas. We shall have music by The Hirelings."

"I will inform them."

"We will play your wonderful new tune. And you must devise a dance for it."

"As you wish."

"And Thomas, our dear Mr Thomas, he must, he must, he must play the bombard."

Now the dancing master laughed, the loudest and fullest laugh she had ever heard from him.

"Except...except," she added, "he is not allowed to play it during my-...during your new tune."

The clatter of hooves and groans of a coach and four interrupted them as it crossed the bridge and rolled towards the inn.

"It is time," she said, and he started to turn.

Still holding the fiddle case, she reached out with her free hand and caught his arm. He turned back toward her.

"Frederick..." she said.

There was the slightest pause, as she waited for his retort which, curiously, did not come.

She went on.

"It being Twelfth Night, I have one additional request of you, sir."

He smiled. Nodded. Inquired with his eyes.

"Mr Worth, I should like to be kissed."

Startled but making every effort not to show it, he turned a little more to fully face her. He drew closer. *So close.*

Placing his left hand on her chin to lift it slightly, he kissed her gently on her cheek.

He stepped back.

She looked at him, smiling, but shaking her head.

"That was a tolerable kiss," she said. "So gentlemanly and chaste. I think it perfect for one's sister, or even one's mother. But I, Frederick, should like a proper kiss."

Worth's jaw dropped but for an instant. His smile, on his lips and in his eyes, was steady.

He reached out and took the fiddle case from her and placed it on the paving.

He moved closer to her. *So close.*

He thought of all the women he had kissed. He had kissed a few: some with affection; some with admiration; some with lust.

But this, he thought, might be the first time that he had ever kissed a woman he loved.

He put his arms around her.

And he kissed her.

❧ Epilogue ❧

An emissary from Mr Murray appeared at the Hanover Square Rooms with the parcel for Mr Worth. Rarely in Town in 1816, the dancing master was sitting in with the Quinns and Mr Thomas, providing music for a fancy-dress ball. During an intermission, Mr Worth opened the parcel and discovered his promised copy of *Emma* with each of the three volumes delightfully inscribed. The first inscription referenced the author as A Lady. The second noted the volume was written by the author of *Sense and Sensibility*. The final volume came from "your friend in music, Miss Jane."

Mr Worth and Miss Austen exchanged letters several times during the year. She inquired about his musical endeavors, asked after the health of the Quinns, and shared her thoughts about the publishing world. *Emma*, for example, had received more critical notice than any of her preceding volumes, yet it was languishing in Mr Murray's catalog. The initial printing of 2,000 copies—too many she feared.

Her letters made extensive inquiries concerning naval etiquette. She wondered about the obstacles that sailors faced when, retired or injured, they returned to ordinary society. Would an admiral just returned from war be inclined or able to let a country estate? And the distribution of prize money—how many years might it take for a captain to capture a comfortable living?

This correspondence has all regrettably been lost. Mr Worth, for his part as we shall see, struck upon some rocks and abandoned nearly all his earthly possessions including these letters from his special friend. And as is well known, Miss Cassandra Austen purged much of her sister's correspondence. Her letters from Mr Worth must have been included among those she thought might earn society's disapprobation.

Mr Worth journeyed to Hull and gained employment for a time, as a music instructor for the children of a prominent barrister. During this sojourn, he was introduced to Mrs Anne Bayfield; the same Anne with whom he had formed an attachment so many years before.

Mrs Bayfield's relations had been correct when they asserted that Anne ought to be able to find a better match. Worth knew this upon seeing her residence. Her husband, Robert Wolsey Bayfield, operated a thriving maritime concern with ships, docks, and warehouses. The magnificence of the home reflected his significant wealth.

Anne herself appeared quite unchanged, however, when he accepted her invitation to tea. She was as fair, as gentle, and as kind as ever he remembered her to be. And whilst the invitation had been for tea, she served him coffee and shared a knowing smile with him. The mother of six children, two boys and four girls, she spoke with great pride of her family. The oldest boy, named Robert Wolsey for his father, was away at university in Edinburgh. Bobby would soon join his father in the family trade. Her younger son, Richard Frederick, was a precocious nine-year-old, always into mischief, she said. The name Richard was, of course, for her father. And Frederick was an uncle in her mother's family and, well, it was a nice name she thought. Mr Worth said he very much agreed.

By August of 1817, Worth had moved further north and was serving as an instructor in music and dance for the family of a glass manufacturer in Newcastle. A tutor employed by the family knew that Mr Worth owned volumes by Miss Austen. He had seen them in the dancing master's room. Had he heard? Did he know that the author of *Sense and Sensibility* had died.

Worth knew that his correspondence with the author had ended, without the foreshadowing of any illness, nearly six months earlier. The news of the author's death affected him severely. He tended his duties and otherwise rarely left his room.

It was, however, the arrival of another parcel on 20 December 1817 that broke his heart.

The package, double wrapped and bound in light cord, showed markings saying it had been conveyed from Mr Murray in London to Mr Davison, the much respected printer of Newcastle. A letter inside the parcel identified it as having been sent to him by Mr Henry Austen.

"My sister would most certainly have wanted you to have this," it said. Four volumes.

Northanger Abbey? He did not recognize the title; yet even in a brief perusal, he recognized the landmarks. *Susan*, he thought. Refitted and reporting for duty.

Persuasion? The new work she had mentioned? Ah, yes. Here at the very first, her leading lady is named Anne.

And a biographical notice. At last. Bother anonymity, what nonsense. Here was the woman he had known, revealed as well she should be, as the author of these and other fine literary works.

In all his free time he read and reread the volumes. *Susan*, as Miss Austen herself had said, seemed slightly out of date and showed signs, here and there, of the worker's hand that had reshaped the manuscript into this new, and he thought grander, *Northanger Abbey*.

The biographical notice. *Oh Henry*, Worth thought. The sentiments were well intentioned, but they came in no way close to giving Miss Austen her due.

"Well, at least he spelled her name right," Worth said aloud, after reading the notice for the seventh or eighth time.

Persuasion was another matter for the dancing master. He found the story in every way perfect, filled with laughter at the characters' foibles, respect for the navy men, scorn for the callous villain and…what was there to be said…a second chance. A perfect ending.

On Christmas Eve, Worth attended the service in Newcastle's Cathedral Church of Saint Nicholas. Taking a seat near the back on the Gospel side, he allowed the service to wash over him; the mighty organ making the ground tremble; this night it seemed just right. After the service, nearly alone in the great church, he silently wept.

The following day, Christmas Day of 1817, Freddy Worth disappeared. He took only his fiddle and a duffle bag, leaving his sea chest and most of his other possessions behind.

Nothing is known of what happened to the dancing master over the following six months. We can only say with assurance that, by some means, afoot or otherwise, he traveled north.

For the next time the dancing master was seen was on the Cowgate in Edinburgh, in a drunken state and in the company of Mr John Ballantyne. Both men were staggering from a public house on one side of the street to a tavern on the opposite shore. Mr Ballantyne, this may be of interest, was the younger brother of James Ballantyne, the printer and publisher of several very popular novels by Mr Walter Scott.

"Another verse, my friend," Mr Ballentyne said. "Minstrels and ballads—I've a friend with a passion for 'em. Let's have some more songs."

There is one other thing we know. A very fine violin of Italian origin, possibly made in Cremona, sat prominently displayed in the establishment of Isaac York, pawnbroker.

What to make of this? Scotland? The seamy, seething Cowpath? How did the dancing master come to be known to this Mr Ballantyne? How did he come to be separated from his precious Mirabella?

All of that, dear Reader, is another story.

The End

❧ Author's Notes ❧

Thoughts on History, Anomalies, and Acknowledgements.
Whilst in my story I have generally hewed to the historic record of Miss Austen's life as closely as possible, scholars and well-informed readers have undoubtedly noted several irregularities.

There is, for example, evidence among her letters that Miss Austen may not have been in residence in Chawton on her birthday in 1815. It is well documented that her business relationship with Mr Murray was much further advanced than suggested in our story, and indeed, we know that *Emma* was already in print in December 1815. Miss Austen *might* have said goodbye to Mr Worth on Twelfth Night with his volumes, inscribed as promised, in his hands.

A close examination of lunar tables may also reveal that dancing master's flight from the dragoons, so ably assisted by Miss Austen, likely occurred on a moonless night and the tide might well have been flowing when Mr Worth ran the smack aground, rather than ebbing as he believed. "Blue light" flares were used in Nelson's navy; a similar military ordnance that a dragoon might have used may exist only in an author's imagination.

The recovery of the manuscript for *Susan*, later revised and published posthumously as *Northanger Abbey*, occurred in the spring of 1816—not in 1815 as depicted herein. Furthermore, Mr Crosby was happy to return the manuscript for the promised ten pounds as his firm was on the verge of financial ruin.

Were there Christmas Eve services at Saint Nicholas in Chawton? And did they sing hymns? Hymns by Mr Wesley in an Anglican parish? Perish the thought. But the scene is such a nice interlude; a calm before the storm.

The musical selections mentioned in the story were all certainly known in the time frame of the story; the degree to which they were popular and might truly have been played in the contexts as described is less certain. The selections from Turlough O'Carolan would have been well known to the Quinns, I think, as they were Irish. Mr Worth would have heard them at gatherings of musicians in Town or even when he was at sea. Whether Mr Bunting included them in his volumes of *The*

Ancient Music of Ireland, I cannot say. But whether there or elsewhere, the music of the blind Irish harper has thankfully survived.

The idea that wee Charlie Wheatstone might have given Mrs Quinn a prototype for his concertina in 1815 is highly fanciful—not impossible, perhaps—but very unlikely as the clever lad was only thirteen years old at the time.

The choreography for Mr Worth and Miss Austen's dance at the Solstice Assembly is similar, in many respects, to Mr Playford's *Well-Hall* (1679). Whilst I, as an author, longed to make that their dance, my advisors on the subject of Regency era dance assured me that such a reference would cause a great gnashing of teeth. I desisted and submitted *The Sussex Waltz,* also known as *Michael Turner's Waltz.* It is widely acknowledged to be derived from a portion of a 1788 suite by Mozart contained in *Austrian Dances* (KV 528 No. 2).

The quotation attributed to Lord Nelson, "Never mind the maneuvers, just go straight at them," is an accurate reflection of the great admiral's approach to naval warfare but it cannot be documented. The estimable Patrick O'Brian put similar words in Lord Nelson's mouth during the course of his 20-volume voyage with Jack Aubrey and Stephen Maturin, the source of much of my understanding of life in the Royal Navy during the Napoleonic Wars. In quoting the admiral, Jack Aubrey says, "I shall never forget it: never mind maneuvers—always go at 'em."

THERE ARE SO MANY PEOPLE FOR ME TO THANK.

My involvement in the world of traditional dance begins with my birthday twin, Lorraine Graves. I will ever remember our 100th Birthday Party Dance; a ball, of a sort, with so many good friends from near and far, a brilliant band, and no murders! Lorraine pointed me in the direction of the Pinewoods Dance Camp where I called my first dance, *Shadrack's Delight* by Tony Parkes.

My mentors, gone and always remembered; Larry Jennings for being cranky and demanding and precise and encouraging, and Ted Sannella, for being Ted. I always save a place for him when I call at the Thursday Night Dance in case his ghost shows up and wants to call a good one. And I shall never forget Mary Kay Friday who always brought joy to English Country Dancing and everywhere else she appeared. TGIF.

The musicians I've worked with so often: Paul Prestopino (who got us backstage passes to meet Peter, Paul and Mary); the *Fiddleheads*: Jim and Willow Sirch, Gary Wikfors and Norman Plankey; Princeton musicians:

Michael Bell, Jane McCarty, Janet and Robert Mills, Ellen and Frank Ruck, Barbara and John Vadnais, Larry Koplik, and so many more; PCD alumni Ben Bolker, Bob Mills and Susie Lorand; great bass players Ralph Gordon and Marco Brehm (bass players are always the coolest cats in the band); Steve Hickman and John Devine; everyone in *SPUDs*, the Phabulous Philadelphia area Pick-Up Band; Mat Clark and Bob P who provide such great backup for singers; John Krumm and his kid, and Tom (the spark plug in *Live Wire*). My ruminations on musician's names reminded me of a missing bass man who played many other instruments as well, Pete Soloway. "Make it loud," he said, when I was doing sound and *Raise the Roof* was playing. And, though he was never a close friend, Bob Mc-Quillan was a musical inspiration. I did get to call a dance with Bob in Concord, NH and actually met Amelia.

Time is fleeting and we are rushing to press; so many apologies for special musicians' names I've missed. We'll catch you in the second edition.

Organizers. Without them, there would not be very many dances. Rich Futyma and Jamey Hutchison hold special pride of place for me; and thanks to Ret Turner who, an a very long time ago, gave me my first big calling opportunity.

Regency dance experts contributed to the authenticity of the text including Alan Winston, who tolerated by first and most foolish questions and prompted the "gnashing of teeth" test for being true to the era, along with Beverly Francis and Allison Thompson. The gifted dance leader Tom Amesse and his wife, Susan, generously created a new dance, *Miss Jane*, to go with *The Dancing Master's New Tune*.

My neighbor and friend, Paul Sanner, was kind enough to encourage members of the church choir he directs to provide us with hymns from our imagined Christmas eve service. The singers included Marnie Ainslie, Teresa Giardina, Barbara Nelson, Kim Taylor, Barbara Vierschilling, and Craig Sanphy.

Librarians are the greatest! Thank you Howard Sykes of the Bristol Central Library, Bristol, UK, for info on backstreets, bars and the floating harbor. And my appreciation to Emma Yandle, Curator and Collections Manager for Chawton House for information about the premises.

Early "beta" readers including Ron Krall, Melanie Axel-Lute, Chris Riemer, Judy Felton, and Don Seltzer helped convince me the story had promise. My advance copy readers were invaluable, providing brilliant feedback. They included Carol Ormond, Ted Garvin, Adam Quinan, Katy Heine, and Jack Marquess. Chari Wessel and Nancy Kaminski were brave enough to read the story twice. Special props to Pam Eidson who helped me steer a steady course and provided constable Claypoole with his lugubrious surname.

On the literary side, special thanks to Austin Kleon for the inspiration (*Steal Like and Artist* and *Keep Going*) to "write the book you want to read." And thanks to Francine Mathews, a.k.a. Stephanie Barron, author of 20 Jane Austen mysteries, for guiding me into the Austen fan fiction world and recommending me to Christina Boyd, my editor who corralled my manuscript into acceptable Regency-era prose and improved everything immensely.

My thanks to Nancy Bailey Doggett for approving my remembrance of Terry. I got you both.

More musicians to thank: Thane Glenn, Kirsten Erwin and Adam Oleska did the heavy lifting in creating the recordings for this volume's "audio illustrations." With luck, they'll be assisted by a bombard player to be named later.

Bill Quern and Sarah Gowan. I have spent more time working with them than another other musicians, and treasured every minute of it. When the dancing master and Miss Austen communicate with the slightest nod, widening eyes or some little quirk, that's how it is communicating with Bill; something akin to ESP. And Sarah, gracious, open and supportive, is always willing to do a musical favor, including creating a brand new tune for the dancing master to play.

Jan Alter, thank you for so many years of friendship and support and for introducing me to the Thursday Night Dance community.

Ben Kennedy: keyboards, recorder, recording engineer, and all around good kid. Not many fathers have the opportunity to hang out with their sons while being completely immersed in something they both enjoy. It's special. Thank you, son.

And my Miss Jane. She keeps me steady, shares her truly wonderful family with me and is, very simply, the best person I know.

Again, my apologies for missing some folk. But, as we noted in the very beginning of this tale, the Gentleman who is telling this story is quite elderly. Perhaps his faculties are failing? Please be kind to him. Anon.

Your faithful servant,
R. Kennedy

CPSIA information can be obtained
at www.ICGtesting.com
Printed in the USA
LVHW030528170322
713568LV00010B/1102